SHADOWS OF JUSTICE

Shadows of Justice

THAMES RIVER PRESS
An imprint of Wimbledon Publishing Company Limited (WPC)
Another imprint of WPC is Anthem Press (www.anthempress.com)
First published in the United Kingdom in 2013 by
THAMES RIVER PRESS
75–76 Blackfriars Road
London SE1 8HA

www.thamesriverpress.com

A CIP record for this book is available from the British Library.

ISBN 978-0-85728-002-2

Cover design by Sylwia Palka

This title is also available as an eBook

SHADOWS OF JUSTICE

Simon Hall

🦢 THAMES RIVER PRESS

For Dad,
For everything.

CHAPTER ONE

At last, it was time. The moment of justice.

The door in the corner of the overly warm room, lit bright with yellow, autumn sun, creaked open and the twelve began filing through.

They had taken the same, familiar walk for so many mornings and afternoons. But this time was different. The procession was slower, footsteps measured. Heavier with the knowledge of expectation and the weight of such a judgement to be delivered.

As one, the eyes of those packed into the room found the foreman, as he politely held the door for his fellows. Each stare studied his expression, waiting to see and wanting to be the first to know.

The story had started with one veteran newspaper reporter, cynical as acid; such is the fate of a hack who spends fifteen years covering the courts. He passed it onto a young, sharp-suited detective, who told a friend of the victim's family, who in turn handed on the golden nugget of insight.

So the ripples of knowledge ran. Like all such adages, each wanted to claim it for their own, and fast the whisper had spread.

Want to know the verdict before it's announced? Keep your eyes on the foreman. If he can look at the defendants, it's not guilty. If he can't...

And so each gaze was set upon this middle-aged, middle-class man, as ordinary as air. His skin was a little flushed, his shirt off-white with wear. His beard sprouted a hint unkempt, his fashionless glasses shined in the sunlight. And, as if he too was aware of the whisper, his own eyes were set away, upon the door, waiting as his eleven peers passed by.

Through one of the skylights, a gang of seagulls screeched a contemptuous call. Sunbeams floated in the still air. The footsteps of the jurors echoed across the old court's aged boards.

And the moment drew nearer.

***

Every seat of the public gallery was full, just as they had been for every day of the hearing. Billboards carried the headlines of the daily developments. Countless thousands of excited words were cast into the ether by radio and television reporters. The web buzzed with the digital traffic of theory and speculation.

Each day, there was a queue outside the court for seats. And as the days went on, the disciplined line, so beloved by the British, would form earlier and earlier and grow longer and longer.

Only two seats were always reserved; those in the front row at the very centre. Around this orderly arrangement had grown a hierarchy of ghouls. The greatest of favours, the proudest of a bore's boasts, be it at dinner table or bar, was to neighbour these seats; to feel the reactions of their occupants played out, so close, so very intimate, as each sting of evidence was aired.

For here was the victim. Someone who had to suffer, wherever they went, the reflex scrutiny that abets notoriety. As subtle as an earthquake, however much they might think otherwise, people would nudge each other and stare.

But at this moment, unique amongst all the weighty parade that had passed here, one seat was empty. The only one in the entire court to be that way; the only domino missing from the long line.

And the most paramount by far. The cog at the hub of the great legal machine. The reason all were here, the focus of every attention, even in her absence.

A weary man rested a father's hand across where she had sat. He leant forwards, almost doubled, face flushed, sweat growing on the baldness of his crown. His eyes were a boxer's: lined, wearied, pummelled and reddened by the repeated blows of the suffering he had endured.

And there had been so much. In the drowning, whirlpool hours of the crime itself, in the long weeks of this trial and in all the onerous days between.

But still, as with everyone else, his sight was set upon the jury box.

And now five were settled.

★★★

At the back of the court a woman sneezed and muttered an apology. But no one turned. On the bench, high at the head of the court, the judge tapped a hand on a pile of papers.

It would be his last case after sixteen years as the resident judge, a career spent dealing with the most notorious crimes the south-west of England had known. He would retire by Christmas, a decision the official announcement put down to a 'desire to explore other avenues in life'.

There was no quote from the subject himself, a silence interpreted as more eloquent even than the laser words he reserved for the malfeasants who appeared here. Or perhaps it was a result of the eccentricities which, the rumours had it, the learned judge had been exhibiting of late. Something the kinder sorts put down to the fraying of the fragile human sanity so often seen in grief.

He picked at the purple blaze of his robe and let a slow stare slip across the cast of the law. Barristers adjusting wigs and gowns in poor impersonations of indifference. Solicitors, clerks, detectives. All waiting, all preparing for victory or defeat.

A pen fell from a bench, rolled an unseen percussion across the wooden floor and rested unclaimed.

At the far end of the tight knot of police officers, a tall, well-groomed detective pulled a distracted finger at the pure white of his shirt. His neck was red, and he itched at it before turning the irritable habit to the thick gold band of his wedding ring. The worth of six months of investigations would be decided in just a handful of seconds.

Decided by not even a sentence; a mere word or two.

On either side of the Chief Inspector sat a woman, one dark haired and a few years younger, and the other with auburn hair and a little older. Each was working hard to favour the other with the thin façade of a colleague's neutral smile, and calm, professional composure. Even if they were far from the feelings pumping in their blood.

Now eight of the jurors were settled. And the ninth, a young man with a tussle of blond hair, was shifting a thin and threadbare cushion ready to join them.

Behind the plate glass of the secure dock a woman sat back, her legs crossed in serenity. Her face was unreadable, unreachable, remarkable for a lack of emotion in this tightening moment. What little expression there might be hovered aloof and detached. It was as if she were a scientist who had set in play this curious experiment, and who merely had to observe the triviality of its conclusions.

One hand rose and a long finger shaped a curl of ginger hair. The sunlight fell on the sprays of freckles which patterned the paleness of her face. Beside sat a man, similar but different in looks. He was leaning forwards, the pull of a T-shirt stretching across the inflated muscles of his chest. His hair stood short and spiked, a cleft pitting his chin. It was the director's look of a classic star, but he was here to play no hero.

So often had it been said, amongst those who filed daily into the public gallery, how very unlikely they looked to be accused of such a crime. She 30, a landmark age that should be amidst the founding times of career and family. Him a year and a half older. And if all the claims and charges were true, such venomous bitterness seethed within the two siblings.

And some said, so very quietly and always checking over their shoulders to be sure of the confidence, if indeed it was true – how they had come to be this way – then perhaps it was difficult to wholeheartedly condemn them.

★★★

Outside the courtroom, along an unseen corridor, a door banged shut. On the press benches a couple of court artists sketched at notebooks. The reporters that encircled them were poised, ready to break the news for which they had been waiting.

Ten jurors were seated now. There was just one more before the foreman would have to turn to the court and all the assembled would see where his look fell. But, as if the whims of fate could never resist one final tease for the earthbound fools of the human race, the last juror was an older lady. She, of course, had to fuss with her jacket and smooth down her skirt before she could even consider the possibility of lowering herself to the wooden bench.

A stifled groan rose from the public gallery. The father raised an arm and rubbed at his chest, massaging circles around his heart. Each breath won felt a wearying battle. The black gown of an usher floated over and, with practice born of experience, passed across the platitude of a glass of water.

Overhead, the thundering clatter of a low helicopter beat across the clear blue of the sky. The judge's eyes flickered upwards with a look that, were it possessed of physical force, would surely have been enough to shoot down the aircraft.

And the stillness settled once more.

On the press benches, at the far end, ready to burst out and break the story, Dan Groves inked and fattened the heading on his notepad.

Verdict – At bloody last.

He picked at the sticky cotton of his shirt. For every day of the six weeks of the trial, Dan had sat here. And for each of the five days the jury had deliberated he had waited. Like everyone else, drinking too much coffee. Trying to read a newspaper or magazine and fated always to fail. Jumping every time the tannoy crackled.

How many calls for barristers, solicitors and witnesses to attend a different hearing had they endured? Or routine reminders of fire safety procedures and requests not to leave bags unattended? How many before finally came the awaited words:

Verdict will now be taken in Court Three.

Eleven of the jurors were eventually, at last, in their seats and settled. The foreman was finally turning towards the court.

And Dan couldn't help himself from reaching out to grip the file – the fat folder containing his notes on this extraordinary case – heavy as it was with details of the intense and chaotic days of six months ago.

The days that had brought them here.

To the silent, resonating roar of this moment of justice.

CHAPTER TWO

It hadn't been a day to bother the mythical creatures who would be his biographers, but it felt all the more enjoyable for that. The simple pleasure of a whole day off, a species so rare it could outdo a cross between a unicorn and a yeti.

And that, Dan reflected as he paced across the classical Devon hillside of the springtime, was the result. His mind was skipping on the treetops. It was as if it had overdosed on the relaxation and was throwing up even more bizarre thoughts than the usual eccentric norms.

The fast scampering of padded feet landed the dream-weaver back in the park. Dan wheeled around, although not quickly enough to evade a whack in the side of the legs. Rutherford had kindly brought one of his traditional gifts, a sizeable stick. The master dutifully grabbed one end, but the Alsatian locked his teeth and hung on more determinedly than a shipwrecked sailor to a lifebelt.

"How many times have we had this conversation now? What's the point of you bringing me a stick if you don't let it go?"

As always, the logic made no headway. Dan fished a treat from his pocket, threw it, picked up the discarded stick and hurled it across the field.

"Stupid dog!" he called after the lolloping canine. "A couple more throws and it's time to get home."

They headed back towards the mansion of Saltram House, its Georgian angles stark in the day's falling sun. The silver stud of Venus, harbinger of the night, had begun to rise in the southern sky. The fields were filling with flowers, a dotted pallet of yellows, blues, purples and whites. Down in the valley, the Plym had fattened with a seasonal high tide, the silver curl of the river spotted with the odd boat and its shard of a wake. A couple of magpies hopped and chattered a courtship jig beneath the boughs of a veteran oak.

"It's that time of year," Dan told Rutherford, who had finally deigned to walk at some approximation to heel. "Maybe we should give Sarah a call, eh?"

The dog turned, wheeling the caber and dealing Dan a sharp blow on the other leg.

"Ouch! Ah, maybe you're right. She is a bit boisterous for a man making a rapid assault on middle age. Perhaps we should give Claire a ring then?"

Early in the years of their relationship, Dan came to understand that Rutherford possessed a vocabulary, albeit limited. In order of popularity, it ran; food, walk, cats, brush, bedtime. The entry of Claire into their lives had added a new word, and one which achieved the unimaginable feat of rivalling participants one and two.

Rutherford dropped the precious stick and let free a run of excitable barks. Dan patted his head and coaxed a couple of phantoms of floating hair from the dog's coat.

"Don't get too excited," he soothed. "I'm not saying we're getting back together. We're just seeing how things go."

Dan stretched, turned his face to the sky and added quietly, "Or should I say, *still* seeing how things go."

There were only a few cars left on the gravel outside the house. Most people had finished their walks and returned home for the Friday treat of a takeaway, a night on the town, or just a welcome chance to unwind. The sun was slipping fast towards the horizon and the evening air setting with a chill.

Dan's mobile began to trill in his pocket. "Maybe I started to relax too soon," he told Rutherford. "I bet it's work."

It wasn't. Not official work, anyway. The name Adam was flashing on the display.

"Evening, Chief Inspector," Dan answered, with some relief. "Are you still on for this beer then? I'm just—"

"This is urgent," came the ruthless interruption. "We've got a kidnapping. I need your help."

★★★

Dan bundled the reluctant Rutherford into the car and bounced it, roller coaster style, over the speed humps to the main road.

The traffic was sticky, tailing back along the embankment, a sweep of red brake lights stretching around the bend of the river. There were rat runs, but they would probably be clogged too. A woman on a bike picked a careful path through the cars, but was making much faster progress than her competitors.

Dan swore to himself and called the newsroom.

The duty journalist, Phil, keenest of the young trainees, began asking questions, but only very briefly. A sharp voice in the background interrupted and the phone was duly passed across to the Mark XIII editor of *Wessex Tonight*.

"Tell me everything," Lizzie commanded, and Dan did. "I want a live broadcast," came the instant reply. "I want a report. I want her parents. I want the cops. I want the lot."

"Ok."

"And absolutely no disappearing into the investigation – again."

"Never, naturally."

From behind, a siren wailed. Cars started easing aside, clearing one of the lanes.

"I mean it this time," Lizzie continued. "I'm fed up with your Sherlock Holmes act—"

Dan rubbed a finger over the car microphone. The line produced a satisfactory crackling.

"Sorry, you're breaking up," he called.

The siren was growing louder. It was a cop car, heading for town. Dan waited for it to edge past, then stamped on the accelerator, pulling hard into the slipstream.

Now they were shifting, cutting through the traffic and almost at the end of the embankment.

The policeman was eyeing his mirror. Dan rummaged in the glove box and found the 'Police Forensics on call' sign. He'd once borrowed it from a scientist, and had stupidly and repeatedly forgotten to return it. He placed it in the windscreen.

The cop nodded and focused back on the road.

The strange convoy sped on.

They were almost at the city centre.

***

The street was cordoned off, a young policeman standing a proudly upright sentry – the telltale sign of the new recruit. Along the pavement, four scenes of crime officers were kneeling and studying a doorway, faces hard to the ground, fingers probing. In the red-yellow hue of streetlight and dusk, their plastic suits shone like human fireflies.

The police helicopter hovered overhead, the beat of its rotors battering the ground. The shameless detritus of an English city centre: discarded shopping bags, parking tickets and penalty notices chased each other in whorls and eddies. The searchlight worked the road with a ring of white, twitching, shifting, swinging to each new target.

Detectives stopped passers-by. Some were let go immediately, others questioned in shouted interrogations, rapid notes taken.

A tall, slim figure walked quickly around the corner and towards the doorway. Even in the gloom Adam was unmistakable, with his upright gait, impeccable hair and mandatory smart suit. He moved like a stork and suffered a similar fondness for preening.

The detective's radar was working as efficiently as ever. Before Dan could wave, Adam beckoned. Like the best of experienced officers, Adam could ask a question without need of a word. His gaze had only to find Rutherford, busily sniffing at the fascination of a manhole cover.

"We were out walking," Dan shouted. "You said it was urgent, so he had to come."

Adam rolled his eyes, but began striding away, bent double to shelter from the assault of the chopper's noise. It echoed from walls, street, windows and pavements. The man-made hurricane of flying air pulled and pummelled at their hair and clothes.

He led Dan to an alleyway opposite the SOCOs. They were concentrating on a large picnic basket. The wicker cradle was on its side and spilled out a series of packets wrapped in cling film. A couple of thermos flasks lay there too, with another resting in the gutter.

The alley was narrow, lined with the litter of cigarette butts and streaked with dark fingers of damp. The mustiness of dirty drains lurked. A spray of graffiti claimed the territory for *Caz*.

The Valkyrie of the helicopter banked east and clattered off into the night, the sudden quiet a release of the booming pressure in the surrounding air.

"This'll have to be quick," Adam said. "The victim's Annette Newman, only child of Roger Newman."

"The kitchens and carpets man?"

"That's him." Adam pointed to where a couple of white-overalled figures were dusting at the doorway, the odd puff of a silver-sparkled cloud lingering in the half light. "She was taken there. A witness saw her being dragged into a white van." A police officer ran past, talking into his radio. In the distance, more sirens wailed.

"What time?" Dan asked.

"Quarter to eight. Just as it's getting dark."

"So the city's got a few people about if you need to blend in, but not too many if you want to avoid loads of witnesses."

"And the roads are still quiet for a getaway."

Adam's mobile rang. "As many as you can get," he said, quickly. "And fast." The detective hung up and added, "Firearms teams."

"So – the soup run?" Dan prompted, nodding over to the SOCOs. "Which would make sense of the sandwiches and flasks."

"You know about that?"

"It was all over the media. A part of settling that well-publicised spat with her dad."

"Right," Adam replied thoughtfully. "Which means…"

"Any criminal would know too. And if she does the same routine each week, there's your opportunity."

"Or invitation," the detective added, grimly.

Rutherford lifted a leg and left his traditional insignia on the alley. It was a mark of the intensity of Adam's focus that this figurehead of the law didn't even comment.

"We've got a partial plate for the van," he said. "Can you do a newsflash?"

Dan was about to head back for the cordon when the fast sound of hard shoes stopped him. He knew who it was without needing to turn around. Rutherford had begun a low whine of delight.

The *z* of *Caz* looked more like a two. Graffiti artists should take better care. Illegal though the art may be, if it was worth the risk of creating then surely it was worth making it understood.

The line of a perfect bob of dark hair edged into vision.

Dan stepped back, a crumpled drink can creaking underfoot. The *C* was far more artistically formed than the *z*. A fine three quarters of a ring. A steady circle suggested a natural talent, or so it was said.

The whining from Rutherford was growing louder. The dog started to pull at the lead.

An elegant figure in a black trouser suit was blocking Caz's artwork and dominating Dan's eyes. He managed a tight smile, before busying himself calming Rutherford, whispering to the dog and smoothing his fur.

As calmly as ever, in her gentle but authoritative voice, Claire said, "Mr Breen, we've got the ransom demand. But there's something very strange about it."

CHAPTER THREE

Darkness. Dense blackness. The tight pressure of thick cloth. Gripping teeth and mouth, binding her head and swaddling her eyes.

No light. No matter how hard she blinked, the blindfold wouldn't move.

Pure darkness.

But noise. A continual rumbling. Wheels running on tarmac.

She was in a car. In the boot. Trussed up in a box of metal, resting above some tools and a spare wheel.

No. She could bend her knees and stretch her legs. There was space. And air.

And it was moving. Fresh air flowing and playing over nose and hands and ankles.

A memory. Bending down. To the tramp. With a sandwich, a smile and a flask of hot coffee, steaming in the evening light. A hand coming up to meet her. A sweet smell and a swirling sickness.

Legs buckling. Falling. Eyes rolling and mind running along a narrow corridor, towards a distant circle of light. Head lolling, too heavy to hold. Arms grabbing. Doors opening, two doors, white doors, more hands. Floating free in a spinning netherworld.

Then blackness.

She felt her stomach churn, snorted in a breath, bit back the bubbling vomit.

A van. She was in the back of a van.

A new noise: a whine of brakes. The engine growling.

A different momentum. Turning.

Her body sliding across the cold metal floor. Faster. Unable to stop.

And now a shock. A presence in the blackness. A sudden pressure in the small of her back. A foot. Pushing her casually away. As indifferent as if she were a sack of rubbish waiting to be discarded.

Someone was there. Hiding in the darkness.

Someone unfeeling and uncaring. Heartless and ruthless. With no picture, no sense of who it could be, still she knew. As surely if it had been tattooed upon her thoughts.

She tried to call out. Form words, force them from her mouth, through the biting gag.

Hello? Who is that? Where are you taking me? What's happening?

But the constricting material allowed only a breathless moan.

And no voice rose in return. There was only the noise of the van. Building again.

But he was here. Alongside her. Studying her.

Eyes caressing her cheeks. Sliding downwards. Across her chest. Stopping, lingering, savouring the sight. To her stomach now. On to her thighs.

And between.

He was moving closer. Just the hint of motion. A creak of the van's floor.

And breath. Into her ear. Hot breath. Creeping across her face. Stinking breath. The curdling stench of a filthy mouth. So close against the prickling flesh.

The vomit rose again. She gulped and heaved. Shuddered, whimpered.

And now a touch. A finger. The scraping edge of an uneven nail. On her neck. Just below the ear. So softly she could only just feel it.

But her skin jumped at the sensation, as if trying to run.

The teasing pressure was toying with a patch of fine down. The dirty, exploring nail. Hovering above a single freckle. Lingering. Circling it. Pressing a little harder.

The rumbling of the van grew again. But joined by the beat of a regular bumping. And the sideswipe of a rushing wind.

A bridge. They were crossing a river, maybe a valley.

The finger was moving again. To her throat.

Her body tensed with an iron tautness. Ready for the soft touch to switch to the sudden slash of a knife. The killing blade slitting through helpless skin.

And to feel the life's blood flood from her.

She waited. And waited. Because there was nothing else she could do.

But still the finger teased her throat.

And now slipped downwards. Over clenched and tense muscle. To her chest. Pushing aside the cotton modesty of her shirt.

Inching towards her breast. Reaching the laced edge of her bra. And rubbing it. Running along the patterned ridges. Picking at the delicate whiteness. Moving towards her shoulder.

Pulling at the strap.

And now back to the swell of flesh. Stopping, hesitating.

Annette tried to curl herself into a ball. But the gripping ropes would grant no refuge.

The finger pushed harder, as if to penetrate her body.

Sweat flooded around it. Tiny rivulets rushing to escape the fearful pressure.

As she waited for the next assault.

But the finger was gone.

There was only blackness. And the incessant rumbling of the van.

But the man was still there. In the darkness.

Close by her side. All around her.

And everywhere inside her mind.

CHAPTER FOUR

Early in his career, Dan learned that an old cliché took on a new meaning in the life of a television reporter. There were storms aplenty, with only a rare few calms to precede them. And a journalist who becomes subsumed into the parallel world of police investigations only exacerbates the storms.

The ageing process wasn't helping. He'd done his best to ignore it, but it was like trying to overlook the influence of gravity. Eventually you had to accept something was going on, however hard it may be to define.

Morning runs with Rutherford, which had been an easy half an hour, were down to an arduous twenty-five minutes. And waking in the morning afresh after a few beers the night before felt like the lost fantasy of a distant youth. School night drinking had been quietly curtailed.

The conclusion was unavoidable: the years were going silently about their insidious work.

With a quiet nod to the importance of vanity, the bathroom light had been reduced in the revealing power of its merciless wattage. But, in truth, it was a poor compensation, as effective as shouting into a hurricane.

Thus Dan would take any precious chance for a moment's respite from the onslaught of the working day. And so, this fine Friday evening, amidst the white water rapids of a major investigation, he found a few minutes to disappear to a place where the mainstay of Plymouth's population had found calm throughout the years.

The great rocky promontory of Plymouth Hoe was at peace tonight. Atop the line of flagpoles the standards of the world hung limp, as if they too were resting in the sanctuary of the darkness. Amidst the harbour of the Sound a couple of merchant navy ships waited at anchor, highlighted by the red and green jewels of the lights of the breakwater.

To the west, above the easy arc of the Cornish coast, a half moon was rising. The waters were dark and still, as black as oil. The dart of a lone yacht made its unhurried way towards the sanctuary of Queen Anne's Battery, the churn of its engine softened by the distance.

Around the road that skirted the Hoe, a single low-slung car boomed its beating way. Dan followed the speeding path. It had always been a puzzle how the drivers of such cars longed to draw attention to themselves, when surely a wiser policy would be entirely the opposite.

The pillar of the Naval War Memorial watched over the Hoe, monument to the sacrifices of the fighting years, the countless lights of the city beyond. Rutherford tugged at the lead, and Dan – after securing a promise of good behaviour, however pointless – set the dog free. On one of the benches overlooking the Sound he settled and took out a photocopy of the blackmail note.

It appeared a simple demand for money, with just the one oddity. The mystery of those two, very deliberate, concluding initials.

★★★

The respite was a brief fifteen minutes, no more. Dan was due at Charles Cross Police Station at ten for a briefing. A report had been cut and left for the late bulletin, and the newsflash just about negotiated, albeit as a perilous voyage through rocks and storms.

After the discussion with Adam, Dan jogged back to the cordon to find exactly the cast he expected assembled. Brothers, if not in arms, then in the words and pictures of the media. Nigel was filming the scenes of crime officers going about their careful work and the policeman on guard duty. The cameraman was dressed in tatty jeans covered in white paint and a pullover upon which many a moth had grown fat. The ensemble was a sure sign of a scramble call.

Next to Nigel lurked the chubby, wild-haired, modern-day Machiavellian court jester that was Dirty El, camera fixed unerringly to his eye. He was wearing a familiar grimy, battered body warmer, bulging and misshapen with spare lenses, cloths, batteries, light meters, and all the disreputable armaments of the paparazzi kind.

"Ta for the tip off," he chirped, without lowering the lens. "Not another snapper in sight and I'm filling me memory card full of cash."

Behind both, sitting in the satellite truck and complaining, as ran the script of his life, brooded the champion misanthrope that was Loud. "What kind of bloody story breaks on a Friday night?" he grumbled, beard twitching in time with the moans. "I was going out for a curry. A hot one, with a nice fat naan bread."

Loud patted his stomach. The blue, red and yellow Hawaiian shirt was already straining to contain his impressive girth. Had the garment known what a taxing fate awaited it, the manufacturers may have riveted on the buttons, rather than sewn.

Dan put on a placating smile, the kind a parent might adopt for a recalcitrant toddler. He took the talkback unit which linked the outside broadcast truck to the studio and slipped the moulded plastic coil into his ear.

Rutherford was starting to pull at the lead again, so Dan pushed him into the safety of the van. The dog immediately started growling.

"Hey, what?" Loud protested. "What's his problem?"

"He's got good taste," Dan muttered.

"What?"

"I said he's not keen on facial hair. But keep still and quiet and he probably won't savage you."

In Dan's ear came the sound of the studio preparing for the newsflash. Nigel had positioned the camera with the police tape and sentry officer in the background.

"This is Emma in the Plymouth gallery," the director's voice broke through. "We're on air in three minutes. We've got 30 seconds exactly."

Dan grabbed a piece of paper and began scribbling notes. The newsreader's introduction would take about five seconds. Following the broadcaster's rough rule of three words a second, he had 75.

"On air in two and a half," came Emma's voice again.

"Move to your left a little please," Nigel said. "I want to get more of the scene in the background."

Dan shifted, but continued working on his words.

Two minutes.

The door of a bar crashed open and shouting echoed down the street. A group of young lads had seen the satellite truck. They tumbled out and began yelling abuse. Some was of a scale that might make even Channel Four think twice about broadcasting it.

Ninety seconds.

The men lurched over, juggling pints and bottles of beer, splashes spilling onto the pavement. One made a play of getting down on his knees to lick up the sacred liquid. Others formed a line and began dancing a conga, singing, *We're all on the telly, we're all on the telly.* Another ran into the background, bared his rear and patted a tune in time. The pallid, pasty flesh proudly sported a Plymouth Argyle Football Club tattoo, and a large one given the expanse of available space.

Yet again a fundamental rule of the TV business had been proven in an instant. The camera is a magnet for the insane, drunk, stupid or simply offensive. Whatever the limits of their faculties, they can somehow sense television being made from a range of several miles and are inexorably drawn towards it.

Sixty seconds.

"We can't go on air like this," Nigel yelled, above the cacophony. "We'll have to pull the broadcast."

"No way. We don't fail."

Dan glanced around. Where the hell was Adam? He'd be able to gather some cops to control the men, but the detective was nowhere in sight.

Thirty seconds.

Dan lurched for the satellite truck, reached in and grabbed Rutherford. The dog produced a movingly loving look, so Dan thrust him towards Loud. The Alsatian bared his teeth and began growling.

Twenty seconds. Dan, where are you? What the fuck are you doing?

He jogged back to the camera. At the sight of the snarling Rutherford the men backed off.

Ten seconds.

Dan sat the dog beside him, just below the camera's shot.

"We interrupt this broadcast to bring you a newsflash," came Craig, the presenter's voice.

Cue Dan.

"In the last hour, a well-known young woman has been kidnapped from this street in Plymouth," he intoned. "She's Annette Newman, daughter of Roger, the millionaire entrepreneur famed for pulling himself up from one of the city's toughest areas to found the Roger's Rugs empire. The police believe the kidnappers got away in a white van. Its registration plate ended in the letters TN. If anyone spots such a van, they're asked to call 999 immediately."

★★★

A young couple walked past, hand in hand. They stopped by the war memorial to steal a kiss.

The woman bent to pat Rutherford, but hesitated. "Does he bite?"

"Only undesirables," Dan replied. "You'll be fine."

The dog accepted a few seconds stroking in that disinterested manner of his, before trotting back to the bench.

"You did well with the newsflash," Dan told him. "Operation Anti-Chav went impressively smoothly. Now, I need to ask you a question – how do you think I did with Claire?"

Rutherford lay down and let out a sizeable yawn.

"Thanks, dog. But you may have a point."

After the broadcast, Claire had stopped at the satellite van. She was carrying a weight of papers and was on her way to Charles Cross to prepare for the briefing. They exchanged an awkward peck of a kiss, then stepped back into silence.

It was one of those emotional stalemate moments, high in the order of human embarrassments. Two people who knew each other so well, but still had no idea what to do next.

"Well?" she asked, eventually.

"Well what?" he replied, with a little shuffle.

"You know what."

"If I knew what I wouldn't be asking what."

Claire sighed. "Will we have a chance to catch up in the next few days?"

The shuffle became a jig. "I hope so."

"But?"

"This case is going to be busy."

"Is that all?"

"Yes," said Dan, in a voice that sounded thin, even to him.

"We are going to have to talk sometime."

The voice dieted further. "Yes."

"Have a think, if that's not beyond your emotional intelligence," she replied, patiently. "I'll see you in the briefing."

On the subject of which, it was time to make for Charles Cross. Dan got up from the bench, stretched, and took one more look at the blackmail note.

We wAnt CasH A million USed notes 4 AnnET WE call Soon 2 arrange DeLivery

The letters had been cut from a series of newspapers. The fonts familiar; the tactic a traditional one. It all looked straightforward enough, a standard kidnapping for money. A mundane crime of which the world saw far too many examples each and every year.

It was just the curiosity of the final line of the note. The letters **PP** which had been placed there, and in such a pointed manner that it could never have happened by anything other than very deliberate design.

CHAPTER FIVE

The back gate to Charles Cross Police Station is an imposing one, heavy with steel bars and topped by razor wire. The barrier grinds open notoriously slowly, and with a persistent groaning and shuddering which harks of a great beast begrudgingly awoken.

The locking mechanism emits the dull clunking required to ensure a visitor is well aware any attempt to hurry it would be the most pointless of follies. Spotlights illuminate the approach and CCTV cameras scrutinise those who come and go with unblinking, electronic eyes.

It's a point sometimes debated amongst the more philosophical of the policing community, whether this is really necessary or more down to psychology. The gate makes an unmistakable statement that the might of the law lies beyond. For anyone brought here as a suspect, the intimidating entrance could be said to mark the first softening up of the interrogation process.

Be all that as it may, the gate is habitually closed. So it was a surprise for Dan to find it wide open as he drove along the back road leading to the police station. He edged the car in and looked for a space to park. For this time of night, the compound was unusually busy. He taxied to the very back and manoeuvred into a narrow slot beside a couple of motorbikes.

As his eyes adjusted to the gloom, shapes began to assume forms, detaching themselves from the darkness. Standing quietly by the four police cars nearest the entrance was a circle of officers. Each was checking a submachine gun. Black and snub nosed, the weights of deadly metal clicked smoothly under careful fingers. Heavy crescents of magazines were loaded with gleaming bronze cylinders. Stocks were extended and folded again, sights lifted to eyes. The flitting red flies of laser dots darted over the blackness of the walls.

Each of the four cars was angled towards the gate. A radio buzzed with a tinny voice, the words lost in the background traffic of the city. One of the officers, a burly sergeant, replied in a gruff voice.

"Firearms teams standing by. We're good to go the second you get a trace."

★★★

On the top floor of the five that make up the block that is Charles Cross lies the Major Incident Room, or MIR. There's the option of the lift to reach it, but it's small, cramped, and takes considerably longer than walking up the stairs. The station gossip has it that it's a deliberate ploy, to ensure the sedentary, desk-bound cops get at least some exercise in a day.

Large and long, the MIR looks out on the city and over Charles Church – the bombed out memorial to the Blitz of Plymouth. Dan slipped to the back of the room, a little detached from the bear pit these briefings could become, and perched on the windowsill.

The congregation reacted to him in its usual way: a mix of hostility and acceptance, roughly divided in equal proportions. Adam's patronage was an effective shield, but many still felt a journalist had no place within another highly sensitive case.

The detective standing just a metre away was a devoted member of the antis. He recoiled at the arrival of the interloper and adopted a glower akin to a gathering storm. The young man had a militarily short haircut and was squat and powerful, with an anvil-like head. He radiated hostility as hot as an electric fire.

Dan busied himself with winding his ever-erratic watch. The tired old Rolex said the time was twenty to ten, so it was probably around five to. Rutherford had been left in the car. It was stretching the limited strain of Adam's patience to bring the dog into the briefing.

Already the MIR had filled with around forty officers, a mix of detectives and uniformed police. It was a testament to one of their detective chief inspector's idiosyncrasies, an insistence on punctuality. The felt boards he habitually used to set out the patterns of a case had also been retrieved from dusty storage and set up at the front of the room. Chatter rumbled, snatches of discussions about the case, theories being aired.

Adam walked in at just before ten, followed by Claire, and the room immediately quietened. "Let's get moving," he said. "We haven't got much to go on at the mo'. We need to start finding something – and fast."

Claire began handing out briefing papers. Detective Anvil Head hesitated and pointedly caught Adam's eye with a question, before reluctantly passing them on.

"We're dealing with at least two people," Adam continued. "A witness saw someone inside the van. He reckons they opened the back doors and helped drag Annette in."

The young detective was taking notes. Tempting though it was, Dan managed to refrain from commenting on how *siezed* would traditionally be spelt.

"Secondly, our 'crims' are calculating. The ransom demand was brought to us by the barman of The Stars, the place along the street from where Annette was taken. It was given to him by a vagrant. The tramp says he was approached by a man and given twenty quid to take the note to the bar."

"Bit of a risk, wasn't it?" a woman at the front asked. "He might just not have bothered."

"The kidnapper thought of that. He told the tramp the barman would give him another twenty when he'd handed over the note." Adam waited, let the moment run. "The tramp also got a bottle of cheap whisky. It's put him well away in drinkland. All he's been able to tell us is that the guy was wearing shades and a baseball cap."

Adam's mobile rang. He held up an apologetic hand, paced over to the corner of the MIR and answered.

Dan used the interlude to flick through the briefing. On the second page was a black and white photograph of Annette, a classical passport shot. Dark hair trailed down her back and her features were shaped in the sort of mystical look the Mona Lisa might have accepted as a decent impersonation.

There was something else about the picture. It was nothing that could be distilled into a thought or description. No attempt to articulate the shape of her face, colour of complexion, or the warmth of the young woman's eyes. Frail words didn't suffice.

Dan tapped a pen on his notepad. It took several seconds before he realised.

It was the joy of embarking on an adventure. The anticipation of striding out into the world, to absorb the understandings it would whisper, and to parade all that she was going to offer to the waiting audience.

As esoteric as it may be, it was that which filled Annette's features: the simple relishing of life.

★★★

Adam ended his call and turned back to the MIR. "Deputy Chief Constable," he said. "To helpfully point out the case is going to be all over the press and a fast result would be appreciated. Those weren't his actual words, by the way."

Laughter tickled the room. Brian 'The Tank' Flood was a former military man, renowned for being as diplomatic as a bare knuckle boxer with a score to settle.

Claire held up a copy of the ransom demand. "Does anyone have any thoughts about the bizarre *PP* part?"

Anvil Head said, "It's often used to mean PayPal." Some of the older officers looked bemused, so he added, "It's a way of transferring money online."

"You reckon that could link in with the ransom demand, Steve?" Claire asked.

"It's a possibility."

Dan was finding it hard to shift his look from the picture of Annette. But he must have been half-listening, because he realised he'd snorted.

"You disagree?" Claire prompted, amusement in her voice.

"No… well, yes, I do. Whoever heard of a ransom demand via PayPal?"

"It's the modern world, mate," Steve replied, with more wit than might have been expected from his appearance. "It's called the in-ter-net."

"And our kidnappers are called cle-ver. Unlike some people," Dan added, pointedly. "How long would it take to trace them if they used PayPal? There's something more to those initials."

The Anvil was beginning to glow. "It's a simple kidnapping case, mate. You make it sound like some film. And who are you again, by the way?"

A couple of sniggers rose in the room. And the reporter and amateur investigator, who had told himself time after time not to rise to the baits of his complicated life, gleefully clamped his teeth on another.

"I'm the man who was solving crimes when you were still fantasising about starting to shave," Dan explained.

"Ok," Adam intervened. "That'll do."

"A quick bit of research throws up lots of other possibilities," Claire said. "A couple of bits of musical, mathematical and computing shorthand, signing a letter on someone's behalf, and a few linguistic and scientific phrases. We're looking at them now."

Adam stepped forward once more and listed the other branches of the inquiry. Roger Newman was being interviewed, to see if he had made any enemies who might want to harm him or Annette.

No forensic evidence, fingerprints or DNA had been recovered from the ransom note. The scene of the kidnapping yielded various strands of hair and plenty of fibres, but they could have come from a thousand passers-by.

A kidnapping expert from Scotland Yard, Katrina Harper, would be here within the hour. She was a veteran of such cases.

The reaction to that was intriguing. Everyone knew the name and greeted it with admiration. A couple of men along from Dan nudged each other and exchanged looks of approval, both professional and personal.

"Who's she?" Dan whispered to one.

"She does all the big kidnaps. Damn good at them, too."

"I've never heard of her."

"Quite," the man replied.

"Ah." Dan jotted a thoughtful note to his pad and asked, "What does she look like?"

"You'll know her, don't worry about that."

To round off the briefing, there was a rapid discussion on where the kidnappers may have taken Annette. They would have prepared a hideout, the consensus had it. Probably somewhere remote, but close enough to reach before police patrols were on the roads. Working on a maximum of a mile a minute, it meant within 30 miles of Plymouth. A sizeable section of the open tracts of Dartmoor was within reach. As was much of the classical Devon countryside of the South Hams – all fields, woods and secluded coastline – and large parts of south and east Cornwall.

"Too big an area to think about searching," was Claire's summary. "We've got to narrow it down."

"So," Adam rallied, "we need to build up some momentum. Don't wait, keep working. Don't hesitate, keep moving. Don't be deterred, keep trying. Work your patch, your informants and your instincts. Be restless and relentless. Follow that trail, trace that lead and sniff out that scent."

He gestured to the felt boards. A large picture of Annette had been placed in the centre.

"She's a young girl. She'll be frightened witless. She's in danger and it's down to us to save her. Her fate's in our hands. Go to it, team."

The energy of the words infused the detectives. The invisible allies of purpose and belief, zeal and determination were riding alongside.

Some officers made for the phones or computers in the corner, others the door. But it burst open before anyone could leave.

A flushed young man, wearing a T-shirt and with flying wavy hair, stumbled in and panted, "We've got the ransom call."

CHAPTER SIX

She could smell his excitement. Could feel the pressure hard against her. Just as it had been with James, that summer night on the beach.

But no moonlit fondness here. No lovers-to-be promise to wait for the moment. No delicious anticipation.

Just fear. Fire and ice. Pulse and throb, pulse and throb.

Knowing the faceless man in the endless darkness would take that which she had so carefully kept. In a second, a moment or an hour. At his leisure, when he was ready.

That sour breath on her face again. The curdled air in her nose.

And a new sensation. A slippery pressure upon her cheek.

At first so soft she couldn't be sure it was there.

And even as it grew more insistent, still she didn't understand.

Or perhaps didn't want to. And feared to imagine.

Until it flicked back and forth.

And stopped.

And she could feel the spittle and saliva. Prickling on her skin.

On her cheek, her ear, her neck.

As his probing tongue tasted her body.

She tried to shout, scream, shift her weight. Turn away, crawl off, shrink back. But the binds were too tight, too strong for the slightest release.

Her flank throbbed from the unyielding pressure of the cold metal. The knot of the blindfold was boring through the back of her skull. The wiry cloth cutting into her temples. Her ankles were raw and weeping where they locked together.

The van slowed, bumped and slewed.

Her hair. A strand was moving, now a lock.

A bunch of hair, gathered and stroked.

Just like Dad did, when she was a girl. When she had hurt her knees in the playground. Or suffered one of the colds of childhood.

As she lay on the bed in her room. Curtains drawn, duvet tucked around.

The comfort of caring. Of being loved.

The way James did now.

But not with this touch. The filthy fingers. The abhorrent, alien claws.

Pulling at her hair. Harder, sharper.

But now flinching and stopping.

Something had changed.

She tried to see through the entombing darkness, hear above the incessant rumbling.

The sound of a siren. Growing.

The sound of hope.

Annette tried to move, cry out, but the merciless ropes refused to relent.

The police knew about the kidnapping. Someone had seen her being hauled into the van.

They'd got its description. They knew the number plate.

Dad had offered a huge reward. A TV appeal for help. People were walking the countryside, watching the streets. All for this van.

And someone had seen it. Reported it.

The siren was growing louder.

The sound of salvation.

She would soon be free. The future she hadn't dared to think about would be returned.

The carefree university years, to live life. To study medicine and become a doctor. Maybe a surgeon.

Or perhaps she would be a teacher.

Whatever, whichever. She would be something. Not a corpse, a headstone, a memory.

It was hers once more. The restoration of life.

The siren was almost upon them. She could sense the man stiffen. Fill with panic.

His turn to know fear.

There would be no violation. No mutilation. No death.

Freedom was only seconds away.

Annette felt tears growing in her eyes.

But the siren was passing.

Moving fast. Fading away.

She wanted to spring up, wave, yell, call and beckon.

But all she could do was lie still and feel the precious hope drain away.

Another noise. Movement, sliding across the van.

Faster than before. More confident.

More eager.

The man was back beside her. Studying her again. Relishing her body.

The touch of his fingertip. In the small of her back. Tracing the leather line of her belt.

And now shifting downwards.

The nausea struck again. And this time it was too strong. An irresistible flood of vomit, purging from her body.

The sickness boiled into her mouth, surged through her nose, sprayed around the gag, spattered across cheeks and chin. Grains of food trapped in her teeth and the sticky, stinking smell filled the tiny space of her incarceration.

But the hands came for her once more.

CHAPTER SEVEN

The kidnappers called at 10.38pm. What they had to communicate lasted just 23 seconds.

Adam led the charge to the control room, a tumbling stampede down the stairs to a basement that could have been a telesales centre. Orderly rows of desks and terminals, operators wearing headsets, calm lighting, even a line of pot plants flourishing on the windowsill.

But in one corner was sprawled an old-fashioned jumble of modern technology. Servers and keyboards, waveforms dancing on a display and a tangle of coloured wiring. It was here they gathered while the young man began fiddling with some leads, his jeans sagging to reveal red and white checked pants.

"Zac Phillips," Claire whispered to Dan. "Head of our Techno Crime department, or 'the Eggheads'. But don't say that to his face. Or backside."

"No rush," Adam hissed, managing to make just two words scathingly sarcastic.

The rear wriggled back towards them. Zac hopped up, hit his head on the desk, cursed, switched on a speaker and tapped at a keyboard.

A phone line buzzed. There was a shallow gasp, then a young woman's wavering voice.

"Hello – hello. Please get this to the police. This is Annette. They've got me. They say they'll…"

The words faded into a gulp. A clunk echoed in the background, followed by what sounded like a grunt. "No, please, please," the voice begged. "Don't…"

Another hum of the line and Annette spoke again, her words so quiet they had to strain to hear. All leaned instinctively forwards, clustered around the speaker. It was obvious she was reading from a script, the words faltering with each line.

"They say they'll kill me unless… you get the money. They want it tomorrow. They'll call then to arrange delivery."

There was a stifled sob and the harsh electronic whine of the disconnection tone.

Adam turned away and swore. Claire stared at the speaker, her usual equanimity ruffled as sure as treetops shifted by an irresistible wind. Zac hesitated, then tapped at the keyboard. The recording played once more.

"Enough," Adam ordered, when it ended. "Why couldn't we trace it?"

"They didn't call us," Zac replied. "They rang the AA."

"Alcoholics Anonymous?" Dan queried.

"Don't be bloody ridiculous," Adam snapped. "This is no time for stupidity. The motoring lot."

"They record all calls," said Zac. "They rang us as soon as it came in and sent the file over. But there's nothing we can do to trace it."

"Smart bastards," Adam muttered.

"They know what they're doing," Claire observed. "Not getting involved in negotiations. Not giving us a chance to drag things out and find them."

"We'll analyse the call to see if there's anything in the background that could help," Zac said. "But I'm not hopeful."

Dan reached for the speaker and turned the volume up to maximum. "Can you play it again?"

"Why?" Adam grunted.

"Just… something."

Annette's frightened voice once more filled the room. One by one, the operators looked over. An older woman began dabbing at her eyes.

"There," Dan said.

Adam leaned further forwards. "What?"

"The last few seconds of the call."

In the background, faint but audible, a bird had begun singing out a tune. It was a rapid, oddly metallic sound.

Sre, sre, sre.

Sre, sre, sre.

"Well?" Adam urged. "What? Have you got something? Come on!"

"Birdsong," Dan said slowly.

"Birdsong? Is that it? In spring? Thanks for the fantastic insight. Now stop wasting my bloody time. I don't have enough as it is."

But Dan was still staring at the speaker and didn't register the tirade. "Birdsong," he repeated to himself, thoughts reaching out their invisible fingers for an elusive understanding.

The door opened and an elegant figure slipped into the control room, moving as easily as a summer breeze. Her steps made barely a sound.

"Katrina," Adam said, warmly. "That's good timing. We need your help, and fast."

The detective shook hands and introduced Claire, Zac and then Dan.

Still drifting, still seeking the something that he knew was somewhere, Dan managed to pull his gaze from the speaker and hold out a distracted hand. It was only then he registered the most mesmeric pair of eyes he had ever seen.

★★★

Adam gruffly announced he required some air, so instead of returning to the MIR they walked outside. The firearms teams were still waiting by the gate of the compound, a couple puffing away at cigarettes, the red tips lighting and fading in the gloom. The occasional hint of smoke scented the night air.

Zac stayed in the control room to work through the recording. He also wanted to be on hand in case more messages came through.

"There won't be any," Katrina said, with such certainty that no one thought to dissent. "They've said what they needed. The pressure's on us now."

The night was still clear, but growing chillier. The brighter stars faced down the challenge of the city lights and patterned the sky.

Claire slipped a jacket over her shoulders. Dan jogged to his car and did likewise, taking the opportunity to give Rutherford a quick break.

"I'm sorry this is taking longer than I thought, old friend," he said. "But it is important, I promise you. We've got to save a young girl and she sounds terrified."

From the overnight kit Dan kept in the boot, he took out a towel and laid it on the back seat to make Rutherford more comfortable.

Adam hadn't bothered to don a jacket. He paced back and forth, never quite still, the agitation allowing him no peace. Every crime the traditionalist detective investigated was forever carried upon his back.

A keen student of his friend, Dan knew that these burdens lay behind a quirk of Adam's character – his use of those felt boards, such an anachronism in an age of computers. He insisted upon a picture of the victim being at the centre of an inquiry, for all to see. It was a continual reminder to his fellow officers of the importance of their work.

For a family man in thought, word and deed, this kidnapping must feel personal. Adam would be thinking about his teenage son Tom, imagining him in Annette's place.

As for Katrina, she was an antidote to Adam's unrest. She stood straight, unmoving in her focus, and with the elegance of a classical statue. Her arms were folded, her fine figure silhouetted by the lights of the police station, one foot angled on the heel of a shoe.

"Would you mind clarifying your role here?" she asked Dan, as he returned.

"Well, I'm—"

"He's a journalist," Adam interrupted. "He's been seconded to the investigation, in particular to help with the media coverage."

"A journalist?"

The words were evenly weighed, but honed with an unmistakable edge.

"Dan's worked with us many times before," Adam replied. "He's trustworthy."

Katrina was studying Dan's shoes, trousers, and now the buttons on his jacket, one by one, her gaze moving slowly upwards. It was as if she were assessing the entirety of his existence in just one look.

And Claire was watching her do it.

Dan found himself shifting awkwardly from foot to foot.

Finally, Katrina said, "In my experience these cases are better addressed quietly, with journalists kept at a distance. They tend to… complicate matters."

"Look, I've—" Dan began, but Adam interrupted again.

"He's fine. He's here on my say so and I'll take responsibility."

Katrina paused, held Adam's gaze. Contained within was an interrogation. *Can I trust you? Is your judgement shrewd? Do you have the drive to see this through?*

And all this in a single, calm stare. After a few seconds, Katrina nodded and began a discussion about the investigation.

Every few seconds, try as he might, Dan couldn't help himself from finding her eyes. They were like two leaves of the autumn; one an evergreen, the other tawny with the turning of the season.

★★★

Across the city, a distant clock struck eleven. The faint sounds of a Friday night crept into the compound. Taxis zipping back and forth, laden with weekend revellers. The odd shout or scream of laughter, and the ubiquitous accompaniment to any night out in every English town or city: the speeding sirens en route to yet another flare of drunken thuggery.

At the back of Charles Cross Police Station, amidst this little group of four, such everyday images had no chance of intruding. Lying on the tarmac between them, the focus of every thought and exchange, was a 17-year-old girl. Tied up, gagged and helpless. Perhaps in the cold surrounds of a cellar or garage, flinching at every sound, however slight.

Standing over her were two, or maybe more, faceless people. Dark outlines staring down at their prize. Weighing up the value of a young woman before they made a final decision on her fate.

"There's just one real oddity to the case," Adam said, and went through the issue of the *PP* at the end of the ransom note.

"That's something I've never seen before," Katrina replied. "If you're suggesting it might be the signature of a gang, I think that's unlikely. It feels… meaningful, but more subtle."

"That's just what I said," Dan contributed eagerly, but to no effect.

"Any thoughts?" Adam continued.

"At this stage, I'm afraid none."

The radio in an Armed Response Vehicle squawked. As one, they stopped talking and listened in. It was a call for available units to deal with a minor crash on the edge of the city.

"You've got the standard enquiries in train?" Katrina asked.

"Everything's covered," Claire replied.

"Then hard though it may be, on that front all we can do is wait."

Adam stopped his pacing. "Wait?"

"Kidnappings are all about patience. We have to wait for their next move before we can make ours. This is the submerged phase. The moment they break the surface, it'll create ripples. Then we can start to circle in. But if we try to do anything now, we're just thrashing around and likely to make the picture more confused."

Her eloquence and easiness with words saw Dan nodding to himself. He slipped out his notebook.

"I'd rather you didn't," Katrina said, without looking at him.

Dan found himself putting away the pad. The voice was soft, but the command clear and incontestable, even if irksome. It was time to progress from being a pet, only talked about but never contributing.

"You said 'on that front'. Is there anything else we can do, aside from the investigation?"

Now Katrina turned, and perhaps with a new interest. "You were listening."

"It's my job – or part of it."

"Yes."

There was a silence. Again, Dan thought he sensed Claire looking from Katrina to him, but in the semi-darkness he couldn't be sure.

"What?" Adam prompted.

"It's just a little… groundwork. A detail of manipulation."

A police car pulled up and a pair of cops climbed out, pulling a young man from the back. Drying sick stained his shirt and blood was trickling from a gash in his forehead. He was so drunk that each limb appeared to be functioning without any central control.

"Regular customer," one of the officers said, as they walked past. "We should start a loyalty card scheme."

Katrina waited until the men disappeared through the doors.

"At the moment the kidnappers see Annette as nothing more than a cashpoint. Which makes it easy to harm her – far too easy. We need to change that."

"How?" Adam asked. "We've got no way of getting in touch with them."

"Not quite."

"Meaning?"

"Her father's the only close family, you said?"

"Yes."

"How is he?"

It was Claire who replied, and with an unusual sharpness. "How do you think he is?"

"Apologies, it was a clumsy question," Katrina countered, smoothly. "What I meant was – might he be composed enough to help us?"

"Like how?" Adam asked.

The charismatic silhouette didn't reply, but instead slowly pointed an elegant forefinger at Dan.

CHAPTER EIGHT

It is the way of the law to begin work early, however inconsiderate.

Dan would commonly suffer a dawn start to follow that staple of a reporter's life: the police raid. It was a standard attempt by any given constabulary to grab a few easy headlines at a time when the news may have been less favourable. Bashing in doors and dragging felons from king-size beds funded by their ill-gotten gains is always good sport.

This morning's early rousing, however, was for a task requiring far more sensitivity. It was Katrina's view – and without the risk of melodrama, she insisted – that a young girl's life may depend upon it.

The hour was approaching six o'clock, the new day inheriting the crispness of the night. Dan jogged around Hartley Park, Rutherford mostly alongside but occasionally sprinting off to investigate the call of an intriguing sound or the lure of a distant scent.

Across the rooftops and through the trees, the rising sun cast her fiery weaves. Hidden birds rustled in the leaves and sang out their welcome for the promise of another fine day.

Sre, sre, sre, Dan trilled to Rutherford. "Why won't that sound get out of my head, dog?"

Another potential clue had been uncovered last night. The analysis of the ransom call had picked up a faraway noise, hidden within the hum of the line. It was thought to be a lawnmower.

Dan was due to meet Nigel and Loud at Charles Cross at a quarter to seven. He hadn't got to sleep until well after one last night.

Initially, in a familiar attempt to claim as much of the sweet, carefree release of bed as possible he'd set the alarm for six. But Rutherford produced one of his specialist never-been-loved looks. Had the dog been able to speak, he would doubtless have raised the issue of the hours of confinement in the car last night. So they'd got up half an hour earlier to share a run.

A couple more laps, then back to the flat to shower and he would set off for the city centre. Dan wanted to be there in plenty of time. An important day lay ahead.

Rutherford returned from a futile mission to catch a pigeon and together they increased the pace, following the ring of a track worn in the morning's dew. Past the line of oak and lime trees, past the children's play area, past the hill of the underground reservoir, heading for the entrance to the park.

In the time remaining, Dan thought through the briefing he'd studied last night: the details of the life of Roger Newman and all his impressive array of achievements. His daughter, her upbringing and their very public difficulties.

But most importantly, the questions Dan would ask in the interview with Roger, and how to shape the ten minutes of television which would be broadcast around the world.

★★★

Loud and Nigel were both waiting in the car park of Charles Cross, as was Adam. He was pacing again and continually glancing over at the gate.

The latest of his best suits was the attire of choice: navy blue and purchased only a month ago. It was the result of a shopping expedition to Bristol. Plymouth had been adjudged as unable to offer the calibre of menswear outfitters suitable for the Chief Inspector's style.

Not to mention vanity Dan thought, but managed not to say. The hint of a television appearance was sufficient to send Adam into a whirl of agonising about the day's couture.

It had been no surprise to anyone who knew the detective that he also returned with three new ties and two new shirts. All boasted the kind of price tags that Dan, a budget shopper at the best of times, would have assumed as an error had he not known otherwise.

Nigel was checking the camera, microphones and lights. Interviews could be knocked off in a few seconds when they were hard up against a deadline, but lighting added tone, depth and class to an image.

"We want this to look good," the kindly cameraman muttered to himself. "The poor, poor man."

He was also wearing a tie, although of a more antiquated variety. It was an appendage Nigel carried in the car, but donned only for the most serious of stories.

"I can't stop thinking how I'd feel if one of my boys was kidnapped," he said. "The guy must be going through torment."

"The thought had occurred to me," Dan replied levelly, trying to ignore Adam who was nodding in agreement.

He hadn't stopped looking at his watch and glancing at the gate. "Newman will be here in a minute," the detective chided, as he hovered. "This is really important."

"Yes, I am aware of that," Dan said, marshalling the remaining forces of his thinning patience. "Would you like to heap on any more pressure, or will that do for now?"

★★★

Katrina was sitting in the MIR, waiting. The brightness of the morning sun collected in the contrasting colours of her eyes.

The *Greater Wessex Police* boards had been set up at the back of the room; a smart and authoritative blue, embossed with a pattern of the force's badge. Two chairs were placed in front, facing each other.

"That should do nicely for the interview," Adam said.

The clock on the wall made the time ten to seven. Nigel started setting up the camera, but Dan reached out a restraining hand.

"Come on, we don't have time to muck about," Adam whined. "Everyone's waiting for this interview."

"Not like this."

"What?"

"Not with those boards."

"What's wrong with them?"

Dan picked up a glass of water and took a swig. "It's no time to bother you with the theory of my job, but... by far the biggest message people take from an interview comes from what they see."

"Yeah, ok, but—"

"If we use those police boards, what does it say to the kidnappers?"

"For God's sake," Adam spluttered. "We're about to interview a man whose daughter's been abducted, who could be killed at any moment, and you're worrying about—"

"Adam!" Dan heard himself shout. "I know all that. Hell, I know it! I'm trying to help."

"And I'm telling you—"

"I think he's right."

The voice was quiet and calm, but it halted the fractious toddlers in a second. Katrina stood up and glided over to the boards.

"This interview – it needs to be all about Annette. Not a hint of the police. We should be silent and shadows."

Dan took advantage of Adam's prevailing state of chagrin to begin shifting the boards; Nigel helping. For a backdrop, they decided on the unnoticeable neutrality of a pot plant and a window.

The time had crept on to five to seven. Dan sipped some more water, sat down and checked through his briefing on the lives of Roger and Annette Newman for one final time.

★★★

Roger grew up on the Eddystone Estate on the northern edge of Plymouth; a place with very distinctive connotations.

At the sight of those words, employers would consign job applications to the simplest of filing destinations. Pizza, Chinese and Indian takeaway drivers generally refused to deliver. The fire and ambulance services would call for a police escort if they had to visit, as often they did. And the unfortunate officers themselves would sigh, curse their fortune and don protective clothing.

As estates go, the joke had it the Eddystone was as sunk as the Titanic.

Unusually, Roger had been born to a couple that actually lived together. But normal service was quickly resumed as the relationship lasted for only the first six months of his childhood. His mother, though, had been determined the young boy should have a decent chance at life and lobbied to get him into a school a safe separation from the estate.

She faced a familiar problem. The all-knowing state was having none of it. With the sympathy, understanding and helpfulness of the massed hierarchy of a faceless bureaucracy, her pleas were rebutted. Roger was allocated a place at Eddystone Comprehensive, an educational establishment the wags described as comprehensive only in one field – its awfulness.

But the young Roger was favoured with a little luck. With the influence of his mother, and the emerging character of a man she described as her *little scrapper*, he managed to steer clear of gangs and the call of crime, aside from one dressing down for fighting. And that, legend told, was with an older and larger boy, who had been trying to steal money from one of Roger's friends.

But perhaps the greatest fortune was a teacher at the Eddystone, a man who recognised a kindred spirit in the youngster and who guided him onwards. Roger performed well in his exams. He went on to take A-levels and suddenly was in possession of something his life had known little of to that point: options, possibilities and maybe even the promised land of prospects.

For what made up a touching CV, this part was marked with the most underlinings in Dan's notes. There had been no history of achievement in his own family either, and it was only the intervention of a couple of teachers that had guided the young Dan to university and his world of today. It was one he could never have imagined all those years ago.

Roger had decided against studying for a degree, pronouncing himself insufficiently academic, but instead left school to go into business. In the sixth form, he'd been given work experience at a couple of local companies. His time there was fondly remembered, largely because of his politeness and willingness to listen and learn, but also one singular feature. He always carried a notepad and would jot down the slightest experience, tip or sliver of advice.

The contacts he made and the impression he left brought Roger the job of a trainee at a carpeting company. It was new and growing, and the future looked optimistic. But Roger stayed for only a year. In interviews afterwards, he said that it was a sufficient length of time to learn all he could from the firm, and more importantly to save up the money required for his next move: the tradition of taking on a market stall.

He worked punishing hours, but fared well. The following year Roger Newman opened his first store on the edge of the city. The year after, it took over the pet shop next door and doubled in size. Twelve months later, a second store opened. And after three more years there were 12 branches of Roger's Rugs across Devon and Cornwall, and plans afoot to begin an expansion outside of the region.

★★★

Roger had never been shy of the media, and the briefing contained a series of interviews he'd given. In one, an admirably cheeky reporter had asked, "Given your success in business, and your wealth, is there anything missing in your life?"

The answer had taken a few seconds to come, the article said. When it did, the words were thoughtful and heartfelt. The desire to have a family was perhaps the sole ambition remaining.

At the time Roger Newman was 28 years old. The company had expanded across much of England and the tally of stores was now 94. The symbolic century would soon be passed.

Then, as if to mark the man's 30th birthday, came a surprise announcement. Roger was engaged. Rachel Hawker was three years his junior and a solicitor. They had been introduced at a dinner party by some friends who had taken upon themselves the quiet art of matchmaking.

The wedding was a lavish affair, at a stately home in Cornwall overlooking the River Tamar. Pictures filled the papers. Faces glowed with happiness. The following year a girl was born, Annette Louise Newman.

All was set fair and Roger's high profile waned. He was devoting his time to the twin demands of business and a young family; plenty enough to occupy any man.

Until the next story came to dominate the news. Rachel had left the family home to live with a barrister, as if one lawyer in a household was not enough. There were reports of attempts at reconciliation, but none budded. In the sad, modern-day way, to the courts they went to contest custody of Annette.

To the surprise of many, Roger won. He could afford the finest of lawyers, but the briefing notes said it was his personal plea which had been decisive. In tears, obviously genuine and all the more powerful for that, he argued he had the means, but most importantly the love and determination to bring up Annette.

Why, he ended his address, should a woman who had left, taking much of his heart, also take his only child?

★★★

Once more, the life of Roger Newman quietened. Annette was growing up and, as he had promised, fatherhood was taking much of the man's time.

But the pain of the separation was still evident. As often happens with people who suffer a loss, Roger looked to put new meaning into his world. He set up a charity to help children born to the kind of background he knew on the Eddystone Estate. Significant sums of money were invested in better teaching, buildings and equipment, and a series of scholarships founded.

Time and again, Roger spoke out as a passionate advocate of the comprehensive system of education.

"Look at what happened to me," he said in one speech to a teaching union conference. "I was made by good teachers. They're an inspiration. We need more investment for more good teachers so we can transform the lives of thousands of children."

As an unlikely alma mater, Eddystone Comprehensive benefited greatly from Roger's generosity. It was refurbished and started to shed its reputation as a dumping ground for problem children. A new wing, dedicated to the study of business, was named after him.

It was rumoured Roger Newman was being considered worthy of an award for his charitable work. Perhaps an MBE, or maybe even an OBE, as the echelons of such an oddity of anachronism go.

But now came the sting, one that has caught many a parent before and doubtless will rise to do so again. Annette reached the end of her days in junior school. The moment arrived to decide where she would spend her years of secondary education.

And Roger sent her to a private school: Imperial, just outside of Plymouth. It was an austere and imposing Victorian estate in the Devon countryside.

Stories immediately littered the press. Business rivals and educational experts fired accusations of hypocrisy. The mooted award of an honour never came to pass.

Roger attempted some justifications. It was essential, he said, that Annette would be able to board at Imperial when business increasingly required him to travel. But the words were lost leaves in the autumn wind. Even to Dan, reading the notes of the time, they sounded half-hearted.

Roger toughed it out. He was a successful businessman, well-used to ploughing a furrow over uneven ground.

But, as so often is the case, it was the attack from within which caused the real damage.

★★★

The teenage changes can bring a spectrum of disorders. Some youngsters barely notice, others plunge off the road in a screaming fireball with much in the way of collateral damage.

For Annette the transition age was 14, and the troubles were perhaps mild to middling. There had been a warning from Imperial after she was caught in a clinch with a boy in the copse behind the tennis courts. Another followed with the discovery of the heinous crime of the smuggling of a half bottle of vodka into a dormitory.

But largely it was the standard adult way. Stern faces and disappointed disapproval in public, amusement in private.

Then, however, Annette discovered the perilous land of politics, conscience and belief. She began to burn with resentment at her privileged surroundings. The injustice of so very much of the world had to be tackled.

Cue, of course, the taking of more deep breaths and dipping into the reserves of tolerance from teachers and father. It was just a phase. It would pass.

And then came the day Annette disappeared from school.

She was missing for almost 24 hours. Fellow pupils, teachers and Roger himself had to endure the sight of police officers beating their way through the woods, divers scouring ponds and rivers. All in a search for that which can never be spoken.

Dan had been away on holiday at the time, walking another section of the South West Coastal Path with Rutherford. They stayed at the historic Bush Inn at Morwenstow in north Cornwall, tackling the toughest part of the trek. Some of the climbs were so steep it would have been little surprise to find the cliff tops capped with snow. Dan was vaguely aware of the story, but it was only a brief episode, a flare of interest, nothing significant to cause it to linger longer in the mind.

Annette returned to Imperial the next day. She just walked back in past two bemused police officers. She had booked into a cheap bed and breakfast, the kind where they take scant notice of the clientele and even less of the frenzy unfolding in the news. The time she had taken, she announced, was required 'to escape these cloying surroundings' and 'find herself'.

What she found instead was a brief suspension, a father both enraged and tearful, and an iron lecture from a superintendent. It was long and stinging, and on the theme that if such a stunt was repeated criminal charges would follow.

The root of Annette's grudge was only revealed the following month when Roger invited the media to witness their reconciliation. It was a bizarre event, but one which was held at Annette's request.

She had been teased about her father's hypocrisy by a fellow pupil. She looked up his eulogies to state education, replete as they were across the internet, and began to simmer with anger. A lesson must be taught she said. And so, she believed, had it been.

The pair were photographed, filmed and interviewed at home, cooking a symbolic meal together. A deal had been reached and mutual forgiveness bestowed. Annette would continue her studies at Imperial, whilst devoting her spare time to good causes. Roger's fortune would be used to fund the work.

One such project was the Soup and Sandwiches Mission for the homeless. Annette insisted it be carried out on Friday nights, to emphasise the inequalities of society. While some partied, others had minds only to seek food and shelter.

And so her work went on. Until yesterday evening.

★★★

The sound of the window being pulled shut summoned Dan back from the past. The clock had ticked around to seven.

Adam, who was watching the police station entrance below, now strode for the door and stepped fast down the stairs.

"He's here," was all the detective needed to say.

CHAPTER NINE

Roger Newman had the firm handshake that must be deemed a job requirement for the successful businessman, but it was laced with a hint of his current suffering. There was a clamminess to the grip which lingered on the palm.

Adam fussed over him, talking about how he understood what a difficult time this was, but greatly appreciated Newman agreeing to the interview.

"Anything," he replied simply. "If it could help."

His voice was husky with tiredness. Adam guided him to the chair and Newman sat slowly, found a silver flask in his jacket pocket and took a long draw. The sweet scent of whisky tinted the air.

"Sorry," he said. "It's just – helping me get by."

Every profession has its uniform and Newman had fulfilled his obligations to the empire of business. He wore a black suit, blue shirt and dark tie. Dan caught Nigel's comment of a frown.

"I usually enjoy being interviewed," Newman said. "Who doesn't like talking about themselves, if they're honest? But this... I've been thinking about it all night."

"We'll make sure it comes out well, don't worry," Dan replied. "On the subject of which..."

"Yes?"

"Your suit."

Newman fingered a lapel which had been lovingly shaped by a doting Italian tailor. "What about it?"

"It's very smart."

"Thank you."

"Great for a business meeting."

"But?"

"This isn't about business. It's about being a father."

"Meaning?"

"A more relaxed approach might look better. We want the kidnappers to see you and Annette as ordinary people."

"This is my best suit," Newman protested. "What you would prefer? Ripped jeans and a baseball cap?" He looked across at Adam, who in turn looked to Katrina. Dan couldn't help thinking it was like a game of pass the parcel – or buck.

"Any advantage we can get, we should take," she said gently. "Sometimes the smallest of details can settle these cases."

Newman got up from the chair and removed his jacket. He was about to sit back down, but Dan let out a pointed cough.

"What is it now?"

The benevolent manipulator tapped at the neck of his shirt and said, "Modern life, modern looks."

"I have a reputation to preserve."

"And a daughter to save."

Newman frowned, but began unlacing his tie. Nigel checked the viewfinder. He made an indecipherable noise, reached into his bag and handed Dan a compact. Newman eyed it warily and took another long drink from the flask.

Behind the camera, Adam checked his watch. The clock had slipped on to ten past seven. Half past was the set time to feed the interview to all the waiting media.

In the textbooks, the preamble to an interview is described as the time to relax the subject. Build a bond, ready to get the best from them. But the man in the chair was tense and tired, condensed with emotion. He was jaded and tetchy in every word and movement, frayed by the pressure.

Any further requests regarding Newman's appearance were unlikely to improve relations. And there was no time for more maneuvering. Dan thought quickly and took a risk. He opened the compact and began sweeping powder across his forehead.

"What the hell are you doing now?" Newman grunted.

"It's in case we need to film any of my questions after the interview." Dan tried a semi-smile, just to see if the ice might be prepared to thaw. "My hairline's not quite what it was and shining skin looks strange on camera."

Newman sat back on his chair. "Think yourself lucky." He tapped his pate, as smooth as a frozen pond. "My hair started going when I was 16. Imagine that. All the other kids are experimenting with mohicans and Nature's clearing the top of my head as if she wants to build a bloody motorway."

Katrina let out a chuckle and Dan smiled too. "But it had an upside, didn't it?"

"You've done your research." Newman sounded easier now. "You're right; it's where Roger's Rugs came from. I thought it'd stick in people's minds. And it worked."

Dan finished his dabbing and held out the compact. "You're welcome to a bit of powder."

"I've never worn make-up in my life."

"Nor had I until I went into TV, I can promise you. But it does make a real difference... and this is a big interview."

Newman hesitated, raised a finger to his skull, then took the compact and began dusting on the powder. From behind the camera, Nigel nodded approvingly.

★★★

There was one more important rule in this interview. Dan wrote it across the top of his notepad, to guard against an easy slip which could ruin the conversation in a second.

Annette is, PRESENT tense. Never Annette was...

"Let's start with a simple question," he began. "Tell me about Annette. What's she like?"

"Every parent would say this, but she's a wonderful daughter. You know how Rachel, her mother, left us? A couple of years ago, she got back in touch and said she'd like to see more of Annette. We discussed it and I said it was up to her. So she invited Rachel round for dinner to talk."

Newman let out a long sigh. "I didn't let Annette know, but I was so nervous. I'd hardly seen the woman for years and that court battle was horrible. We had supper and it was all ok, even fairly pleasant. But at the end Annette said – and I'll never forget this – 'Thanks for getting back in touch. It's good to know you're there and I'm happy to give you a call occasionally. But I'd ask you not to bother Dad and me otherwise. He'll find it too upsetting and we're very happy as we are'."

Dan let the power of the words resonate while he composed the next question. "And since then – how has she grown up? It's an important time in her life."

"She's doing well at school, really well. I don't know where she got the brains from – not me, certainly. She wants to go to university. Annette keeps talking about doing medicine, but she says she likes the idea of teaching as well."

Even through his suffering, the pride was sufficient to prompt a tired smile. "She reckons that'd be in the family tradition. With me and my little 'educational crusade', as she puts it."

In the reflection in the window, Dan could see Katrina nodding. The questions were hitting the target, the replies ticking the boxes.

And it mattered, how it felt it mattered. This was no standard interview. It was being haunted by a ghost of the living.

"On the subject of crusades, Annette's got one of her own, hasn't she?"

"Her charity work? You know how it all came about? Our little spat because I sent her to a private school. We talked about it… 'Everyone's a secret hypocrite,' I said. 'Not me,' she replied. 'Wait until you're a bit older,' I told her, 'and then you might think differently.' Anyway, that was how we left it. But being Annette, she said I had to pay a price. She decided the best way to punish a businessman was to hit him in the wallet, so we did a deal. The Soup Run was her idea. And she's got other plans, as well."

"Such as?"

Newman almost managed a laugh. "Annette has decided Roger's Rugs has to become carbon neutral. How we're going to make that happen with all the vans and warehouses I have no idea, but she's insistent. I'll probably end up having to plant at least a couple of forests."

Dan took a glance at his notes to find a gap to think. They were approaching the difficult ground. The kingdom of thought-fear.

"You've given me a picture of a fine young woman. But Annette's a teenager and she's human; both dangerous traits. There has been... friction?"

"Oh yes," the heart of the father replied. "There was her disappearance from school. That was one hell of a way to make a point. And she's been in trouble for having a few drinks and dabbling with boys. But what young girl hasn't? She's got a boyfriend now – James, he lives in Manchester, they met on some trip – and do you know what she announced? She said she's going to have him to stay, and in her room, too."

Such familiar battles of the generations, aired so publicly. It would have prompted laughter, had it not been for the context of the interview. Annette was all around them. Those eyes, which relished life, now filled with dread. And looking here, to this room, this conversation and these few minutes for help.

"And what did you say to her... suggestion?"

"I said she would do no such thing. When she was 18 we might think about it, but not before. I tell you this: sometimes I wish I'd had a son. Daughters give you no end of trouble."

Dan had matched Newman's smile, but now let it fade. They were moving towards the end of the interview. It was time to change the mood, to ingrain the message which would fill the airwaves.

A great professional and a sensitive mind, Nigel felt the shift and gently zoomed in his shot for the power of the close-up. Newman's face would fill the screen, the moistening of his eyes emphasised by the dark circles of sleepless fears that surrounded them.

"And worries are what we're talking about here," Dan said softly. "Difficult though it may be, can you tell us what you've been going through?"

With each answer before, Newman had taken a second or two to consider his words. But now the reply was instant. This was the only thought, the sole feeling, the one consideration.

"It's been torment. There's no other way I can describe it. Every minute, every second, I'm thinking of Annette. I'm wondering where she is. And…"

His voice cracked and almost broke, but he gulped in a hurried breath and rallied.

"I'm wondering what's happening to her. Fearing it. Dreading it. I see her face everywhere, even when I close my eyes. Every time the phone goes, I think it's someone calling to break the news – to tell me…"

Dan nodded at the unspeakable, unthinkable fear, but kept quiet; let the denouement of the interview play out. And it did – how it did.

"I can't eat, I can't sleep," Newman continued. "I can't do anything. I'm so lost. So damned helpless. All I can do is think about Annette. I'd ask – please, please, if anyone has her, or knows where she is, please help me get her back."

★★★

Adam held open the door and they walked across the compound to the satellite van. On the road outside, amidst the white haze of a cherry tree, Dan saw a glint of polished glass.

"Ouch!" he yelped, bending down to massage his knee.

Adam, Newman and Katrina stopped too. "What?" Adam asked, impatiently. "Come on, we've got to feed the interview."

"Only a touch of cramp. It might not have been such a good idea to go for a run this morning."

It was 7.28 when Dan handed the memory card to Loud. "Cutting it a bit fine, aren't you?" the engineer grumbled, holding up a list running to several pages. "You wouldn't believe who's waiting for this."

They'd left Nigel in the MIR to pack up the camera and lights. A police driver was ready to give Newman a lift home, but he said he would like to see the interview being fed.

"I've spent more than enough time at home lately. All I've got there are thoughts of Annette."

Loud started to explain how the pool feed worked, but it sounded like a lecture from the final year of a physics degree, so Dan eased the van door closed and translated. For major events, when there was no benefit in rival broadcasters all providing their own camera crews to get exactly the same footage, one organisation would be designated to provide the coverage.

It was commonly used for royal, presidential or prime ministerial visits and had the added advantage of not offending the regal dignitary with an unseemly gang of cameras and journalists.

Newman watched the interview being replayed on the monitors. "You were right about the open neck," he told Dan. "And the powder. I look almost human, for once. Sorry if I snapped at you."

Dan patted the man's shoulder. "It's no problem. I would say I know how you're feeling, but how could I?"

"You only asked a few questions. Will that be enough?"

"Six or seven minutes are plenty. Most radio and TV stations and websites will run the interview in full to start with, then use clips later. The newspapers will lift some of your quotes."

"And use one of their old pictures of me to illustrate it?"

"Something like that," Dan replied, trying to keep his voice neutral.

"I can't believe you got all that stuff out of me. About Annette, and well…"

"All I did was let you talk."

Newman reached out a hand, took Dan's and shook it hard. "Nice try, but I'd say there was a bit more to it than that. If you ever get fed up with this TV lark, just call. I could use a man like you. I don't know how you do it. You always look so calm on camera."

"I usually think of it as a tissue thin layer of bluff," Dan replied. "It hides the panic in my head."

★★★

They walked back upstairs to the canteen to get a coffee. It wasn't yet eight o'clock, but already felt well into the working day.

Newman had gone home with his police escort. Adam and Katrina had a couple more questions first. They wanted to know if he could see any possible significance in the letters *PP* in the ransom note. Newman thought hard and long, but said he couldn't.

Katrina raised the issue of whether he might have been targeted as part of a grudge, or if there was a location which had special meaning for him and Annette. Some kind of second home or favourite escape, somewhere the kidnappers might consider as a hide out to taunt him. But again Newman was unable to help.

On the way upstairs they checked the TV, radio and internet. The interview was everywhere. In major news events, there is often a remarkable unanimity amongst journalists about the headline. *Father's Emotional Plea to Kidnappers over his Missing Girl* was running on most stations.

The websites were using a photograph of Newman in his open necked shirt. It had clearly been taken in the police station's backyard.

"Anything to do with you, that?" Adam asked, wryly.

"With a story like this there are bound to be snappers trying to get a shot of Newman," Dan replied, as innocently as he knew how. "Anyway, isn't it what we want? Maximum exposure?"

Adam chose to answer by folding his arms and adopting a knowing look.

Dan fetched the drinks. He had spent many pained years failing to get used to police tea and coffee. They were invariably of a potency sufficient to prompt paint to peel from the walls. And today, he faced the worst of fates. The canteen wasn't open, so he had no choice but to chance the machine.

It grumbled and gurgled, as if suffering chronic indigestion, and eventually produced three small cups of jet-black liquid. Dan picked them up, pointedly holding the offerings at arm's length and carried them over to the table. In the best tradition of the police service, Adam added milk and a couple of sugars. Katrina took hers pure black and bitter.

"That was a very moving interview," she said, as Dan sat down.

Nature does have a habit of flaunting her achievements. A total eclipse, a meteor shower, even the earthly wonders of a mountain range or a mighty waterfall are difficult to overlook. On a smaller scale, the colours of a rainbow or the unique sparkle of a diamond are equal fascinations.

Proud Mother Nature hadn't missed the opportunity to emphasise Katrina's eyes. She was one of those people who blink at a rate approximately half the average for the human race, and it accentuated the different shades.

Be it that, the surprise of the compliment, or perhaps the potent mix of the pairing, Dan was left with no option but to flounder.

"Oh, was it? Oh… thanks."

"It really brought Annette to life. I felt I got to know her from your questions."

"Um, yeah, well… thank you."

"And it was clever, the way you led Newman into putting some powder on."

"Yeah, it wasn't bad at all," Adam agreed, rather begrudgingly. "He made her out to be a bit more of an angel than she actually is, but otherwise it was ok."

"In what way?" Dan asked.

"Annette's got a caution for possessing cannabis. It was after some party. It wasn't much, and I'm surprised we even bothered. You have to have enough to get half the city higher than the clouds these days."

The rancour of the detective's disapproval could have soured the air. Dan had to look away to hide a smile. He was sure Katrina was doing the same.

"But I suppose it wasn't really relevant to the interview," Adam conceded, loftily. "Now, enough of this self-congratulation. Annette's still missing. So – what next?"

"We keep waiting," Katrina replied. "To see how the kidnappers react to the interview."

"And that's it?"

"It's all about patience."

"I never really got the hang of patience," Adam said, sulkily.

And now Katrina and Dan exchanged a look, and a smile too.

A trio of policemen walked into the canteen. At the sight of a senior officer, all made a play of collapsing onto chairs with the exhaustion of their law enforcing endeavours. One seat squeaked loudly. The sound was reminiscent of a fledgling bird.

Dan stood up, knocking over the remains of his drink.

"Be careful, will you," Adam protested. "This suit's new."

"Get me a car." Dan said. "Now."

"What for? Where to?"

"Our studios. I've just realised how I know the bird song in the ransom call."

CHAPTER TEN

Like one of the family who has never quite fitted in, the news library lived life a little detached. It was to be found in the far corner of the *Wessex Tonight* studios, part of a modern annex to the Victorian edifice. The library overlooked the garden; an accident of appropriateness. It was one of the few calm havens in a building more familiar with looming deadlines, running feet and shouted commands.

Dan had long mused on how much knowledge was contained in one small room. He discovered a bond with the library early in his career. The simplicity of its peace appealed in days that could feel filled with incessant noise. It was also an unspoken asset that Lizzie seldom visited. The clash of characters between her and this room made an effort to enter like coaxing a demon onto holy ground.

The delightful anachronism of the metal cabinets filled with card index files lined one wall. For years now, records of all the stories *Wessex Tonight* covered had been saved on computer. But there dated back many decades of the earlier times of the programme, and all were remembered in these files.

A project to transfer them to the far less evocative destination of a hard drive, or set of memory sticks, had been mooted for many a year. But in the great tradition of the British, it had never quite been *got round to.*

Dan was quietly pleased by this, and would always argue for any available resources to be directed elsewhere. Computers may be faster and more efficient, but they lacked the soul of these indexes; the yellowing colour of the card and the smell of the history they told.

All of which made precisely no impression on the pragmatic detective with a missing young woman to find.

"So we're in a library," Adam complained, as they strode through the door. "So what?"

He'd been carping for most of the short drive. In truth, although Dan could remember covering a story featuring the mysterious *sre, sre, sre* birds, he wasn't sure exactly where and when. More importantly, he had no thoughts at all about what relevance it could possibly have in finding Annette.

As Adam so deflatingly put it, "We're hunting kidnappers and you've got me following a lead which consists of some birds singing?"

"Well… yes."

"It doesn't sound great."

"No," Dan conceded.

"Not even anywhere close to remotely approaching great."

"Well, no."

"So why are we doing it?"

"Just – a feeling."

It was Katrina who again took on the role of referee, one she had fast realised was required when dealing with the odd relationship set before her.

"There's nothing else we can do at the moment," she soothed. "So we're not losing anything and we might just make a gain."

The journey up to the studios had been a five minute interlude. Adam drove, intermittently wondering aloud whether the kidnappers would have heard Newman's interview and bemoaning the tenuousness of the lead. Dan sat in the back, trying to remember the story and the enigmatic birds, but instead found himself studying Katrina.

It was another fair morning. The traffic was light, with almost as many buses on the roads as cars. But that was common for Plymouth: a city of historically low wages, and so – even in this automobile-obsessed society – relatively light car ownership.

The fine hair on the back of Katrina's neck made for a chevron. It took no Olympian leap of Dan's imagination to envisage an inviting path downwards.

He focused instead on a couple walking past. Both were rotund, to push the art of euphemism to its limits, and sweating in the day's warmth.

The straps of Katrina's bra bevelled through the white of her blouse. They were edged with patterns of lace. Dan wondered if it was silk or cotton. The former, he suspected. It was far more her.

The strolling couple were sporting skimpier clothes than might have been advisable. The exposed flesh shone like a snowfield in the sun. The male of the species lit a cigarette, which it passed to the female.

The outline of a dark shape patterned the back of Katrina's shoulder. It was subtle, difficult to make out through her blouse and no bigger than a few centimetres tall, but looked like a tattoo. Dan thought he could see the details of a figure, perhaps a loop on top of a cross.

Subtlety was not a concept that came easily to the smoking couple. Much of the available area of legs and arms had been inked. It was as if they'd made a block booking at the tattooist. Perhaps the parlour had been attempting to work up some trade and running a *Buy One, Get Lots More Free* offer.

Tattoos, Dan reflected in one of his common philosophical moments, were all very well for now. He was not, however, looking forward to a generation of tattooed grandparents.

But Katrina's looked strangely intriguing. And probably meaningful too, knowing what little he did of the woman.

★★★

As if fate were also sceptical of his hunch, the duty librarian was the one Dan was expecting and dreading. Brenda was a lady in her very late 50s, whom Lizzie had taken against and set about ushering towards retirement. Part of the deal was weekend work, which suited her well. It wasn't taxing and didn't usually demand any rapidity of response.

Today, instead of replacing tapes in the archive or unearthing long forgotten sequences of pictures for reporters, they found her gazing out at the garden. In terms of enterprise, Brenda was polishing the spoons of the library tea set, a fine old combination of china and silver. She truly was the last empress of a forgotten world.

"Daniel," she exclaimed softly, as he walked in. "How lovely to see you again, and your friends too." She surveyed Adam with a maternal smile. "Is this your brother? He looks like you."

The detective's snort was far more communicative than mere words.

"And this must be your wife. I'm sorry, partner we say these days, don't we?"

There was an odd silence before Dan stuttered, with a triumph of unconvincing wit, "Err, no, I'm afraid no such luck."

He hastily introduced the two police officers, and yet again had to request Brenda not use the name he viewed as reserved for maiden aunts, tax demands and court summonses.

"But Daniel is so much nicer," she objected, with all the force of Neville Chamberlain on a bad day. "Now, would you like a cup of tea? I've got a lovely lot of fruit teas. And some sponge cake I've just made."

"I'm sorry, we're in a hurry," Dan interjected, before the chatter could gain momentum.

"You young people always are," she replied, sadly. "The pace you go, you miss so much of life."

"It's called news," Dan hissed under his breath, before adding, "If you wouldn't mind helping me look out some stories? I need ones from my time covering environment."

Brenda's face warmed with nostalgia. "I loved the reports you did then. Lots of ponies and otters and our wonderful countryside. So much nicer than now. These horrid murders and kidnappings and—"

"I know what you mean. But can you find the stories I did on birds, please?"

"Are you sure you wouldn't like a cup of tea?"

The ominously lurking Adam emitted a noise that sounded like a rocket preparing for take-off.

"Yes," Dan said. "Sorry, I mean no, we don't want one. As I said, we are in a hurry."

Brenda nodded slowly, put on her glasses and tapped at a computer.

"Puffins!" she said, happily. "You were on the Isles of Scilly. Such beautiful birds. Lovely, coloured beaks."

"Yes, that's puffins. What else?"

"Oooh, look! Choughs. Such character – those funny red legs."

"Yep, that's choughs. What else?"

She tapped at more keys. "Ah, red kites. Wonderful birds of prey, absolutely majestic."

"And not what I'm looking for. Any others?"

The computer screen scrolled. Page followed page. Slowly. Very, very slowly.

"Cirl buntings!" she exclaimed. "What striking little birds. Such a lovely, vibrant yellow; just like the flowers in my garden."

The ramble continued, but Dan wasn't hearing it. His eyes were set on the screen.

"That's it. Cirl buntings."

Adam was at his shoulder. "Cirl buntings?"

"Yep."

"You've brought us here to look at some scabby little bird. That's it?"

With admirable restraint, Dan ignored him. "Brenda, could you get the tape please?"

"Now?"

"Yes. Now."

She ambled over to a storeroom. Invisible footsteps paced back and forth and Brenda returned with a grey plastic box. Dan opened it and loaded the video cassette into one of the players.

"A beta tape?" Katrina queried.

"It's one of the great ironies of TV. Back in the '80s, when there was the format war, VHS won the mass market, but the television industry chose beta. We thought it was better quality and more reliable."

Dan skimmed through the stories. There were floods, government cutbacks, health warnings about the dangers of sunbathing, county shows.

And now a group of small yellow birds in a tree, all singing.

Sre, sre, sre.

Dan paused the tape. "That's it. The noise from the ransom call."

Adam stared at the screen. "Well whoopty-doo," he grunted. "I can't say how overwhelmed I am at this dramatic breakthrough. A boy scout bird spotter's badge to us."

"Adam, for fuck's sake, shut up!" Dan snapped. "I've had a bellyful of your whining."

"Don't you dare tell me to—"

"Don't either of you ever use language like that in here," Brenda intervened, with surprising steel. "Now look at the report nicely, or you can leave."

Katrina reached between the petulant pugilists and set the tape playing. Her shoulder brushed Dan's. It felt firm and toned. He could smell the freshness of her perfume.

The screen flickered with a countdown and a familiar voice began a commentary:

"Once common, cirl buntings are now sadly rare. Loss of their habitat and changes in farming methods are being blamed. But the Royal Society for the Protection of Birds has begun a project to try to increase numbers. They're recruiting landowners to help, by managing areas in a bunting-friendly way. It's not such a big job as you might think. Cirl buntings are now confined to only a small part of South Devon, around the village of East Prawle."

Dan turned, readying a triumphant look from the very summit of his stock of *I told you so* expressions. Victory in The Battle of the Little Yellow Birds was his and it was time to parade it.

But Adam was already on his mobile and heading for the door.

★★★

Once more, the guardian of the gate into Charles Cross stood wide open. Just inside, by the armed response cars, the officers were again checking their guns. But where before it had been routine, a drill – rehearsed a hundred times or more – this was the call to arms.

It was in the eyes, focused and sharp. It was in the movements, calm, practiced and precise.

And there was no banter. This was reality, not rehearsal. This was their time.

Cops jogged from the police station's back doors. One carried a weight of body armour, his head hidden behind the mass of reinforced plastic. A woman bent low with the burden of a small, metal battering ram. Another snapped open boxes and pulled out snub-nosed taser stun guns. Helmets, gas canisters, a loud hailer joined the armaments.

A line of police vans stood, their back doors open, waiting. A sergeant convulsed back and forth, shouting instructions. A spin of blue lights cascaded around the compound.

A group of officers were bent over a patrol car, a map spread across its bonnet. From the windows of the police station, faces stared out. A modern day army was readying for battle.

Claire jogged from the back doors and picked her way over. From the urgency, the impetus of this unflappable investigator, it was clear there would be significance in her words.

Dan thought of Roger Newman and Annette. Another interview with the businessman, but this time carried out in the past tense. Tears and regrets in place of hope.

He could see the spectre with Adam and Katrina, too. The way they waited, the fear of what they were about to hear. But instead, silent dread was replaced by relief, like rainfall in the desert.

"Sir," Claire told Adam, "I think we've got a lead on the kidnappers."

CHAPTER ELEVEN

He was still there. Silent and unmoving, but she could sense him.

A black shape in the tarry darkness of this eternal night.

Watching her. As he had from the start. And would until the end.

And that moment was coming. It was in the air, all around her.

But no easy ending. Just an inescapable agony.

The smell. So ordinarily everyday, but here and now so fearful, so heavy with fate. In her nose and ears. Her eyes and mouth. Unmistakable, unavoidable, no matter how she turned her head to try to escape.

Petrol. Volatile, vicious petrol.

And the sound. The easy innocence of a soft rustling. Like the English countryside on many a summer's day. From the walks she had taken with Dad, through fields and over stiles, on their weekend outings from the city.

The dry sound of golden straw.

And one more noise to reinforce her certainty. To know what surrounded her, and the end which awaited.

Newspaper. Ripped into strips. And crumpled into balls.

Rolled, shifted and positioned. With exacting certainty. To encircle her helpless body.

Ready to feed the flames of the pyre.

Annette tried to gulp, but the gag allowed no respite. She could see nothing and say nothing. She would die blind, mute and immobile.

Able only to wait for the fire. And helpless, feel her skin bubble, blister and burn.

She had expected the end so many times. In the van, when she was sick. When the cloth was pulled from her mouth. She was ready for the knotted knuckles of a flying fist.

A lesson. A beating. A punishment. Blood flowing and teeth breaking. The blows growing more frenzied, the pain whitening until the grateful release.

Never to come around.

But there was only the thrust of a rag. The sickness wiped away. And the sudden shock of a cold cascade of water.

How she gulped it down. Chewed it from the air, each sluice, every drop.

Until the binding gag was restored.

Then once more readying for the end. When the rumbling slowed and quietened, and the doors opened.

The breeze on her face, the hands pulling her, the arms lifting her, carrying her through sightless space. The sound of seagulls in the sky.

She had expected to fly. Soar from the clifftop, at last unbound, until the killing impact. Twisted and broken, her forsaken body claimed by the gentle undertaker of the creeping tide.

No headstone here. No loving memorial to young Annette Newman. No forever remembered and always missed. No last resting place recorded, no black-clad mourners to lament her passing.

But she had found only cold, hard floor. And distant noises.

The creak of a stair. Whispers in the darkness. Perhaps a plane flying by. Maybe a bird's cheerful song.

A secluded door closing. The muted burble of a quiet radio.

And always the sound of time passing. The blasting silence of the indistinct, immeasurable, hours.

She was cold now. Shivered, twitched to shift her weight. Her flank was numbed, lying on this slab of a floor. But she was trussed too tight to move.

A trickle of blood ran down her ankle.

Dust was starting to settle in her nose, mixing with the petrol, forming the paste of the coming death.

She would smell herself burn.

Annette tried to imagine. To find a refuge in her mind.

James, that night on the beach.

Anywhere. Any escape. Anything.

But the darkness was too filled with the dancing terrors of her taunting thoughts.

CHAPTER TWELVE

They ran for the back door. Dan had been expecting a rapid clambering up to the MIR, but Adam headed downwards, towards the basement.

These corridors of the police station were much less trodden than others. There was no banter, none of the continual sound of feet which characterised other floors. It was quieter, darker, had the air of a lair.

The catacombs of Charles Cross, Dan thought, with a reporter's whim.

In the car park, Adam had cornered the sergeant who was attempting to organise the melee. "How long?"

"Five minutes, maybe ten."

The detective didn't reply, instead turned and set off, Claire, Katrina and Dan following.

"What're we doing?" Dan asked. "Where are we going?"

"You'll see."

Adam passed the entrance to the control room. They turned a corner. Now they were approaching the end of the corridor. Ahead was a fire exit and next to it another door, a little smaller. It was plain and bore no sign to betray its purpose, but was strong and well-secured.

Only one of the strip lights was working, and it grumbled with a low buzz. Daylight was a stranger to this part of the station. The corridor was tainted with dust and smelt musty. Many of the floor tiles were cracked and chipped. The gossamer patterns of a spider's web stretched from the top of the door.

"What's going on?" Dan asked. "I didn't even know this place existed."

"Quite," Adam replied.

He fumbled in his pocket, found a fob of keys and picked one out. It was fatter than the rest, shinier and looked little-used.

With a begrudging clunk, the door opened.

★★★

Around the walls were propped signs, an unofficial history of concerns long-forgotten. Several appealed for witnesses to road crashes, others muggings and one a robbery. Most carried the everyday warnings of the business of policing: the risks of ice, pickpockets operating in the area and the ever-present danger of leaving valuables in your car.

In the corner was a ramshackle stack of old desks and chairs. There were a few abandoned computers too, some which harked back to the days of the ZX Spectrum. Dan reached out to touch one. It was like laying a finger on his past.

The teenage Dan had bought an early model, second hand, with the money he'd saved from a Saturday job picking tomatoes on a fruit farm. The lasting memory was of more crashes than a banger racing weekend, and a keyboard which resembled long-dead flesh.

A couple of stacks of traffic cones teetered by the door, their hoops smeared with dirt. Guarding them was the incongruity of a line of gnomes. A note attached to the hat of the tallest read, *Nicked by students, owner to collect next week.* It was dated nine years ago.

At the far end of the room was a metal filing cabinet, and it was to here that Adam stepped his careful way.

Dan found Claire by his side. "The twilight files," she whispered.

Adam was delving hard into the cabinet. Wisps of dust took to the air. Katrina began coughing.

Claire's radio crackled.

Two minutes to the off.

Adam was still bent double. It was as if the cabinet was making an attempt to swallow him.

The click, click, click of turning metal filled the little room.

Finally, the detective stood up. He was holding a stained manila folder.

"Got it," he said.

***

Katrina took the wheel, but in a manner that was both unexpected and a little alarming. She worked the gears like a racing driver who's trailing the pack. The car hugged corners and cut a straight line across bends. They had to wait a couple of times for the rest of the convoy to catch up.

"Where did you learn all this?" Dan asked, in a voice which he hoped disguised his qualms.

"Advanced driver training. If you need to speed it pays to know how."

"Is that how you got down to Devon so fast?"

"Not entirely. I caught the train. It's better for thinking through a case. Besides, it's only about three hours from London to Plymouth." She glanced over, her face unreadable. "Very easy to pop back and forth."

Dan thought he heard Claire make a kind of strangled noise, but it might have been the percussion of another of Katrina's gear changes.

She'd insisted on driving. It made sense, she told Adam. He was the officer in charge of the case. He needed to be free to make phone calls. He could also read out the contents of the file, tell them about the two people who were suspected of kidnapping Annette.

As his deputy Claire should sit alongside. Which left Dan in the front, next to her.

The logic was incontestable. Yet Claire appeared unimpressed, her face flinty. It was most unlike her, a woman with a natural warmth for the world, even on the most difficult of days. Dan wondered if she wasn't feeling well. She was wearing more make-up than usual. Perhaps it was to cover for the effects of some bug.

The convoy left the police station, crossed the bridge over the River Plym and headed into the open countryside of the South

Hams. Adam was about to start reading the file when Dan saw his moment and interrupted.

"I've got an idea."

"Why does that make me worry?" Adam replied.

"Call it a way to make up for my stupid clumsiness."

As they jogged out of the police station to rejoin the convoy, Dan spotted an officer carrying a video camera. In the blindness of his preoccupation with the case, he collided with the man, knocking the camera to the floor. Bumped off balance, Dan had also trodden on it, breaking the lens. It was all down to the rush; he apologised repeatedly and perhaps over-effusively. *Wessex Tonight* would pay for the repair, or a replacement.

"That's not the bloody point," the officer remonstrated. "It's the only one we've got."

Adam was eyeing Dan with his special detective's look. It was loaded with all the suspicion of more than twenty years as a policeman, a generation's experience of deception.

"Get on with it," he said. "You're not fooling anyone."

"It's just – video can be such powerful evidence."

"Really? Thanks, I'd never have thought of that. It is why we bring a camera along – or try to, anyway," he added, pointedly. "What are you up to?"

"Nothing, nothing at all. Only that – maybe I can help."

"Let me guess. By getting Nigel along to film?"

"Oh! What a brilliant idea. Just to help you out, of course. To make up for my little accident."

"In return for which, you get exclusive pictures?"

"Well, I never imagined it like that. My only thought was for the interests of justice. But since you come to mention it…"

Adam clicked his tongue. "What do you think, Katrina?"

She accelerated the car around a bend, generating g-forces akin to a roller-coaster. "Dan is right, a recording could be useful."

"All right," Adam said, when the offending reporter had finished his performance. "Now, if you're quite done with your devious little manoeuvers, would you like to hear who we're up against?"

CHAPTER THIRTEEN

A cinema of the mind formed within the car, as the detective narrator began chronicling a criminal CV.

"The story of Brian and Martha Edwards," Adam recounted. "An extraordinary and I suppose sad one, too – if it wasn't for the way it turned out."

Even the drive through the marvels of the Devon springtime didn't distract from the story. The trees were lit with candle buds and rained blossom. In the fields, cows and horses watched the wailing convoy pass with that magnificent detachment of the animal world. The meadows and pastures were full of the colours of the warming land, prompted from hibernation by days once more blessed with light.

The Edwards were born in Plymouth and remained in the city for their growing years. Both were educated – if that wasn't too optimistic a word – at Eddystone Comprehensive, the same school Roger Newman attended.

"Interesting," Katrina noted.

Their criminal careers began modestly. It was clear from the notes that, initially, they were considered relatively small time. They were assessed as not violent, nor a significant danger to the public.

One remark from the first of the cases, written by a junior detective, said, *All this was about was taking the piss.*

"Hang on," Dan objected. "What's that kind of comment doing on an investigation report?"

"Because," Adam replied emphatically, "none of this exists. Our little storage room is there for a reason. It's off computers, off the books and beyond the reach of Freedom of Information and Data Protection laws. And particularly journalists. Ok?"

"Well, I—"

"That's only if you want to hear more. I could just stop."

"Ok," Dan submitted, a little peevishly.

"In which case, do you want to know the remarkable thing about the Edwards?"

"What?"

"We think they've committed plenty of crimes," Claire replied. "But guess how many convictions we've managed to get?"

"How many?"

"It's a round number," Adam said. "Very round, in fact."

"That bad?"

"Yep."

"How come?"

"If you let me finish the briefing, you'll find out."

Puerile as it may be, sometimes the infantile pleasure of the sticking out of the tongue is hard to resist. Dan contented himself with a shake of the head, but deigned to be silent.

Martha was 22 years old and had just completed a three-year course in Forensic Science and Computing. She graduated with a third class degree.

"Not exactly a criminal mastermind," Katrina observed.

"So you might think," Adam replied. "But after a few crimes which we thought could be down to the Edwards, a detective went to talk to her old tutors. Their view was unanimous. She was by far the brightest and most talented student in her year, and one of the best they'd ever seen."

"She flunked the exams?"

"She certainly did. But as to why – we think it was deliberate. She didn't want to draw attention to herself with a shining academic record."

They passed a farmyard, a couple of men working on a tractor, a sheep dog skipping around their feet. At this speed, East Prawle lay twenty minutes to the south-east. There, on the outskirts of the village, the convoy would draw up and the strategy for the assault be formulated.

Adam returned to his notes. The Edwards' first suspected crime involved housing benefit fraud, but with a twist.

They had invented scores of people and bank accounts into which the money could be paid. The fraud lasted for just a few months and was closed down before the council became aware of it. Only following an audit later in the year was the alarm raised. Tens of thousands of pounds were stolen.

"Pretty mundane stuff," Dan commented. "Housing benefit fraud is hardly new or particularly clever."

"That's true," Adam replied. "But – the Edwards chose a council which had just been involved in a child abuse scandal. Its social workers failed to prevent the deaths of a couple of kids."

"You think the council was deliberately targeted?" Katrina asked.

"We're sure it was. Because of the money the Edwards stole, we reckon they only kept half. Our investigations didn't get very far, but there was one thing we did establish. The Edwards made a big donation to some children's charities. The amount was about half the total estimated to have been stolen."

The next case was an attack on some large insurance companies. A couple of towns in the Midlands had suffered flooding after torrential rain. Hundreds of residents were forced to leave their homes. The repair bill would run into many millions of pounds.

As people began to make claims, there came a development which will surprise nobody who has ever tried to scale the edifice of an insurer to retrieve some of the money they had spent years paying in. The firms started to spin, wheedle and squirm.

Spokesmen claimed there were exemptions. Some acts of god – or at least a peculiar type of deity who looked kindly upon insurance companies – were not covered. Excesses on a scale sufficient to pay a premiership footballer applied. Climate change was a specific area which could not be covered. Homeowners should have had the foresight to fit flood defences. The list went on and on, and then on some more.

The Edwards took advantage of the companies' preoccupation with repelling the selfish hordes who had the audacity to expect assistance. Quietly, they began to build up a series of motoring claims. They were relatively small and so were hardly checked. But the quantities involved made for significant sums.

Once more, the result was the Edwards keeping half the money, the rest going to a fund set up to help the flood victims.

★★★

The convoy was approaching the village of Churchstow. Signs pleaded for careful driving. Katrina slowed the car and switched off the sirens. Even those from outside the two fair counties instinctively understand it is a rule of Devon and Cornwall life, that the sacred peace of a small community must not be disturbed.

In the field beside a school a group of children halted their kick about to watch the cars, vans and motorbikes. This was a place that very rarely saw a police officer, let alone a convoy.

Sunshine flared inside the car. Dan rolled down a window, Adam doing the same.

★★★

Now came a sense the crimes were growing bolder. The Edwards moved on to target banks.

It was a time when the titans of finance had been trying to persuade customers to make greater use of the internet. It was quicker and more convenient the banks proclaimed, omitting to mention it was also much cheaper to administer. As for concerns about security, they could be happily dismissed with the airy wave of a banker's trustworthy hand. The systems were invulnerable.

Such a claim is a temptation too far for any hacker that has ever set finger on a keyboard. The Edwards were amongst them. This time, it was mortgage fraud. A series of online applications were made for relatively small amounts, which attracted less scrutiny. Again, many thousands of pounds were stolen.

When finally one of the grand repositories of the land noticed, Greater Wessex Police were called in. But so sure were the banks of their impregnability, it was difficult to convince them they had been conned. And when, at last, the arrogance faltered and they accepted the inevitable, the matter was hushed up. The men in bespoke pinstripe suits decreed that no further proceedings were required. It would be too damaging for the sacred share price.

There were a couple more notes on the case. The banks targeted had been identified as the worst for customer service, whilst still managing to pay staff the kind of bonuses which could fill a calculator's screen. This time, it was estimated the Edwards took only 15 per cent of their haul, the rest going to a range of charities.

A note from one of the investigating officers read, *15 per cent, a standard agent's fee. So, make of that what you will. On this one, I can't find myself too bothered we're not trying to bring charges.*

★★★

Adam checked his watch. East Prawle is Devon's most southerly village, just inland of the heady cliffs of Prawle Point and the vista of the English Channel. They were fifteen minutes away. The car bumped as it crossed a bridge over a muddy tidal inlet.

"There's another note below that last one," Adam said. "'We *will* be pursuing the Edwards, make no mistake. Because once they get a taste for crime, we don't know where it could lead.'"

The detective stared out of the window, before adding quietly, "I was the senior officer reviewing the case. I wrote that. And it turned out to be bloody portentous."

All in the car was silent as they waited for an explanation. But Adam said only, "There are a couple more bits I want to read you, while we've got the time. They should make clear what I'm talking about."

The Department of Health was the next target. A controversy blew up about the amount of money being paid to top civil servants when NHS services were struggling with cutbacks. The predictable denials were issued. But the mandarins' salaries would not be revealed, a clipped spokesman announced. They were strictly confidential.

The next week they were published on a website, much to the frothing glee of the media.

Another note commented – *What investigative journalists couldn't manage, I reckon the Edwards did in an afternoon's hacking.*

"We're getting towards the end of this part," Adam said. "But there's one thing to note here – the shift to a focus on health issues."

The media live for a row, and the next case concerned some large pharmaceutical companies. They were accused of being *merciless and pitiless*, for not allowing a range of expensive products to be sold at cost price in developing countries. Thousands of lives could be saved, campaigners protested.

A barrage of expensive spin was thrown up to counter the claim. Developing the drugs was hugely expensive. Money had to be made so profits could be reinvested in the next generation of medicines. But, in fairness, a concession was offered, however much it may have been a single grain of sand on a mighty beach.

The drugs could *perhaps* be sold at a small discount, the announcement ran. But of less prominence in the proclamation was how that might be achieved. It could only follow the report of a focus group, a working party, a committee, a sub-committee, a commission of inquiry and the executive board, and all after a series of fact-finding trips and a good lunch or two.

With the prospect of progress a galaxy away, the controversy dimmed. That was until the following month when a new website was launched. It listed some of the products in development. Many were highly lucrative. The companies' futures looked prosperous.

But the site had a sting. It detailed confidential information on how the trials were progressing, picking out the problems which made the release of many of the products years away.

Share prices slumped. Billions were wiped off corporate values.

The authors of the website were never traced, despite the best efforts of the fuming companies. But the Eggheads were of the view the scandal fitted with the way the Edwards liked to work.

The final case Adam had to relate was a simple act of mockery. A tsunami caused widespread destruction in the Far East, with the loss of thousands of lives. Even more were left homeless. The British government was criticised for failing to offer sufficient help.

A week later, a mysterious glitch in the centralised supply system saw hundreds of government offices going without supplies of toilet roll.

***

The convoy entered a green tunnel, sweeping through the interwoven branches of the bowing trees. Blue lights smeared the new leaves.

"I'm starting to like the Edwards," Dan grinned.

"Are you now?" Adam replied, and there was something in his voice. It was like the way the air changes before a storm, a perceptible shift in the pressure.

Dan found himself faltering. "Well, yeah, I mean—"

"Because they're Robin Hood types, aren't they?" the detective continued, with that unsettling, constrained anger. "They're lovable rogues. Robbing from the rich to give to the poor in just the way you reporters think is great."

"Well, given some of what they did, you can't deny—"

"And what about kidnapping a 17-year-old girl? Terrifying her and tormenting her dad?"

"Ok, that's out of place, but—"

"I bet you think she'll be safe in their hands? These Edwards wouldn't hurt a fly, eh? It's all just a harmless little game?"

The menace in Adam's voice was overwhelming. It left Dan speechless and looking to Katrina for help.

"That's what you think, isn't it?" the detective powered on. "But you're wrong – very wrong – because it always ends up the same."

And perhaps to save Dan from any more discomfort, or simply to hear the conclusion of a story which had been stoked with such a build-up, Katrina cut in, "Adam, maybe you should just tell us what you're trying to say."

***

A page turned. The division from what went before was stark, like a curtain coming down and a new act beginning.

The Edwards tried another attack on a bank. And they were nearly caught.

"I was still twitchy about what they might try next, so I had the Eggheads put surveillance on them," Adam explained. "Martha must have realised she was being watched and pulled out. I might have got her on some paltry charges, but it would have been community service at best. And given what she's gone through, maybe not even that."

"What she's gone through?" Dan queried.

"I'll tell you more about that later. Anyway, there was something different about this case. It looked like the Edwards were chasing serious sums of money."

Now came a lull, the first in the chronology of crimes the siblings were thought to have carried out. For four months, nothing was heard.

Until the night of 13 September and the break-in at the headquarters of the South West Peninsula (Subdivision) Regional Health Strategic Oversight Authority; a masterpiece of bureaucratic nomenclature if ever there was one.

As Adam went through the story, Dan understood the reason for his friend's anger. He turned, held the detective's look, and received a nod of forgiveness.

★★★

The convoy slowed for the town of Kingsbridge, all inlets and creeks. It was market day, and a busy one with the sunshine, colourful stalls filling a car park and lining the main street.

They followed the road through the throng, then back out into the countryside and on to the village of Frogmore. It was another in the well-fed register of Devon names that raised more questions than could ever perhaps be answered.

They turned off the main road and onto a single tarmac track, fattened only by the occasional passing place. The earth banks of

Devon hedges closed in, their green bulk speckled with the blues, purples and whites of springtime.

One by one, the accompanying sirens fell silent. They were moving slowly now, furtively, unwilling to risk alerting that which they had come to hunt.

"I can just finish the story," Adam said. "It's time to show you what the Edwards really are."

★★★

He was a security guard in name, but it was a Hall of Mirrors description of the job. A caretaker in uniform would have been more honest.

Albert Fisher was, by unanimous account, a gentle man. He was 63 years old, greying in the hair, expanding in the waist and earning a little extra money to ease the transition into retirement. He and his wife Janet both had reasonable pensions and planned to downsize, selling the house in Plymouth and moving to the kinder climes of the Lizard peninsula in Cornwall. A twee white cottage had been identified. The garden was fruitful without being overly taxing and the conveyancing was underway.

The couple had always been the fabled outdoor types and planned to do their best to defy the ageing process by staying that way. The Lizard was a wonderful place to walk, with its unique heathland and spectacular coast. Even that great headland could be just a base for exploring the rest of Cornwall. A good life's final adventure beckoned happily.

The motive for the break-in was unclear. A theory that the Edwards might have been looking for confidential documents was aired, or maybe trying to steal official stationery for some purpose unknown. Perhaps they wanted to access the computer systems.

Such were the thoughts, but none were ever proven as facts. All that could be concluded was money wasn't the objective. There was only petty cash stored in the offices.

Albert had found a storeroom open and walked in to investigate. His reward was a cosh on the back of the head. The medical evidence was clear that he had been hit at least twice more as he lay unconscious.

That the Edwards were responsible was conjecture, a supposition based on evidence so flimsy there would never be a point in putting it before a court. They had no alibis for the night and an informant had whispered that they'd been talking of some kind of attack at an important building. Martha's knowledge of forensics, the theory went, would have equipped her with the ability to break in without leaving the giveaway fingerprints, hairs or fibres.

Albert had survived, but he hadn't lived. There was extensive brain damage. It left a man who had been proud, independent and eloquent unable to walk, communicate or care for himself.

In a reflex of emotion, Dan remembered the story. When it became clear the police investigation was making no progress, Janet had spoken out in an attempt to bring witnesses forward.

Dan could recall very few reports on *Wessex Tonight* that were not his own. Most were fillers, of little consequence, forgotten in seconds. But some stood out. And for him, they were always the victims' stories, the tales of lives ruined in a second's viciousness or violence, stupidity or negligence. On the darker nights, lying sleepless in bed, those that Dan had himself covered often returned to taunt his restless mind.

Janet put on a little make-up to help her brave the camera and had just about got through the interview. That she kept breaking down only made it more moving. She described the life the couple were planning to lead together. Spoiling grandchildren by day, walks on the beach by night, just like when they first married almost 40 years ago.

"And now…" she'd stammered, "all he's got… after all those years… all those hopes… is a living death."

Martha and Brian Edwards were interviewed at length. He would say nothing at all, retained an unbreachable silence.

A note on the file read, *Suspect Martha drilled it into him. Usual story. Say nothing and we're safe. Psychologist believes he's totally in her thrall. He was probably the one who did the actual beating, but on her orders. Evidence for this – as ever – none. Just another theory.*

Martha said almost nothing. Only when she was told both siblings were being released had there been a brief exchange.

Martha Edwards – *You bastards have been going on at me as if I'm a criminal. Where were you to investigate what happened to me?*

Detective Sergeant Franks – *That's not what we're talking about.*

Martha – *And that's the fucking problem, isn't it? No one's ever talked about it. No one's ever cared.*

Franks – *For the last time, do you have anything to say about Albert Fisher?*

Martha – *I'm sorry for what happened to him. But…*

Franks – *But what?*

Martha – *Who's sorry for what happened to me?*

Franks – *About Albert Fisher?*

Martha – *He worked for the government. You work for the government. You make your choices and you take your chances. Fuck you all.*

Franks – *He was a 63-year-old man. Beaten as he lay helpless on the floor.*

Martha – *And I was a 5-year-old girl!*

Franks – *Is there anything you want to say about the attack on Albert Fisher?*

Martha – *Just let me out of here.*

★★★

Adam finished reading. They drove on in silence. The rumbling of the car was the only companion to their wandering thoughts.

Finally, Adam said quietly, "No Robin Hoods. No lovable rogues with hearts of gold. Just criminals."

The road turned down a hill. Ahead was an expanse of sea. They were approaching East Prawle, angles of roofs reaching above a line of trees.

Katrina drew up in a pub car park. The rest of the convoy followed. Police officers began clambering out of the vans and cars.

"Just one thing," Dan said, as Adam opened the door. "What changed? To turn them from mockery to effectively murder?"

Adam hesitated, then said, "Later. It's not what you need to hear when we may be about to face them."

CHAPTER FOURTEEN

It began like a phoney war.

The procession of vans, cars and motorbikes moved slowly along the narrow road. There were no racing engines, no squealing tyres, no sirens. Only the silent intensity of pure concentration.

Every officer was watching. For a surreptitious or panicked movement. The guilty twitch of a curtain or hasty shutting of a door.

They would move into the centre of the village as furtively as possible. And from there they would storm outwards, a radius of motion, through houses, cottages, caravans, shops, sheds and barns.

A tattered old wooden sign welcomed them to East Prawle. A homely and embracing sight for generations of locals and holidaymakers, but surely never to have witnessed visitors like this.

The Devon hedges tapered to the ground, as if curtains falling on their arrival. Around was the expanse of open countryside and the great dome of the sapphire sky. Fields filled with the hues of crops.

Ahead a promontory jutted a dark finger into the sea. Prawle Point, southernmost tip of Devon; an impertinent jab of land into the waters' realm. The line of the cliffs embraced the bay, the sun at its zenith, its only challenge a couple of brushstrokes of cloud. In the far distance the tiny dots of a disciplined line of shipping ploughed a path along the English Channel.

The road opened out once more. Houses were beginning to rise from the earth. A man guided a young child on a bike, newspapers, bread and milk piled in its basket.

The air was full of the sound of gulls. One picked at the discarded packaging beneath a litter bin. A jackdaw watched from atop a Georgian post box.

It was quintessential England, exemplary Devon, an archetypal village. But hidden somewhere, amidst the rustic veneer, was a secret.

Silence had filled the car, Katrina, Dan, Adam and Claire too focused on their surroundings to speak.

But now Adam muttered, "Are you sure about this? You and your bloody weird inspirations. Cirl buntings indeed."

Dan didn't bother to reply. It was an echo that hadn't the decency to fade. They must have been through the conversation half a dozen times. After the moment of revelation in the news library, Adam sent a couple of detectives to check on the key claim of the report, the tiny scope of the birds' sole remaining habitat.

Dan tried not to grow irritated at the challenge to his journalistic honour, and then smug as the call came back. It was entirely true. The story of the cirl buntings was renowned within the birdwatchers' world.

If it was cirl buntings the police needed to find, they could confine the search to East Prawle and its immediate surroundings. And given that faint noise of a lawnmower in the background of the ransom call, it had to be the village itself.

Ahead were a couple of shops and a pub with a large earthen car park beside them. One by one the vans, cars and bikes pulled up. And across the grass and tarmac and paths and tracks spread the flood of the operation to save Annette Newman.

★★★

That the briefing had been quick was a mark of its urgency, with Adam managing to confine his oration to only a few seconds. He stood on the step of a Land Rover, the breeze toying with the dark strands of his hair, with the officers all gathered around.

There were a hundred or so, as many as could be mustered in a short time. The convoy had grown as it travelled. Cars lingered in lay-bys to join, others screamed up behind. The police helicopter had also been scrambled. It was waiting in a field, ready to join the hunt.

At the heart of the gathering was the knot of armed officers. Even they were showing hints of the anticipation of what was to come.

One man dabbed at a trickle of sweat as it twisted its way down his forehead. Another clenched and unclenched a fist.

As befits a village hiding in the cambers of the Devon countryside, and at the extreme of its long miles of beauty, there was but one road into and out of East Prawle. A couple of officers were pulling barriers from the back of a van and blocking it. Another laid out bollards and *Road Closed* signs. Two more stood sentry duty.

The trap was laid.

At the back of the group Nigel filmed, camera steady on his shoulder. He too had joined the convoy, pulling out just as it left Kingsbridge.

"What's the plan?" he whispered to Dan.

"I don't have a plan. We've no idea what's going to happen. Just follow and film everything we can."

Adam was gazing into the ring of the crowd, a leader's look to each of his officers. The sun had angled behind him, casting a darkness across the detective's rugged features. Shadows filled his eyes.

"I won't say much, because there's not much to say," Adam rallied, the authority of his voice carrying easily across the car park. "We get one chance at this. When we pull up, storm the area. Be restless and relentless. Use your eyes and your instincts. Spot the sign that leads us to the kidnappers. That gate closing, the feet running or the person who can't look you in the eye. Get out there – and save Annette!"

***

In each direction officers ran, filled with the energy of their purpose, like sparks flung from a Catherine wheel.

One made for the shop, the kind of all-encompassing affair of many a village monopoly. A blackboard advertised the sale of newspapers, cigarettes, milk, lottery tickets, greeting cards, beer and wine, vegetables, light bulbs, logs and kindling. Even a variety of creams for every purpose; ice, sun, insect and Devon clotted.

Through the reflections of the glass, the officer pushed his way past the queue of three, quite a rush in the terms of the Devon countryside. He began talking to the woman behind the counter.

An Alsatian trotted past, his handler striding hard to keep up. The dog could have been Rutherford's cousin. A spaniel sniffed along the path beside the pub, stopping occasionally to check a scent, its busy head a smudge of golden motion.

Outside the pub, a detective spoke to a squat man wearing a grubby T-shirt and shorts. His arms were folded, resting on the support of his ample girth and his voice loud.

No, nothing. Nothing unusual at all.

The village filled with the barrage of the police helicopter. It rose from beneath the cliff line and hovered overhead, rotors threshing the air.

At the axis of the momentum Nigel filmed, whipping the camera around time and again, panning back and forth, trying to capture the human blizzard that was the hunt.

"It's chaos," he gasped. "Where do we go?"

Dan didn't reply, just kept his look set on Adam. The leader had become the observer, the analyst, the interpreter. Amongst all the officers going about their frenetic work, he alone stood still, a cool pillar of composure. All the experience of his generation of policing was in that look; scrutinising, feeling for the trail they sought.

A young cop was half way up a ladder, calling questions to a man digging out a gutter. He was waving a picture of Annette. A woman was checking the cars parked around the back of the pub. A stream of officers knocked on doors, hard and demanding, firing questions at the householders who emerged.

"Adam?" Dan prompted. "Adam?"

No answer. Slowly, the detective was turning around, his narrowed eyes taking in each detail of the storm he had unleashed. He was with every one of the officers, sensing what they sensed, seeing what they saw.

"We'd better follow the cops and get more action," Nigel said.

"Yeah, but which ones? How the hell do we know where Annette is?"

"If she's here at all."

"She's here."

Dan was surprised at the certainty in his voice. He had no time to wonder if it was true faith or an attempt to convince himself.

"When they find her, that's the shot," he continued. "The picture that'll be splashed around the world. If we're here and we don't get it, it'll be humiliating. We'll be the nearly men. So near and yet so far."

"Very lyrical, very you," replied the practical cameraman, anchor to the earth. "So – what do we do?"

"Adam?" Dan prompted again.

And now the detective spoke. "We wait."

Claire and Katrina headed off to join the search. They went separate ways, Claire heading down the hill, towards the coast and a group of bungalows. Katrina made for the pub and cottages behind.

As they ran, both women looked back. Dan quickly busied himself wiping a grain of dust from his eye.

The helicopter banked and headed west, to the edge of the village and the open countryside, rising higher into the sky.

A cop was leading a woman towards an old-fashioned garage, white stone and black wooden gates. She unlocked them and he disappeared into the darkness.

Nigel took a step forward, the camera trained. "This is it. I can feel it."

They could hear the sound of metal moving, grinding and groaning. A line of officers jogged past, heading for the northern end of the village. All were sweating hard in the day's heat.

Another noise from the garage. This time a dull thud. Nigel edged closer.

A car chugged past, heading out of Prawle, an older woman driving. A detective stepped into the road, stopped her, checked the boot and waved her on. In this net, with these stakes, no one was beyond suspicion.

From the garage the cop emerged, brushing dust from his shoulders. He was shaking his head.

"So much for your hunches," Dan muttered.

His mobile rang. "Yes, there is an operation going on in East Prawle," Dan replied. "I know because I'm in the middle of it. Yes, Lizzie, we are filming it. Thanks for the tip, I would never have thought of that."

Beside him, Adam shifted position and peered into the brightness of the sky. To the north and east, no more than a quarter of a mile away, a thin trail of dark smoke was rising above a line of trees.

★★★

Adam was away, running, moving fast. Dan didn't hesitate. He followed.

They crossed the road, dodged a couple on bicycles and found a gap between a line of houses. A dry mud track, just wide enough for a car, led over the brow of a small hill. It was lined with trees.

From above, Dan thought he heard the song of a cirl bunting. He tried to pick out a shape in the foliage, but there was no sign of any birdlife.

Nigel was panting hard from the slope. Dan reached out and took the camera.

To either side were the back gardens of houses. A child careered down a slide. A woman watched while talking into a mobile phone.

They were nearing the crest of the hill. The smoke was thickening, a fattened smear on the blueness of the sky.

"What're we doing?" Dan gasped to Adam.

"A hunch."

"But – should we be leaving the main search? Most of the houses are back there."

Adam just kept running. Dan stumbled on a clump of thick grass, the dense weight of the camera nearly dragging him over.

"Surely it's just a farmer, burning rubbish?"

"A fire's the best way to destroy evidence. As someone who'd studied forensics would know."

They rounded a corner. Now the green lane was filled with smoke. Its acrid tang prickled the tongue and stung the nose. Through a barrier of bushes loomed the hazy outline of a cottage.

The thatch of its roof was aflame, orange spears rising into the air, circling the stone of the chimney. The fire was spreading fast, roaring out its hunger. More flames danced from an upstairs window.

Nigel took the camera, hoisted it to his shoulder and began filming. Overhead the helicopter swooped, sending flames leaping and smoke swirling. Adam waved frantically and the great beast banked away.

"Help's coming," Dan yelled.

"We can't wait. She could be dying in there."

Next to the cottage was a garage. Adam lurched towards the double doors and pulled them open. Black smoke bellowed out, enveloping him. The detective began choking and coughing as he squatted down to escape the fumes.

Inside, swathed in smoke and with flames leaping around it, was a white van. Paint was starting to blister and peel from its bonnet and the windscreen was blackening. As they watched, it cracked with a whipping snap. The stench of burning rubber and petrol was like an attack. Dan felt his body shake with a burst of wracking coughs.

Adam span and headed for the door. All of the thatch was alight now, greedily sucking in the air. The heat assailed them, beating at every inch of exposed flesh, singeing eyes, throats and lungs.

The door was ajar. Adam kicked out. It smashed into the wall, a pane of glass breaking with the impact. They tumbled inside.

The cottage was fast filling with murderous smoke. The momentum of the fire was growing relentlessly. Embers of burning straw floated past.

Ahead was a staircase, a threadbare carpet with pictures lining the walls. The way was blocked by a bank of flames. It was impassable.

"Shit," Adam moaned. "If she's up there…"

He pivoted left, along a stone-flagged corridor. A barometer crashed to the floor, tiny spheres of mercury speeding from it.

They were in a small lounge. A sofa, an easy chair, a television and a rug covering the floor. A leaning standard lamp. But no sign of Annette.

From above came a low creaking, followed by a thud, then another. Flaming straw fell past the window.

"The bloody place is coming down!" Dan shouted. "Adam, we're going to die in here!"

He clutched for his friend, but too late. In the far corner of the room was a small door. Adam leapt for it, pulled it open. Shelves, a vacuum cleaner, some pillows and blankets. He span and headed back for the corridor. The merciless heat was everywhere and growing always more intense.

They burst into a kitchen. Adam pulled open a row of cupboards. He groped blindly inside, arms flailing. Cans, pots and pans tumbled out, clattering a discordant rhythm on the stone of the floor.

Dan leant back against the sink and tried desperately to catch some breath. The air was full of singeing, cloying smoke. A bottle of wine dropped and shattered. Another groaning thud echoed from the roof.

"Come on, come on!" Adam panted, lunging for the end of the kitchen, glass crunching under the hard soles of his shoes.

Another black wooden door faced them. It was a store room, also stone floored, the shelves full of packets and tins and the air blissfully cool. And on the floor, on a tartan blanket, was the curled shape of a person, hair seeping onto the flagstones. It was motionless, no sign of life.

"It's Annette!" Adam yelled. "Help me! For fuck's sake!"

Dan tried to breathe, felt his stomach heave with the effort. He bent down, battling to fight the bile of the rising nausea. The air was clearer by the ground, free of the sticky, suffocating smoke. He gulped it in.

"Her legs!" Adam ordered. "Come on man!" His voice rose to a scream. "Now!"

Dan fumbled to get a grip, managed to grab a fold of jeans, then an ankle. He felt the warmth of Annette's body through the material and had to concentrate to force himself not to let go. Clouds of dense smoke billowed around them, stinging his eyes. They were watering so hard that he could barely see.

"Lift!" yelled Adam. "For Christ's sake, lift!"

It felt like an immense, immovable weight. He managed to half-lift, half-drag the flaccid legs towards the door, following Adam and shuffling towards the hazy light. Ahead was the sweetness of the clean air, the breeze like the most rejuvenating of balms.

Dan urged his leaden muscles to take one step, then another, to wade through the hellish smoke and heat and stench of fire. He was vaguely aware of arms helping to pull him, Nigel's contorted face looming. Someone was shouting, but the words made no sense.

He nearly fell but steadied himself, forced another couple of steps from his faltering legs and they were out in the light. The blessed, beautiful sunshine. Dan collapsed onto the lawn, struggling to breathe in the sudden shock of freedom.

Adam sunk to his knees beside Annette. He tapped gently at her cheek, then harder. But there was no reaction.

The spirit of the reaper chilled the air. The darkness of his outline lurked in the corner of each set of eyes, beckoning to the young woman trapped in the twilight between life and death.

Another flare of fire arced from the cottage roof, smoking fronds filling the sky. Adam leant back, let out a low groan, grasped Annette's shoulders and shook them, then again, harder now.

There was still no reaction. He tried once more, then stopped and stared at the prone figure lying lifeless on the grass.

Annette's eyes twitched and opened.

In all of his lifetime, Dan never forgot that sight. Choking for breath on his hands and knees amid a perfectly cultivated lawn on a beautiful Devon day, a voracious fire devouring the cottage and sirens screaming around him, yet all he could see were the eyes of a young woman.

He took long weeks trying to understand what it was he found in them. Finally, many months later, when all was at last done with the story of Annette Newman, when he could summon the courage to revisit that day, Dan decided.

Her eyes were filled with newborn demons.

CHAPTER FIFTEEN

Annette's face froze, lingered and disappeared. The television screens faded to blackness, only the red jewels of the standby lights showing in the darkness.

The flames that had filled the inside of the cottage, which had leapt from the monitors and around the old room, were gone. The roaring of the inferno that had sounded from the floorboards and walls was quietened. The blinds were drawn back and the lights in Courtroom Number Three turned on once more, a horde of the shadows of the past running before them.

The pictures Nigel filmed that spring day, six months ago, had made for one of the most dramatic parts of an extraordinary trial. And now, at last, they had reached the denouement.

The eleven in the jury box sat silent. Only the foreman remained standing. He took off his glasses and polished them with his thin, acrylic tie. Around him, all waited to see where the man would look.

The old adage was everywhere. At the Edwards, or elsewhere. Guilty or not guilty.

But still the man was resolutely staring downwards, rigorous in the pursuit of the slightest speck of grime on those oversized, outdated spectacles.

And the courtroom waited.

Eyes automatically found that one, vacant seat. And the father who sat beside it, bent double now, a polished shoe turning on the carpet tiles.

On the press benches Dan squirmed as a sweat spread across his back. Ahead sat Adam, his dark hair newly cut for this final week of the trial and his flushed neck turning ever redder. Beside him Claire toyed with a pile of folders.

Still, six months on, they hadn't talked. The occasional walk, yes, the odd drink, yes, always on the neutral territory of moorland or a pub, but never the conversation which threatened. Always he was too tired, or she too preoccupied by a case.

To Adam's other side Katrina sat back, her arms folded. Her hair was a little longer than six months ago, perhaps with the hint of a shading of colour. On her shoulder lay that legendary symbol.

Dan found his pen sketching an outline of the tattoo. He knew what it was now, he had made the discovery precisely ten days ago. And in what extraordinary circumstances.

The foreman finished buffing his glasses and was replacing them carefully upon his nose. At last he was starting to look up.

And then a noise as shocking as a thunderclap. A hammering at the courtroom doors. A random, relentless beat. Panicked hands with pummeling fists.

And the sound of a cry. The voice of a young woman.

"Let me back in! I have to know!"

The doors shook under the attack. Judge Templar tapped a finger on the gavel, balanced upon the bench.

Another rocking of the doors. "Please! Please!"

Furrows pitted the judge's brow. "Such an occurrence is most irregular at this point so pivotal in the trial," Templar announced. "The doors of justice are locked only occasionally, but always for good reason. However, the young lady is understandably distressed and the court will make allowances."

The usher slid over, unlocked the doors and in tumbled Annette. Her face was blurred with tears and taut with lines of misery. Her father rose and she collapsed into him. There they stood, intertwined, Roger's arms squeezing the breathless moans from his daughter's body.

One final anguished wail emerged, the sound of a spirit close to breaking. And as for Roger Newman, his eyes had closed as if no longer able to fight the weight of such an infinite burden.

Rays of sunlight streamed into the court. It was growing ever warmer.

The usher stepped carefully across and handed Newman another plastic cup of water. He took a sip and passed it to Annette.

With trembling, hopeless hands she tried to drink, a cascade of droplets staining dark circles on the carpet tiles.

From aloft on the bench the judge watched, silent and unmoving. But eyes never resting. Over the foreman, the Newmans and the Edwards.

The players on the stage of justice. For this, the final act.

One of the solicitors began to cough, quickly stifling the sound.

Behind the glass of the dock the Edwards sat hand in hand, both intent on the foreman. Brian jiggled a knee. Martha was still, that green gaze set on the man who would decide her fate.

Beside the dock a prison guard shifted her weight. A heavy fob of keys jingled.

And the clock ticked on towards the hour.

★★★

Amongst the hacks, the consensus was for a not guilty verdict.

Proof beyond reasonable doubt was what the law required in that delightful legal way of leaving a galaxy of scope for expensive dispute. The more analytical of lawyers took the words to mean two thirds convinced, or 67 per cent. The journalists' view was that the Edwards were certainly guilty, but the evidence against them wasn't quite strong enough – perhaps adding up to 55 or 60 per cent.

What they all agreed on was that it was a close call. The jury might well see it differently. They often did.

For the first time in his life, Dan had been called to give evidence. He'd tried to convince himself it would be a straightforward experience. He broadcast live to half a million people with a nonchalant regularity. What could possibly be the problem in telling a roomful of maybe a hundred about what he had witnessed?

"Some advice," Adam said, on the morning before Dan was due to take the stand. "Just answer the questions, but watch out for the defence. He'll try to discredit you. Make out to the jury you can't be relied upon. Just stick to what you know and don't get involved in a row. And no matter how much it might go against your grain, on no account whatsoever try to be smart."

"I think I can manage that," Dan smiled.

The look which came back was far from convinced. "Just remember what I said. Whatever you do, don't try to be clever."

That morning, Dan found himself unusually preoccupied with his attire. It wasn't normally a prerogative. In his personal list of priorities, the purposes of clothes were – (1) warmth, (2) modesty, (3) comfort, and (4, by far) fashion.

"What do you think?" he asked Rutherford, as the dog thrust his nose into the rarely explored depths of the back of the wardrobe. "A suit? Or does that look like I'm trying too hard? Just my usual trousers and a jacket? Or does that look like I don't care enough?"

Rutherford sniffed at the clothes and sneezed. "There's no need to be so rude," Dan chided. "What about a tie? Do we go bright, or does that look untrustworthy? Or darker? Or does that make me look like I'm going to a funeral?"

The dog padded off to deal with the more important business of curling up in the sunshine of the bay window. Eventually, Dan chose a light blue shirt, dark blue jacket and a plain, mid-blue tie. At Lizzie's behest, he'd once suffered one of those colour assessment courses. A heavily made-up woman had fussed over him, held various swatches of ridiculous shades next to his cheeks, clucked a little and finally pronounced that blue was undoubtedly his hue.

Since then, Dan had bought little else. It was the fashion equivalent of not knowing much, but knowing what you like.

★★★

The art of throwing skunks is well-practiced in the legal profession, in particular the champions of the lawless. And Piers Wishart QC could have been an Olympian. The purest of waters, the most clear cut of cases, could be muddied by his creative tampering.

Dan stood in the witness box, trying not to look at Adam, and definitely not Claire or Katrina. Instead, he kept his eyes set on Wishart's well-fed, cigars and port features.

"So, you were with the police for the entirety of the operation to rescue Annette?" the barrister began.

"Yes, sir."

"The whole of it?"

"Yes, sir."

"You saw absolutely everything that went on?"

"I believe so."

"Right up to the moment Annette was rescued?"

"Yes, sir."

"And as the footage in that remarkable video we've seen shows, you were actually there."

"Yes, sir."

"And in the aftermath? When the police searched the area?"

"Yes, sir."

Wishart paused, flicked a ginger curl back under his wig and gestured to the dock. "And did you see any sign of my clients?"

"Err... no, sir."

"None at all?"

"No, sir."

"Not a trace?"

"No."

"No hint whatsoever?"

"No, sir. But that doesn't mean they weren't there."

Wishart's face warmed. Behind him, Dan could see Adam had closed his eyes.

"Really, Mr Groves?" the barrister boomed. "I do apologise, I must have misheard. What is your profession again?"

"I'm a reporter, sir. A journalist."

"I'm sorry, I thought you must be an experienced detective. An accomplished investigator, no less."

"No, look, what I was saying—"

"It's just..." the barrister interrupted smoothly, "No one saw my clients there. As the trial has heard, there was no evidence they were there. No fingerprints, no footprints, no forensics – nothing.

But your special insight into the case means you can stand here and tell us they may have been there?"

"Well, they could have... err... fled."

Wishart turned to the jury and raised an arm.

"Fled?" he mocked. "*Fled*? Past a hundred police officers? Who were on high alert, busily searching for them? Past police dogs? Past roadblocks? Past a helicopter? I think perhaps the only way they could have fled successfully is if they had one of those devices in which Dr Who travels through space and time – a Tardis, I believe?"

Even some of the jury chuckled. Dan caught a warning glare from Adam and just about succeeded in biting back a retort.

He spent the rest of the day seething, but managed to secure at least some revenge when Wishart left court that evening. He was suffering a nasty cold sore on his chin and Dan made sure Nigel filmed a close up of his face to feature in the day's report.

★★★

Even Adam agreed that the case was finely balanced. Fifty-fifty was his estimate of the chances of a conviction.

The fire in the white van had consumed any forensics there and they'd found nothing useful in the cottage. The combination of the voracious blaze and thousands of gallons of water from the firefighters' hoses had destroyed any evidence. The forensics officers had done their best, but eventually had to concede the scene was hopeless.

The recording of the ransom demand provided no assistance. That there was someone in the background when Annette spoke was clear, but exhaustive analysis came up with the unhelpful conclusion that it could have been anyone.

The kidnappers had been clever. Adam worked up a theory about how they'd got away, but that was all it was, just a suspicion.

With only one road into East Prawle, he thought Martha had been hiding somewhere, watching it. When she saw the police approaching, she'd called her brother. They used untraceable pay-as-you-go mobiles, discarded later when they had escaped.

They had petrol and kindling ready to destroy the van. Brian had probably been living in it to avoid the risk of leaving any traces in the cottage. Together, the Edwards had dumped Annette in the storeroom. Martha left to watch the road and Brian camped in the van, returning occasionally to check on Annette, to give her water and force her to make the ransom call.

Dan had wondered whether they intended to kill Annette? It was a moot point, the subject of some heated rows between the detectives and the Crown Prosecution Service.

Adam thought they probably didn't mean to kill her, that Martha would have expected Annette to be found before the fire razed the cottage. But even so, he argued strongly that it was tantamount to attempted murder to be so reckless as to start the blaze with her lying tied up in the storeroom.

Adam originally wanted that to be the charge, but the CPS had vetoed the idea. It would be hard enough to secure a conviction for kidnapping on the available evidence.

How had Brian escaped? It wasn't by car, the only road out of East Prawle was sealed. He was physically very fit and had possibly fifteen minutes head start on the police.

He could, Adam suggested, have simply walked. The area was networked with paths. It was a fine day and he would have blended in with the hundreds of other ramblers enjoying the Devon countryside. The warm weather meant a hat and sunglasses wouldn't have looked out of place; an excellent disguise.

A rowing boat had been discovered, sunk in a creek near the town of Salcombe, around four miles from East Prawle. Adam suspected Brian may have taken that and rowed to safety. But the boat had long been scuttled by the time it was found and any evidence destroyed. It was another theory that could never be proved.

The case fell back on circumstantial evidence. The Edwards had disappeared for the couple of days of the kidnapping, only resurfacing afterwards and professing astonishment at being arrested. They refused to answer any questions, just as Adam predicted.

Silence had served them well when interrogated about the attack on Albert Fisher. They expected it to do the same now.

The mobile phones registered to the siblings were switched off for the whole time Annette was missing so there were no location traces to help the investigation. The CCTV of Annette being abducted from Catherine Street showed two indistinct figures who an expert testified were *similar in build and manner* to Martha and Brian Edwards. There were shoe prints from the scene matching their sizes, but the shoes themselves were never recovered.

There was also intelligence from a couple of police sources that the Edwards had been boasting of some spectacular project in the days before the kidnapping. But the informants were criminals, unwilling to give evidence. It was all temptingly suggestive but a very long way from conclusive.

★★★

The prosecution's best hope was an alleged cell confession by Brian Edwards. He was being held on remand in Exeter Prison and had shared a cell with a young drug addict and burglar called Ernie Smith. Brian had taken some of Smith's heroin and afterwards talked about *the big story of the year, that young girl being kidnapped and what a fine job it was.*

There was a whole morning of legal argument about whether the jury should even hear Smith's evidence. He was a career criminal, hoping to win some reduction in his sentence by inventing a story, said the defence. No, a man of dubious past, but one who had finally decided to do the right thing, claimed the prosecution.

Finally, Judge Templar ruled that Smith's testimony would be heard. Adam's sigh of relief carried across the courtroom. The odds on a conviction had changed in an instant. But it was the falsest of dawns.

Smith was young, nervous and faltering. His hair was cut short to the point of extinction, one ear was perforated with a line of metal hoops and he hadn't shaved. In fairness, possibly as a gesture to the importance of the moment, he had at least the decency to wear his best track suit.

"You are a thief, aren't you Mr Smith?" was Wishart's gentle opening.

"It's just – well, I didn't have much in life and—"

"I suspect some members of the jury believe that at some point they didn't have much in life either. But that didn't prompt them to begin breaking into people's homes."

"I was going through a bad time."

"As do many people, Mr Smith, but they don't turn to crime."

"I want to set the record straight and—"

"And you're a drug addict."

"It's not easy in prison."

"For whom no one is responsible for you being there but yourself, Mr Smith."

"Well, yeah, but—"

"And you are a self-confessed liar, are you not?"

"Yeah, but who doesn't tell the odd lie?"

Whishart let the words wander through the air, before turning to the jury box.

"And that, members of the jury, says it all. Ask yourselves this – can you really put any trust in this man?"

Based upon the look of the two lines of faces in the jury box, Dan began sketching out a script for a not guilty verdict.

CHAPTER SIXTEEN

In his years of observing the stately processes of the courts, Dan had come to the conclusion that he was, at very best, disillusioned with the legal system.

When arguing the point he would cite the way the law dealt with those who should be most central to its attentions. But for a victim, the English concept of justice was entirely capable of piling anguish upon suffering upon torment upon ordeal.

It was the night after one rape trial that Dan found himself sitting on the great blue sofa in the flat, sipping whisky and trying to forget what he had witnessed. The woman, whose misery lurked everywhere before his eyes, was in her early 30s, married with a young son, and was known in court as Wendy.

It was an early evening in the wintertime. She had been walking home from a coffee with a friend after work and was set upon. Wendy was pulled from a street near her house, dragged into a lock-up garage and raped.

The defence barrister questioned her at length about the attack, and unsurprisingly she broke down. Without her testimony, as is so often the way, the case collapsed. The alleged attacker, a body builder with a neck like a rhino's and an attitude to match, swaggered out of court and made for the nearest bar to celebrate. As for Wendy, she had been left sitting in a bare ante room, crying.

Before finally going to bed, Dan looked up *victim* in the dictionary. He stared at the words, before picking up a pen, crossing them through and scrawling, *Person to be treated with contempt, preferably humiliated, and left as a pile of human wreckage.*

Other experiences of the courts had softened his definition not at all.

Lizzie had, on one occasion, allowed Dan to take up an invitation to join a public panel to debate the workings of the criminal justice system. It was a mistake never to be repeated.

It might have been the complimentary wine, but his comment – "I don't have a great problem with householders attacking burglars. If they don't want to get hurt, the answer is simple – don't break into people's homes" – caused a minor controversy and created a flurry of interest in the local press.

Dan was aware of his views and so careful when reporting that most essential moment of a trial, the victim's evidence. The morning Annette took the stand was, then, one for which he had been preparing himself.

In the weeks that followed the kidnapping, he had got to know a little more of Annette. Dan's role in the inquiry was largely over, employed as he was as a kind of freelance assistant investigator. Now it was for the real detectives to build a case against the Edwards.

But, at the invitation of Roger Newman, Dan had been asked to meet Annette, to be thanked for his help in saving her. It was an encounter he tried not to think about, given the woman he found.

The meeting was in the MIR, just a few feet from where her picture had stood on one of the felt boards, and it was brief. To say Annette had changed was to compare a shift of the weather from Mediterranean summer to Antarctic winter.

***

It was Katrina who took the lead in questioning Annette. But even her experience was faced by damage of a degree she had seldom before encountered. The interviews were marked by long silences and frequent breaks.

Dan only heard about it second hand from Adam at a couple of their regular discussions. During the last, over lunch, he had to ask to hear no more. Some roads are best left untravelled.

A psychologist had carried out an assessment. It took several months to prepare, despite the urgent need, because it was many weeks before Annette could speak about what she had gone through.

The Greater Wessex Police specialist, 'Sledgehammer' Stephens, produced a report with all his usual subtlety.

The subject is suffering SEVERE EMOTIONAL TRAUMA, Stephens wrote, and for once his fondness for capitalisation was justified. *Her mental fragility is STARK and a matter of EXTREME CONCERN. Counselling and treatment appear to be having LITTLE EFFECT.*

Her symptoms are classically those of someone who has suffered a NEAR DEATH EXPERIENCE. In simple terms – POST TRAUMATIC SHOCK.

The sense of helplessness is PALPABLE. As a consequence, a growing state of PARANOIA has taken hold and will, in my judgement, be EXTREMELY PROBLEMATICAL to address.

Annette has been suffering with continual MOOD SWINGS. She has a CONTINUAL, HEIGHTENED and EXAGGERATED fear of being abducted again. No amount of work has been able to ameliorate this.

She is experiencing VIVID and REPEATED NIGHTMARES. Sleep is intermittent and elusive, contributing a PHYSICAL FRAILTY to her psychological problems. She hardly eats. The deterioration in her CONTINUES.

FLASHBACKS are commonplace, and form with EXTREME DETAIL and REALISM. They are particularly triggered by smell, a reaction to the petrol which was set around her, one of Annette's most fearful memories of the abduction.

Annette seldom ventures out. All strangers are viewed as POTENTIAL ENEMIES. She is DISTANT, WITHDRAWN and DIFFICULT TO REACH. She has an almost insurmountable inability to discuss and share feelings.

As with many such subjects, her personality has CHANGED MARKEDLY. Prior to the abduction, Annette was a virgin. Since, she has sought sexual experience and had a series of partners.

I note one further area of EXTREME CONCERN. Annette has, on two occasions now, confessed to suicidal thoughts. She should be

CAREFULLY MONITORED, to ensure these do not grow and take an irreversible hold.

"17 years old," was Adam's final comment, as he and Dan left the pub. "She had everything in life to look forward to. And now everything's become an ordeal."

★★★

Even the shortest of walks can be made to feel very long.

From her seat in the public gallery to the witness box, Annette had to cover perhaps fifteen metres. But the anticipation of the moment hardly helped. All in the court knew it was coming, but announced it had to be anyway. Just to be absolutely certain everyone was staring at her.

When someone suffers a crime the system insists they relive it, and never just the once. First they must be interviewed by the police, and a statement taken. Afterwards, there are many follow up visits. And then comes the climax of the torments: the court case. Once again the victim must go through what happened, and in a very public arena.

Even after all that there comes an added sting, just for good measure. The final revisiting of the crime must be carried out in full sight of the perpetrator, and usually only a few metres from them.

And so it was for Annette. The sound of her name being called came like an impact, an invisible blow, a physical recoiling from a dreaded moment. Roger reached over and gave her a hug. His daughter's body was trembling hard.

And all this in front of every watching, staring eye.

Roger got up, gently pulling Annette. By her side floated the black robe of the usher, a kindly, guiding hand leading towards the witness box. She fixed her face ahead and began the walk. Each step felt like an effort of supreme will.

At first, she trod lightly, as if intimidated by the sound of her footfall on the wooden boards. But suddenly, her pace increased.

Annette was approaching the plate glass of the secure dock. Watching her, as she passed only feet in front, were the Edwards.

Annette never gave them a glance. There was an impenetrable wall of fear to her side, created of the condensed blackness of the countless nightmares and flashbacks. She kept her gaze set upon the witness box, walking faster and faster, reaching out for its sanctuary, until she stumbled over the low step and up and into it.

And there the young woman stood, breathless, hands gripping the curve of the carved wooden rail. And there she waited to relive her ordeal one more time.

CHAPTER SEVENTEEN

On this mid-morning of a kind September day, the sun was making the most of the waning days of her reign. Radiance filled the skylights of Courtroom Number Three. As if they had been arrayed, ready for this moment, the brightest of the natural spotlights fell directly onto the witness box and the 17-year-old woman standing there.

Judge Templar produced a judicial smile; one of those intended to communicate warmth and understanding in the possession of great authority, but which never quite convince.

"Ms Newman, the court is aware of the ordeal you have suffered. We have no interest in adding to it. If at any point you would like a break, please say. Mr Munroe will take you through your evidence."

The prosecution barrister was a short, chubby man, whose wig suffered a tendency towards a lopsided outlook. Stature being a strength in legal circles, Munroe had borrowed a trick from his female counterparts. As they might indulge themselves in stilettos, so he wore bespoke shoes with stacked heels.

Nature being a generally fair benefactor, Munroe had been compensated with a rich baritone voice of which an opera singer would have been proud.

He began the examination gently, taking Annette through her statement. For a victim of such a crime, it was remarkably short. There was little she could recall about the abduction itself. In the subsequent hours she was kept tied up and blindfolded. She had overheard no voices and had no recollection of anything which might be construed as real evidence.

The only detail upon which Munroe fixed was Annette's view that she believed two people were involved in the kidnapping. One was driving the van, the other in the back with her. The barrister held a long look with the jury, and then pointedly let his eyes slide over to the Edwards.

Being bereft of facts, the majority of Munroe's questioning concentrated on Annette's feelings. Dan had seen it time and again. Everything the best of advocates did was designed to win the sympathy of the jury.

"Forgive me for this question," Munroe said. "But some could perhaps think you came out of all this entirely unharmed?"

Annette stared at him. Her complexion, pale throughout the trial, had turned to milk in the witness box.

"Unharmed?"

"Yes."

"As if – I didn't suffer at all?"

"Just so."

And now came a hiatus. There had been many in Annette's testimony as she struggled with the recollections, but this felt different. It was the pause before the step into the land of shadow.

"I did suffer – I have suffered."

"I appreciate from the medical report that it's something you find hard to talk about," Munroe replied, gently. "But – can you try to give us an idea?"

Another hesitation in the thick stillness of the courtroom. But when the words emerged, they came in a tumble, a rush of release.

"I hate the world! I daren't go out. I'm so scared. I keep thinking it's all going to happen again. I used to have loads of friends. Now I don't have any. I used to have hobbies. Now I just watch TV. I think about what happened all the time. The only chance to escape is when I try to sleep. And even then it all comes back again. I'm afraid to sleep! But I'm afraid to be awake too, because it's always there. It's like, well… I'm just afraid to live."

The tears were forming and Annette dabbed at them with a sleeve. The brightness of the court, the mix of sunshine and fluorescent strips channeled the light onto her cheekbones.

They were once so very fine, had made her the subject of a couple of photo-shoots in her sixteenth year. But with the shock of her suffering, they had tightened to gauntness.

"I'm sorry that this is upsetting," Munroe continued, sympathetically. "But it's important for the jury to understand this was not a story with a simple happy ending – you being rescued and returned safely to your father."

He adjusted the neck of his gown. One of the jurors, an older woman, was wiping her eyes with a lace handkerchief. In the dock, the Edwards sat still, listening. Roger Newman was again bent forwards, only his face raised to his daughter.

Munroe cleared his throat and said quietly, "During all this, you were never physically assaulted, were you?"

"I was – touched."

"The fingers on your skin you told us about? The tongue?"

Annette gulped. "Yes."

"Some might think it's very little to truly worry someone."

She pulled at an ear lobe and reached for a glass of water.

"Take your time, Ms Newman," Templar intervened.

Annette managed a couple of trembling sips and set the glass back down. The thud was loud in the quiet of the courtroom, amplified by the microphone above the box.

"I don't know how long I was held," she said. "They tell me it was less than a day. But it felt so much longer. And every second, every minute…"

The words faded. Munroe waited, then prompted, "Yes?"

"It felt like I was going to be – to be…"

"Yes?"

"Raped! Strangled! Beaten! Murdered! I knew he was there. He was with me all the time. I could hear him. I could feel him. Looking at me. His eyes all over me. I couldn't stop thinking about what he was going to do to me. Every second I thought it would come. I was waiting for the hands on my shirt, ripping it open. On my jeans, pulling them down. Every second, every single second I was waiting, expecting it to come."

Annette glanced over at her father with fast, frightened eyes. She grabbed for the glass again and drank hard at the water. Munroe waited and let the words adhere to the old wooden panels of the court.

Raped. Strangled. Beaten. Murdered.

"Finally Ms Newman, we've seen the video of how you were rescued. Can you tell us what you went through then?"

And now, for the first time, the answer came instantly. Annette's voice was breathless, but stronger.

"I knew I was going to die. I heard him building a pyre around me. I could smell the petrol. I heard the match being struck. I could hear the flames. They were roaring, all around me. Even through the blindfold I thought I could see the fire. I could feel the heat. I could hear the house starting to collapse. Every second, I was waiting for the flames to touch my skin. Melt my body. I was waiting to die! I was helpless, I couldn't move, I couldn't cry out and I knew I was going to die in agony. That's how it felt! Ok?!"

Once more Munroe waited and allowed his gaze to roam over the Edwards and to the jury before turning back to Annette.

"That's all I need to ask, Ms Newman," he said.

★★★

Wishart rose from the bench. He oozed empathy for the distress Annette had suffered and apologised for having to question her, before picking up on the first of his points.

"Would you mind taking us back to the moment you were abducted?"

"In the street?"

"Yes."

"I had some sandwiches and I was walking towards this tramp who was sitting in a doorway. I bent down, and he pushed a—"

"I'm sorry," Wishart interrupted. "Did you say *he?*"

"Well, I—"

"You did say he, didn't you?"

"Well—"

"Because it's the prosecution's case that it was Martha Edwards dressed as a tramp. And that Brian was waiting in the van."

Annette hesitated. "I'm not sure. I say he, but it could have been a she. I don't really remember properly."

Wishart nodded understandingly, but glanced towards the jury.

"Now, regarding the van. You are of the opinion there were two people involved in your abduction?"

"Yes. One driving and one in the back with me."

"Could it have been more than two?"

"Well, I—"

"Because you didn't actually see anyone for the whole of the time you were kidnapped, did you?"

"No, but I just thought it was two people."

"But it could have been more? Again, you see, it's the prosecution's case that it was just Martha and Brian Edwards working together. But it could equally have been someone else, couldn't it? There could have been anyone in that van. And later, in the house where you were held."

Annette gripped hard at the wooden rail. The sunlight fell into the lines of her face, far too scored for someone of her age.

"Yes, I suppose there could."

Wishart picked up one of the folders on the desk. "You've told us of your fears about what might happen to you. But, just to be absolutely clear – you were never actually assaulted, were you?"

"No."

"Not touched in any indecent way?"

"It felt like it! All the time! That it was coming."

"I understand. But in actual fact – you were not?"

"My back. The top of my chest. My neck. And the breathing on my face."

"But not touched indecently?"

"No."

"And you think that it was a man who touched you?"

"Yes."

"How do you know?"

"I just – thought it was."

"Why?"

"I assumed it was a man."

"Assumed?"

Annette's eyes again shifted to her father.

"Ms Newman, look at me please. Why did you assume it was a man?"

"I just thought it was."

"But you have no evidence for that."

"I just—"

"No evidence?"

"No, all right?! No bloody evidence!"

"Thank you."

In the jury box the foreman adjusted his glasses, pushing them up to the bridge of his nose. Roger Newman's hands were knotted tight together. Adam's face was set hard, a finger pulling tetchily at the collar of his shirt.

The unyielding wood of the witness box was shifting, closing in on Annette, trapping, squeezing and crushing her. With the brightness of the sunshine pouring onto her, the small square of space had become a crucible.

Once more, Wishart checked through his file. "Let me bring you on to the matter of the phone call you made, the ransom demand. You were reading from a script which had been prepared for you?"

"Yes."

"But still you saw nothing of who kidnapped you?"

Annette stared down at the floor. 'I... I don't know if I can do this.'

"Please, take your time."

"It's bringing it all back!" she yelled. "I can't, I don't want to, I can't go back there again!"

Few were the fathers who could sit through such suffering of their own flesh. Roger Newman leapt up from his seat and was striding forwards. A security guard tried to grab him, but Newman was too quick, too intent and dodged past.

Annette jumped down from the box and into his arms. The usher was following, his black gown billowing, trying to stop Newman.

Munroe was on his feet. 'Your Honour, is this questioning really necessary?'

Newman was hugging Annette tight. Adam was rising, Katrina standing too, reaching out for Annette's hand. The court was filling with noise, hubbub and melee growing into cacophony.

"Order!" Templar called from the bench. "I'm calling a recess for lunch. We shall reconvene in one hour."

★★★

Dan's hopeful suggestion of something to eat earned only a derisive look from Adam. He spent almost the entirety of the lunch hour stalking the corridor, muttering unpleasantries about the law. Even the coffee Claire brought him remained untouched.

Annette was taken to a waiting room, to sit with her father and try, as best she could, to find some calm. Katrina joined them for a brief chat. Through the gap in the door, before it closed, Dan saw Annette give Katrina a long hug.

The usher who had intervened to try to stop Newman introduced himself as Jonathan Ivy. "It happens sometimes, that," he told Adam. "I've seen it often enough. It's not surprising, given what people have to go through."

"You're not wrong there," Adam grunted.

"Anyway, thanks for helping to calm it all down. Judge Templar is no fan of disruptions I can tell you, particularly lately."

Katrina emerged from the waiting room, looking flushed. "Annette's struggling, but I think she'll just about get through," she said in response to Adam's look. "I told her there's not much more to come."

"Bloody lawyers," was the detective's sullen response. "As if she hasn't suffered enough."

"Templar's a decent judge," Katrina soothed, to little effect. "He looked after Annette as best he could in there. I know him from his days as a barrister in London. He's one of the good ones."

"Didn't know there was such a thing as a good lawyer," Adam grunted. "From what I hear, Templar's going off the rails. It's no accident this is one of his last cases."

A line of solicitors filed past, all dressed in identikit suits and carrying regulation leather briefcases. Claire looked to Dan, and without hesitation reached out and gave him a cuddle. "Sorry," she apologised, disengaging. "I just needed that."

Katrina muttered something about getting herself a drink and walked away.

"Maybe we could catch up later?" Claire whispered. "I could do with a chat."

"Me too," Dan said. "But it'll depend on work. And given what's been going on in court, I suspect I'm going to be busy."

"There's no pressure, as ever," Claire replied, her voice tinted with sadness. "But if you do have an hour, it'd be great to see you. We are going to have to talk sometime."

She smiled and Dan managed to find a passable imitation in return. The tannoy announced the resumption of the case and they paced back towards the court. Katrina stood by the doors, finishing the remains of her coffee, with an expression as aloof as the highest mountain top. She didn't once look at Dan.

★★★

For a woman who was diminished enough at the start of the trial, Annette had shrunk further with each day.

The clothes she wore enveloped rather than fitted, as though they were bought for a different person. There was no colour to them, no personality, no spirit or sparkle. She wore no make-up or jewellery, no detail, no adornments. It was as if she wanted to fade from sight, be as nondescript and indistinct as were ever possible. Own no individuality, suffer nothing distinguishing about herself.

And now she stood once again, in the tomb of the witness box, waiting for the final assault.

"The last matter I must raise is the ransom demand," Wishart began, when the court had settled. "Can you tell us how that happened?"

The break had brought none of the life back to Annette's face. She was sickly pallid. Her voice, quiet throughout, was now close to imperceptible.

"I heard a door. And feet behind me. Then these hands grabbed the sides of my head and held me so I couldn't move."

Annette stopped abruptly and reached for her ear lobe in that reflex, comforting twitch. The microphone thudded dully with the movement.

"Ms Newman?" Wisheart prompted.

"I thought I was going to be killed! I thought they were going to take a knife and slice my throat open. Ok?!"

"And then you saw the note?"

"Yes."

"And?"

"This hand pointed to it. There was a phone. I heard a voice answering. Something tapped me on the back of the head and a finger pointed to the note again. So I started reading."

"And then?"

"The phone disappeared and my blindfold and gag were put back on."

"And you saw no one?"

"No."

"Did you not try to look around?"

"My head was being held so I couldn't. And—"

"And?"

"I didn't dare to! Ok? I was too scared. I thought—"

"Thought what?"

"That I'd be killed. From that note, I knew – knew they were serious. What they said they'd do to me. I thought I was going to die."

Wishart smoothed his robe. "It is the case, is it not, that throughout your ordeal you caught no sight of the person, or persons, who had taken you?"

Annette was struggling to form the words. "I…"

"You didn't see anyone, did you?"

"No."

"So these two people in the dock. You can't possibly say they were in any way implicated in this crime, can you?"

"I… I think—"

"I'm not asking for an opinion, Ms Newman. I'm asking for a fact."

"Careful, Mr Wishart," intervened the judge.

The barrister paused. "Let me rephrase the question. I'm putting it to you that you can in no way connect these two people in the dock with your abduction? Can you?"

Annette's lips were trembling. The sunshine which had surrounded her faded as a cloud drifted over the courthouse.

"It's a simple fact, is it not?" the barrister continued. "You, the subject of this crime, you can in no way link these two people to it? Can you?"

And now Annette leaned back in the witness box and slowly lowered herself onto the seat. Torment upon ordeal, bombardment upon barrage had taken their toll. All fight was extinguished, any remaining spirit broken. When she answered, her voice sounded exhausted.

"No. I can't."

Several of the jurors had been taking careful notes. Now, in unison, they rested their pens.

CHAPTER EIGHTEEN

Thursday was a point of the week which threw up a dilemma for Dan. Usually he'd see it as a gateway to the weekend and pop out for an evening beer. A drink or two to relax, ready for the welcome embrace of Friday.

This particular Thursday, like Janus, he faced two ways. One instinct was vociferous: to head straight out and get drunk. Only such a numbing experience could ease the emotion of the day in court.

The more cerebral side counselled caution. Another busy day loomed tomorrow, with more of the case to report. The end was nearing, the tension growing. A hangover would be a highly unwelcome companion.

To help him decide, Dan ran a familiar track. Rutherford was placed upon his lead and together they crossed Eggbuckland Road and walked into Hartley Park.

The light was beginning to seep from the sky. The trees rustled with the sound of roosting birds. Dan performed a couple of perfunctory stretches and began running, Rutherford keeping an easy pace alongside. They had the park to themselves and delighted in it.

There was, however, one irritant, an annoying thought which kept popping uninvited into Dan's mind like an unscratched itch. It was a memory of an unanswered question, one which had needled him for six months. That elusive *PP* in the ransom demand.

In the police interviews, the Edwards had looked blank and refused to answer questions about it. Despite all the inquiries, all the detectives who had worked on it, the meaning of the two letters had never been discovered.

Dan had come to wonder if it ever would be, if even perhaps it signified anything. It could just have been a game, a taunt, the reddest of herrings. But that had never struck him as the Edwards' style.

He distracted himself with different thoughts. The report of the day's proceedings was the lead story on *Wessex Tonight*, and rightly so. Dan felt he had done Annette justice in showing how she'd suffered, no matter what doubts the defence may raise.

"So, it wasn't a bad day," he told Rutherford, as they completed a lap. "It was just the little issue with Katrina which tarnished it. I don't think I'll be getting anywhere with her now, after that hug from Claire. Not that I probably should, anyway. It really is about time to have that talk with Claire, don't you think?"

At the mention of the sacred name, Rutherford jumped up and wheeled his paws in the air.

"That's a deal then dog," Dan panted. "We'll sort it out by Christmas, ok? Assuming she's still interested in us. And who could blame her if she wasn't? What sane woman would want to take on you and me?"

They managed to hit the target of ten laps before heading home. As they left the park, Dan said, "So, what am I doing? Having a beer or not?"

Usually, when they went for a run, Dan took his mobile along. Long experience had taught him a call was most likely when it was least wanted. But on this occasion he'd left the phone in the hallway.

Its little message light was flashing a welcome. Dan sighed and picked it up, readying himself for a summons to a breaking story.

But it was a text message, and from a number the phone didn't recognise.

Fancy a drink tonight? K

★★★

The bus dropped Dan off at Royal Parade, in the midst of the city. He could have travelled on a couple more stops, but the time was only twenty to nine. He had already breached the etiquette of cool texting and didn't want to compound the crime by arriving early.

The message from Katrina was ten minutes old by the time Dan saw it. He managed to make himself wait the five minutes of a rushed and agitated shower before suggesting Leo's Bar, on Sutton Harbour, for nine.

It was twenty-five long minutes before the answer came back.
Fine.

Dan was on the bus a few seconds later. As he sat, rumbling along Mutley Plain, home to the unholy trinity of students, cheap bars and kebab houses, he realised the favourite shirt he wore was the one Claire bought last Christmas.

The night ran by. Local legend had it that Plymouth possessed more pubs per head of population than anywhere else in England, possibly a hangover from the days when the Royal Navy dominated the city.

The streets were milling with people, a parade of colour wending its way to the bars, clubs and restaurants. Cabs trundled along Royal Parade, stopping to unload their laughing, tumbling cargoes. Music pumped from open doors, lights flashing in time. Bouncers eyed those passing with all the suspicion of the experience of a thousand drunken fights.

The Parade marks a sharp divide, almost a tarmac river in the city centre. To the north the glass fronts of the rows of stores denote the start of the shopping district. Opposite lies the open promenade to the Hoe and the view to the red and white hoops of Smeaton's Tower, the old lighthouse which once guarded the treacherous rocks of the Eddystone reef.

At the eastern end stands one of Plymouth's most iconic landmarks. As much of the city was razed in the bombing of the Second World War, the stately stone of St Andrew's Church was not spared. Only the walls and tower were left standing, six hundred years of Plymouth history largely destroyed in a single night.

Amidst the rubble and debris of a once proud city, laid low in a few hours of barbarity, a headmistress nailed a wooden sign above the remains of the door. Upon it was carved simply *Resurgam*.

I will rise again.

To this day, the entrance is known as the Resurgam Door, a granite plaque now replacing its wooden ancestor.

Dan crossed the road and, as was sometimes his habit in this city which had become his home, stood thinking.

The urban bustle passed by, as always it does. But in this small space the ghosts of the past gathered, whispering the lessons they tried forever to pass on to the unlistening ears of every modern generation.

★★★

A zig-zag walk through the narrow backstreets brought Dan to Sutton Harbour and the cobbles by the Three Crowns pub. A line of fishing boats had moored along the wharf, dark shadows of men moving over one deck. The smell of fish filled the still air.

A couple sat on a wooden bench overlooking the water, eating from bags of chips. A pair of swans glided towards them, necks arched in an elegant begging.

Dan walked on, past a café and the drifting notes of a saxophone, then on to a couple of pubs and a discordant karaoke. The doorman wore a thickset grimace. "I'd rather be scrapping with drunken louts," he grunted.

Ahead loomed the Citadel, the great block of the Napoleonic fort, built to protect Plymouth from the invading hordes gathering across the channel. And just beside it, as if sheltering, was Leo's Bar, the windows dim with suggestive lights.

Beneath a yellow streetlamp, in the mirror of a parked lorry, Dan checked his hair, shirt and, with an afterthought, his teeth. The amount of food which could sometimes be found stored there was remarkable. He started walking again, then stopped, started again, and hesitated once more.

"Come on, Groves," he told himself. "You're just going to meet a friend for a drink. That's all."

The time was five past nine. Perfect to be a little cool, but not rude or uninterested.

The bouncer began a scan program, from the peak of the highest follicle to the edge of the longest toenail. The man's face set in concentration as he went through the calculations regarding shoes, jeans, shirt, severity of haircut and predominance of tattoos. The eventual answer proved acceptable and the door was pushed open.

★★★

Sometimes in life, you can feel a spotlight illuminating your doubts for all the world to see. So it was for Dan as he lingered in the doorway.

He checked along the polished wood of the bar. A pair of businessmen. A group of three women. A waiter. A barman, buffing knives. No Katrina.

Next, it was the stools by the window. A young couple, steepled together. A man eating some unidentifiable snack.

Now the chairs and tables at the back of the bar. Dan squinted through the darkness. One day, he'd have to conquer the snowy mountain of vanity and get some glasses. But he could just about make out at least two or three people at each table.

Finally, the leather sofas. A couple picking at some olives and sharing a bottle of wine. A man reading a paper, sipping at a bottle of beer. No Katrina.

Eyes were starting to stare at the newcomer, standing in the doorway. It could only be seconds before the dreaded whispers began.

It's that man on the telly. He's been stood up. He's got no friends.

From behind came a gentle cough. "Would you like to join me, or would you prefer to just stay there?"

Dan was about to reach out to shake her hand, but managed to stop himself as she stood for a kiss.

Their mouths moved together, slow, slow, slow, until Katrina suddenly turned her face. And then they sat, as if a peck on the cheek was all that had ever been envisaged.

The leather sofa was large enough for two, but only just. Dan angled himself into one corner, Katrina the other. Their knees brushed as she reached for the menu.

"Do you like wine?"

Dan tried to ignore the tempting range of bottled ales beckoning from the foot of the sheet. "Yes."

"Red or white?"

"Both. But not in the same glass, please."

She raised an eyebrow, but ordered a bottle of red. It was the second most expensive on the list.

"Interesting," Dan mused, sitting back.

"In what way?"

"Most people choose the second cheapest wine. I'm wondering what picking the second most expensive means."

"It means it's my favourite."

They talked a little about the bar. It had only opened a few months ago. Smart, but trying to be relaxed and just about succeeding was the consensus.

The waiter arrived and poured Dan a measure of wine to taste. Katrina was going to take it, but he got there first. It was time to show off the legendary Groves' wit. He held the glass to the light, made a play of sniffing hard, then sipping and rolling the liquid repeatedly around his mouth before pronouncing, "Yep, that's definitely a red."

The waiter didn't smile. But that mattered not at all, not in the slightest, not an ounce nor an atom, because Katrina did.

"Tell me about yourself," she said, softly. "There's hardly been time to talk about anything apart from work."

Dan described his college days as a disc jockey, then moving on to radio and television news. Katrina talked about her career with the Metropolitan Police and kidnapping cases she'd handled.

"It's 23 now. And each one is still like a flame burning in my mind. You never forget."

"Just like I never forget an interview with anyone who's suffered a bereavement. Whether they've lost someone to a drunk driver or a murdering thug, it doesn't leave me."

"It's the intensity of the emotion. It carves the memory into your mind."

The bar was growing busier. The wine had evaporated with remarkable rapidity, as bottles do when you reach a certain age. Katrina ordered another.

They discussed the trial, how it was going and Annette.

"You've grown close to her," Dan noted.

"It's difficult not to. She's suffered terribly."

"It's just that?"

"Meaning?"

"You don't have any children, do you?"

Katrina rolled the wine around her glass. "You're a perceptive man."

"I just – notice things."

"It's more than that. It's partly why Adam always wants you around. He relies on you a great deal, you know. You see things that he can't."

Dan felt his cheeks reddening. It must be the drink. He was scarcely used to wine, let alone such a heady vintage as that which was currently dancing across his tongue.

"I don't know about that," he managed, at last. "But I can tell you this… it feels like a hell of a burden some days. It's like the whole of the world is waiting for me to sort out its problems."

Katrina excused herself and made for the rest rooms, as they had been styled. Dan stared out at the view, lights shimmering on the smooth waters, the outlines of people passing by. It was a surprise when a bell rang and the barman called last orders.

"I'll be heading back to London in a few days," Katrina said, as she returned. "When the case is finally over."

"That's a shame."

She leaned forwards. Now their legs were touching, and with a firm, persistent pressure.

"Is it?"

"I think so."

"Doesn't it make your life easier?"

"In what way?"

"With Claire."

Dan didn't reply, instead sipped at his wine.

"She loves you very much, you know."

"What?"

"You heard me."

"She told you that?"

"She said you'd had a few problems, but you were working it out. *You were meant to be together.* Those were her words."

"Err…"

"I think she was warning me off."

Dan found himself getting up from the sofa. "I think it's time I was getting home."

"Sit down a minute."

Back down he sat, without a thought to demur. The light was catching Katrina's eyes, pooling in the contrasting colours. It was difficult not to stare into them.

"Do you like my eyes?" She asked.

"Err, well – yes, of course I do. I thought…"

"What?"

"It's nothing."

"Please tell me. I'd like to hear."

"I was being silly. It must be the wine."

Slowly, her lips formed the words. "Tell me."

Dan hesitated, but said, "From the first moment we met, I thought they were like two different shades of autumn. The turning leaf next to the evergreen."

She sat back and finished the remains of the wine. A kiss of lipstick lingered on the rim of the glass.

And amidst the quiet and half-light of the bar, the supernova exploded.

"Would you like to spend the night at my hotel?" Katrina asked.

"What?"

"Would you?"

"Um, well…"

"I'd surmise that as a yes."

"Oh, err…"

"But there's a little game you have to play first."

"I'm sorry? A what?"

"Call it – a test."

"A test?"

"You have to answer a question."

"A question? What question?"

"This question – what is *heterochromia iridis*?"

"What?! What's what?"

She repeated the words, spelt them out, then sat back and crossed her legs. And now Katrina waited, elegance and poise, beauty and mastery, effortless in body and mind. It was all Dan could do to mumble an apology and make for the rest rooms.

With the door closed and surrounded by the safety of the stark, white tiles, Dan stared at himself in the mirror. He splashed some water onto his face. It made no difference to the nonplussed expression gawping back.

Time passed, although how much, he could never say. A man walked in, went about his business and cast a quizzical look, but Dan didn't come close to noticing.

He straightened his shirt, ruffled his hair, wiped any traces of wine from his lips and reached a decision. After just a few seconds he found the answer to Katrina's question and returned to the bar.

CHAPTER NINETEEN

One of the great advantages of being reasonably well off is that it limits the necessity for the dreaded walk of shame.

Dan's sufferance was just a couple of hundred yards, from the hotel to taxi rank. But, as if to penalise him anyway, fate sent a dagger of conscience in the form of a demonic driver.

The time was half past six and the crimson spectacle of a young autumn dawn already established in the eastern sky. Dan had hardly slept. In part, that was due to Katrina, but more to do with the traditional wondering whether this was really such a good idea. There was also a modicum of guilt, but, in truth, it was by far the junior partner.

"Thanks for an interesting night," she murmured sleepily, as he vanished from the room. Dan couldn't help but think it wasn't the finest eulogy of a send-off.

Upon the opening of the heavy, black door the cab driver didn't bother to drop his tabloid. Instead, he immediately chirped up with exactly the kind of comment you really don't want to hear in such a situation.

"I know you, don't I?" the man asked, with the faux cockney accent that some younger people see as an important fashion accessory.

"I don't think so," Dan replied, climbing hurriedly in.

"I've driven you before. You're that man on the telly."

The star of the small screen attempted to shrink into the seat. "Yeah, that's me, 'the man on the telly'. Hartley Avenue, please."

"You do all them crime stories. I always watch *Wessex Tonight*. You got some nice birds."

"Good. Thanks."

"You go out with that detective woman, don't you?"

Already taken well aback, Dan now retreated further. "What?"

"The really pretty one. Gorgeous, in fact. Ever so nice she is. Great figure, beautiful hair. A lovely woman, really kind. Clever too.

I've driven you two to her place on the Hoe. You're well lucky having a bird like that."

"Would you mind if we got going? I've got a busy day ahead."

The man produced a grin so lecherous that even the director of a *Carry On* film might have found it excessive. "What you been up to then? Get lucky, did you?"

"Hartley Avenue, please," Dan replied, weakly.

So browbeaten was he by the man's assault that Dan even gave him a tip. "You should be in the diplomatic service," he muttered, as he unlocked the door.

Rutherford leapt up and went through his usual fusillade of barks. Dan grabbed the dog's muzzle.

"Shh, old friend! I've been a bad boy and we don't need anyone else knowing. I conned my way into a woman's bed when she asked me some ridiculous question I had no hope of answering. But with a bit of the old Groves' craftiness, I got it anyway."

Dan made for the bathroom and a protracted process of trying to wake up. He needed to rejoin the pace of civilisation. Today could be a very important one in the trial, perhaps even providing the moment which would decide its outcome.

The word was that Martha Edwards would be called to give evidence.

★★★

The case had reached its closing stages. They were into some routine character evidence about the Edwards and the proceedings were plodding along at the rate of a sullen mule.

It was far from exciting, and on the press benches the hacks stirred restlessly. It was just that lingering possibility which kept them waiting.

There had been constant rumour that at least one of the Edwards would be called to testify. A couple of the braver journalists had asked Wishart what he intended. "I'm considering the defence's position," was all he would say.

It was a game that had been played out many times before. One of trial tactics. A fine judgement that could nudge the verdict either way.

If Wishart didn't call the Edwards, the jury would be told they could infer that damaged the siblings' claims of innocence. The simple argument – what did they have to hide? But if he did, the prosecution had an opportunity to cross-examine them. And for some defendants that could be akin to giving them the keys to lock up their own cell.

Wishart finished reading the evidence of a Dr Andy Lovejoy, tutor in Forensics at London Metropolitan University. He had submitted a statement about Martha's skills and character.

A quiet student who tended to keep herself to herself, but nonetheless a dedicated one. She was clever and talented and showed herself to be extremely capable. As to her character, she always behaved impeccably in college and I saw no signs whatsoever of any criminality or anti-social tendencies.

Judge Templar scribbled a note and looked up at Wishart.

"That, I think, concludes the list of witnesses for the defence," the judge said. "So, we proceed to the closing speeches. Unless…"

Wishart shuffled some papers and turned to the glass dock. "Indeed, Your Honour. Unless…"

Like all the best barristers, Wishart was a master of drama. He studied Martha as she sat, hands in her lap, looking calmly back. In her eyes wasn't anger, not even defiance and certainly not fear or concern. It was a look of neutral and detached curiosity, the expression of a scientist.

"I call Martha Edwards!" intoned Wishart.

Fast breaths ran around the courtroom. People leaned forwards to take a better look at this fabled creature, freed for the first time from the glass confines of her cage.

The woman portrayed over these days of the trial as cold, bitter and ruthless. The one who would kidnap a 17-year-old girl and leave her to an agonising death in the inferno of a burning cottage.

But also the one who had herself suffered so much. Who knew all too well the cruel interlude of medical history which the prosecution claimed as her motive.

A security guard unlocked the dock. Martha drew herself up and, with an exaggerated care, walked step by precise step, to the witness box.

★★★

How a day can make a difference. Yesterday, over the hours of testimony, the old wooden box had edged inwards until it crushed Annette. With Martha, the shining panels kept a respectful distance.

She stood, her hands resting calmly on the grooved ledge, facing Wishart and the twelve watchful faces of the jury. The flow of her hair had been loosely tied and held in a copper tail. The light found the blanched and freckled landscape of her face.

"Let us first deal with the basics," the barrister began. "The prosecution have outlined the crime they believe you committed. What do you say to that?"

"It's not true."

"Did you kidnap Annette?"

"No."

"Did you hold her in a cottage in the South Hams?"

"No."

"Did your brother, Brian?"

"No."

"Did either of you have anything whatsoever to do with the kidnapping?"

"No."

"So you are both totally innocent of the charges against you?"

"Yes."

Martha's voice was clear but husky, the words curiously soothing. There were no nerves, no hesitation and no pauses. No scent or sound of evasion or deception.

"Let us now deal with the so-called *evidence* against you," Wishart continued. "The prosecution say you left no forensic traces because your expert knowledge meant you knew how to avoid doing so. What do you say to that?"

For the first time, Martha's face formed an expression. It wasn't quite a smile, more an edge of amusement.

"It's nonsense. If there's one thing you learn studying forensics, it's that the techniques are so powerful you can always find some evidence. A basic principle I was taught was – if you can't find it, it's not there."

Around Dan, the hacks underlined the phrase in their notebooks. Such a memorable quote would feature heavily in their reports.

"Moving on," Wishart boomed, "What explanation can there be for the fact that you disappeared at the time Ms Newman was kidnapped? And that your mobile – along with your brother's – were both turned off?"

"I can explain that. But this part I... find difficult."

"Please, take your time."

She sipped a little water and closed her eyes, as if summoning the memory.

"It was a beautiful couple of days so we went to Dartmoor. I love it there. There are lots of places where you're alone in perfect peace. I like to watch the sunsets over the tors. They give me strength. And at night, the silence. It's like a medicine to me."

Wishart let her words float over the rapt court. In the jury box at least a couple of heads were nodding.

"And Brian took you?" the barrister prompted.

"Yes. He has to be there in case..."

"We'll come to that in a moment. But – you stayed up there on Dartmoor?"

"Yes."

"Camping?"

"Yes."

"And your mobiles were off because?"

"They intrude. They spoil the peace and beauty."

Wishart turned again to the jury. "'Peace and beauty'. Something all of us seek at some point in our lives. Hardly the way of a ruthless and embittered kidnapper, I think you'll agree."

He turned back and found a page in his file. "One further matter, Ms Edwards. It's about Brian. He won't be giving evidence?"

"No."

"I know the jury will be asking themselves – can you tell the court why?"

"He's found all this very difficult. He's not quite as good at coping as I am, or expressing what he feels. He thinks we've already suffered enough. He can't understand how, after all that we've been through, we can find ourselves…"

Her voice faltered and she drew in a long breath of the warm air.

"How we can find ourselves… here. On trial. Accused of a crime we didn't commit. Having to go through yet another ordeal in our lives. It just doesn't – well, it doesn't seem fair."

Wishart nodded his agreement. "And fairness is something which has sadly eluded you in life, has it not? "

CHAPTER TWENTY

The court shifted in time, pulled back 30 years in a few seconds of Wishart's words. Eyes dulled as minds imagined their way to another world.

In his university days, the less than committed student that was the young Dan Groves, had taken a course on the history of science. It looked an easier option than some of the intimidating alternatives. They were laced with warning words like *Advanced*, *Quantum* or *Mathematical*.

It did turn out to be amongst the more worthwhile uses of his university time, and one lesson stayed with him.

Always beware with the keenest distrust the person who is absolutely certain.

When arguing the point, Dan would talk of radioactivity. In the early days of the discovery, the fact that it made a liquid glow was taken as proof of great benefit to the human body. People were fed gallons of the stuff and grinned their delight to the cameras.

It was only when the unfortunate subjects' bones became so fragile they would shatter under the slightest pressure, or the foulest of tumours began to develop, that the scientists realised their incontestable conclusion may have been a little awry.

The lesson could be extended to any field of life. Another favoured example was the insistence by learned statesmen of the past; that a small German chap with an odd moustache and unbecoming haircut could best be handled by giving him whatever was wanted.

Dan was reminded of his little maxim as Wishart spoke. The barrister lowered his voice, in the best traditions of a storyteller, and reminded the court of one of the greatest scandals in the history of British medicine.

★★★

Wishart began gently. "Tell us about your childhood."

"Which part?"

"From your earliest recollections. How you compared to other children."

The arrow hit the invisible target. The moment changed. It was there in Martha's face, the paleness of those green eyes. A different door had opened. It led inside, to a part of the person previously unreached.

Where before she had been calm and relaxed under questioning, a strain began to show in Martha's voice. It was no longer soothing and easy, but muted and faltering. The answers took longer to come and were offered without reassurance.

Her fingers, once still on the shining wood of the ledge of the witness box, now twitched and played. Her feet shifted on the boards.

Wishart had broken through. The defences that stood for so long, which repelled charge, battering ram and boulder had fallen under an assault of roses. Kindness had succeeded where cannonballs failed.

"You were different, weren't you?" the barrister prompted.

"Yes."

"Tell us what you remember."

"I must have only been three or four. I'm not sure. I remember being…"

"Yes?"

"Lonely. I wasn't allowed to play with the other children. I had to stay in my room. I wasn't allowed to do anything like climbing or running around. I just sat, watched TV and drew pictures."

"And all this because you weren't well, were you?"

"No. I wasn't."

Martha said no more and Wishart didn't try to push her. Instead, he turned to the jury.

"My client finds this understandably difficult, so perhaps it's best if I tell you the facts."

He looked up to Templar and received a judicial nod of approval.

"Martha Edwards suffers from Von Willebrand disease. It is similar to haemophilia. It means the person bruises extremely easily and the blood does not clot properly when they suffer an injury. In the most serious cases it can be life threatening. And Ms Edwards' case is amongst the most severe."

The faces of the jury studied the woman, standing in the witness box. She said nothing, just closed her eyes and slowly nodded her head.

"A sad case,"Wishart continued. "But there was hope – or at least, a hope of hope." He turned back to Martha. "Was there not?"

"Yes."

"Can you tell us what happened?"

"It's difficult…"

Wishart glanced to the judge sitting impassive above him, the red and purple blazes of his robes bright in the sunlight.

"You can take all the time you need," Templar decreed.

"Well – my memories from that time are blurred. But they're all about men and women in white coats. It was as if they used to float around me. Sometimes, they'd hurt me, with needles and tests. But they were kind. Always told me how brave I was, and that it was all to help me get well again. And then one day…"

"Yes?"

"One day they said they'd found a way to make me better. So that I'd be like the other children. So I could go outside and run around and play with them. And be…"

"Yes?" Wishart prompted again.

"Just – normal. That was all I wanted. To be like the others."

"You must have been excited?"

"I was so happy. It was all I'd ever wanted. Every Christmas and birthday I'd ask to be like the other children. To join in with them, instead of watching through a window. That's how I felt: I was a window child."

Even through the microphone and speakers, Martha's words were growing close to imperceptible. Wishart waited for her to find some composure before asking, "So – what happened?"

She took a long breath "They told me I had to go into hospital. I didn't mind, because all these clever people told me I was going to be better. So I went in and they did all these – things to me. And they told me I just had to be patient and in a few weeks I'd be like all the other children."

It is an underrated art to nod sadly, but the barrister managed it. "But it didn't turn out that way?"

"No."

Again the words were thin and faint. Martha rubbed at her eyes with a careful hand.

"Can you tell us what happened?"

"A week passed. Then another. I kept asking when I'd be better. But there was no answer. These people with their white coats, the ones I'd trusted. The ones who promised they'd make me better, they didn't answer. Then they just seemed to fade away. They disappeared. And I started to understand I wasn't going to get better."

"That must have been bad enough. But, in fact, it was even worse. Was it not?"

Martha may have tried to speak, but her lips hardly moved.

"Take a moment, Ms Edwards," Templar intervened. "Perhaps Mr Wishart can take us through what happened next."

The barrister took a drink of water, turned to the jury and picked up the story.

It was the late 1970s and early '80s. Blood products to treat those who suffered from hemophilia, Von Willebrand disease and others like them, were being imported from America. But controls were lax and a scandal was in the making.

To attract donors a payment was offered, and many drug addicts and prisoners came forward. Some of the blood they gave was infected with HIV and hepatitis. Almost five thousand people in Britain contracted the illnesses.

Government procrastination was an exacerbating factor. Evidence started to emerge of the contamination, but it was ignored. The blood continued to be imported.

Martha was one of the last to be infected before the negligence was exposed. She had to live with the knowledge that, if action had been taken sooner, she would not have suffered.

She was, in a way, lucky. Unlike some, her death sentence would take years to be executed.

Courtesy of the misguided, and perhaps even reckless, efforts of the state and medical profession, Martha Edwards contracted hepatitis.

★★★

The judge called Wishart's narrative to a halt. Martha had sat down on the seat in the witness box, her head bowed. Only a flow of coppery hair showed above the lines of wood.

All in the court saw it, but no one said. No one could.

It was precisely the same stance as Annette had been reduced to after her testimony.

In the jury box, the foreman tugged at a tuft of beard. Wishart held a whispered conversation with a solicitor sitting behind.

"Ms Edwards, I have only a couple more questions, if you think you could manage?"

She stood back up. "Yes."

"It is another difficult matter, but…" a hesitation, then softly, "How advanced is your illness now?"

She swallowed hard. "It's reached the terminal stage."

"And it makes you physically weak?"

"Sometimes, yes."

"And would have done so six months ago?"

"Yes."

"So – not exactly the ideal condition for a ruthless kidnapper, the like of which the prosecution have attempted to paint you?"

She cast a disdainful glance at Adam. "Not exactly."

"And as to your treatment? The doctors are doing all they can?"

"Yes."

"You trust them – despite what happened to you as a child?"

"Yes."

"You're being given the best of medication?"

"I think so."

"I ask because the prosecution say part of your motive for kidnapping Annette was to get money for a new drug treatment."

"No. I think I'm being treated as well as I can be."

Wishart scribbled a note on a piece of paper.

"There is one final matter I must put to you. The prosecution claim you kidnapped Annette, in part, for revenge. Because she and her father in some way represent *the establishment*, something you hate because of what it did to you all those years ago. They say another element of your motive is resentment and anger, to hit out at someone who has so much in life when you do not. What do you say to that?"

Martha stared up to a skylight, a rectangle of perfect blue held within. Sunbeams danced down upon the court, riding in the circling breeze.

"It's not easy sometimes, but I try not to be bitter about what's happened. I've often wondered why some of us are picked out to be healthy and happy and seem to have everything they could ever want in life. And yet others are picked on and just seem to suffer."

Another hesitation, another careful sip of water. "For me it comes down to this. You can either shout and scream and let what you've gone through destroy you. Or you can come to terms with it and still do the best you can with the gift of life you've been given. And, however tainted it may be, I believe it's still a great gift."

Once more Wishart let the words linger in the silent courtroom, before he pronounced quietly, "An embittered woman, members of the jury? A ruthless kidnapper? Or a victim every bit as much as Annette Newman?"

He produced a sombre smile. "Thank you, Ms Edwards. Please remain in the witness box. I know the prosecution will have some questions for you."

★★★

Adam was the first out of court. He strode from his seat and beckoned to Dan, who picked his way through the crowd to follow.

Templar had called a fifteen minute recess. Then Munroe would have his chance to question Martha.

The detective was waiting by one of the small interview rooms. He closed the door firmly and drew the blind too.

"I know you're angry," Dan said, calmingly. "Ok, Martha came across as very decent and human. And yes, it probably did make an impact on the jury. But given what Munroe's like, I bet she won't be looking quite so angelic by the end of the day. And another thing—"

"It's not just that."

"What?"

"It's not to do with the case. I just don't need any more complications."

"Err – what?"

Adam sat on the edge of the table. The shadow of his beard was already growing dark, despite the early hour.

"You need to start thinking up a good excuse."

"An excuse?" Dan floundered. "What are you talking about?"

The detective produced one of his lofty looks. "Last night."

If Adam not wanting to talk about Martha's testimony was a surprise, this was a shock. Ice in the stomach and a vice on the heart.

"Um – what about last night?" Dan dissembled, hopelessly.

"You look tired out. Whereas Katrina—"

"What about her?"

"Looks like she's had a double measure of the elixir of life in her coffee."

"What are you saying?"

"I don't think I need to be saying anything, do I?"

Dan shifted his weight busily from foot to foot. He studied the sole decoration in the small room, a faded print of some water lilies.

"And another thing," Adam added. "If you've always exchanged a chatty hello with someone, and then one morning you mumble something and can't look at her, it's the kind of thing a detective might just spot."

"You mean when we were coming into court?"

"Affirmative."

"Bugger."

"Which I'd say about sums it up."

A feeling was building fast inside Dan's body. It started around the heart and spread rapidly outwards. Every nerve, bone and vein felt like a guitar string being mercilessly tightened, tightened, tightened.

"Do you think... did Claire... would she have..." he stammered.

"I tapped her on the shoulder and asked her to check something when I realised. I think you've probably got away with it. But I can't be certain."

Adam got up from the table and reached for the door. "We need to get back. I reckon Munroe's about our only chance of a conviction now. I just hope he can tarnish the holy glow of Saint bloody Martha."

He hesitated, and then added, "One more thing. Just another bit of advice, if you're up for listening?"

"I think I'd better."

"I think you're right. Look, beware of Katrina. I've seen what she can do."

The magus of a chief inspector ruminated briefly upon the wisdom to be delivered, then his face warmed with one of those smug expressions in which he specialised.

"I'd remember this. Beware of putting the lure of passing lust ahead of the endurance of love."

CHAPTER TWENTY-ONE

Edward Munroe QC was one of the stars of the South West's legal circuit. He'd made a name defending career criminals, the kind Dan and his peers might refer to in their headlines as *Mr Big*.

The barrister had once been as popular as ants at a picnic with the police, until the day of an unlikely transformation. It was long analysed and eventually summarised by a detective wit, who christened it a *Road to the Supreme Court* conversion.

Munroe was an ambitious man whose CV was replete with his talents at defence work. The opinion was that he needed some high profile prosecution successes to set him fair on a journey to becoming a judge. To the surprise of the police he offered to switch sides, and was welcomed with little hesitation. Whatever the detectives may have thought, Munroe was a charmer of juries, a ruthless dissector of evidence, and on the big cases he tended to get the brief.

He was a little stocky, but fit; a middle distance runner of a decent standard and he was always impeccably shaved. Munroe carried a razor to court and would set aside ten minutes at lunchtime to applying it. The theory, he once explained to Adam with a meaningful nod at the detective's beard line, was that juries put more trust in a clean complexion.

With a case as finely balanced as this, Munroe's opinion had been sought on the chances of success. He considered and then pronounced a similar view to the solicitors and detectives. Fifty-fifty, no more and no less.

But Munroe added something else that Adam said was much responsible for the trial being held. He asked whether either of the Edwards would give evidence. Knowing of her eloquence, and the story she could tell a jury about her suffering, it was thought likely Martha would.

In that case, Munroe said, he would like to take the case. And so, many weeks ago, the scene was set for today.

The barrister was silent and unmoving with concentration in final preparation for the coming duel. The twelve jurors watched, several with notepads poised.

Dan tried to force himself to focus. This may well be the pivotal moment in the trial. But he couldn't help looking three rows ahead and to the women either side of Adam.

He'd made a point of standing by the doors as the court reconvened, mobile clamped to ear – a little curious, as there was no one on the line, except maybe his conscience.

Katrina walked past and Dan smiled, open and easy. Claire approached and he put down the phone and breathed out hard.

"Are you ok?" she asked, with concern.

"Rutherford was sick most of the night. That was the vet calling. He's ok, thankfully. It was probably just some bug he picked up in the park."

A caring hand found Dan's shoulder. "I thought you looked tired. You poor thing. I'd love to see that daft dog again – and his master, of course. Maybe a walk at the weekend?"

"Yeah, that'd be – err, good," the great deceiver managed, awkwardly.

★★★

The court was still, only the slightest of seeping breezes relieving the denseness of the heat. All knew what was coming next.

One more whispered conversation with a solicitor and Munroe finally got to his feet. Martha eyed him coolly. They were just a few metres apart.

"You've told us about your condition, but I'd like to know a little more, Ms Edwards. How did you feel when you understood you were infected with hepatitis?"

Her face twitched with scorn, and it overflowed into her voice. "Mmmm… let me think. Oh, that's it – overjoyed. Absolutely delighted. Really! How do you think I felt?"

Like any professional player, Munroe's expression didn't change. "I don't know, Ms Edwards. I've never had the experience. Nor have the jury. So perhaps you could tell us – and a little less sarcastically?"

Martha looked to the judge. "He's entitled to ask," ruled Templar, "Whatever you may think of the question, it's part of the prosecution's case regarding your alleged motive."

"Well, if I must. Initially, I suppose I didn't really understand. I was very young. But then I started to realise. When I still couldn't go and play with the other children. And I think I knew then I never would. I think…"

"Yes?"

"I felt like I'd never be a proper person. It's like I was semi-detached from life."

Munroe nodded and found a sympathetic tone. "A difficult time."

"Oh, well put. Brilliant in fact." Contempt filled Martha's voice. "Yes it was, as you so very rightly say. A… difficult… time."

From the barrister came no reaction, only a brief, sideways look to the jury. It felt as though he was telling them – *trust me. Follow me. I might have something interesting to show you.*

"Let me take you on a few years. You decide to study forensics. May I ask why?"

"Because it interests me. Because I hope it might lead to a career, something worthwhile."

"And does it?"

"No. No way. No one wants to employ someone like me. There's no room for a freak in any company I ever managed to find. It was never said, of course. It was always, 'you gave an excellent interview, but we regret to inform you there is someone better qualified', or 'many thanks, and we will keep your application on file'. All that sort of…"

"Sort of?"

Her expression tightened, the pale skin whitening further. Martha knew where she was being led, but couldn't resist.

"That bullshit!"

More understanding soothed from the barrister. He had seen into Martha and realised that he, himself, was one of the greatest provocations she could face. Successful, privileged, healthy, a part of the establishment – they were his goads and spurs.

"I see. Well, I was going on to ask how it felt, but…"

"Have a guess!" she interrupted, savagely. "I bet you never could. Someone with your job and life. This is how it felt – we'll give you this incurable illness. Then, instead of helping, we'll dump you. Instead of having the decency to say sorry, we'll gloss over our little mistake, secure in the knowledge it won't be around long to embarrass us. Soon the problem'll be solved… 'coz it'll be dead."

Munroe half turned to the jury. "Pretty bitter, then?"

"Yeah."

"Disillusioned with society?"

"Just a little."

"Angry?"

"Yeah."

"So… that was when you decided to take revenge?"

Martha glared at him, briefly closed her eyes as if to cast off the animal of her anger. "I've never taken any revenge on anyone."

"Really?"

"Really."

"So, the forensics degree – the computing too – they weren't to provide the knowledge you'd need to be an efficient criminal?"

"No."

Munroe absorbed the setback. He turned a couple of pages on his notes and ran a hand over the smoothness of his chin. Now the pace of his voice changed. It became quicker, sharper with a new angle of attack.

"What do you think of Annette Newman?"

"What?"

"What do you think of her?"

"I – I don't think anything of her. I don't know her."

"You don't pity her, for what she's been through?"

"I…"

"You don't feel anything for her? After her tears in the witness box? The nightmare of the ordeal that still haunts her?"

Martha glanced at the jury. She might have been searching for a hint about the right answer. For the first time, there was discomfort in her voice.

"I suppose I… feel sorry for her."

"Suppose?"

"What?"

"You just suppose?"

"Yeah."

"And feel sorry?"

"Yeah."

"Just sorry?"

"Yeah."

"For the torment you inflicted?"

"Yeah… no! You bastard, you're trying to catch me out."

Munroe said nothing, just settled upon the ground he had won. He let his eyes run along the twelve expressionless faces in the jury box. And now his tone changed again. He had become an uncle, helping a favoured child with some homework.

"What kind of an outcry was there about you, and thousands of others, being infected with hepatitis and HIV?"

Martha studied him, unsure where she was being lured this time. "You know damn well."

"Tell us."

"Just about none."

"None?"

"No. None. Not a bit. Zip. Absolutely zero."

"That must have struck you as rather unfair?"

"No shit."

"That no one seemed to care?"

"Yeah… no one cared."

"Society least of all?"

Martha snorted unpleasantly. "Not a bit."

"So, you took Annette to demonstrate the contrast. The very different reaction to what happened to her?"

The forced calm was back. "Don't bother trying that. I did not take Annette."

Munroe accepted the block to his parry. He pushed the silvery wig back a little from his brow, gave himself some thinking time.

"A final question, if I may?"

"If you must."

Munroe rode the jibe. He didn't react, instead unfolded a large sheet of paper. It looked like a map. He made a point of studying it, and with obvious affection. And then his expression changed, hardened with determination. He focused upon Martha's eyes.

"So then – Great Mis? Vixen? Cox? Sheep's?"

"What?"

"Bellever? Pew? North Hessary? Gutter?"

"What? What are you talking about?"

"Leeden? Yar? Laughter? Leather?"

"What the hell are you talking about?"

Munroe waved the map. "Tors, Ms Edwards. They're all Dartmoor tors. What's your favourite tor?"

"What?"

"You're a Dartmoor lover, according to your evidence. That which you swore was the truth – remember? You delight in the moor's natural beauty, or so you say. I just wondered which tor was your favourite?"

"I… I…"

"You have no idea, do you?"

"I do – I like… Hay Tor."

"Hay Tor?"

"Yes."

"Hay Tor – Dartmoor's most visited. The one that probably anyone could name. That's your favourite?"

"Yes."

"You said you love seclusion. Peace and tranquillity. Is that why you like Hay Tor?"

"Yeah."

"Despite it being a tourist honeypot? Having two large car parks, a visitor centre and an ice cream stall?"

Martha glared at Munroe. Her hand clutched at the polished wood of the witness box. Behind her, in the dock, Brian was leaning forwards, agitated. He looked as though he was in pain.

"I like the views," she said finally.

"You are a liar, Ms Edwards. You kidnapped Annette Newman and you and your brother held her in a cottage in East Prawle."

"No—"

"You did so because you wanted money for drugs which might help your condition, but most importantly as part of your crusade for revenge."

"No."

"Annette was an embodiment of the establishment, so you took her and delighted in making her suffer."

"No!"

"Because of the attention given to her abduction and the lack of interest in your own plight."

"No!"

"It was your personal version of justice, wasn't it?"

"No!"

"You are a liar, Ms Edwards. Despite what you might believe of your lofty purpose and perverted morals, you are nothing more than a common criminal."

Martha's face had flushed an angry red. "I am not a common criminal!"

And now Munroe lowered his voice once more. "And that's exactly how you see yourself, isn't it? No common felon, but an avenger. Bringing justice to a world that can't manage to find its own. But I can tell you, Ms Edwards, that you are a criminal. Perhaps not common, maybe even rare, but a criminal nonetheless."

"No! No, no, no!"

The barrister held her look. "No further questions, Your Honour."

Dan finished a final note and looked to the jury. The eyes of every man and woman were fixed on Martha Edwards. He thought he could sense a change in some of the expressions. It was nothing readily perceptible, nothing that could be written down, but perhaps the beginnings of an understanding about what truly stood before them.

For the first time in the weeks of the trial, Dan found himself starting to believe that the distant land of a guilty verdict might just be within reach after all.

CHAPTER TWENTY-TWO

The great labyrinth of the legal maze had at last been navigated. Evidence and testimony, speeches and learned arguments, all finally exhausted. Now there just remained a choice of the two doors.

The moment of justice.

The foreman was still standing, head a little bowed, one hand fingering a wisp of beard. In another place, another life, he could have been a geography teacher patiently waiting for a class to quieten.

All eleven of his peers had settled for the final time on these inhospitable wooden benches. All were looking to him, *primus inter pares* of this randomly assembled dozen.

And all the rest of the court looked, too. The judge, high up on the bench, framed by the dancing lion and unicorn. The opposing ranks of the law, the barristers and solicitors of each side. The Newmans on the front row of the public gallery, the Edwards in the dock, awaiting their fate.

All in the gift of this man's voice.

And now it was time.

The foreman was drawing himself up with all the height he had available. The whole court could see the rise of his chest. His hands were gripping hard at a small piece of paper and his look was lifting. Upwards, degree by degree, taking in the wooden bench before him, still rising, and heading for the well of the court.

He had closed his eyes, just a brief blink, as if in anticipation of what was to come. And now he was looking directly into the court.

Straight at the Edwards.

★★★

Templar nodded to a woman, sitting below him. The Clerk to the Court rose, her black robe flowing to the floor in waves.

She was young, perhaps no more than thirty, but nonetheless donned a pair of half-moon spectacles more befitting a woman double her age.

"Mr Foreman of the jury," she called. "'Have you reached a verdict upon which you are all agreed?"

"We have."

Solicitors looked to their colleagues. Detectives did the same. Strangers in the public gallery nudged each other. Annette cuddled into her father, face buried in his shoulder. Behind the glass of the dock the Edwards held hands.

And so came the question, the answer and the moment.

"Mr Foreman – do you find the defendants guilty or not guilty?"

Just one more hesitation. A final tease, a last procrastination, as the man took another deep breath.

"We find the defendants... not guilty."

An instant's freeze seized the courtroom. A rushing, tumbling, beating, battering silence. So loud it could have drummed on the wood and blown out the skylights.

One, sole, single second, the time for synapses to click and nerves to react. Time to understand, to realise and to know.

The Edwards began hugging each other. Beside Adam, Katrina patted his shoulder and Claire laced around a comforting arm. At the front of the court, Wishart and Munroe shook hands.

A sudden babble filled the room. Unleashed, it echoed and amplified from the old wooden boards. Amongst the hacks there were final scribbled notes and fast fingers on keypads, flashing the copy to newsrooms and on to the world.

And in the public gallery sat a middle-aged man and a young woman; the only two unmoving in the growing melee. Locked together, as though trying to shelter, to protect each other from yet another torment railed upon them.

To their side Ivy, the usher, was waiting, a single ally in the uproar. A reporter approached, but Ivy pushed the man away.

By the dock, the security guard was searching for a key. The steel that would unlock the plate glass and open it to the Edwards' freedom.

Amid all this, Templar was unmoved. Sitting aloft, scrutinising the court. In his face was something indefinable. It was in the lines worn of experience and the knowing of his eyes. Perhaps a regret at this ending to the case – his last? A farewell to all the years of his career? An empathy for the Newmans, a distaste, maybe more, for the Edwards? And pride or disillusionment with this profession which he had served for so long?

But he was watching, observing, as a voice struggled to penetrate the whirl of noise.

"Listen! Please! I want to say... There's a but! A but—"

It was the foreman. He was trying to shout above the crowd with the thinness of a voice that was never designed for such a task. The woman beside him pushed at his arm, urged him on.

"But!" he called again. "There's a but!"

And now people were noticing. Turning. Hearing him.

Templar banged his gavel on the bench, the crashing harshness of the sound a shock, stopping the courtroom in a second. "Order!" he called. "This case has not yet reached its conclusion."

The judge let a slow look fall upon the foreman. And once more, however unexpectedly, the attention of all was set upon this nondescript man.

He glanced at Templar, a quick, nervous glimpse. It was a check for disapproval, but one which received only an imperious stare. Emboldened, the man gripped the piece of paper, the one he had held so tightly. And now came the reason why, as he read aloud its extraordinary contents.

"We, the jury, believe we have carried out our duty as demanded by the law. We have tried the accused on the evidence put before us and have decided that we cannot, beyond reasonable doubt, find them to be guilty."

He studied the sheet one more time.

"However," the foreman added, "However – that is not to say we believe the defendants to be innocent."

★★★

Amongst the most garrulous species of the earth, lawyers and journalists must surely rank in the top three. Perhaps the dubious trade of the politician is the only serious rival for the highest of the podium positions.

So it was that the foreman's words, remarkable in themselves, were enhanced by an additional accolade. They reduced the creatures of the law and media to a puzzled silence.

Barristers looked to their solicitors for opinions, or the guidance of precedents, but received instead shrugs. Reporters did the same with their rivals. And the only answer was more vacant looks.

Unique amongst all this were the Edwards. No longer in the clutches of the court, no longer prisoners of the proceedings, they would soon be free.

Initially, they too struggled to comprehend the foreman's words. Then Martha's face broke into a smile and a laugh, until it rang with rich contempt. She relaxed back into her seat, placed her hands behind her head and beamed at the confusion. It was the delight in superiority that a child might enjoy from poking an anthill and watching the insects run around in confusion.

"Order!" called Templar, above the uproar. "That concludes these proceedings. Members of the jury, may I thank you for your careful consideration of this case and your verdict – however unorthodox."

He turned to address the dock. Martha was still chuckling, playing a hand across the glass in front of her, tracing circles. The guard stood by the door, keys in hand, readying to open it.

"Martha and Brian Edwards, you are free to go," Templar intoned. "However, before you do, I add this. It may be true that the needs of the law were served here today. But as for the needs of justice, that is quite another matter."

CHAPTER TWENTY-THREE

The next hour would return to taunt Dan for the rest of his life. The image of what happened never faded with the years, unlike the fragility of so many memories. It stayed sharp and clear, as horrifying as the day they captured it on film. Some ghosts of the mind refuse to rest.

From the occasional conversation they dared to risk in the times afterwards, he knew it was the same for Nigel, even the normally impenetrable Loud. In any talk about the notorious Edwards' case, this moment was never mentioned. It had been censored, shamed and hidden. What they saw would stay with them always, but with them alone. It was not something for sharing.

The media pack careered out of the court in the disorderly stampede of their ramshackle way. It was important to get ahead in case any of the main players in the drama, the Edwards or the Newmans, tried to escape before they could be photographed and filmed.

It mattered not if they didn't want to speak out. Theirs was not the choice. Frenzied questions had to be thrown over the ranks of cameras. Often, mere expressions could tell the story more eloquently than words.

Nigel had positioned himself at the centre of the arc of the press pack. There must have been forty or so there, the cameras in the middle and reporters clustered around. He held out the microphone to Dan who squatted and shoved himself a space beside his friend.

Amongst the media, Plymouth Crown Court is popular for a happy pairing of reasons. The first is the Pepperpot Coffee Bar on the concrete plaza outside. It's conveniently close, always refreshing and a guaranteed source of legal gossip. The second, and nominally more important, is that the court boasts but one entrance and exit.

The victims of the press have no choice but to run the gauntlet of the cameras.

All they had to do was wait. And wait was what they did.

Dan used the time to phone the *Wessex Tonight* lawyers. Never before had he known a verdict like that which the jury had delivered. Judging by the reaction, neither had the duty solicitor. She called back twenty minutes later, having waded into the ancient waters of the law library, checked the modern repository of the internet databases and spoken to colleagues.

The nearest interpretation the mass of legal minds could provide was that the jury had effectively adopted the Scottish verdict of *Not Proven*. In other words we think you're guilty, but there's not quite enough evidence to return that verdict.

The sun was dipping in the western sky, but the day was still warm. From the tower of the City Council offices on the opposite side of the plaza stretched the block of a long shadow. Pigeons paraded the pavements in their restless search for the joy of a discarded crumb. The intensity of the sunlight flared on the glass doors of the court. Each time a figure moved inside the pack tensed.

The satellite truck was parked just over the road. Lizzie wanted a standard news *doughnut*; a live introduction from Dan followed by his report on what happened in court and a summing up.

It was half past four, two hours until *Wessex Tonight* was on air. Time was already growing tight.

"It's one hell of a story," gloated El, who was next to Dan. "It's gonna be worth some wonga from the papers. Hope all our little players come out soon."

Nigel asked about what happened in court and Dan gave him a quick summary.

"Those poor Newmans," he said, in his fatherly way. "The ordeal just goes on and on for them, doesn't it?"

"Action stations!" El burbled.

The doors opened and Adam strode out. He was as immaculately presented as ever, but his face was dour. He looked like a man who had sworn he would never smile again.

"I have a short statement for you," he said, peremptorily. "Greater Wessex Police respect the jury's verdict. But I can add this. It is a comfort to us that, although no one has been brought to justice for the crime, Annette was found safely and returned to her father. I'd also like to say that we will not be looking for anyone else in connection with the case. In the police's view, the words of the foreman and judge speak for themselves."

The usual burst of shouted questions rose from the pack, but the detective had turned and begun walking back into the courthouse. He'd reached the third of the six concrete steps when Martha stepped out of the doors.

Adam stopped. She stopped.

"Shit, she's done that deliberately," El whispered.

Claire put a hand onto Adam's shoulder as if to guide him past, but the detective didn't move. Martha eyed him, the paleness of her face coloured with a smirk.

"Hello, Mr Chief Detective," she chirped. "Been explaining to the press how the clever criminals outwitted you?"

Still Adam said nothing. Now Katrina wound an arm around his shoulders and tried to channel him into the doors. But the detective had become a block of stone. He refused to move.

"It must be really galling," Martha continued. "All that work to find those nasty people who kidnapped Annette. And then to have a jury tell you that you almost got it, but not quite."

Katrina mouthed something that Dan couldn't catch. It looked like *bitch*.

Adam took a step towards Martha. Brian was at her side, ready to repel any attack. And from the look of Adam, it could come. He was a man who prided himself upon being in control, cool and professional, but not here, not this time. He was balanced upon the edge of an assault which would destroy his career, but may still be a temptation too far to resist.

The pack edged closer, wanting to witness each word. The detective stared into Martha face. His neck was flushed and his fists were bunched into tight knots. The sum of all his furies was contained in these few seconds.

Quietly, the words only just under rein, he said, "We'll be watching you. Make no mistake; we'll be behind you, everywhere you go… for what little time you've got left."

★★★

The doors closed on the detective's back. With the narrow precision of a sniper's shot, the single sentence had penetrated the certainty of Martha's defences. Her smile faded and the dancing brightness of the green of her eyes dimmed.

Brian leant gently over and whispered into her ear. She nodded and turned to the ranks of the assembled media. The mask was back.

"What a bad loser. And who likes one of those? So then, press people – what do you want to know?"

"How do you feel?" came a voice from the back of the pack.

Dan tried not to wince at one of the worst clichés in the journalist's handbook. But Martha neither noticed, nor cared.

"I feel fantastic! I feel like this is the best medicine I've ever known. And I've had plenty pumped into me over the years."

"And what will you do now?"

"Brian and I are going to get drunk – or the best I can do given my condition and my poor liver. We'll eat well and toast our freedom. And we'll do it all on credit, because tomorrow I'm going to sue the police for six months of wrongful imprisonment."

Dan's mobile warbled with a text message. It was from Adam and could have been possessed of a voice, one which screamed from the screen.

Fucking get her will u

Beside Dan, the lens of El's camera loomed forwards to capture every detail of the grin on Martha's face. It was the picture which every paper would print, and juxtapose with Annette's misery.

Winners and losers, the media way.

"You're hardly exonerated, are you?" Dan called. "The jury said they thought you did it, but that it couldn't be proved."

It may have been intended to wound, but the question only offered more entertainment for Martha.

"And isn't that the sweetest of victories – if, of course – *if* it were the case? A criminal plots a plan so perfect the police know exactly who did it, but can't prove it. It's not a bad form of—"

"Revenge? The revenge you denied in the witness box you wanted?"

Martha hesitated. More quietly now, she said, "Maybe... education. Exposing the rottenness in this country. Perhaps it's like – knowing how someone had committed a dreadful crime, but being unable to act against them."

Her voice changed again, filled with a different emotion now.

"Maybe it's like infecting an innocent child with an incurable disease and no one ever being brought to justice for it. Despite their suffering, and thousands of others, too. And despite it being there, horribly apparent, utterly obvious for all the world to see, people dying in front of them, no one is to blame. No one is ever *found guilty*. In our fine, upstanding, so very civilised society, something like that would never happen. It'd surely be unthinkable... wouldn't it?"

The journalists were silenced by the speech – a rarity for a press pack. Perhaps it was the potency of the emotion, or the knowledge of the clock counting away Martha's life. But even safe in the comfort of their numbers, no one could find a question to challenge this woman.

When a sole voice spoke out, the source was a surprise. From behind the camera, Nigel called, "So how does it help to create more victims? What about Annette?"

Martha's smile faltered. This time her answer wasn't measured, but snapped.

"Annette will be fine. She's young, her Daddy's rich and she's got her health. She'll get over what happened to her – unlike me."

★★★

The pack remained set in formation, that semi-circle lurking at the bottom of the grimy, chewing gum blossom steps. The cameramen and photographers may have laid down their weapons for a few seconds rest, but all were still intent on the doors, waiting.

The time had edged on to five. Across the city, above the urban backdrop of the ubiquitous traffic, bells began to ring out the hour. The streets filled with people hurrying their way home.

By no means for the first time, Dan reflected on another of the quirks of his job. As many were finishing for the day, his work was intensifying to its most critical moments.

He stood beside Nigel, fluffy microphone under one armpit, notepad in hand, trying to scratch out a script. If he had a draft ready, Loud could start editing as soon as he was back at the satellite van. Every second saved counted with the beast of a deadline breathing fire into your face.

He tried composing an opening line, crossed it out, attempted another and scored through that too. Dan noticed he kept doodling *PP* in the margin.

"How's the writing going?" Nigel asked.

"It's not going anywhere. It's like trying to build a house with only two thirds of the bricks. We need to hear from the Newmans."

Nigel rested the camera carefully on a step and stretched his arms. "It's going to be darn tight to get on air if they don't come out soon."

"You know, I hadn't thought of that," Dan replied heavily.

The cameraman smiled an apology. "Sorry."

"Anyway, what was that about, throwing a question at Martha? I've never known you do anything like that before."

"You didn't mind, did you? I know it's not my territory, but—"

"It was the best question of the lot. You were the only one amongst us who landed any sort of blow."

And now this kind and gentle man was blushing, despite all the years on the road and his vast library of experience. "It just – came over me. I suppose sometimes suffering in silence isn't an option."

Dan glanced over at the van. Loud was sitting in the front seat, his feet up on the dashboard reading a tabloid. He tapped pointedly at his watch and grimaced.

A couple of kids on skateboards trundled past. Nigel picked up the camera and balanced it back on his shoulder. "I'm glad I only do the filming. I don't fancy your job, particularly not on a story like this. I just point the thing, check the picture looks ok and hit the big red button."

Dan patted his friend's back. "Nice try, but it's not quite that simple. If you can make me look half decent, there's a fine art in there somewhere."

El polished the lens of his camera and let out a loud belch.

"Another fruit fancy, Great Aunt Ethel?" he giggled. "Sorry, me stomach does that when we're hunting. It gets all excited."

Dan was about to reply when the doors of the court swung open. Roger Newman walked uncertainly down the steps, a tight arm around Annette's shoulders. Her eyes were circled with a red soreness. Behind them, protectively close, stood the usher.

"I... I have a brief statement," Newman began. "I – we... want to say that this was our last hope of justice. Of being able to believe we could start again. And now..."

His voice faltered. He looked down at his daughter and pulled her closer.

Annette was crumpled and shrunken. Defeat and despair filled every cell of her existence. The young woman had become old in the two days of the kidnapping, the months of waiting for the trial, the weeks of the hearing itself and the final killing thrust of the verdict. The erosion of decades had done their work in only half a year.

Her body was trembling hard and her face ashen. She was struggling to breathe, a hand fluttering to her heaving chest. It was as if she wanted to retreat into herself and hide from the world forever.

The cameras were all zooming in to capture the single shot that told the story in an instant, the summary of a young woman's torment.

A moan escaped her mouth, an inhuman, unearthly sound, and Annette tensed with the shock of a sudden decision. She sprang down the steps, half stumbled but righted herself, began sprinting hard, dodging around the fringes of the pack, moving fast, her long legs flying across the grey paving stones of the sunlit plaza.

CHAPTER TWENTY-FOUR

Through the sticky heat of the late afternoon they ran.

The plaza was a mirrored box, relentlessly reflecting the sun's power. From the silvered windows of the courthouse, the Civic Centre and the concrete paving, the withering rays attacked them.

Roger Newman stood stunned, overwhelmed by yet another ordeal in days which had become filled with so many. He shouted for his fleeing daughter, then began running after her, calling her name, time and again.

"Annette! Please! Annette!"

Even through the disguise of the breathlessness, the apprehension and incomprehension in his voice was pitiful. The scales had tipped a little further against a man's sanity. Ivy was alongside Newman, running too, that dense usher's robe a black cloud in his wake.

Dan grabbed Nigel's shoulder and pulled him to join the pursuit. Other journalists were following. Some strained even to take the steps to get underway, an ignoble testament to an increasingly sedentary profession.

Annette was running towards the tower of the council building. She was still moving fast, filled with the strength of youth, but something else too – that strange spirit which had come upon her.

They rounded a couple of park benches and an old lady resting there, her coat pulled tight around her shoulders despite the day's warmth.

Nigel's face was streaming with sweat. They'd discarded the tripod, but the camera remained a dense, unforgiving weight. Dan reached out, took it and received a nod of thanks. The scarce breathing air was too precious to waste with words.

Annette passed the grey, sixties monolith of the Civic Centre. From the glass doorways people watched the careering procession.

She was still running determinedly; she hadn't even glanced back, despite her father's shouts.

They passed under a couple of thin and pasty trees, this concrete expanse no place to live a fulfilling life. The temporary seconds of the shade were a relief from the pervasive heat. The concrete of the plaza had spent the day baking in the sun and was keenly releasing its stored energy.

Their reddened and breathless reflections passed in one of the algae-green, rectangular ponds. A couple of seagulls bobbed and ducked, their whiteness stark in the grimy waters.

They were nearing the Theatre Royal. Annette dodged around a line of traffic, crossed the road and tumbled through a yellow door into the multi-storey car park. Her father stumbled and crashed into a young couple carrying shopping bags. He ignored the cries and careered through the door after her. Ivy hesitated, pulled off his gown, screwed it into a ball and followed.

Dan lurched to a halt.

"What're we doing?" Nigel gasped, as best he could. "We're running out of time. Shouldn't we be getting the story on air?"

"Maybe. But I'm getting one of those feelings about this."

The rest of the pack were catching up; a couple more reporters and El at their head. All were panting hard.

Above, they could hear running feet. Through the concrete panels of the car park walls, a tall, thin silhouette was still sprinting. A hundred yards behind were a couple more figures. They were on the sixth floor, one below the roof.

Dan handed the camera back to Nigel. He stepped back to get a better shot and began tracking the line of runners. Annette was jogging up the final ramp which led to the open air. Her pace was easing. A car passed, then another. One hooted a horn.

Newman and the usher were fifty yards behind. Echoes of Roger's shouts resonated from the walls of the car park.

"Annette! Please, stop! Annette!"

A group of onlookers were gathering. A couple of young women, a man dressed in a suit, a trio of schoolchildren. A woman pushing a pram joined them, a young boy biting hard into an ice cream at her side.

The sun dipped behind the Civic Centre. The plunge into sudden shadow could have been a dive into a cooling sea.

Annette emerged onto the roof level. She was walking now, but still moving determinedly, even robotically. She looked thinner than ever and her hair stuck up in spikes against the clear background of the sky.

The two figures of her pursuers were closer, perhaps twenty yards behind. They'd also slowed to a walk. Roger was reaching out his arms.

"Annette! Come on love, let's stop all this, eh? We'll get through it, like we always do – together."

The young woman had reached the corner of the level. There were no cars here, all now retrieved by their owners after a day's work or shopping. A low fence ran around the concrete wall, the odd tuft of moss colouring its mundane, functional greyness.

Roger was stepping carefully towards his daughter. "Come on Annette. Let's go home – please."

The silhouette turned. A palm raised. Newman stopped, the sun flaring from the pate of his head.

"Come on love, this is silly. Let's go and get something to eat and have a bottle of wine. We can get through this."

He was trying to catch his breath, the words coming in staccato gulps. Ivy made to walk forwards, but Newman stopped him.

The dark outline of the young woman stretched out to find a foothold and pulled herself up onto the wall.

As one, the crowd of onlookers gasped.

"Annette," Newman pleaded. "What're you doing? That's dangerous. Please, come down."

She ignored him and turned her face forwards. Towards the court building and the statue of justice looking back at her.

Upon those below, the understanding of the look was lost. It could have been contempt, loathing, sadness or simple incomprehension. But at the proud lady, and her sword and scales, Annette stared.

"Shit," El whispered. Nigel too was groaning. Beside him a man called 999. The woman was pulling her son away. But he was resisting, trying to turn back.

"Is she going to jump, Mummy?" the boy asked.

In the distance a siren wailed. At the top of the car park, perhaps seventy feet above them, Annette spread her arms wide.

And now Newman's voice was filled with panic.

"Annette! You're frightening me. Love, please come down. We can do whatever you want. We can go out for a meal. Or we can go home and talk. Just come down… please."

A seagull screeched in the sky. Newman took a careful pace forwards, then another.

The figure of his daughter began to rock back and forth.

"Annette! Don't do this. You're scaring me. What about college? What about the company? You've got so much more to do with it."

Another siren joined the first. Newman stepped forwards again, Ivy beside him. The usher was crying silently, tears streaming down his face.

"Please Annette!" Newman begged. "Don't do this."

The silhouette turned. A hand raised, as if waving. An easy breeze gently ruffled the spikes of Annette's hair. It could have been nature's fond goodbye to one of her beautiful creations.

The young woman's feet shuffled on the narrowness of the ledge. A couple of loose chippings fell and clattered down to the pavement.

The crowd drew in a collective breath. They had become one in fear and dread. People began to reach out for the comfort of friends.

Annette looked down, studied the expanse of the concrete below. The patterns of the paving stones, the dark waters of the ponds, the trees, the lines of benches.

And gazing over them all, the guardian statue of justice.

To the cloudless sky, Annette lifted her head. She took in one final taste of the sweet air and caress of the warming sun. And then she fell, pitching forwards in a graceful dive, plunging in a curving, elegant arc, flying in freedom through the perfect, autumn's day until her body smashed into the pavement.

Dan managed one look. Just a brief, half-second, no more than a snapshot, but enough to capture that vision for always.

The shattered body. The fingers of fresh blood stretching from the lifeless head. The cracked porcelain of those fine cheekbones. The one open eye, more contented in death than it was in life.

He fell to his knees and was violently sick.

CHAPTER TWENTY-FIVE

In the unlikely refuge of the satellite van they sought shelter. Away from the ambulances and the hopeless efforts of the paramedics. Away from the police officers, stretching out the plastic tape of a cordon and trying not to look at that which they were protecting. Away from the gossips, gathering to share their thin and faux horror.

And away from Roger Newman, crying into the arms of the usher. A blanket around his shoulders, despite the heat of the day. A mug of tea thrust into his shaking hand, from which he had taken not a sip. A policewoman trying to guide him to one of the vans parked beside the multi-storey.

As sleepwalkers, Nigel and Dan trudged back to the court. Not a word, not a gesture, just weighted legs moving in automatic time. A pair of friends and colleagues, united over years by the bonds of humour, professionalism and a savouring of life, now with nothing to share except that of which they dare not speak.

So much they thought they had seen and faced down, so much they had come through. But never like this. A black cloak had been cast over them, excluding all light from the world, even on this sunshine day.

It was half past five. An hour until *Wessex Tonight* took to the air. But never had a deadline felt so inconsequential. It was as important as a wash prior to the guillotine or watering the garden minutes before Armageddon.

Nigel pulled the door closed. It was a time for shutting out the fear of reality. In the van they stood, and stood was all they did.

On every wall, the windscreen, the seats, even on the clocks, there was the broken, lifeless face of a 17-year-old woman. A personal ghost, to be with them always.

"What do we do?" Loud asked, quietly.

"Who cares?" Nigel replied.

He stepped across to the front of the van and sat on the passenger seat, head bowed between his knees. Loud folded his arms and sucked at his teeth. Dan reached for a bottle of water and swigged hard. It cleared some of the tang of sickness, but he could still taste bile. He poured a cascade over his head. Some splashed onto Loud and the edit desk, but the engineer didn't react.

There was only stillness and silence. And it was enough. The safety of the half light of the cramped space. A place that was not *out there*, an unwanted existence where young women were so traumatised by the evils inflicted upon them that they could embrace death from the top of a car park.

Dan's mobile rang. Mechanically, he answered. It was Lizzie. One of the news agencies had put out a flash about Annette's suicide.

"Did you see it?"

"Yeah."

"Did you film it?"

"Yeah."

"Bloody hell."

"Yeah."

"Are you ok?"

"No. I'm fucked up."

"Ok, we can talk about it later. You'd better get on with editing the report."

The thought had hardly occurred to Dan. "The report?"

"I know you've had a traumatic time. But it's a huge story and it's your job – your duty – to get it on air."

"Whatever."

He cut the call and turned the mobile off. The silence returned. The clock ticked around to twenty to six.

"What we going to do, then?" Loud asked.

"I'm going home," Dan replied. "I'm going to get so drunk I won't remember my own name, let alone…"

He didn't need to finish the sentence. From this moment, he never would. The sight must be banished, exiled, confined to a corner of the memory from which it could never escape.

A banging on the door made them recoil. It was Adam, tie low on his collar, face streaked with sweat.

"Did you film it?"

"I wish people would stop asking me that!" Dan shouted. "Yes, we fucking filmed it, all right? She landed a few feet from me. She died a few feet from me. Splat, dead, dead, dead, right by me. We saw the lot. We filmed everything. I've even got some of her fucking blood on my trousers if you want a look. Ok?!"

"Don't you start—"

"Then don't you start coming in here and—"

Dan felt a pair of arms around him. The grip was firm, but kind. It was Nigel.

"Calm it down," he said. "We've all had a shock."

"No bloody shit," Adam grunted.

"Yeah, right," Dan snorted.

"We're all supposed to be on the same side, here," Nigel continued.

"What are you going to do?" Dan asked Adam. "Are you going after the Edwards?"

"What's the bloody point? I couldn't even get them for kidnapping. I hardly stand a chance of pinning Annette's suicide on them. What about you?"

"I'm going home," Dan replied, determinedly.

"Home?"

"Yes, home –where I live. The only place I want to be right now. Curtains closed, on the sofa, bottle of whisky in hand. And oblivion, ASAP. Anything but this."

"Like hell you're going home. We need you to tell people what the Edwards did."

Dan picked up his satchel and stepped deliberately down from the van.

"I'm out of here. I quit. From the TV and your bloody police work, too. I can't take this shit any more. I never asked for it and I don't want it."

Adam grabbed Dan's jacket and slammed him back against the side of the van. He tried to slap the detective's arms away, but he was too strong, too intense, hurtling too fast down the red tunnel of his rage. His eyes were wild and his breath smelt stale.

"Get back in that fucking van and start telling people what happened here today."

Flecks of foaming spittle flew with the words. Adam was set rigid and staring, veins standing out dangerously, the hot blood pumping hard. His arms were locked, his look with them.

As for Dan, his heart was hammering, his head pounding. But despite that he felt numb and detached, so far away from the world, drugged with the horror he'd seen.

Nigel tried to push between them, muttering calming noises. But it was an ineloquent rambling from an unexpected source which broke through the flaming trance.

"I dunno, but... well, I know it's not down to me, but... I reckon he's right."

Loud was leaning out of the truck. He looked surprised with himself, but also determined with the discovery of what was right. "I mean – if the law can't get 'em, then we're the next best thing – aren't we?"

Nigel was nodding too, and holding out the memory card of the pictures they'd filmed. He kept it at arm's length, as if fearful of the horrors confined in the nondescript plastic box.

Dan let go of Adam's jacket, took the card, and stepped back into the van.

★★★

The merciless turning of the clock had taken the time on to a quarter to six. But for once, the pressure of the deadline was welcome. It allowed no time to think or feel, only to react.

"We'll do the report chronologically," Dan told Loud. "It's the quickest way. Put down some pictures of Adam coming out of court, then we'll go to that bit of his statement about the words of the jury and judge speaking for themselves."

He used the couple of minutes to sketch out the rest of the script and accept a decision he knew was already made. Upon both shoulders were demons, whispering and urging, pushing and pleading, telling him to give in. For the sake of Adam, Loud, Nigel and Dan, himself, but most of all for Annette.

He should resist, remember the rules. The mantra learnt and repeated from the earliest days onwards.

Never get involved.

But in life, there were times to cross the line.

After Adam's words, Dan wrote one more segment of script. 'As the police made their views clear, the Edwards emerged – apparently deliberately – and there was a confrontation.'

Loud inserted the exchange between Martha and Adam. Then it was time for Martha's interview, her reaction to the verdict. Her gloating face filled the monitors.

"Blimey," Loud grunted. "That's going to make her look bloody evil, given what happens later."

And to that, Dan's only reply was an iced smile.

It was ten past six. They had reached the most difficult part of the report. Dan took a few seconds to think, while Loud laid down Roger Newman's garbled statement, followed by Annette running away.

Over that shot Dan said nothing. The action of the pictures, the camera rolling as they ran captured the drama in a way commentary never could. Less is more, one of television's golden rules.

"Now the tricky bit," Dan said to himself.

Loud edited the pictures of Annette running along the car park and to the roof, her father and Ivy following.

A few words were scribbled down, crossed out. Dan tried a few more. They still weren't right. Not for something this important.

The clock measured off another minute.

6.20.

Dan tapped his pen on the notepad and took a swig of water. Outside, Nigel was setting up the camera. He kept looking at his watch. Loud glanced up at the clock.

And still the seconds passed.

"Don't try to be clever, idiot. If in doubt, just KISS – Keep It Short and Simple," he muttered and began writing.

"Clearly distraught, Annette ran to a nearby car park, her father in desperate pursuit. And then, in the middle of a city, in front of hundreds of onlookers, on a beautiful, cloudless day, came the moment that despair drove a young woman to take her own life."

Loud went to lay down the shot of Annette jumping, but Dan reached out and stopped him. "We don't show people dying on the TV, my friend," he said kindly. "At least not at half past six, with kids watching. Stop the sequence when she's standing on the ledge. That's plenty enough."

Nigel was standing outside the door watching. As the last shot of the report was laid, he leaned forwards and gave Dan a gripping hug. Loud watched for a moment and then joined in.

★★★

In years of enthusiastic practice, Dan had come to realise an unexpected truth about his passion for beer. Drunkenness can be much more about mood than intake.

The younger version of today's man had noticed he could grow tipsy on just a few pints, if he was feeling buoyant. But if he was down and dour, even a swim in a lake of ale was unlikely to make an inroad on his sobriety.

Thus it was this evening. Dan had supped a few pints and they hadn't shifted his mood in the slightest.

In truth, it was worse even than that. He had partaken of a fair measure of spirits too, although he could probably claim that was a professional requirement. The caring cameraman and guardian that was Nigel had jogged to a corner shop and bought a half bottle of cheap whisky.

He offered it across as Dan prepared for the live broadcast. The gift was so gratefully received it was difficult not to snatch. The amber firewater restored colour to the complexion, roughened the voice and steadied the nerves. And so, once more, they'd got away with it.

Lizzie rang afterwards and pointedly didn't mention Dan hanging up on her. But she managed to do so in such a way that the omission was painfully obvious. It was always there in its absence, like a tooth newly missing from a mouth.

The editor-beast pronounced the report *pretty acceptable*, but went on to issue a catalogue of demands for a follow up story tomorrow. Dan made soothing noises, pretended to take diligent notes of the insane litany of demands and ended the call as soon as he could.

Some days, enough was more than enough.

He went home, gave Rutherford a cuddle, took the dog for a short run around Hartley Park, showered, changed, caught a bus and headed for town. As an afterthought, Dan ordered a burger and chips from a stand. The day's disarray meant he'd forgotten to eat.

In the hideaway of a forsaken corner of a backstreet bar, Dan sipped at his beer, gathered his fortitude and slowly allowed the memories to return. The pub was quiet and he was left undisturbed.

It was as he began operations on the third of the succession of pints that Dan reached a resolution. He took out his mobile and sent Katrina a text message. With a woman like her it had to be finely judged.

Hell of a day. Horrible what happened. I know you were close to Annette – hope you're ok?

It took another half a pint's debate before Dan added a kiss and sent the message. He sat back and finished the drink. It was time to move on.

He began walking, towards the plaza and the courts. If there was to be any chance of sleep tonight this stampede of screaming thoughts would have to be calmed.

The Chancellery was the nearest bar to the courts, its frontage looking out on the plaza. And it was to there that the weary and woebegotten traveller of the soul slowly headed.

★★★

The city was filled with the night. Caves of darkness dominated with only the rare intrusions of streetlights and shop windows. People passed, chatted and chuckled. Taxis, cars, buses and motorbikes rumbled and buzzed.

Life went on. It always did.

The air was still warm but sharpening as the memory of the sun's benevolence faded. From the cellar of a club came the piercing sound of a band tuning up. A line of joggers puffed their way by, each wearing a reflective vest flaring in the occasional flash of light. Pigeons watched from ledges, cooing their contentment as they settled for sleep.

Dan paced a circular route to the Chancellery. First, he walked down Catherine Street, passing the doorway where Annette was taken. He knelt and ran a hand over the pavement, following the cracks and undulations. The space where the white van had parked was empty. A couple of women walked past on the other side of the road, giggling together, not noticing the strange man staring into space, his eyes lost in the past.

He turned and walked back to the plaza. Past the courthouse and the Lady of Justice, a half-moon hanging above her sword. A couple of lights shone upstairs, a window filled with the outline of a person dutifully pushing a broom and another carrying some boxes.

On Dan walked, to the fearful destination of the car park.

There was no police tape left, no sign of what happened here only so very few hours earlier. Cars trundled around the multi-storey, their headlights flashing through gaps in the concrete panelling. A young man emerged from the wooden swing doors and headed for the shopping centre, walking fast.

Life went on as ever it did, and always would.

By the side of a wooden bench the penitent knelt, bowed his head and whispered an apology. And there he stayed, until his knees and back would bear no more. He stretched and trudged up the steps to the Chancellery, nodded to the pair of rectangular door staff and pushed open the door.

And there, at a table, sat Martha and Brian Edwards.

★★★

Dan stopped, stricken. He half-turned, ready to make an escape, but Martha was on her feet. "Come and join us."

Spread across the tables was an array of tapas. Olives, tomatoes, cheeses, some prawns, ham, artichokes. And a couple of bottles of the finest of champagnes, two fluted glasses alongside.

"No hard feelings," Martha went on. "Have a drink on us."

"What?"

In the one small word was disbelief and incredulity, anger and rage. And although Dan rarely used the word, thought it tired and rarely true to its meaning, now it was precise. There was hatred, a bubbling cauldron burning within, filled with the flames of a thousand fires.

"No – thank – you," he managed.

Music was playing, a Mediterranean guitar sound. Fans turned in the ceiling, spinning shadows from the spotlights. The place was busy, all the tables taken and people were standing at the bar. More were coming in, pushing their way past.

And now the enmity beat down the disbelief, overwhelmed it effortlessly. The gale filled his sails, irresistible, even if he had a thought to tame it.

Dan stepped over to the table. "You heard what happened? To…"

Martha shrugged. "Yeah."

"So?"

"So what?"

"You're still out celebrating."

"This is our first night of freedom for six months. It's nothing to do with Annette."

"Nothing to do with her?"

One of the bouncers had sensed the gathering storm. He stepped into the bar and was lingering behind Dan.

"You come in here, yards from where she died. You eat and drink and you say it's nothing to do with Annette?"

Martha picked up a prawn and swallowed it. "I'm moving on. It's something I've had to get used to. Maybe you should do the same."

Dan took another step forwards. He was within feet of the Edwards. The bouncer followed. Brian stood up, inflated himself, ready for the attack he knew was coming.

"Don't you feel anything? Not even any remorse?"

"Remorse?"The word could seldom have sounded so incredulous. "Look, shit happens in life. It certainly has to me and I've managed to tough it out. If other people can't, maybe they don't deserve to."

She took the champagne and began topping up a flute. Dan lunged forwards and knocked the bottle from her hand. It went rolling across the table, bubbles flowing on the wood.

The bouncer sprung, steel arms grabbing Dan's shoulders and pulling him away. It was all he could do to flail a leg. It hit the table and upset the flutes. One fell to the floor and shattered, crystal ice flowing over stone.

The bar was silent. Everyone watching the little scene.

The bouncer dragged Dan out of the door. All he could hear was the echo of Martha's laughter and her voice calling for more champagne.

★★★

The darkness of a bench outside the court was the only possible niche to try to find some calm. The clock aloft a bell tower said the time was just after ten.

Dan checked his mobile. No calls, no messages. No Katrina. No nothing, no one.

A tramp walked past swigging from a bottle of cider. He picked up a cigarette butt and asked for some change. Automatically, Dan dug into his pocket and handed over a few coins.

A plane droned overhead, navigation lights winking on its wings. He watched its path, hesitated, then scrolled down the phone's address list and found the name.

She answered quickly. "Are you ok?"

"No. Not a bastard, bloody bit."

In a rush of words Dan told her about the evening.

"Do you want to come round?"

"Yeah. Well, no actually. I do want to see you. But…"

"But?"

"I need to be in my flat. With Rutherford, and just… safe."

"I'll see you there in half an hour."

"Just one more thing."

"Yes?"

"It's not for – well… you know. It's just for a cuddle – if that's ok?"

"That's fine. I'll see you soon."

Dan got home only a few minutes before she arrived. They sat up until well into the early hours, staring at the moon, fussing over Rutherford and talking about nothing. It was just a chance to live somewhere else, far from today.

When finally they got to bed and at last to sleep, they must have known a couple of hours rest at most. The ringing of the phone jarred both awake.

"Dan, it's Adam. Where are you?"

"Err – what?"

"Where are you?"

"In bed. In my flat. As you might expect, given you've called my home number."

"Don't try to be smart. I was checking you hadn't diverted the phone, or something like that."

"Adam, what are you talking about? Why are you so interested in where I am?"

The detective ignored the question. "And you've been at home for the past few hours? After your little showdown with the Edwards?"

"How did you know about that?"

"It doesn't matter. Is there anyone who can confirm you've been at home tonight?"

Dan struggled to sit up. "Adam, what the hell are you talking about?"

"You're going to be a suspect, otherwise. Which means I won't be able to use your help. And I think I'm going to need it."

"A suspect? Adam! For what?"

"Before I tell you – can anyone confirm you've been at home for the last few hours?"

Dan glanced over to Claire, rubbing her eyes and yawning. She was wearing one of his old T-shirts and looking far better in it than he could ever have imagined achieving himself.

"That won't be a problem. Now, what are you talking about?"

"The Edwards. Half an hour ago there was an explosion in their street. In their house, in fact. It was a big one. It's wiped the place out. They were blown to pieces."

CHAPTER TWENTY-SIX

Almost as if it was a matter of ego, the biggest stories tend to make themselves known from afar. The Edwards' house was in Cattedown, just south-east of the city centre. It was probably four miles from Hartley Avenue, but a warning of the explosion was in the air soon after they left Dan's flat. The darkness of the night sky was daubed a rhythmic blue with the ranks of emergency lights, all reflecting from a haze of drifting smoke.

Dan headed for the driver's side of the car and was stopped by Claire in full police officer flow. "How many drinks did you have last night?"

"A couple."

She gave him a detective's look. It was the equivalent of wearing a T-shirt bearing the legend *You're lying and I'm well aware of it*.

"We're headed for a place swarming with cops. Ones who might not be as understanding as me."

With no further fuss, Dan handed over the keys. Several years ago, when their relationship was skipping hand in hand across the meadows of springtime, he'd picked through the mire of bureaucracy and nominated Claire an authorised driver of the car.

Many times since Dan had been more than grateful. Claire rarely minded not having a drink. She was happy to drive them home from country pubs where a quick half had mysteriously transformed into several pints, as can be the cunning way of beer.

In these dark, early morning hours of a breaking story it was a godsend. The short drive was filled with Dan ringing Nigel and tipping off Dirty El. He also put in a call to the newsroom. Young Phil had landed the dogtime shift, as befits the trying life of a trainee, and was his usual fireball of keenness.

"I'll call a cameraman."

"It's done."

175

"I'll ring the police to get more info."

"It's done."

"I'll ring Lizzie to let her know."

"Don't. There's nothing she can do and she won't thank you for being woken."

"What shall I do then?"

"Just leave it to me."

"So why did you bother ringing?"

The question made Dan pause. In his last appraisal, Lizzie had dared to accuse him of being a *control freak*. It led to quite an argument as he hadn't been able to resist the retort of hypocrisy.

He'd eventually, and reluctantly, agreed to try to be more of a *team player*, whatever that meant. In fairness, he had – several months ago – made a round of teas for half a dozen colleagues, much to their surprise. But the momentum of the zeal was soon dissipated. The appraisal form hadn't since emerged from under the pot plant, where it was usefully soaking up any stray water.

"I'll definitely need your help later, Phil," Dan replied finally, and not entirely winningly. "I could probably do with someone to… err – pick up the pictures so we can get the story onto the breakfast bulletins."

"Four years at university, a year in journalism college and I'm coming to pick up a memory card?"

"Better go," the champion diplomat lied. "I'm nearly at the scene."

The streets were almost deserted, just the odd early worker making their unenthusiastic way and an occasional rumbling post van. Claire accelerated through some traffic lights that were just turning red. Dan felt his stomach lurch. He took a couple of gulps from a water bottle and crunched some mints.

They crossed a roundabout, navigated a sharp corner and pulled up outside Homely Terrace.

★★★

The Edwards' house had come close to being erased from existence. It was as if it had been a toy, flicked away by a mighty, reckoning finger.

The roof was entirely gone, destroyed in the eruption of the explosion. Plates and shards of broken slate littered the road, some lying across the bonnets of parked cars. Dan bent down and picked one up, a dagger of a piece. It was still warm. Even here, at the end of the road, there were plenty of scattered fragments; a testament to the force of the blast.

Cattedown grew up around the docks; its southern, waterfront side heavy with the metallic sounds and oily smells of industry. Above it rise the stout towers of the gasworks, and further out is filled with lines of streets. The houses are compact and largely terraced, apart from a handful of favoured roads. The gardens tend to be small and separated by narrow alleyways, usually filled with the flying feet of children at play.

The Edwards' place was on the end of the terrace. A *For Sale* sign had been knocked over in the garden of the house next door. Otherwise it was remarkably untouched, apart from a couple of shattered windows. A diagonal line of jagged bricks, the remains of what was once its neighbour, swept down from the eaves to where the living room window had been.

The bricks traced half of an empty rectangle, a couple of warped prongs of the window frames drooping at wilting angles. What was once a supporting wall now stood only knee high, blackened with fire and ash. Leaning across it was the charred wooden stump of a standard lamp, topped by spindly wire, its shade consumed in the flames. Inside, the hint of an easy chair and sofa were piled together against a wall along with a table, layers of wallpaper peeling above.

A couple of shoots of orange and red flame flickered inside the house. Arcs of water from the jet hoses swung to their new target. Grey and black smoke and white steam mingled and rose together from the ruin. The air reeked with the acrid tang of burnt plastic.

Dan sniffed hard and thought he could sense another, more subtle, odour. He coughed hard, swallowed and tried again. This time he could scent it more clearly.

He tapped Claire's shoulder. She too sniffed the air and nodded.

The street was filled with fire engines, police cars and vans. Arc lights had been set up, illuminating the terrace and the ragged wound in its flank. A constable loomed into view, ushering arms aloft, his intent instantly neutered by the shield of Claire's warrant card.

At the end of the road Nigel pulled up, grabbed the camera and tripod and began filming. Even after the turmoil and emotion of yesterday, and the early call out, he looked fresh and worked fast. He had the spirit of a man less than half his semi-century of years.

Dan edged along to where Adam was staring at the remains of the house. "A revenge killing?" he asked.

"It could have been an accident."

More convincing explanations had issued from the mouths of politicians drowning in the quicksand of yet another scandal.

"All right, that looks most likely," the detective conceded. "But it'll be a while before we're sure. It's one hell of a mess. It's a gas explosion."

Claire nodded. "We thought so. It's still in the air."

"The Edwards?" Dan asked.

"Didn't stand a chance. The bodies are in there. But... it's not pretty."

An unspoken question rose from the ruins of the house and wound its way around them.

"I suppose we've still got to find out who did it," Dan said, at last.

"Yes, we have," Adam replied, firmly. "No matter who suffers it, or who commits it and why. A crime's a crime."

"Is it?" was Dan's quiet rejoinder.

★★★

The standard news editor's question to any reporter covering a fire is – *Did you get to film any flames?*

It's a measure of how fast you are on the scene, and so how impressive the pictures are. The problem is the fire brigades are always a foe as they tend to selfishly extinguish the conflagration as soon as possible.

Nigel took only minutes to get to Homely Terrace and was happily filming not just with flames, but also the evacuation of the rest of the houses in the street. Which left Dan the simple task of pouncing upon those who could best be charmed or browbeaten into providing an interview.

He captured three. The first was an older lady, who spoke of the night "being like the Blitz", a statement which will be familiar to journalists throughout the kingdom. A younger woman talked of the explosion shaking the foundations of her house. Her partner agreed and eloquently described a fireball reaching up into the sky and debris clattering to the ground.

Powerful though the descriptions were, it was something else that marked the interviews in Dan's mind. All three of his contributors were awake when the explosion happened, despite the time being around four o'clock in the morning. The reason was a car alarm which had gone off only a few minutes before.

Light was shading the sky. The time had edged on to twenty to six. The first of the breakfast bulletins took to the air at half past. Lizzie was renowned for shaming the lark, and one of her first instincts was to check the world of *Wessex* news. Getting a report together was the next priority.

Nigel was mouthing some words, but Dan wasn't hearing. He was staring at the space in the terrace where the Edwards' house had once stood.

"Are you ok?" the cameraman called, a gentle hand shaking his thought-miner of a reporter's shoulder. "I said – you'd better get going to the studios."

"Sorry, I was… somewhere else."

"You're not trying to be a detective again, are you?"

They were interrupted by an ambulance driving fast up the street. Nigel span the camera to follow it.

"Bit late that, isn't it?" he asked.

El had materialised from the shadows of the dawn, as was his way. "I'd have reckoned so. From what I hear, the Edwards are toast."

Two paramedics jumped down from the cab and headed along the pavement, towards the remains of the house. Adam was nowhere to be seen, so Dan called him.

"What's going on?"

"We've found a body."

"The Edwards?"

"No, they're still in the house. It's someone else. Buried under rubble at the front.'

"Who?"

"No idea, yet."

"Alive or dead?"

"Alive – just. Look, I've got to go."

"Just one more thing," Dan interrupted. "Because you'll want to hear it. I reckon I know how the Edwards were killed."

CHAPTER TWENTY-SEVEN

Amidst the surroundings of the ruined house they reconvened.

It was Adam's idea, and often his way, to consider a crime in the place where it had been committed. Dan put this down to an extension of his insistence that a photo of a victim be placed in the Major Incident Room. It was a continual reminder of why they were going about their work.

A couple of fireman walked past, taking off their helmets and wiping smears of ashy sweat from their foreheads. Katrina climbed down from the police van and joined them. There was a quick chat about how the investigation would be run before she added, in a voice loud and clear, "I'm sorry I didn't answer your text last night."

"Err, what?" Dan replied.

"It was kind of you to send a message, thank you. But I was – a little lost in myself."

Dan managed to mutter something about it being no problem. He glanced over at Claire, but all he could see was her back.

The house had been made safe, an operation which was eased by the paucity of the remains. The fire was out and the ruins rigorously damped down.

Dan had quickly discovered the rivalry running between the three emergency services, most pointedly that which divides police and fire. Many cops quietly referred to firemen and women as *The Window Cleaners*. They often thought that far more pumps were produced and water sprayed around, than was actually required.

As a senior officer, with diplomacy to consider, Adam had never echoed the view. He commonly spoke highly about the bravery of those who would enter a burning building in search of survivors. But on a couple of occasions, Dan had witnessed the detective's exasperation at the hopeless contamination of a crime scene by the thousands of gallons of water played upon it.

Now was one such occasion. Scenes of Crime Officers were already at work, but the early opinion was that Adam should expect little assistance. A fire investigator was also picking through the debris and promised a briefing later. But here too, the difficultly of drawing any meaningful conclusions from these cases had been emphasised. The power of the explosion and the aftermath of the fire-fighting effort were a ruthless combination in the extermination of evidence.

All that Adam had been presented with so far was confirmation that a gas leak was responsible for the explosion. It was a gem of information, as much a revelation as the opinion that sex can lead to pregnancy.

The bodies of the Edwards had been removed from the ruin. Dan turned away to avoid the image imprinting upon his mind, but a smell is far harder to evade.

A stillness fell upon the site, but it was not one universal in respect. A couple of fire officers watched, one shrugging his shoulders and the other flicking a dismissive hand at the body bags. Amongst the crowd of onlookers that still lingered at the end of the street, some made more explicit gestures. Adam stared, his arms folded across his chest. Katrina gently shook her head. Claire was expressionless.

As Dan turned away, he'd tried to catch her eye but she pointedly avoided looking over. Out in the sea of times ahead, a storm was brewing.

At least there was some comfort in the morning's television work going well. With a little rushing around, Dan cut a report for the breakfast bulletins and then headed to the studios' canteen. He bought himself and Nigel a well-deserved coffee and bacon sandwich, with a side order of beans for dunking. It was their traditional treat on an early start.

Lizzie professed the outcome of their efforts *not bad*, but instantly demanded a return to the scene in order to prepare further reportage. Although he didn't say so, this suited Dan well. With their endeavours of the night, the mainstay of the journalism was done. He could concentrate on working on the investigation.

While they were sitting in the canteen, young Phil asked if he might pull up a chair and join them. With a faltering tone, he proceeded to pour out an impressive torrent of rue and insecurities.

"I do my best, but Lizzie never seems to notice. I try hard, I come up with story ideas, I make sure my bulletins are good, but she never says anything."

Nigel began going through a series of reassurances, with all the kindness of a practiced father, but it was to Dan that Phil was looking in a vulnerable, almost beseeching, manner.

"You're doing well, don't worry," he said, feeling the strange stirring of an unexpected heart. "It's just Lizzie's way. A no comment from her is damned good. She'd soon say if she saw something she didn't like."

"Really?"

"You've seen some of the stories I've turned in?"

"They're legendary."

"Ah, well, I don't know about that," Dan had the decency to at least semi-deny. "But the point is, about the best I've ever heard from her is 'not bad'. And even then she immediately goes on about wanting more. Take it from me, you're well respected here and you're doing fine."

It's always an unsettling experience to see someone in such pomp of life laid low. Phil was perhaps in his mid-20s, tall and athletic. He boasted the sort of blonde hair and blue eyed chiseled looks that has women fanning themselves and men muttering into their beers.

The resulting gush of thanks was perhaps a little excessive although still gratifying. But the next question was even more unexpected.

"I've been meaning to ask this for ages…"

"Yes?" Dan replied, trying not to sound wary. "If you need a loan, I'm a bit hard up at the moment," he added, with a reasonable attempt at a smile.

"Do you think – might you… mind mentoring me a bit? Not a lot, obviously, I know how busy you are. But just – the occasional bit of advice, maybe?"

A look of such earnest devotion was hard to refuse. Dan shook Phil's hand and magnanimously agreed.

"Are you ok?" Nigel asked, as the canteen door closed behind a considerably happier young man. "You're not in danger of becoming human, are you?"

★★★

In the corner of the small back garden of what had been the Edwards' home they stood, talking and watching the investigators go about their work. A couple of rose bushes climbed the wall, many of the delicate petals littering the paving, shed by the force of the explosion.

Dan pulled himself up onto the wall. It was low, rising only a few feet, and took no great exertion.

"Most people would be able to get over it without a problem," he said.

Adam pushed the gate. There was no lock and it opened silently and easily. "Or they could just have walked in," he replied, sniffily. "Come on then, tell us your theory."

Dan eased himself down from the wall. Fragments of scattered slate cracked under his feet.

"The Edwards are out on a bender to celebrate their acquittal. I know, I saw them."

"Plus," Claire added, still without looking at Dan, "They announced it to the world via that little press conference on the steps."

"Our killer's already angry about what happened in court," Dan continued. "Justice hasn't been done. That anger grows to a rage as the Edwards do their bragging. And when Annette kills herself, the rage becomes an overwhelming fury. A murderous one."

They waited while a couple of workmen carried a table out of the ruins of the house. The garden was already full of furniture, blackened and charred.

"There has to be vengeance," Dan resumed. "But how? Our killer isn't a professional assassin. They don't have access to a gun or explosives. So they're faced with a problem – how to kill both the Edwards in one go? If they try a knife, or something like that, it's never going to work. They won't be able to kill two people without them fighting back and the attacker themselves probably being killed. So – what to do?"

Adam rolled his eyes. "This isn't a television drama. Perhaps you might just get on with it."

"Ok, our killer's thinking – what do they know that can help them? To start with, they know where the Edwards live."

"Because it's on all the court documents," Katrina interjected. "On public display."

"So that becomes the focus of the plan. I reckon the killer might have carried out a reconnaissance along the street yesterday evening, while the Edwards were out. It would have been nothing obvious, just a drive, only stopping for a few seconds. They would have seen the house isn't particularly secure – the locks are just latches. And they'd have seen the flue on the side of the house, so they know the Edwards have got a gas supply. That's when the plan starts to come together."

A couple of dining chairs joined the sorry pile of furniture along with a rolled up mat, still dripping water. Wisps of ash continued to drift in the air, colouring the ground with the dirty greyness of running charcoal.

"Our killer does a bit of research, probably at some internet café so there'll be no record on their own computer. They find the information they need. I checked when I was in the studios earlier and it's all there, online. Then, they wait."

"Enough of your storytelling," Adam urged. "I don't know if it's escaped your notice but I've got a double murder to investigate."

"The killer waits until the early hours. They know the Edwards will be home and in bed, sleeping off their night on the town. They break in and find – well, this is where I'm starting to guess…"

"It all sounds like guesses to me," Adam grumbled. "More of your daydreams."

"Or insights," Dan corrected, pointedly. "Which is why you want me here, isn't it?"

"Just get on with it," the detective replied, huffily.

"The killer finds the cooker, or fire, or maybe both. And they turn them on. Then they slip back outside again and wait. I reckon maybe twenty minutes, perhaps half an hour."

"And then?" Katrina prompted. "How do they trigger the explosion without being caught in it?"

"That's the clever bit. The killer sets off a car alarm outside the Edwards' house. They bump up and down on the bonnet and then escape. The alarm wakes up one of the siblings, they switch on a light to see what's going on and…"

"Bang," Claire added quietly.

Adam kicked at a portion of brick. "Call me Mr Picky, but your evidence for all this would be what?"

Dan gestured around. "The explosion. The car alarm going off just beforehand. And there's something else."

"Which is?" Katrina asked.

"Four years ago there was a case in Plymouth Crown Court. I vaguely remembered and looked it up online earlier. An elderly man died in a gas explosion in his bungalow. The gas company was prosecuted for not fitting the boiler properly. As part of the evidence there was loads of detail about how long it takes to fill a house with gas, exactly how much there has to be for an explosion, all that kind of thing. In other words—"

"An instruction manual for how to cause an explosion," Claire concluded. "All there for whoever needed it."

"Yep. And guess what else?"

"What?" she asked, rather abruptly.

"The judge presiding over the case – it was Templar."

★★★

At the front of the house a couple of tipper trucks arrived, men jumping down to begin assessing the rubble. Adam's mobile rang.

"That was one of the lads at the hospital. The person we found is in a critical condition. From what we can tell she's entirely innocent.

She was walking to work and got caught in the blast. Her name's Amy Ailing. She's a trainee baker, only 19 years old."

Dan took out his notebook and was hit by a warning look that could have been propelled by a cricket bat. "That's not for broadcast," Adam ordered.

"But it's an important part of the story…"

"Which you can wait to report. I need to make sure all her family know before it goes out on the TV. Now, Katrina, I think you had something to tell us?"

She pushed a stray lock of hair behind an ear. "I had a coffee with Templar yesterday evening. Just for half an hour."

"And how was he?"

"He was – odd, to say the least. When I knew him in London, he was very straight, very calm. Whatever case he handled, he could be detached. But yesterday, he was…"

"Angry?"

"More than that – he had a kind of controlled fury about him. But when we went on to talk about old times, he changed. He became really jolly, laughing and joking."

"He's going to be a suspect, however unlikely," Adam replied. "Given what he said at the end of the case about the needs of justice not being served. And from how angry he was about what happened to Annette."

They went on to talk about other suspects. The foreman also received a mention in dispatches, given his little speech about thinking the Edwards were guilty but not being able to convict them.

"But the prime suspect," Adam said, "has to be Roger Newman. Who else has a more powerful motive?"

There were nods all round. "We'd better look at his friend, Ivy, as well," Claire added. "He was trailing round like a puppy after Newman. He's got a decent motive, too."

They began walking for the gate. "First order of business, then," Adam said. "Let's see who on of little menu of suspects has an alibi for last night."

CHAPTER TWENTY-EIGHT

In a profession with the pomp and preening of the law, office would be far too mundane a word. So it was in Templar's chambers that Dan and Adam awaited the arrival of the learned judge.

The room was grandiose defined. One wall was lined with a dense mass of books, and by no means the bestseller, beach-read kind. Rows of aged and comfortably worn leather backs stared loftily down, replete with the wisdom of hundreds of years of the precedents which guided the calling. A large window looked out over the plaza. In front of it squatted the dark, shining curves of Templar's hardwood desk.

But amongst the majesty of the room there was a reassuring humanity. The desk was strewn with ramshackle piles of papers and the silver balls and strings of a sizeable Newton's cradle. There was also a photograph of a couple in a large, silver frame.

The carpet was as thick as the lawn of an idle gardener and a set of leather armchairs were arranged around the desk. Neither Dan nor Adam made a move to settle. It was one of those rooms where relaxation felt out of bounds.

Enquiries into the deaths of the Edwards were already well underway and were being directed by the diligent hand of Claire. She had returned to Charles Cross to assemble the usual team of detectives, all of which had been arranged without a single glance, or word, towards Dan. It was as if his presence had been airbrushed from the world.

Katrina had gone to talk to Roger Newman. Not a formal interview, Adam stressed. The businessman was distraught and needed no further additions to his suffering. Katrina had got to know the Newmans from her work with Annette following the kidnapping. She was best placed to tell Roger what had happened to the Edwards and gently to find out whether he had an alibi for last night.

At least Katrina, as she left the Edwards' house, did favour Dan with a look. But as ever with such a woman, a reliable interpretation was impossible. She was like trying to break a code.

The usher, Ivy, would also be spoken to, as would the foreman of the jury, to see whether they had alibis sufficient to free them from the clutches of the inquiry.

Important news had already come from the fire investigator. The Edwards' cooker was found in the ruins of the kitchen, and one of the hobs was turned on. It could have moved in the explosion, but that was thought unlikely. The amount of gas which would have been released was quite sufficient to cause the blast.

The problem was that the information, in itself, meant nothing. It could easily be the familiar story – that the Edwards fancied a snack when they got home. They were considerably the worse for wear and may have omitted to turn off the ring. Such a scenario had been responsible for more gas explosions than the investigator cared to recall. It was one of the most common methods of involuntary suicide.

The scenes of crime officers had examined the controls of the cooker and taken seconds to conclude that any attempt to lift fingerprints would be folly. It had been burned, scratched and beaten in the rubble and dowsed with jets of water. On top of that, given the scenario the police were considering, the killer would have to be thoughtful. The chances of them touching the dial without using gloves or a tea towel were negligible.

Which brought them to the interviews with the suspects. Adam had decided to see Templar personally. The judge was a prominent and powerful individual, perhaps able to cow detectives of lesser ranks. There was also the question of Templar's eccentric behaviour, something which may require sensitive handling, to which Dan had raised the obvious question of whether he should come along.

"Yes, but keep quiet," was the reply. "Try the Victorian child model, however much it might go against the grain."

Dan thought of responding with some form of indignation, but decided against it. He'd started to feel jaded after the beer and limited sleep of last night. It was another fine autumn day, and the cheerful morning sun was blazing through the window, making the room a little too warm.

The comfort of the chairs beckoned with their allure of a few minutes peaceful rest. But there was no chance of that. Heavy footsteps, that somehow managed to sound impatient, announced the arrival of Judge Templar.

***

In Dan's experience of almost every interview carried out by the police, they had the initiative. The subject was often nervous or apprehensive, and nearly always on the defensive. But not here, not with Templar.

"I wondered how long it'd be before you arrived," he barked. "Got me down as a killer, have you? A double killer in fact, damn it."

"No, Your Honour," Adam soothed. "But you'll appreciate—"

"Of course you bloody have, man!" Templar interrupted. "I could scarcely have made myself more of a suspect, with my little speech about justice not being served. I could have gone on a fair bit more, I can tell you. Bloody juries and their nonsense. You'd be a fool if you didn't want to speak to me."

Adam's chosen attempt to defuse the bomb was to proffer a hand. Templar eyed it disdainfully before engaging. Dan did likewise. The eyeing went on for double the time and the handshake was transitory, at best.

Adam began to introduce Dan and explain his presence. The words came easily through familiarity. *Police assistant, co-opted to help handle the media.* But again Templar cut in.

"I am aware you conduct your inquiries in an unorthodox manner, Chief Inspector. It has become a matter of some renown. But I lay down this warning. If one detail of our discussions becomes public, through the medium of…"

He hesitated before pronouncing the word, and when it came it was ridden with rank distaste. "… television, I shall instantly take up the matter with your Chief Constable and the Attorney General. In fact I may even trouble the Justice Secretary with it. Do I make myself clear?"

"Yes, Your Honour."

Templar paced around to his desk and prodded disdainfully at one of the teetering piles of paper. "Bail applications, I loathe them with a particular passion. A bunch of neer-do-well miscreants and their dribbling advocates trying to convince me they should be set free, no doubt to commit more crimes. I usually manage to find reason to refuse them."

He sat down, extended a bony finger, pulled back one of the silver spheres and set the cradle swinging. The metallic click of the rebounding balls beat with a clock's tempo.

Click clack, click clack…

"Look at that!" he exclaimed, face changing instantly to a delighted grin. "Splendid, isn't it? I've been wanting one for ages, but you can't get them anywhere. Then I looked them up on this new-fangled internet thing, and blow me – one's here in a week."

He rubbed his hands together, the beaming smile growing. "It's damned good if you like a round, too."

"I'm sorry?" Adam replied.

"The internet, man! Golf! I take it you don't play?"

"Err, no."

"I thought not. You hardly look the type. But you must have heard of St Andrews? A wonderful, ancient course."

"Yes, Your Honour."

"Every year they set aside some tees for amateur players. But they're damnably in demand. They make you apply by email, you know. Noon, the thing opens, and I was stuck in court. So, do you know what I did?"

"Um, no Your Honour."

"I set up a little program! To send my application at one second past noon. And within minutes back came the answer that I'd got a tee. How splendid is that?"

Adam shifted his weight and tried to put on an expression of polite interest, although with limited success. "Wonderful, Your Honour."

SIMON HALL

The judge discarded his wig and threw it onto a chair. He leaned forwards and gazed at the silver balls, busily swinging back and forth.

Click clack, click clack…

Dan realised it was the first time he had seen Templar without a wig. The judge was in his late fifties, maybe sixty at most, with tightly cropped, silver hair and a keen shrewdness in his expression. He had the face of an aged, but still formidable, bird of prey.

"Your Honour," Adam began, but was once more sliced through with all the efficiency of a newly sharpened scythe.

"No, I haven't."

"I'm sorry?"

"I haven't got a blasted alibi. For last night. I take it that's what you want to know?"

"Well, yes."

"I looked up the story. His *Wessex News* website thing." The judge pointed an accusing finger at Dan. "About four o'clock in the a-m, wasn't it? The explosion?"

"Yes."

"I was at home. I think I was online. I don't know for sure. But I don't have an alibi."

"You were awake?"

Templar reached out and stopped the flight of the silver balls. Slowly, with unexpected tenderness, he angled the photograph to face Adam and Dan. It was black and white and showed a couple on their wedding day. The bride had long, light hair and was beaming at the camera. The handsome young groom was the Templar of perhaps thirty-five years ago.

"Eileen, my lady wife," he said quietly. "I lost her last year. Since then, I've been – struggling to sleep. I sometimes pass a few of the long nighttime hours on the computer."

Adam nodded understandingly. His fingers went to his own wedding band and shifted it up and down.

"I'm sorry," he said.

"Everyone is. Everyone's sorry."

192

The judge tapped a hand on the wood of the desk, the reflection of the movement rising to meet it. His gaze was way afar, not for the two visitors, not for this room, not even for this time. The smile was gone, as though it had never existed and could never be resurrected.

"Your Honour," Adam said, after a long pause, "your computer could help us. It will probably retain a record of what you were doing, and at what times. It would help us to eliminate you from the investigation if we might take a look?"

The question didn't register, was a mere whisper against a wall. Whether subconsciously or deliberately Templar began to toy with his own wedding band, eyes following every shift of the dull metal.

"I've never taken it off. I never will, you know." He looked back up. "I see you have a wife, Chief Inspector."

"Yes."

"Make the most of her is my advice. You never know what the world has in wait."

Adam didn't reply. Templar studied him and waved an irritable hand of acquiescence.

"I should make you apply for a warrant," he announced, as though addressing a courtroom. "But as I'd probably have to sign the bloody thing myself, I might as well save the trouble and say yes. You may examine my computer."

★★★

They emerged from Templar's chambers to a surprise. Jonathan Ivy was sitting directly outside the door.

"Not listening in were you, by any chance?" Adam asked.

"No!" The usher sounded genuinely taken aback. "One of your colleagues has been on the phone and said you wanted to see me."

Adam gave him a cool look but allowed Ivy to lead them down the stairs, along the corridor and to an interview room. Dark portraits of judges past, stalwarts of the local legal system, watched them go. All were men and all were glaring. Even the hint of an accommodating expression was clearly not the done look within the higher ranks of the profession.

The detective had turned off his mobile for the duration of the interview with Templar. As he switched it back on, it bleeped with a series of messages.

All three were from Claire and contained news of useful, and perhaps even important, developments. The flow of the investigation was in their favour.

Two more interviews had been set up, both for this morning. One message confirmed that Jonathan Ivy was at work and would be expecting them as soon as they had finished with Judge Templar. There was also a rapid briefing on the man, impressively thorough and quickly compiled, even by Claire's standards.

The second informed Adam that the foreman of the jury was an Ian Parkinson. He worked for the City Council in the tower block of the Civic Centre, just across the plaza. He was in his office all morning.

The final message was the most interesting. The fire investigator had called and said it was urgent. An important and highly suggestive discovery had been made in the ruins of the Edwards' home. It couldn't be properly explained over the phone and had to be seen.

CHAPTER TWENTY-NINE

The interview room was small and clinical, but full of the ghosts of emotion. It resounded with anger, remorse and fear, all emanating from a couple of rough carvings on the wooden table.

One professed an undying love for Janet. The other had some highly offensive words for the police.

Dan sensed a young man sitting alone, head in hands. A barrister had been here. He'd told the man the weight of evidence meant continued denial would only see him found guilty anyway, and receive an even more severe sentence. He should plead guilty and prepare himself for long years in prison. He'd been permitted ten minutes to consider his predicament.

Similar fates had befallen many in this intense little cube of space, and would find more again in future days.

The room was entirely plain, just the table and four plastic chairs. Ivy explained it was used by lawyers for talking to their clients and so there was little incentive to make it comfortable. At this point he tried a smile but it was unsuccessful and faded as fast as a match struck in a gale.

Ivy was an odd looking man. Dan tried to sum him up and an image arrived in mind that even he thought was unkind, but which nonetheless lingered. The usher had a face like a satellite dish. The complexion was pale and the shape round and cursed with an antenna of a nose.

Unlike his friend Roger Newman, Ivy had kept his hair but it was a sandy shade of nondescript. He was carrying a magazine, *DIY Monthly*, and a copy of the *Daily Mail* folded inside.

"Sometimes we have to wait about for juries and that sort of thing," he said, placing the indispensable contributions to the library of world literature on the table. "I always bring something to read. I imagine it's the same in your job?"

Adam didn't take up the invitation to conversation. Dan had a clear sense he'd taken against the man from the moment they found Ivy lurking outside Templar's chambers. Instead, the detective asked what he was doing at about four o'clock this morning. The predictable answer came back, that the usher was at home.

"Can anyone confirm that?"

"No. I live alone. My wife and I, we – separated a few years ago."

It was more than a few according to Claire's briefing. Twenty would have been the honest answer. There was still loss in his voice, and he hadn't been able to use the word divorce. Jonathan Ivy had spent a long time waiting to move on.

He'd lived a difficult life in several ways. Claire's research found that Ivy had been the victim of a sizeable con. An invitation to make money aplenty on some investments which couldn't possibly lose was offered by a friend of a friend. The trusting Mr Ivy had duly invested and the couple's life savings – several tens of thousands of pounds – disappeared.

Marie Ivy had left home and not returned. The theory was that the marriage had been in difficulties beforehand and the loss was the catalyst for a divorce. Since then, Ivy had worked at a variety of jobs, from sales, to management at a waste disposal company, to local government administration. For the last nine years, he had been an usher at Plymouth Crown Court.

"I enjoy it – most of the time," was his verdict on the position.

"Most?" Dan queried.

"I can make a difference; do something to help the poor victims. And it's always interesting to see the cases played out. Sometimes we even manage to get some justice done."

There was a bitterness in Ivy's words which Adam noted down but didn't comment upon. The detective was looking thoughtful and disinclined to venture another question. He could sometimes be that way, saying he learned more from observing than talking. In which case, Dan was aware of his part and carried on with the interview.

"How do you know Roger Newman? You seem close."

"We grew up together. We got on from the start."

Ivy had a tendency to rub a nervous hand over the furrow of a scar on his forehead. He saw Adam watching and explained, "I got that at school. I was bullied a fair bit, being, well – not the best looking. Some kids threw this rock. It could have killed me. Roger used to look after me, though. They didn't mix it with him."

"He was a tough lad at school?" Dan asked, as neutrally as such an inquiry allowed.

Ivy saw the point of the question and hesitated. "I wouldn't say that. He could just look after himself. He wouldn't have killed those Edwards, however much they might have deserved it."

Adam looked up. "I don't remember anyone saying he did."

"But that's why you're here, isn't it? He's got to be your prime suspect. I'm on the list too, as his friend. And Judge Templar as well, because of what he said in court." Ivy tried another thin smile. "It's the gossip of the building, you coming here to speak to us."

Adam went back to his notes, so Dan resumed the interview. "You think Martha and Brian Edwards deserved to die?"

Ivy rubbed at his scar, before saying defiantly, "Yes, I do. You saw all the anguish they caused. They were going to get away with it. I don't have a particular problem with what happened to them."

"Really, Mr Ivy?" Adam interrupted. "And what about the young woman who was walking past their house when the explosion happened? Because that's the problem with revenge, isn't it? It's never clear cut."

Ivy's face flushed. The moon was turning red. "Oh, let me guess. I suppose you'd say people should leave the law to you and the courts?"

"Yes, I would."

"You didn't do so well with Annette, did you?"

"Look, Ivy—" Adam snapped, but the usher had found a theme and wasn't to be interrupted.

"That's the problem with this place. It's a court of law, not justice. I get sick of seeing victims treated like criminals, while everyone does all they can to look after the offenders. And it's getting worse."

Ivy's rant faded. His chest was heaving. Adam looked back down at his notes and said, with a determined calm, "We were talking about your alibi, Mr Ivy. So – no one can confirm what you were doing in the early hours of this morning?"

"Maybe."

"Meaning?"

"I don't have to tell you."

"That's true," Adam said gently, before delivering the punch. "Just like I don't have to arrest you and let you sit in the cells, but I still might."

The threat prompted a hasty reconsideration of the rebellion. "I was up most of the night, like I usually am. I was online a bit. Sending a few emails. And…"

"Yes?"

"Well…"

"Yes?"

"Watching some porn, if you must know."

Adam's lip curled like an old parchment and the usher added quickly. "It's not illegal. Just some women doing—"

"And it's not what I'm interested in," came the sharp interruption. "You suffer from insomnia?"

"Ever since I was a kid. I've never had a proper night's sleep in my life."

The detective made a clicking noise with his tongue. "What a coincidence. Judge Templar suffers from sleeplessness too."

"So?"

"So – it's interesting, isn't it? That two people, who might just have a motive to murder the Edwards, and who work in the same place, both suffer insomnia?"

Ivy shrugged. "It's more common than you think. I have tried to help His Honour, but it's one of those things you have to face alone. It's a cruel illness."

Adam thanked Ivy and began to get up, but the usher stayed sitting. "Going to see Roger now, are you?"

"That's a matter for us, Mr Ivy. But yes, we will see him in time."

"Let me save you the effort – and him the upset. Don't bother. He didn't kill the Edwards."

"Really? And how would you know that?"

"Because he couldn't. It's just not him. Can I tell you something about the kind of man he is?"

"If it's quick."

"It will be."

Adam stopped in the doorway. "Go on."

"Two weeks before I was due to get married, the hotel rang to say they'd double booked us. They wanted to palm us off on this other place miles down the road. It wasn't anything like as nice. Marie was in tears. I poured it out to Roger, and he just said he would handle it and not to worry. The next thing I know, the hotel are back on the phone, apologising and giving us an even bigger do to make amends."

Adam was edging through the door, but Ivy wouldn't stop. "Roger even offered to bail me out when I got conned. He's a great man. He could never be a killer. Look at all the charity work he does. He's kind, loyal and thoughtful, too. I'd do anything for him."

And now Adam stopped and gave the usher an impenetrable look. "Would you, Mr Ivy? Would you really?"

★★★

They broke up the short walk to the Civic Centre by stopping at the Pepperpot café to get a coffee. Dan sat at a table in the sunshine and checked his watch as Adam waited to be served. The time was just before half past eleven.

"Don't worry," the detective said, without looking round. "We'll still make it to the Edwards' place for lunchtime. I take it you want to do some kind of live broadcast, as well as being in on the fire investigator's briefing?"

Dan had long given up being surprised by his friend's powers of observation. "Yes, please."

The café wasn't busy and the coffees arrived quickly. It was a wise tactical move. They tasted fresh and strong, far better than anything likely to be on offer from the Council. No public sector drink of Dan's experience had ever compared to that produced by free enterprise.

Adam spooned some chocolate froth into his mouth, took a sip and emitted an approving noise. "So, discussion time. What did you make of Templar and Ivy?"

Dan swirled his drink. "That gossip about Templar's eccentricities looks like it's true. He was so up and down with his rants about justice, his misery about his wife and then glee at the bizarre Newton's Cradle thing."

"Agreed. But the chances of him being the killer?"

"He's got the expertise to do it without leaving any clues given all the cases he's presided over, particularly that other gas explosion trial. On the other hand, judges don't often become criminals."

"That's true. But it's interesting both he and Ivy have trouble sleeping."

"That could just be a coincidence."

Adam's face wrinkled at the sound of a trigger word. Many times he had lectured Dan about how detectives tended not to believe in coincidence. It was a favoured theme; that they often pointed the way to successful prosecutions.

"Ivy was obviously bitter about the legal system," Dan went on. "As was Templar to an extent. They've both had years of seeing justice not being done. That could give them motives. There's also Ivy's closeness to Roger – perhaps even devotion might be a better word. Would he kill the Edwards to avenge the death of his best friend's daughter? That might be pushing it a bit, given that he struck me more as a follower than a leader. But whatever, I think he and Templar are both still suspects."

"Agreed. So let's see what we turn up when we look at their computers."

Adam ushered a couple of pigeons from under his feet and headed towards the Civic Centre. As they approached the building, Dan looked up. In one of the many windows of the towering edifice, he was almost sure he saw the bearded face of the foreman of the jury, watching them.

★★★

Reception was staffed by a man and woman who had forgotten how to smile. Dan and Adam politely introduced themselves, were begrudgingly directed to the fifth floor and, with an afterthought, given security passes.

"That should sort out any terrorist threat," Adam commented.

The lift looked like it dated from the early days of coal mining. It grumbled and ground in a far from reassuring manner so they took the stairs. It was one of the mysteries of the man that was Adam Breen that he did so without growing at all out of breath despite the lack of any regular exercise in his life. When once Dan had raised the question, Adam pointed to the management of a teenage son as being sufficient to keep anyone trim.

The door they found was old-fashioned, wooden and plain and decorated only with the name of their suspect. Adam was about to knock when it opened and a hirsute head appeared. They shook hands and were escorted to two spindly wooden chairs.

The office was small, just a desk, an overflowing bookcase and three faded watercolour prints on the walls. A strip light buzzed in the ceiling and continual footsteps echoed from the corridor outside. The Civic Centre had the sense of being built in a hurry and with the cheapest materials available. On the desk was a picture of a middle-aged woman, also wearing glasses, her arm around a younger man whose hair hung down on his shoulders.

"Kate, my wife, and my son Chris," Parkinson explained. "He's backpacking around the world before he goes to university. He's in Thailand at the moment, having great fun according to his emails. I try not to think about it. Kate's on her way out to see him. She left the day before yesterday. I couldn't go, obviously, not with..."

Parkinson was wearing the same suit that he had for every day of the trial. Before Adam could pose a question the former foreman of the jury said forlornly, "I saw it, you know. I saw it all."

He pointed to the window. The view looked out across the plaza and to the multi-storey car park from which Annette had jumped.

Such was the emotion in Parkinson's voice, it was an effort not to try to comfort him. Adam attempted a few, well-worn introductory remarks; that this interview was a matter of routine, nothing to worry about. But they made no headway into easing the man's unhappiness.

"The main point we need answered, Mr Parkinson," said Adam, when he had reached the end of his patience – a process which seldom took long, "Is what you were doing at around four o'clock this morning?"

The question came as a surprise. "What I was doing?"

"What and where, in fact."

"I was in bed, of course. Asleep."

"At home?"

"Err, yes. At home. Where else would I be?"

"Alone?"

"Yes. Alone. As I said, Kate's on her way to visit Chris. Chief Inspector, why do you ask?"

Adam said nothing, just raised his eyebrows knowingly. It was another detective's look.

"Oh!" exclaimed Parkinson faintly, tugging at a sideburn. "It's about that explosion, isn't it? You think I—"

"Not think, Mr Parkinson, but we have to check."

"I – I don't know what to say. Am I a… a…" He found the word difficult and it took time to form. "Am I a suspect?"

"It's purely routine. But you'll appreciate with what you said after you delivered the verdict it suggests you might have a motive."

Parkinson stared out at the courthouse as if it were a mortal enemy, perhaps even Hades itself, situated across the concrete of the plaza rather than the River Styx.

"I didn't want any of this," he lamented. "I've always been just an ordinary man, living an ordinary life. That was the first… well, unusual thing that's ever happened to me. I didn't ask for it and, to be frank, I didn't like it and I didn't want it. The other jurors elected me foreman because – well, because I wore a tie. And my position, too."

He pointed to a nameplate on the desk. It said *Deputy Assistant Director, Parks.* Dan bowed his head to stifle a sudden urge to giggle.

Adam had decided he'd heard enough. He began thanking Parkinson for his time, in a rather abrupt manner.

"Just one further thing," Dan interrupted, before they exited this bastion of supreme executive power. "Did all of the jury think the Edwards were guilty?"

"Oh yes," came the emphatic reply. "That was the view of every one of us. But we also all agreed we didn't have the evidence to convict them."

"So whose idea was the 'Not Proven' verdict?"

For the first time, Parkinson looked less persecuted, and even a little proud. "That was mine. I thought it was a fitting way to get across what we really believed, so that at least a semblance of justice could be done." He nodded hard to underline the point. "I was determined the Edwards should suffer at least some kind of punishment, absolutely set upon it."

CHAPTER THIRTY

Homely Terrace had come to resemble a building site. Tipper lorries rumbled back and forth, laden with dusty rubble, the penetrating beep of their reversing alerts filling the narrow street. A swarm of workmen attacked the pile of debris where the Edwards' home had stood.

The forensic investigations had been concluded and the house was being demolished. It was a merciful end. There was little left to save and the authorities had reached a speedy and sensible decision. Even the faceless planners and their beloved birds' nests of bureaucracy had soon resolved the question – who would want to live in such a notorious place?

It would suffer the same fate as others which had housed murderers or hosted their crimes. A terrace that had stood intact for more than a hundred years would shrink a little, a whispered book of stories rising where the masonry had fallen. It would become one of the tales of the city, another urban memory.

At the back of the ruins, shielded as best they could from the noise, stood Adam, Claire, Katrina, Dan and the fire investigator. The message that he had some important findings to pass on proved accurate in all but one respect. The assumption of a junior detective that the person known as Indy was a man.

"Stephanie Sarnden," she introduced herself. "Or Indy, as most people call me."

No one else was going to ask, but curiosity was a vice Dan could rarely resist. "Because Indiana is where you born?"

"Go back a bit further. Nine months in fact, and the parents' honeymoon."

Dan had come to notice a common feature of women in the enduringly male-dominated emergency services: they could often become more laddish than the lads. It was something from which

Claire never suffered. That, he had once proudly thought to himself, was a credit to the strength of her character.

Less happily, such fortitude was currently exhibiting itself in Claire positioning herself as far from him as possible, and continuing to treat Dan as a mere disturbance of the air. She hadn't once looked over despite his attempts to offer a winning smile.

The day was growing warmer, the sun rising to its zenith in the sky. Indy unbunched her strawy hair, shook it down and took off her jacket to reveal a fine figure. She was in her mid-thirties, with a cute, freckled face and full lips, a combination which was only highlighted by the fine powder of the dust streaking her face.

Naturally, Claire chose that moment to finally look at Dan. He, in turn decided a deep study of the remains of the house would be more appropriate than any surveying of the charms of Indy. As he looked away he noticed Katrina had been watching him too.

Sometimes in life, all you can do is sigh.

"Let me get your theory straight," Indy said, when she'd mopped the residue of the building site from her face. "Someone breaks in, turns on the gas cooker, gets back out, waits and then sets off a car alarm. One of the Edwards switches on a light to see what's going on and ignites their own funeral pyre."

"That's our best guess," Adam replied.

"It's plausible. But if it's right, your killer's been even more methodical than you suspected."

She delved into the depths of a sizeable black plastic tool box and held out an evidence bag. Inside were the remains of an old fashioned light bulb, the kind beloved of the British until the European Union intervened. The glass was cracked and a patch of the protective sphere missing.

"So?" Katrina said. "It probably got smashed in the explosion?"

"I don't think so. The damage would be far worse. This is too precise. I reckon your killer did their research. This is the light from the hallway, outside the Edwards' bedrooms."

Adam's brow grew as furrowed as a farmer's field. He was an appreciator of science in that it could tell him who had committed a crime, but a long way from being a comprehender. "Which tells us what?"

"The person you're hunting knew about gas explosions. They wanted to maximise the chances of it all going off in a big blast. So they tampered with the bulb by chipping away some of the glass. The exposed filament would arc briefly at a very high temperature – more than enough to ignite the gas and cause a hell of a bang."

"It looks like your theory is holding up," Adam said to Dan, a little begrudgingly.

"And there's something else to back it up," Indy added.

Like a magician with a top hat, she reached once more into the box, but this time produced a sheaf of papers. It was a manual on fire investigation and the properties of natural gas.

For an explosion, there had to be a specific amount of gas in the atmosphere of a house. Between about five and fifteen per cent, according to the scientific papers which Indy brandished. Below five and there was insufficient gas, above and there wasn't enough oxygen for detonation. She also cited some research on how fast gas can spread around a house, depending upon its age, ventilation, the number of open doors and the source of the gas.

"And that's easily accessible information?" Claire asked.

"The research is all online."

And now, amidst the noise of the lorries, the shifting of rubble, the beat of a radio and the shouts of the workmen, in this little group of five there was only silence. All eyes were turned inwards, and all were seeing the same images.

The killer's rage as the Edwards were acquitted. The growing fury at Annette's death. The resolution upon vengeance.

A quick reconnaissance of the Edwards' house. Some calculations. A wait until the early hours. Breaking in to the house and setting the gas running. Checking the level of ventilation. Perhaps opening a door or two to increase it. Cracking the light bulb, just to be sure. Slipping back out, waiting, setting off the car alarm.

And then hearing the blast a couple of minutes later as the new-found murderer headed for home.

★★★

It was only the arrival of a waving, shouting Nigel that reminded Dan of his day job. The time was half past twelve and the lunchtime news on air in an hour. He received a hasty set of instructions from Adam about what could be broadcast and jogged over to the satellite van.

The report was easy to cut, as was often the way with the strongest of stories. Dan used the pictures they had filmed in the darkness of the early hours to talk about what happened. He included snatches of interviews with people in the street describing the power of the blast. There was also a clip of Adam, being as diplomatic as ever, saying a revenge attack was one of the police's foremost lines of inquiry.

The time sped on to ten past one. Dan stepped down from the van, straight into Indy.

"Do you mind if I have a quick look?" she asked. "I find TV fascinating."

"Really?" He replied, unsurprised to suddenly be sporting his best smile. "I usually find it baffling."

Loud was busy laying down the last pictures, so Nigel gave her a quick tour. It was too complex for Dan, with its oscilloscopes, satellite frequency locator and the rest of the equipment. It might as well have been science fiction, but she nodded knowledgably.

The lecture was in its final stages when a fizzing, rushing pop from the top of the van interrupted. The antenna on the satellite dish was ablaze, a run of flames dancing an orange path.

"Fire in the hold!" Loud yelled. He grabbed an extinguisher, unleashed a cloud of white powder and the flames died.

"What was it?" Dan asked.

"Waveguide," the engineer muttered. "It's shorted out. Bloody cheap rubbish."

"What does it do?"

"What do you think? It guides the waves, dum dum. The poor electromagnetic ones that have to carry your ugly mug up to the satellite."

"Can you fix it? Are we going to be ok for the broadcast?"

"No chance."

Dan vented a few creative profanities. They were the lead story, and an important one at that. Fail to appear and Lizzie would undergo spontaneous human combustion.

"How long to the studios from here?" Dan asked Nigel.

"Seven or eight minutes."

"And the report's cut?"

"Yeah," grunted Loud. "It's just not going anywhere."

"There's just time. Set up the camera."

Without hesitation Nigel did, looking back on the rubble of the house. Dan took his position and tried to fix a few words in his head.

"Recording," Nigel said.

"This lunchtime, the police have named the woman who was injured when she was caught in the explosion. She's Amy Ailing, who's 19 and from Plymouth. She's in hospital. Her parents are at her bedside. Dan Groves, *Wessex Tonight*, Plymouth."

Loud held out the memory card that contained the story. Nigel grabbed it, jumped into his car and headed off.

"He should get to the studios by 1.25," Dan said to himself. "Take five minutes to add that piece to camera to the end and it'll still make the lead story – hopefully."

He leaned back against the van, took a deep breath and stared up at the calming expanse of blue sky.

"Bloody hell," Indy commented. "Is it always like this?"

"No," Dan replied, with feeling. "This is one of the more straightforward days."

★★★

It was a lesson hard learnt. Investigations were not all as authors would have them; not endless action, excitement and a glamorous tearing around in pursuit of suspects. There could be periods that Dan had come to think of as *treading water*. And this afternoon, however irritating, was fated to be one.

"Just wait, will you?" Adam snapped in reply to Dan's petulant question about what was going to happen next.

"I don't like waiting."

"Funnily enough I'd noticed that, what with being a detective and all. But on this occasion you'll have to."

They were still at Homely Terrace, but had retreated to an incident control van at the end of the street. It was the only way to escape the noise and dust. With all the radio and CCTV equipment, it was a dark and cramped space. Blessed as he was with impressive stature, Adam was forced to adopt a permanent stoop.

Claire had returned to Charles Cross to coordinate inquiries and Indy had left for her next assignment, a suspicious fire in a cottage on the beautiful Roseland peninsula in Cornwall. No one was hurt, but the fine old building had been destroyed. Young arsonists were suspected.

Here, the afternoon would be taken up with the dull routine of checks. The Eggheads were currently working on Templar's computer, and would also examine Ivy's, to see if the men's internet activities could provide them with alibis.

Templar was already looking less of a suspect. He'd made a phone call to his bank around the time of the explosion, it being one of the 24 hour variety. The exact details were still being verified as the bank would take a couple of hours to retrieve the recording from its data storage system.

Katrina's investigations revealed that Roger Newman was certainly at home for some of last night. Several witnesses had seen him in the local pub where he sat alone, drank a succession of strong beers, picked at a meal and spurned any offers of company. He was also seen returning to his house. A kindly neighbour had kept an eye on him, but that only accounted for his time until around half past eleven.

After that, Newman said he simply stayed in. He tried to sleep, but couldn't. He sat up, watching a film, but couldn't follow it.

He tried to read, but couldn't concentrate. Eventually, he sought comfort in the whisky bottle and, by his account, became more and more drunk.

Newman had no recollection of time, but insisted he hadn't left his house. As to an alibi, he claimed that at several points he became so distraught that he sobbed, shouted and screamed and even threw pots and pans at the walls.

Detectives had been sent to talk to Newman's neighbours, to ask if they had heard a disturbance. The findings would be known later this afternoon, as would the results of the Eggheads' work. But for now, the only option was waiting.

"I do have an idea," Dan said airily, and explained.

"And it's nothing to do with making a good story?" Adam asked, wryly.

"It could help the inquiry," Dan replied, as neutrally as possible.

"I'll see how things go with some straightforward investigating before we resort to the shadowlands of your devious imagination."

A phone call from the Deputy Chief Constable hadn't helped in improving Adam's fractious mood. There was the usual helpful pointing out that the case was a very high profile one. The eyes of the world were, apparently, set upon Greater Wessex Police, waiting for the perpetrator to be revealed.

This particular missive from on high, familiar as much of it was, contained a surprise. A film company had been in contact. They wanted to begin work on an epic, designed to capture the *natural drama and pathos* of the story of the Edwards and the Newmans. Some well-known actors had already been lined up to play the parts in what was being billed as "a tearful tragedy – a Shakespearean story of modern times."

For senior officers, concerned with the standing of Greater Wessex Police, only one ending was acceptable. The heroic cops must arrest the villain and the forces of justice emerge triumphant. It would duly be appreciated if Adam could get a move on and clear up the case as soon as possible. All of which left the detective with a throbbing neck and a disgruntled scowl.

"We might have to try your idea, after all," he told Dan, tetchily.

The time was coming up to two o'clock. An updating of the story for tonight was required, but that would only mean an amendment to the end of the report and was half an hour's work. The satellite van and its mischievous waveguide would take a day to repair, sparing Dan a live broadcast.

The tiredness was gaining, casting the sloth of its net. Dan yawned hard and an idea began to whisper slyly in his mind.

The lunchtime report had made the lead story, albeit by the breadth of seconds. Lizzie was sated, for now at least. A couple of disappearing hours in the comfort of the flat would be a fine respite from the cares of the world. The beautiful songbird of a little sleep was singing its beguiling melody.

Dan was about to bid his goodbyes to Adam and Katrina when she sprung the surprise.

She had, Dan suspected, been waiting for the moment. Even when she'd finished recounting Roger Newman's alibi, Katrina looked as though she had something more to say. It was in those extraordinary eyes. But to conclude her story then might have been too straightforward for such an enigmatic woman. Now, even the noise of the building site abated for her words.

"You remember that strange *PP* on Annette's ransom note? I think I might have finally found out what it meant."

CHAPTER THIRTY-ONE

Sometimes, an enchanting idea can start to feel so real it could take on a physical form. As though it holds out its hands and draws you into a loving embrace.

And so it was with Dan's plan to enjoy a sun-blessed siesta this afternoon. He'd driven back to Hartley Avenue and was reaching wearily for the sanctum of the door. He could hear Rutherford and that low whine of delight it was the dog's habit to emit upon sensing the arrival of his master.

The tiredness was a heavy suit now and there would be little hope of a respite this evening. Adam was determined to work until significant progress was made in the case.

An hour and a half's snoozing should just about restore enough energy to see Dan through. In his mind he was already stripping off his shirt, ready to lower himself into the warm bath of beautiful sleep.

Instead of which, with shameless inconsideration, Dan's mobile rang. It was Adam, destroying the dream like a bully snatching away a bag of sweets. He was in urgent form, and the vision of a sleepy break was ruthlessly shredded.

"The Ailings – they'll do it. Can you get up to the hospital?"

To some questions you know the answer even before you ask, and no matter how much you might dread the reply.

"Right now?" Dan asked, forlornly.

"Right now. And can you get it on tonight's news?"

Dan checked his watch. It was only mid-afternoon. There was no space for excuses.

"Yep."

"I'll make the arrangements then. For – what we discussed."

"Ok."

"Before you go, there's one other thing. The Ailings are a little nervy, so I said I'd send someone to look after them. Claire's on her way. She'll be waiting for you at the hospital."

★★★

Dan Groves had once considered himself a brave man, but the way life ran in earlier years had exhausted his reserves of valour. And so, on this particular occasion, he had no hesitation in choosing the coward's way.

Dan called Nigel and asked if the cameraman would pick him up. "It gives us a chance to work out how to do the interview," he explained, trying to pretend the rationale was purely professional. "It's going to be an emotional one."

Nigel was as accommodating as ever, and promised to be at the flat in fifteen minutes. Dan used the time to give Rutherford a cuddle, which the dog quite likely appreciated, and a quick run around the garden, which he probably preferred. The sight of the stupid canine careering around, snapping at the odd phantom in the air, was almost as good a tonic as sleep.

"It makes perfect sense, Nigel and I going together," Dan told Rutherford, as they walked back up the steps to the flat. "I want no suggestion that being with him will mean Claire doesn't have a chance to get me alone."

As Nigel drove the ten-minute trip to the northern edge of the city, they discussed the interview. Experience had equipped them with a way of working in the most sensitive cases. Dan would chat to the Ailings to try to build up a rapport. As invisibly as possible Nigel would set up the camera, microphone and lights.

As was his way, Nigel spent a few minutes in empathy, rueing what a dreadful time the Ailings were going through and then slipped into a silence to prepare himself.

The landmarks passed. The battlements of the old Crownhill fort, built to defend Plymouth from Napoleonic attack, the modern day business parks, the glass ship of the Western Morning News building.

On the horizon ahead, Dartmoor glowered, the natural boundary for the ever-sprawling city.

The parking at Tamarside Hospital could be an added ordeal for a visitor. But on this day they were lucky, turning into the car park as a young couple with a baby were reversing out.

Even through the sunshine and mass of hurrying humanity, Dan could make out the figure of Claire, standing at the main entrance, arms folded and waiting.

★★★

Nigel was greeted with a fond kiss and a long hug. He and Claire had always got on, united as they were in being that curious breed of the optimist. Dan was permitted only a fleeting peck on the cheek. It was an experience as transient, ephemeral and lacking in warmth as an English summer.

Claire led them along a series of corridors. The off-white tiles reflected their rapid footfall. The smell of antiseptic lingered everywhere. Most faces they passed were set, a few in tears. There was little room for smiles in a hospital.

A couple of trolleys rattled by, each carrying a comatose figure, gangs of nurses marching alongside. A woman stood, staring out of a window, her hand in a young boy's.

Claire stopped by a door and clicked it open. "I just need you to sign a disclaimer," she told Dan.

He nodded resignedly and stepped into the room. And Claire was in his face, right in it, wincingly close.

"Have you been seeing Katrina?"

"What?"

"Have you been seeing her?"

There was no choice but to hold Claire's look, with her eyes so close and so very bright, but it wasn't easy.

"Hang on, what is this?"

"Answer the question."

"I've been working with her, if that's what you mean."

She snorted, the sound bitter with disbelief. "Why did you text her yesterday?"

"Because – well, it's just that I knew she was close to Annette. That's all it was, and—"

"Was I second best?"

"What?"

"The back up? The reserve?"

"What?"

"Was I your fall back?"

"No!"

"You couldn't get her, so you called me?"

"No! Claire, you'd never be—"

A finger was up at eye level, very large, very close and remarkably unwavering. Dan tried to back off, but the room was small, the wall unyielding and he was trapped by the onslaught of feeling.

"I've had enough messing about. I'm not waiting for you any more. You're pathetic. You stick your head up your backside and won't pull it out. You seem to think you're the only one in the world with problems. You and your murky little pond of self-pity. You'd better snap out of it and get yourself sorted."

For once, Dan found himself struggling for words. "Well, thanks for the lovely, relaxing build-up to an important interview—" he managed, but was instantly overridden.

"Don't give me that crap. It's time someone told you the truth and I'm damn well going to do it. Get yourself together. And now you can go and do this interview and do it bloody well."

Dan tried desperately to find some rejoinder but he was mouthing helplessly at Claire's back. The door was open and she was striding out.

"Disclaimer all sorted then, is it?" Nigel asked, with a hint of a smile.

***

Ronald and Elizabeth Ailing were sitting quietly together, holding hands. Dan had seen it so many times, but the cold squeeze on the heart never lessened.

Good people, singled out by a sole second of malevolent fate. Picked for no better reason than that they had lived decent lives, tried to make their way and bring up a family. And yet still be made to suffer an incomprehensible wrong that they had never deserved. While on the other side of life's street strolled a grinning procession of the wasters and the worthless, forever untouched by ill-fortune.

The couple rose in time and shook hands. Claire carried out the introductions and Dan went through the familiar words which never helped. He was sorry for their pain and distress. He would do his very best not to add to it. He hoped their courage in speaking out may be of some comfort and help their cause.

And through all of this was the unspoken understanding. On the floor below this sterile waiting room, lying on a bed in the Intensive Care Unit, her body bound and pierced by tubes, was Amy.

The Ailings were in their mid-forties, both softly spoken and earnest. Elizabeth's face was drawn and tired, Ron's ruddy with an anger which was beyond his wife. Often that was the way with couples, the women collapsing inside themselves with grief, the men looking to hit out at its cause.

Nigel adjusted the camera while Dan chatted; about the weather, what a fine hospital Tamarside was, the dedication and talents of the nurses and doctors, and gradually onto the more dangerous ground. How Amy was, and how they were coping.

"Do you have a picture?" he asked. "It would help me to get a sense of her."

Ron opened his wallet to show off a photograph. "It was taken on her eighteenth birthday. It's my favourite."

Amy stood, a couple of colourful streamers draped over her shoulders, her arms laced around her parents, smiling at the camera. It was an open and genuine expression, something few could manage when asked to pose. She had long, dark hair and a pretty, warm face, with the hint of mischief in the corners of her mouth.

"She's a beautiful girl."

"Yes," Elizabeth replied, because nothing else needed to be said.

"She looks like you."

"When I was younger, maybe."

Dan matched the sadness of her smile. "I know it's a lot to ask, but – could we film the photo? It would help the viewers get a sense of Amy."

The couple exchanged a look and Ron held out his wallet. Nigel adjusted a light and took a couple of minutes to capture the image.

"We're going to run this interview after my report," Dan said. "We'll have about two minutes, which may not sound long but is quite a while in TV terms. Are you ready to give it a try?"

They both nodded, but didn't speak. Below the camera's shot the squeezing of the Ailing's interlaced hands had become a grip.

"I know it's difficult," Dan said, "But could you tell me what you went through when you heard what happened to Amy?"

And then a pause, as ever in these interviews. Because it was so very hard to find mere sounds and syllables to describe such shock and suffering.

"First, it's like – just numbness, disbelief," Ron began. "You can't understand, you can't comprehend anything like this could happen. Then it's fear – you're overtaken with it. The police were marvellous. They rushed us up to the hospital. But for the whole of the trip – it was only short, but it felt like ages – we were dreading what we were going to find. We were expecting to get here, and be told that Amy was… well, you know."

Dan nodded. He knew, the Ailings knew, the viewers would know. A doctor with a practised look, a kindly hand leading them to a private room and the dreaded, final words.

"Moving on, and most importantly," Dan asked gently, "How is Amy now?"

"She's getting better, thankfully," Ron replied. "Bless her, she's a fighter. She's off the critical list and she's stable. The doctors say they expect her to recover. It'll take a while, but we don't care. We'll be there, however long it takes."

Understanding and encouraging, Dan smiled. "Mrs Ailing, if I can ask you…" He waited, to allow Nigel time to pan the shot onto her. "What kind of a woman is Amy?"

She swallowed hard. "Amy's lovely. She's a little quiet and shy, but she's so kind and gentle. She was delighted to get the baker's job. She was loving it. And then – well, what happened with the explosion… we couldn't believe it. It just seems so… terribly wrong. We thought – why us? Why our family? What have we done to deserve this?"

And, as ever, there never was, and never could be any answer. Not in this little hospital room, not outside, not anywhere at any time. Here was the age-old saying that *life's unfair* encapsulated in the anguish of one small family.

Dan let a couple of seconds slip past. Calm and measured was the only way here, and another difficult question had to be asked. "You know the police believe the explosion was probably a revenge attack. What do you think of that?"

The couple's grip grew tighter. Yvonne looked to Ron. He studied the floor, took time to find the words.

"I can understand someone wanting revenge for what the Edwards did. But that's the problem with revenge. It's never so simple. Someone else always gets hurt – and it always seems to be someone innocent."

★★★

They walked in silence back to the hospital's main entrance. Nigel received another hug from Claire, and Dan the penance of another cheek peck. But this time he got a meaningful look, too.

Before Dan could head for the car, Claire reached out and asked him to wait. He steeled himself, expecting another fusillade, but was spared.

"I've got a message from Mr Breen," she said. "He needs to know for certain whether that interview is going to be broadcast tonight?"

"Very much so. It'll be the lead story. Very high profile."

"In which case, he says the operation is ready to go." Claire paused, looked him over. "So come on then – what are you up to?"

CHAPTER THIRTY-TWO

Dan found himself a nook at the back of the MIR, and was doing his best to shrink into it. Never had he felt at ease here, the very nexus of an investigation, despite Adam's assurances. But this evening the issue was more one of embarrassment.

Television has come to take on a strange role in modern Britain. For a country with a decline in faith, Dan often saw it as a replacement God. In the celebrity stakes he counted himself not even an aspiring Z list, just a humble reporter on a small, regional television station. But even then, sometimes those he met would stare and point.

One man had approached in the street, mouth agape, and stammered, "It's you, isn't it?" – as if Dan were the ghost of Elvis. A woman had once stopped him in the supermarket, peered into his trolley and gasped, "So that's what you eat!"

Of such embarrassments he was reminded now. A television had been set up in the corner of the MIR and Adam, Katrina, Claire and Zac were gathered around.

"Are you not coming to join us?" Adam asked over his shoulder.

"No thanks. You enjoy it."

The *Wessex Tonight* theme music boomed out and the titles began to play. As with many of the strange species known as news editors, the headlines were a compulsion amongst obsessions for Lizzie. She described them as the programme's shop window and insisted the most careful thought was given to selecting the best material. Tonight, after a couple of shots of the fire blazing in the Edwards' ruined house, came a long clip of Yvonne Ailing. In a faltering voice, she asked the world why it should be her family who suffered.

Adam tapped the table in appreciation. Dan remained steadfastly in his corner. Craig, the presenter, read the introduction to the story and it rolled. Dan tried to watch the passing world, down below, in the city centre, but the Ailings' words kept intruding.

"That was very powerful," Katrina observed when the sequence had finished.

Claire said, "Yes, it was impressive," and added pointedly, "I thought between us, that *we* handled them well when we were at the hospital together."

Zac just nodded, his waved hair bouncing with the movement, while the ever-practical Adam concluded, "So let's see what happens."

He picked up a radio. "Base to the Eyes, report in please."

And one by one, the surveillance teams which had been assigned to watch Templar, Newman, Ivy and Parkinson confirmed they were focused upon their subjects.

★★★

"Right," Adam said, brusquely, "while we wait to see the suspects' reaction to our little prompt, let's start thinking. First, Katrina – your theory about that last mystery of the kidnapping."

From her bag, she produced an envelope and unfolded a letter. There were two typewritten sheets. The paper was faded and gave off a musty smell. It was dated fifteen years ago.

Dear Mr Newman,

Hello! I know you're busy and I'm sorry to trouble you, but I'm writing to apply for one of your bursaries. There was something I had to tell you in person, something I couldn't put on the form. I know you have many requests for help, but I believe mine is different.

Like you, I grew up on the Eddystone Estate, with the ambition to make my way out, just as you did. I have researched your life and find it inspirational. I admire the business you have created and all your charitable work. I would love to have the opportunity to follow in your footsteps.

I suspect you hear similar words all the time. So let me confide something which may surprise you.

I am seriously ill, and through no fault of my own. I was born with a blood disease, which the doctors thought they could cure. But they made it worse, by infecting me with hepatitis. When I ask how long I have to live, they don't answer.

But, like you, I have resolved to overcome my problems and do the best I can with my life. I hope to go to university and study for a career. My family is not well off and a bursary would make that possible.

I tell very few people about my illness. It's difficult for me, as I know you'll appreciate. I have only mentioned it here so you can understand my needs, and my hopes.

I thank you for your time and look forward to hearing from you.

The signature was faded and near illegible. But no one reading was in any doubt who had written the letter.

"The reply is attached," Katrina said quietly, holding out another sheet.

Dear Ms Edwards,

Thank you for your letter. I regret to inform you this year's bursaries have been allocated, and, given the difficult state of the economy, there are, as yet, no plans to provide more for the coming years.

I'm sorry if this is a disappointment, but let me take this opportunity to wish you all the best for the future.

Yours truly,

pp
Roger Newman

★★★

Katrina had spent the morning with Roger Newman. They talked in his office, during which time a secretary had bustled in with a pile of papers to be signed. They were applications from students for one of the businessman's bursary schemes.

"I haven't got time to deal with them at the moment," Newman said. "Just *pp* them for me, will you?"

"I made an excuse about needing to check his records for the inquiry," Katrina recounted, as she laid down the letters. "He was distracted enough not to spot what I was thinking."

Newman allocated an assistant to help. In a dank and cold storeroom, it had taken a couple of hours to find the letters.

"Martha opened up to him," Claire said, softly. "All those years ago. In return she got a standard letter, which Newman hadn't even taken the time to sign himself."

Katrina angled a foot on one of her heels. The room had begun to feel stuffy. Adam pulled at his tie. Dan pushed open a window.

"What could that have meant at the trial?" he asked. "If we'd known, if the jury had been told… And then – Annette, and all that's happened since…"

A sudden breeze rattled the room. Zac fiddled with a roll of hair. Claire rubbed at her eyes.

It was Adam who broke the silence. "It's no good going back over all that. What's done can't be undone. We need to get working on who killed the Edwards."

★★★

On a table were some bundles of documents. They contained a report on the suspects' alibis. Judging by the methodical detail, the typescript might as well have been replaced by Claire's elegant handwriting.

Timings
The explosion happened at 3.59am, from the evidence of a couple of CCTV cameras. Although none cover Homely Terrace, a couple which monitor the city centre picked up the fireball in the background.

The car alarm was set off at 3.57am. This is the independent evidence of several people in the street who were woken by it.

The lock on the Edwards' back door was a latch and unsophisticated. The house was relatively small. The estimate is for the killer to take no more than five minutes to get inside, set the gas running, crack the light bulb to expose the filament and leave again.

Less straightforward is the question – how long would it take to fill the house with the amount of gas needed to cause an explosion? Given the research available, and the fact that the cooker was the killer's chosen source of gas, the calculation of the fire investigator is approximately 25 minutes.

All the suspects live in and around Plymouth, and no more than ten minutes journey from Homely Terrace. Which means the critical time for the suspects' alibis is between 3.15am and 4.10am.

Next, to the movements of the suspects themselves:

<u>Ian Parkinson</u>
Claims he was in bed, but no one to verify this. Lives in the Lipson area, no more than ten minutes from the Edwards' house by foot, or perhaps five by bicycle. Has no car and says he bikes everywhere – this is verified by colleagues and neighbours.

A tinny voice broke into the room. Claire got to the radio first. "Go ahead."

"How expensive is this operation, ma'am?" the voice asked.

"Damned dear enough," Adam snapped. "What are you talking about man?"

"I've been on more exciting stake outs, sir."

The man was watching Judge Templar. He had sat at a long, wooden table, eating supper, watching *Wessex Tonight*. He showed no reaction throughout and merely carried on with the meal. As soon as the report ended the judge poured a glass of wine, switched off the television and finished his food slowly and thoughtfully.

Now he was washing up in a large kitchen built for entertaining, a cave of a space. The task took only seconds, with just one plate, one knife, one fork and one glass. He returned to the dining room, settled in a chair, selected some music and took out a notepad and pen. Occasionally his face would bunch into a scowl, but sometimes Templar would let out a chuckle and even begin laughing.

"I think I got a glimpse of the title of what he was writing," the man whispered, through the radio.

"Go on," Claire replied.

"These binoculars are pretty good, but if you really want to kit us out for surveillance…"

"Just tell us," Adam ordered, tetchily.

"Sorry sir. I reckon it's called *A Peculiar Justice*."

★★★

Newman

Both neighbours interviewed. One a deep sleeper – heard nothing. Other believes she heard crashing and shouting from Newman's home at about 3.45am (he claims he was drunk, raging and throwing items about). She was, in her words, half asleep and listened for a little longer, but heard nothing else and was quickly sleeping again.

She's about three-quarters sure it was Newman's voice she heard. The timing of 3.45 is certain, as she has an LED alarm clock which is always accurate.

Newman lives on the Barbican, by Sutton Harbour, in the city centre. The walk to Homely Terrace would have been no more than ten minutes, the journey by car barely two or three.

Adam had placed his radio on the table while he read the papers. Now, it squawked again.

"Sir, action," came a woman's voice. "It's Newman. He's being weird."

They bunched around the tiny speaker. First came a hurried report of Newman's reaction to the *Wessex Tonight* story. He sat on a sofa and sipped hard at a hip flask. He said nothing, but flicked a V-sign at the screen when pictures of the Edwards' ruined house were shown. During the interview with the Ailings he shook his head and appeared to groan.

"And now?" Adam prompted.

"He's staring out of the window, towards the sea. He's pressing his palms up against the glass. Now he's pushing his face against it, his cheek, really hard. It's as if he's trying to break through. He's… shit!"

Adam grabbed the radio. "What? What is it?"

"He just span round and kicked a light off a table. Now he's stamping on it. It's one of those multicoloured glass things. He's smashing it into pieces. Now he's slumped back on the sofa, glugging at that flask again. He's just lying there, drinking."

Adam told the officer to keep watching and make sure Newman didn't do "anything silly."

Dan said, "What does that mean? Guilt-ridden anguish for killing the Edwards?"

"Or perhaps just a father's suffering at the loss of his daughter?" Claire added quietly, with a note of admonishment.

Adam picked up another pile of papers. "We'll talk about it in a minute. Let's finish our suspects' alibis first."

CHAPTER THIRTY-THREE

The police station quietened, as it often did at this time of the evening. The day-staff were happily home. The night shift was yet to arrive, ready for the sad policing rituals of dealing with drunken fights, petty criminals and domestic violence.

From the corridor outside came the odd chirpy bid of "goodnight" and the measure of feet, always lighter than in the moments arriving for work.

But the MIR was a bubble, insulated and cocooned. Here, this little group were intent upon the radio which linked them to the surveillance operation going on in four quarters of the city and the bundles of documents outlining the suspects' alibis.

<u>Templar</u>
Checks reveal a nighttime history of internet use and emailing, dating back to shortly after his wife died. Doctors verify insomnia induced by grief is a common complaint.

On the night the Edwards were killed, Templar sent several emails in the early hours. The Eggheads have retrieved copies (enclosed). Of most interest are exchanges with Jonathan Ivy.

<u>Templar, 1.24am</u> – *This Death by Dangerous Driving case next week, I'm thinking of saying a few words of warning to other young motorists. If I talk about "A car being a deadly weapon in the wrong hands, little different from a gun or knife," do you think that would be excessive?*
<u>Ivy, 1.39am</u> – *I think that's absolutely fair. It's a terrible case and will be widely reported. A warning would be appropriate.*

<u>Templar, 1.44am</u> – *And have you made arrangements for the victim's family to be kept segregated from the defendant's? They have an unpleasant reputation.*

Ivy, 1.58am – *There will be a police presence in court to make sure there are no disturbances.*

Templar, 2.07am – *Thank you.*

Both the men's computers reveal they have commonly exchanged nighttime emails in previous months and always relating exclusively to court matters. The pattern is of Templar using Ivy as a sounding board for comments.

Following the above exchange, Templar makes various internet searches for foreign holidays and sends two more emails:

3.20am (to professionalsinlove.com) – *Thank you for the information, but I am not interested in meeting women from Durham and Liverpool. Please confine any further suggestions to the South West England.*

3.39am (to the Ministry of Justice) – *Regarding my recent communication on concerns about defendant transfer times from Exeter Prison to Plymouth Crown Court, may I enquire whether the matter has yet been brought to the attention of the Minister?*

Finally – *At 3.49am*, Templar calls his bank to instruct them to pay a credit card bill and transfer funds between accounts. Records reveal it is commonplace for him to make such calls in the early hours since the death of his wife. To access his accounts, Templar must give a password and personal information. The recording of the call has been checked. It is, with absolute certainty, Templar. The call was made from his home landline.

Templar lives in Turnchapel, on the eastern fringes of Plymouth. Journey time to the Edwards home would be about ten minutes by car, perhaps a little less.

Ivy

Aside from the emails to Templar (documented), his computer reveals a series of internet searches, timed from *2.33am – 3.38am*. They divide into two categories: the hunt for a new car and also a foreign holiday in one of the resorts in southern Spain.

At *3.45am* the internet searches change to pornography. Several sites are viewed. A Personal Identification Number is entered and a members-only *site visited. It specialises in young girls (although all are over the age of 18). A film is watched.*

Ivy lives in Greenbank, an estimated 15 minute walk from Homely Terrace, or perhaps five minutes in a car.

Note – All the suspects' home and mobile phone calls and email accounts have been checked. There is no record of any communications between any of them after Annette died and before the explosion at the Edwards' house.

***

Adam picked up the radio and requested the final reports on the suspects. Demanded might have been a better word. He looked tired and sounded irritable. The pressure of the case was squeezing a temper which was never his strongest asset.

In a snatched moment earlier, Dan had asked the classic question – if his friend was "doing ok?"

"No, I'm bloody not," came the snappy reply. "I've got three corpses so far, one of them an innocent young woman who I couldn't manage to find any justice for."

"You can't blame yourself for Annette's death," Dan attempted to soothe, only to be cut off by Adam's venting.

"That's what I keep telling myself, but I don't believe it. I can still see her face after she hit the concrete. Plus, I've got the High Honchos all over me, demanding a result."

A crackly voice on the radio informed them that Jonathan Ivy had paced back and forth and appeared disturbed as *Wessex Tonight* was broadcast. He watched the interview with the Ailings with a hand over his mouth. When it had concluded, he flopped down in a chair, lay back and closed his eyes. The watchers reported they thought they could see tears on Ivy's face, but couldn't be sure.

Since the broadcast he had made a halfhearted effort to prepare some food, but succeeded only in making a sandwich, most of which he left. Ivy was currently staring forlornly at the television and had been doing so for the best part of an hour.

Ian Parkinson watched the report through the gaps in his fingers, as might a child confronted by a frightening film. When it had concluded, he walked slowly into the kitchen and made himself a cup of herbal tea. Parkinson was talking to himself. The windows were open and the Eyes were close enough to overhear. They believed he kept repeating, "This is all my fault."

He tried to call his wife, but received no reply. Parkinson was now reading a book entitled *The Unseen Life of the Larch*. On a couple of occasions he had switched the television back on and watched a recording of the interview with the Ailings, shaking his head the whole time.

★★★

Katrina pleaded the need for a comfort break, which Adam begrudgingly granted. When riding on the express train of a major investigation this focused detective disliked making stops.

To prepare them for the discussion which lay ahead, Dan slipped to the canteen and bought a round of coffees. They were as grim as ever, but at least harboured hints of a vague coffee smell.

Zac helped carry them back, quiet and diffident as was his manner with everything aside from technology. Upon returning, he asked Adam if he was required any longer. Since the computing part of the discussion was over, Zac duly departed.

"First off, then," Adam said. "What do we make of our suspects' alibis and their reaction to that interview with the Ailings?"

"They were all watching," Dan said. "So we're probably right. It looks like they've concluded my closeness to the inquiry means my reports are a good indicator of how we're getting on."

"But as they were all watching, that doesn't help us narrow down a suspect," Claire observed, deflatingly. "Parkinson has to be a decent bet. He's got no alibi. And watching that interview repeatedly and his talk about it all being his fault is suggestive."

"Or that could just be him thinking his 'Not Proven' verdict began all this," Adam replied.

"And," Dan added, "he just struck me as too much of a mouse to be a killer."

"Mice can do plenty of damage, you know," Claire countered.

"Ok, but he just didn't feel like a killer to me."

Adam picked up a marker pen and clipped a sheet of paper to one of the felt boards. He wrote: *Parkinson – still suspect, although too timid?*

"Right, onto Newman."

"He's less of a suspect, if his alibi holds out," Katrina observed. "It puts him at home when he'd need to be at the Edwards' place."

"But it's not a full alibi," Claire pointed out. "75 per cent at most. That's plenty of room for doubt and he's got to be the one with the strongest motive."

"Agreed," Adam replied, and began writing again.

Newman – semi-alibi, but most vengeful of bunch?

He scribbled the words fast, most unlike his usual neat style. This was no time for tidiness.

"Next then – Templar."

"He looks pretty much out," Dan replied. "His alibi is the strongest of the lot."

"We're assuming he can't have faked that email stuff and the chat with his bank? He knows about computers."

"I don't see how he could," Claire objected. "I listened to the recording of the bank call. It's Templar, there's not a doubt. He chatters away with the assistant about some new golf club he's bought. It sounds like one of those manic moods of his. And the timing is precise."

"Unless," Katrina said gently, "He's involved in a conspiracy with one of the other suspects. Putting them up to the killings, or helping in some way."

The MIR fell quiet as they considered the idea. Another theory, another suspicion had been added to the countless thousands born and raised here. The tatty old room was a nursery of criminal imagination.

"It's possible," Adam said. "But it doesn't look like there were any phone calls between our suspects after Annette killed herself and before the explosion. Plus, experience tells us to go for the simplest explanation first. And that's one person acting alone."

This time, he wrote: *Templar – probably out, but not definitely.*

"And finally, Ivy?"

"He certainly seemed agitated after the broadcast," Dan noted.

"But he's got another strong alibi," Claire said. "Although it's not watertight. Again, he could be part of a conspiracy with one of the others."

"And if I let my perception off the leash, Ivy doesn't feel like the kind of person who might do something alone," Dan mused. "I think he'd need to be led."

"Which brings us back to my point. About starting off simply with just the one killer, before we go complicating things with a conspiracy," Adam said. "So, let's say for him…"

Ivy – less likely, but by no means impossible.

"And where does all that leave us?" the detective concluded, edgily. "No bloody further forward, I'd say."

The time had moved on towards nine o'clock. Dan yawned, as did Katrina, although she had the decency to cover her mouth with an elegant hand. But Adam was in no mood to allow any leeway for such a triviality as fatigue.

"We've come back to the same old problem," he said. "We've got theories, but few facts. And that's how it's going to go on. Unless we start forcing the issue."

"Meaning?" Dan asked.

"Our two best suspects are currently Newman and Parkinson. And of the two, Newman has to be the most likely. So let's stir him up a little."

"In what way?"

"Bring him in and see how he reacts to questioning."

Claire frowned, an expression rarely seen in the serenity of her face. "Sir, are you sure that's wise? He's a grieving father."

"And our prime suspect."

"Yes, but—"

"There's no room for sentiment in a murder inquiry, Claire. You know that."

"Ok, but maybe we should investigate a bit more before we bring Newman in."

The gaunt express train was building momentum and set upon a destination. "The pressure's on for a result. Plus, if he is the killer, who knows what he might do next? We can't wait around."

Adam looked to Dan. He nodded gently knowing the decision had been made. But Katrina stepped forwards until she was alongside Claire.

"Yes?" Adam said.

"I agree with Claire. Newman just doesn't feel the type."

"On what basis?"

"I've got to know him the best of all of us."

"Maybe you've got to know him too well."

A hiss escaped from Katrina's mouth and those eyes darkened. "I'm offering you my professional judgement," she said, coldly.

"And here's mine," Adam replied, with his own frosted steel. "Newman's the most likely killer. And we've got nowhere else to go. So, tomorrow morning we arrest him on suspicion of double murder."

CHAPTER THIRTY-FOUR

There is an odd divergence of views amongst senior detectives at the point of an arrest. Some eschew it, almost as if the actual detaining of a suspect is somehow tawdry. Others relish the experience and insist upon being there.

Adam was of the latter breed. One of his pet sayings has it that an arrest is a senior officer's prerogative. Not only did he like to be present, he would carry it out himself. It was possible, in Dan's view, that Adam took some vengeful, judicial pleasure in informing a suspect about what was happening and reciting the ritual words of the caution.

The detective's defence was that the instant of arrest could be a powerful indicator of guilt. Just the slightest of reactions, the flicker of an eye or the quiver of a mouth, might give them away.

Katrina excused herself from the arrest. She had seen Newman suffer enough she said, in a cutting voice, and turned and left the room without a backward glance.

And so it was that Adam led the way, followed by Claire and Dan. He always found an arrest highly unnerving, a potent harbinger of many years in prison, and so tended to lurk in the background.

It was just past nine o'clock on another bright September day. Newman was back at work, saying he preferred to try to take his mind off all that had happened. He was in Roger's Rugs city centre store, just off Royal Parade.

It was by no means the biggest of the empire, but important as it always took stock of the latest deliveries and attracted a large amount of footfall. He would usually start the day there, as it was closest to home and gave him a chance to decide what new offerings should be displayed.

The store boasted a long window, which was dominated by the latest whirlpool bath. A necessary luxury to ease the chills of the coming winter and all at an affordable price, the marketing claimed. A choice of matching showers, sinks and toilets surrounded it, accompanied by mats and rugs of the highest orders of fashion. The shop faced directly into the rising sun, a series of replica orbs blazing from the plates of polished glass.

Newman was at the counter, talking to a woman who was checking through an inventory. When he saw them walk in, he froze. His eyes flicked to his side and the darkness of a store room. Adam spotted it, increased his pace and closed the distance between them rapidly.

The businessman was trapped and he knew it. But he stood his ground, ready for the fight. There was a sense about Newman of someone who had little left to lose. And such people were always the most dangerous.

"I didn't do it," he said.

"Didn't do what?" Adam replied.

"Kill the Edwards."

"I never said you did."

"But that's why you're here – isn't it?"

Adam didn't answer, instead said, "You'll appreciate there are some questions we have to ask."

Newman shrugged. The gesture was somehow aggressive rather than uncaring. It was loaded with menace, a hurt that would never end.

"Go ahead. It's not as though I've got a family any more. It'll be a change to have someone to talk to."

He was wearing another dark suit but no tie. He hadn't shaved well, patches of bristles picked out in the glare of the sunlight. Newman was sweating too, a gathering moisture growing on the pale skin of his crown. He looked tired and drawn, and a faint smell of the sweetness of whisky tinted the air around him.

Newman leaned back on the counter, produced a hip flask and took a long swig. "Don't say a word," he muttered, in response to Adam's look.

"I appreciate it's been a difficult time," the detective replied, but without sympathy.

And now, with only the slightest of pressure, the eggshell of control cracked. The toxic bitterness was running free.

"Do you?" He snarled. "You've had a daughter kill herself before your eyes, have you? You've seen the people who wrecked your life walk free and crow about it? And then you've had the police come to call you a murderer?"

"Calm down, Mr Newman," Adam said, heavily. "No one's accusing—"

"Bollocks, Breen. It's written all over your damned faces. I didn't kill the bastards. But I'll tell you this – if you do find out who did it, let me know because I'd like to shake their hands. And if you think it's me, you're going to waste your time here and that means the real killer gets away with it, that's just fine."

Newman took another swig from the flask and set it down on the counter. The woman reached out a hand to his shoulder, but he pushed it away and stood glaring at Adam. He was swollen with his suffering, and there was so much of it, filling body and mind.

"Come on then."

"I'm sorry?" Adam replied.

"Arrest me. Come on – do it."

"Mr Newman—"

"Come on, be a man. Do it. And I tell you what—"

"Now, look—"

But Newman wasn't to be interrupted. There was something else he had to say, and he was going to say it. "I hope you have as much success getting me as you did the bloody Edwards."

The arrow of the goad hit the very heart of the target. Adam visibly stiffened at the impact on his professionalism and pride. And all restraint was shed. "Roger Newman, I'm arresting you on suspicion of the murder of Martha and Brian Edwards," he intoned. "You do not—"

He got no further. Newman's voice was a shout, a screech and a scream, all in concerto.

"Fuck you!"

He swung a fist, propelled towards Adam's head. But the detective had faced these moments too many times to be caught so easily.

He stepped inside the blow, grabbed Newman's arm and pushed him against the counter. Claire lunged forward and reached for Newman's free arm.

But they were fighting a storm. Newman was a man possessed with an inhuman strength. The pumping power of repressed rage was running through him. The unleashed anger was filling his muscles and veins with an infinite energy. Even with Adam clinging to one arm and Claire the other, he was still moving, shaking them off. With one great heave he broke free, sending them both stumbling backwards.

Newman let out an anguished yell, vaulted over the counter and disappeared into the storeroom, slamming the door in his wake.

★★★

Dan went to pick Claire up from a pile of carpet tiles, but she pushed him angrily away. Adam was hammering at the storeroom door. It was solid, unmoving, locked fast.

"Where does it go?" he barked at the woman behind the counter.

"Stuff you," she said, defiantly.

Adam turned, headed for the front of the shop. He lurched into the street, scanned left and right. Around a corner, fifty metres ahead, Newman appeared. He was running hard.

"Come on, after him!"

The city was quiet, only a few early morning shoppers walking the pavements at a leisurely pace. They turned to stare at the strange procession chasing past. Newman jumped over a barrier and turned another corner, into Royal Parade.

"Claire, get some back up here," Adam panted.

They were running fast, but not closing the gap. Newman was still well ahead, his long legs and fervour giving him the advantage. He passed a grocer's, a restaurant, a baker's, the people in the windows all watching.

He swerved and clipped a man carrying a couple of bags. Apples and oranges rolled across the pavement. Newman didn't break stride, just kept running. Dan danced his way through the strewn fruit. He was sweating in the heat.

"Where the hell's he going?" Adam gasped.

A lorry had pulled up on the kerb, the driver carrying a pile of boxes into a newsagent's. Newman dodged around him and careered across the road. A car jarred to a halt, its horn blaring. Adam didn't hesitate and ran across the road too.

They were on the plaza between the courts and Civic Centre, heading towards the Hoe. The sun made a silhouette of Newman's fleeing figure. It was quieter here away from the traffic, the sound of their sprinting shoes echoing around the square.

"Roger, stop!" Adam yelled. "Stop!"

But Newman was insensible and kept running. He weaved through a couple of benches and past one of the ornamental ponds. Crows took to the air to escape the cascading insanity. He was heading towards the theatre.

"Oh no," Dan panted. "No, no, no. Not again."

"What?" Adam barked.

Newman ducked under the low boughs of a tree and disappeared through the door into the multi-storey car park.

"Shit," Adam groaned. "Claire, get onto the fire brigade. And make it quick – damned quick. Dan, with me."

"But I don't want to see another—"

"Don't argue. He liked you. We might need that."

They pushed through the swinging wooden door, into the stairwell. It was dark after the brightness of the open air and smelt dank. They could hear Newman running up the stairs, all footfall and panting.

Adam began following, but a little slower now. They passed a woman holding the hand of a young child. Both eyed them nervously. The detective wielded his warrant card and apologised.

Newman was still moving. The shadow of his figure flitted on the dirty white walls. They reached level four, then five. At the top of the stairs they heard a door open and slam shut again, a sharp boom of a sound.

"Shit," Adam groaned. "He's on the roof."

They jogged up the last two flights. At the doors Adam hesitated, reached out an arm and made Dan wait.

"Let me go first. Just in case."

It was a suggestion Dan was never going to dispute. He hastily took a couple of steps backwards. Adam gave him an exasperated look but crouched, ready to fight, and pushed at the doors.

There was no reaction, no screaming assault, no hurtling attack. Nothing. He stepped out into the brightness.

Ahead was Newman, walking slowly to the far corner of the car park. It was the one where Annette had jumped to her death.

***

Pace by measured pace, they followed. The roof was deserted, too high yet for the onrush of the day's shoppers. It was just a concrete plain suspended in the sky, bounded by a low wall.

Newman was still walking. He hadn't once looked back. His steps were automatic, as though he were in the tunnel of a trance and could see only the destination of that far corner. Overhead, birds soared in blue freedom.

The end of the car park had become a shrine. It was piled with bunches of flowers, thoughts and gifts in Annette's memory. Some had notes attached, words of rue for a life lost far too soon. Cuddly toys hid amongst the colours of the blooms; a smiling cat, a grey goose and a hedgehog, peering out from behind some stems.

The concrete floor was patched with the dark stains of dried oil. Occasional graffiti picked out patterns on the walls. A couple of sweet wrappers played in the breeze.

Newman had reached the corner. And there he stood and looked out. To the green expanse of the Hoe, the cliffs, the sea, the city and the plaza so far below.

They kept walking, more slowly now. Took in the distance watchfully. They were twenty metres away, fifteen, then ten.

Newman raised a hand. "No closer."

Adam stopped abruptly, Dan likewise.

"Roger," the detective said. "What are you doing? This isn't you."

No reply. No reaction. Nothing. Just blankness.

"Come on, Roger," Adam coaxed.

On a floor below a car engine started and faded away.

"Roger," Adam said again. "This is pointless."

"Is it?" came the answer, the words soft and faraway. "I don't know what's the point of anything anymore."

"Come on. Look at all the good you've done. The business, the people you employ – they rely on you. All your charitable work."

"And where's it got me?"

Adam didn't answer. Perhaps he couldn't.

"I'll tell you where it's got me – nowhere. I've worked hard, tried hard, tried to do some good, and what happens?"

There was a strange distance to the words. It was as if the man was fading away from existence.

He reached down and picked up a picture of Annette, which had been left amid the flowers. Newman pulled it to his chest and looked back out at the city.

"Roger," Adam said again. "How does this help anything?"

"You think I killed the Edwards."

"Look, I'm not saying—"

"You were going to arrest me for it."

"That was just – it was a… routine thing."

Dan winced at the hollowness of the words. Below, he could see police officers running across the plaza, ushering people away. A couple of fire engines had parked on the road. Two large yellow bags and a pair of pumps were being carried to beneath where Newman stood.

"You think I killed the Edwards," the businessman said again.

"All I'm saying, Roger—" Adam called, but he was interrupted once more.

"So, if I die now – you'll be sure I killed them. And whoever really did it will get away with it."

"Roger!" Adam shouted, but Newman had already levered himself up onto the wall.

"Dan, for fuck's sake, say something," the detective hissed from the corner of his mouth. "Try anything. Just stop him!"

So many times, Dan had delighted in the new life that being part of police investigations had brought. But he'd also come to taste the bitterness of what it could really mean. The truths they don't tell you in books, or on the television. The hopeless impotence of being utterly helpless in the face of so much unwarranted suffering.

And here, on the roof of this grubby concrete block of a car park, and now confronted with this broken and suicidal man, he could have grabbed Adam and screamed into his face.

Why me? Why drag me into this? Why me?!

"Roger!" Dan heard himself shout. "You once offered me a job. Are you still serious about that?"

Newman turned. "What?"

The words were pathetic, embarrassing, even humiliating. And Dan knew it. But he was shaking from the heart, terrified of what may again come to pass here. And if his rambling, nonsensical flailing offered the prospect of an edge of hope, then he would take it.

"It's just – I reckon I might have had enough of this policing lark. I'm starting to think it's too much for me."

And however absurd the attempted conversation, Newman was listening. "I liked you, Dan. You were honest with me. About how I looked and how to try to get Annette back."

"I liked you too. I, err – thought we made a good team."

The breeze pulled at the lapel of the businessman's jacket. "But you think I killed the Edwards too, don't you?"

"Well, I—"

"It's not just Breen. You think so as well. Don't you?"

Below, the yellow bags were filling fast with air. They looked like the bouncy castles of children's parties. But they were still less than half inflated.

Dan took a second to consider Newman's question. It was all he could afford. But when the answer came, it was a surprise.

"No, I don't think you killed the Edwards. I don't think it's in your character, Roger."

Adam drew in a breath, but Dan ignored him. Newman was listening and that was everything.

"And I don't think this is in your character, either," Dan continued. "You're no quitter."

"You're right, I've never quit. But now I just don't see what I've got left to fight for."

Newman shifted his weight and teetered on the ledge.

"Roger!" Dan called, trying to hold back the fear in his voice. "Is this... is it what Annette would have wanted? Is it?"

But there was no reply this time. Newman was staring down at the plaza and the expanse of concrete, as hard and pitiless as iron. His body had begun to sway, back and forth.

"Roger!" Dan shouted, desperately. "What about the business? All your staff! Your charity work? What's going to happen to all that? Roger! For fuck's sake, don't!"

But the pleading was nothing. The resolution was reached and the ending set. The man had spread his arms to fly, just as his daughter did before. Adam lurched forwards, started sprinting, but it was futile, the distance too far, far too far.

And Roger Newman pitched forwards and fell.

CHAPTER THIRTY-FIVE

Seldom could the inhospitable confines of a police station have felt so welcoming.

Dan couldn't stop fidgeting and kept scratching at imaginary itches. Even Adam was clearly ruffled. His collar was open, his tie well down his neck, and his dark hair spiky and wild, a legacy of the chase through the heat of the morning.

They hadn't said a word on the way back to Charles Cross. They didn't need to. The unspoken understanding was clear.

Just leave, escape, get away. From this dirty, mundane, multi-storey car park, distinguished only as a place which can host the unspeakable. Not just once, but twice. And worse, so much worse, to a family, a young woman and her father.

The walk back was blind and fast. It was more of a flight, an automated escape from the unimaginable and incomprehensible. And mute too, because sometimes there are no words to say.

Claire was waiting in the MIR. At the wretched sight of their arrival, any hostility or criticism was forgotten. She ran over, hugged Adam and then Dan. There was no holding back and neither man resisted in the least. She brought them cups of hot coffee. And despite the heat of the day they cuddled the warmth to their chests.

In the MIR they sat and tried to find some composure amidst the wildfire of what they had faced. First Adam's mobile rang, then Dan's, but neither man answered. They just sat, sipping occasionally at the coffee and staring out of the windows. At the line of pigeons on the fume-rotted sill, the limp blue standard hanging from the rusted old flagpole, the bank of silver cloud gathering on the western horizon.

Anything which was not their lives of the last hour.

More cups of coffee arrived. The originals were little touched, but had turned cold.

Claire's mobile rang. She asked a couple of questions and hung up. Next to Adam she sat and rested a gentle hand on his shoulder.

"Sir? Sir!"

No response.

"Mr Breen? Sir!"

Adam took a long drink of the coffee, rose laboriously and walked to the windows. He opened one by all the few centimeters that the Health and Safety regulations would allow and breathed in deep lungfuls of air.

"The Deputy Chief Constable's on his way," Claire said, when she sensed some return of life. "He wants to talk to you about 'how the case is going'."

Adam swore. "He's heard about our triumph in the plaza."

"Yes, sir."

"It's all over the media?"

"Yes."

"He's going to throw me off the case."

"He didn't say that."

"And probably give me a disciplinary."

"He didn't say that either."

"He didn't need to. He's not coming here to bring me a bouquet and a medal. I should have taken back up."

"You weren't to know Newman would run. And that he would…"

Adam closed his eyes and Claire spared him the remainder of the sentence. "There's something else."

"Yes?"

"Jonathan Ivy's downstairs in reception. He wants to talk to you."

The detective's demeanour changed in a breath. "Does he now? What about?"

"He won't tell me. He says it has to be you he talks to."

★★★

243

For Dan, since the early days of their friendship, he had always found Adam a reassuring presence. Whether it was because he represented the authority of the law, or his long experience in dealing with just about every trauma that can be imagined, he had an aura of protection.

On this day, Dan noticed he kept unusually close to Adam as they walked down the stairs to the front desk. It felt like being a young boy alongside his big brother, running the gauntlet of bullies but safe in his comforting stewardship.

Ivy was sitting on one of the plastic seats, fixed to the wall. He was tapping his feet in a distracted way and looking up every time the door opened. His face was flushed, the tip of his long nose curiously red. He didn't come close to resembling a man bowed with contrition, about to unburden and confess how he had killed a brother and sister.

The desk sergeant buzzed open the secure door and Adam stepped into reception. As if detonated by a trigger, Ivy leapt up and sprang for him, arm held high, ready to strike.

And at that instant, however ridiculous it might be, Adam did something strange. He let out an exasperated sigh.

The distance Ivy had to cover was way too great for an effective attack. And he was far too inexperienced an assailant. With embarrassing ease, Adam ducked under the blow and pinned Ivy's arm against his back. Carried by his unwieldy momentum, the man crumpled to the floor. And there he stayed, either unwilling or unable to fight back.

"That's the second time someone's tried to attack me this morning," Adam said, heavily. "And it's beginning to annoy me. So – a couple of words of advice, Mr Ivy. Firstly, only in films do whirling dervishes succeed in their ambushes. It's generally considered an ineffective way to surprise your victim. Secondly, that was assaulting a police officer, a very serious crime. But, as I wanted to see you anyway, I'll put your little transgression down to shock at what happened to your friend earlier. Now, we'll go and have a little chat. If you can manage to behave yourself?"

Ivy scowled, but picked himself up from the floor and meekly allowed Adam to lead him into the police station.

★★★

Interview Room Two was the smallest of the pair. It was the coldest, darkest and most intimidating, and Adam's favourite for those very reasons. The room was blessed with the talent to squeeze the resistance from a suspect with its oppressiveness.

Ivy's face had lost some of its warrior's hue, and he looked more sulky than aggressive. A truculent lip protruded. It was not as pronounced as the impressive reach of his nose, but not far off.

"It's a disgrace, what you made Roger do," Ivy began, but Adam was in no mood for more criticism.

"And it's not what I want to talk about. So unless you'd like me to charge you with assaulting a police officer, keep quiet until I ask you a question. At which point, confine yourself to answering it, and make it short, sharp and truthful. Nothing more – got that?"

The diving board of Ivy's lip edged a little further out, but he didn't demur.

"It's this simple," Adam said. "Did you play any part in killing the Edwards?"

"No!" he exclaimed, as if offended.

The detective leaned forward, so he was peering directly into Ivy's eyes.

"You had nothing whatsoever, in any way, to do with it?"

The usher inched his chair backwards and turned away. And Adam seized on the discomfort and was upon him.

"Why can't you look at me?"

"Because I don't like you getting too close. I don't like my personal space invaded."

"Is that all?"

"Yes. Yes!"

"So you had nothing to do with killing them? And you know nothing about who might have killed them?"

This time Ivy returned Adam's look, straight and unflinching. "Nothing."

Claire opened a file. Ivy glanced nervously towards it. Carefully, she handed Adam a piece of paper. From his station, next to the door, Dan could see it was an expenses claim.

"Well, Mr Ivy, this is interesting," Adam announced, in a meaningful tone.

"What is?"

"Our little piece of research."

Dan squinted through the gloom. The detective was tracing a hand over some car parking charges.

"What research?"

"Your background. A bit of psychological analysis, too. And guess what it says?"

"What?"

"That you're easily led. A born follower. So – this is how it goes. Roger decides to take revenge on the Edwards."

"No—"

"But he knows we'll come straight to him, because he's the obvious suspect."

"He wouldn't kill them. You don't know him. It's just not him."

"So, he needs an alibi."

"No!"

"He comes to you. He tells you about his idea. He convinces you to go along with it – after all, it's no more than justice, is it?"

"No—"

"You agree."

"No!"

"Between you, you come up with a plan to kill the Edwards. In fact, do you know what? I think it's your idea, the gas explosion. Because we know you were working in the courts during that last case, where the gas company was on trial for the explosion in the bungalow. You've got all the information you need. You suggest it to Roger and you decide to do it."

"No! That's not Roger. He'd never do something like that."

"But you would, wouldn't you?"

"No! I was on the computer all night. I couldn't – I wouldn't."

"Really?"

"Really. Honestly!"

"You know, we detectives usually think that when someone says 'honestly', they're definitely lying."

"No! It's the truth! I swear!"

Adam held the man's look. And Ivy looked right back. He was defiant, holding fast to his denials. And they had nothing on him. No evidence, just the theory of a motive.

It was a conclusion Adam must also have reached, even if he couldn't resist a little more pressure. "Alright, Mr Ivy, you can go. But if I were you, I'd have a think about what you've said, and whether it might be in your interests to come back later and tell us the truth."

★★★

From the MIR they watched Ivy walk out of the police station and make his way towards the courthouse. He moved hurriedly and occasionally glanced back over his shoulder.

"What was that about asking him to come back later and tell the truth?" Dan asked.

"No idea," Adam grunted. "Just a desperate bluff, I suppose."

Claire put on a knowing half-smile. "Do you think he had anything to do with the killing?"

"No idea to that one, too. You?"

"I don't know, either. I wasn't sure if he was lying or not in that interview."

"Mr Perception Man?" Adam prompted.

"Likewise, I'm afraid," Dan replied. "He's one of those I can't read."

Adam stared silently out of the window and picked distractedly at a thread on his trousers. Mobile phones tended not to work in the interview rooms, situated as they were in the bowels of the building.

Dan took advantage of the revival of the signal to check his messages. There were three, all from Lizzie.

The first demanded a follow up story on the Edwards' deaths. The second informed him about Roger Newman jumping from the car park, insisted that it was reported on the lunchtime news and asked why he wasn't aware of it.

"I was aware," Dan muttered. "All too bloody aware."

The final message was a rant. If he could not be relied upon, she was sending the bright, up-and-coming talent that was young Phil to cover the events of this morning. Amidst the barrage of words was the threat of disciplinary proceedings for deserting his post at a time of national emergency, or words to that effect.

Dan pulled a face at the phone and deleted the messages.

"We're in the same leaky boat," he told Adam, and related the reckoning which now hung above him too.

"Don't worry," the downcast detective replied. "All we need do is solve the case in the next few hours. That way I make the Deputy Chief happy again and you get an exclusive to placate your editor."

Further attempts at levity were, by tacit agreement, redundant so they lapsed back into a sullen silence.

Claire had been on the phone to some of the other detectives working on the inquiry. After a few minutes she returned with news, she said, both good and bad.

"Give me the good first," Adam replied resignedly. "I could do with it."

"Deputy Chief Constable Flood got held up authorising some phone taps. He won't be here until later this afternoon."

Adam's hand went to his tie and straightened it. "The patron saint of detectives is back on the beat. We've got a bit longer to crack the case and save me from death by disciplinary."

"But then there's the bad news," Claire added, carefully. "Judge Templar wants to see you in his chambers as soon as possible."

***

They found Templar engaged in an experiment. He was attaching varying sized pieces of Blu-Tack to the balls in his Newton's Cradle and timing the effect it had on the swing of the spheres.

Dan was reminded of the Eggheads' analysis of his computer, and that curious mix of personalities. The businesslike note to the Ministry and his membership of a dating club. Dan was surprised to feel a sympathy stirring for the judge, and a wondering of what the future might hold when the foundations of work were removed from his life.

Adam stood quietly while Templar concluded his observations. The final test involved a huge lump of the blue mass being stuck to one of the balls that then hardly twitched under the swinging attack of its colleagues.

"I'll show Newton how to conserve momentum," the judge chuckled. "Oh, this is so much better than locking up the lawless. I'm just sorry I didn't discover it before."

He wrote a note, looked up and saw Adam. Dan was a short, but nonetheless very deliberate distance behind. Templar was unsettling at the best of times, and this clearly wasn't one.

"What are you doing here?"

"You asked to see me, Your Honour," Adam replied, patiently.

"Did I? Ah yes, indeed I did." The warmth in Templar's face fled, a taper snuffed by a single pinch. "You've really excelled yourself this time, haven't you?"

"I'm sorry?"

"Getting that Newman chap to jump off the car park. Even by your standards of melodrama, I'd say you've plummeted to a new low."

"It wasn't my finest hour, I'd agree," Adam replied, painedly.

"So, are you going to actually bother clearing up this case? The killing of the Edwards, I mean. I think we all know who did for poor Annette."

"I'm working on it, Your Honour."

"Are you making any progress?"

"We have some leads."

"I believe I've heard that one before, have I not?"

Adam didn't reply. His hands were interlinked behind his back and Dan could see the pressure of the grip intensifying.

Templar unstuck the blue mass from the silver sphere and set the cradle in motion once more. A rhythmic *click, clack, click, clack* filled the room.

"Am I still a suspect?" the judge asked.

"You and the rest of the world, Your Honour."

"Like that, is it?"

"Yes."

"Well, come on then, interrogate me," he snapped. "Use your wit and skill to ensnare me in my own words and unmask me as a murderer."

Click, clack, click, clack.

Dan thought he heard Adam groan. "Did you have anything to do with the killing of the Edwards, Your Honour?"

"No!" Templar chirped, gleefully.

"Did you fake an alibi with those emails you sent, and that phone call you made to your bank?"

"No!" came the reply again.

"Then I think, if it's acceptable, I'd like to get on with the investigation."

There was no reply. Templar was too entranced with the swinging of the silver balls. Adam contorted himself into a poor impersonation of a bow and slipped out of the door.

★★★

Commonly quiet when thoughtful, Adam now took upon himself an impenetrable silence. It was akin to that at a memorial service, dense and demanding of respect. He walked slowly out of the courthouse and sat on a bench in the plaza, deliberately facing away from the car park.

The clouds which had edged into the western sky were massing their forces. The sun's reign, so unexpectedly long for mercurial

September, was coming to an end. A growing breeze stirred some remnants of litter and leaves.

Dan considered getting a coffee from the Pepperpot, but he'd had more than enough caffeine this morning. He contented himself with sitting, watching the procession of the world pass. There had been little time for rest of late.

As they left the court, across the plaza he saw Nigel and Phil interviewing a man who must have been a witness to Roger Newman's jump. Dan sat close to Adam, but on the opposite side so the pair wouldn't spot him.

"It's no good just sitting around," the detective said suddenly. "As we're here, let's go talk to Parkinson. If we don't get anywhere I reckon we're left with the same old conclusion. That it must have been Roger Newman who set off the explosion."

★★★

Parkinson looked flustered at their unexpected arrival, his beard twitching with concern.

"But you didn't make an appointment."

"Killers don't, detectives don't," was Adam's memorable, if somewhat cryptic reply.

"I've got a meeting in five minutes."

"Cancel it. This is a murder inquiry."

"But it's about a major new tree planting initiative."

The resulting look would have withered a rainforest of the kind Parkinson doubtless championed, and proved a sufficient answer.

"I don't know how else I can help you," the Deputy Assistant Director prattled. "I've told you all I can."

"I've got bad news for you," Adam said coldly, and perhaps with relish. "You're the only one of my suspects who hasn't got an alibi."

Parkinson could have been hit by a fist, such was his recoil.

"Am I?" he asked, weakly.

"You are."

"Well... I don't know what to say."

"You could try saying you didn't do it."

"I didn't do it."

"You've told me that before. Now convince me."

"How?"

"Try."

Adam left a silence after the merciless thrust of the words and let it run. Dan had always been an admirer of the way the detective could make a mere absence of sound so very menacing, but this was a virtuoso example. It was an emptiness filled with flaming arrows and raining boulders.

"I was in bed," Parkinson stuttered. "I was asleep. I don't know what else I can say."

"Try."

His oversized glasses were starting to mist. It was clear the man was only seconds from tears, and possibly a substantial quantity.

"I never asked for any of this," he gulped. "I don't know why it's happening to me. I didn't want to be on that jury. I've never done anything wrong in my life. I've never had so much as a parking ticket. It's just not fair! If I had killed them I'd tell you, I promise I would. It would save me all this damned torment!"

Parkinson took off his glasses, wiped them on a greying handkerchief and dabbed miserably at his eyes.

Adam stood up from the chair. "Thank you," he said.

"What?"

"We're leaving."

"You're not going to arrest me?"

"No."

"So, was – that it?" the unlikely master criminal asked.

"That was it. With all due respect Mr Parkinson, you're not the most difficult subject I've ever had to interrogate."

"Oh, thank you, thank you," he gushed. "I feel like an innocent man again. Thank you so much."

And with that, they left the daredevil man of parks to the excitement of his tree planting initiative.

★★★

They returned to the bench in the plaza. The time was coming up to noon. Cloud was beginning to dominate the sky. Nigel and Phil had disappeared, probably to return to the studios to edit the story for the lunchtime news.

"I don't care," Dan whispered to himself, entirely unconvincingly. "It was just a job. Good while it lasted."

"In reverse order then, our suspects," Adam said. "Just for the sake of completeness – Parkinson?"

Dan forced himself to focus. "Out. Unless he's the finest actor known to man, I can't even begin to contemplate him being a killer."

"Templar?"

"A better bet. He's got the knowledge about how to cause a gas explosion and leave no evidence behind. And he's either already off the rails or in the process of leaving them. He's also got a decent motive – all those years of seeing justice not being done."

"But he's got a hell of an alibi. The best of the bunch."

"True."

"So – Ivy?"

"He claims not to be a violent type, but he took that swing at you. And he's got a good motive, too. Like Templar, he's seen too much of justice failing. Plus he was close to Roger and Annette."

"But he didn't give me any indication of guilt in that interview, earlier. And he's got a good alibi."

"Yep."

"Which again brings us back to where we started. The most likely killer all along – Roger Newman."

Adam's phone rang. He got up, paced around, as is an unwritten rule of using a mobile, and returned to the bench.

"Interesting, very interesting," he mused. "That was Claire. The neighbour who gave Newman his alibi – or seventy five per cent of one, to be exact. She rang in. She's worried she might have misled us. She says she was quite sleepy and reckons she can only be about half sure it was Newman she heard shouting. It could just have been someone in the street."

"Really?" Dan said, slowly. "That is interesting. So it becomes more and more possible that Newman did kill the Edwards."

They sat in silence for a couple of minutes. A gang of pigeons pecked busily around their feet. A queue formed at the café, then waned again.

Adam stood up. "That settles it. Let's get up to the hospital. Newman should be in a reasonably fit state to talk to us by now."

CHAPTER THIRTY-SIX

For twenty minutes the car waited in queues, or trundled at an orthopaedic pace around the great tarmac lot that surrounded the northern fringes of Tamarside Hospital. Adam grew more and more agitated. "Come on, come on!" he urged. "We don't have enough time as it is."

It was lunchtime, a peak visiting hour as they were finding out. The demands upon the Deputy Chief Constable dictated he wasn't due in Plymouth until late afternoon. But, as Adam put it, "That still only leaves a handful of hours to save my backside."

Dan gave him a sorrowful look and the detective added, "Sorry, our backsides."

Claire decided to drive. She welcomed the chance to escape the MIR where she had been coordinating inquiries because there were few inquiries left to coordinate. The investigation had hit a hiatus. The only suspects in town remained their list of four and every conceivable investigation had been carried out into their movements and backgrounds.

No one else had appeared on the radar of law enforcement. No one else with any kind of motive had been found. It was just a question of discovering which of the four was responsible. But that was one of those disarming statements which sound simple but are rather more tricky to achieve.

Partly to distract Adam from his frustrations, and himself too, Dan began another recap of the case.

Roger Newman was a very lucky man. The firefighters had positioned their inflatable bags in just the right place and managed to force enough air into them to break his fall. One leg hit the concrete and was badly broken, but that was his only injury. A call to the hospital confirmed he was sitting up, in pain but entirely in possession of his faculties. He was fit enough to be interviewed once more.

Claire let out a high-pitched noise, which was a mixture of surprise and relief. A man was backing a Jeep out of a space. It was odd how a few square feet of tarmac could resemble the promised land.

"Just one more thing before we see Newman," Adam said to Dan, as Claire manoeuvered, assisted by the covetous glares of a queue of other drivers. "When we were at the car park. You said you didn't think he killed the Edwards. Did you really mean that?"

Dan gave himself a minute to think. He knew the answer that was expected, even required of him. But he couldn't give it.

"Yes, I did mean it," he said, slowly. "I don't think Newman killed them."

★★★

The walk to Torridge Ward was dominated by Adam reeling off a catalogue of reasons why Newman could be the killer. They came faster and more forcefully than promises from a politician at election time.

Of their suspects, Newman had the strongest motive by far. He had no real alibi. He was a successful businessman and you had to learn to be ruthless in business. That could feasibly extend to committing murder. His mental balance was disturbed by the loss of his daughter.

As for the argument that it wasn't in his character, look at Newman's reaction when they went to arrest him. He'd thrown a punch. So, he could be violent. He'd tried to escape, a credible sign of guilt. On top of which, Newman tried to kill himself. That was – partly at least – in remorse for setting off the explosion.

Dan listened patiently and had to agree with all Adam said. It made perfect sense. But he still couldn't escape the indefinable feeling that Newman wasn't the killer. And he could see Claire felt the same way.

"We'll see in a minute," a disgruntled Adam huffed, when he'd given up trying to convince them.

They followed a long and well-polished corridor, around a corner and into a newly built part of the hospital. It overlooked the sizeable gardens on the southern side of the grounds, an expanse of neat hedges and lawns.

The windows were large and the wing light. The occasional sound of hammering and drilling drifted through the walls.

Ahead was a pair of swing doors. They were almost at Torridge Ward.

★★★

Newman was out of bed. He was sitting in a wheelchair by one of the long windows, looking out over the grounds.

Debate as they may the nature of Newman's character, his popularity wasn't in doubt. In just a few hours, word had spread of his attempted suicide. For some, it would have attracted only contempt or even bare hostility. But not for Newman. His bed was surrounded by cards from well-wishers and several bunches of flowers.

One was from his housekeeper, another from the staff at Roger's Rugs. Some of the cards were from the schools he had helped with his charitable work. But by far, the majority were from young people who had received bursaries and gone on to fine futures they might otherwise never have known.

Adam's eyes roved across the display. But his expression said it made no impact on his resolve. He coughed loudly and Newman turned.

Dan hadn't been sure what reaction to expect. More anger and defiance he thought most probable, perhaps another tirade. But Newman was humble and contrite, and it felt genuine. He said quietly, "I'm sorry. Please, sit down and let me try to explain."

Claire settled on a chair, Dan sat on the end of the bed. Adam remained standing.

"You're sorry for what, Mr Newman?" he asked.

"Not what you're thinking."

"That depends what I'm thinking."

Newman smiled. It was a weary look, but honest enough.

"You're waiting for me to pour it all out and say sorry for killing the Edwards. But I can't – because I didn't."

Adam said nothing, just waited for Newman to continue. And he did, without any reservations.

"I'm sorry for losing my temper, and for trying to hit you."

"It's an occupational hazard," the detective replied, wryly. "You get used to it."

"And for running from you, too. And for – well, you know. That business on the roof."

Adam's demeanour made it clear he wasn't going to be tempted into any concessions, so Newman turned to Dan. "You understand, don't you? I wasn't myself. I'd been drinking. What happened with Annette…"

Dan spared him the need to finish the sentence. It was difficult not to empathise with the man.

"I can certainly understand that, Roger."

"And I wanted to thank you."

"Thank me?" Dan couldn't keep the surprise from his voice. "For what?"

"For trying to stop me jumping. For doing your best to talk me round. For all you've done, in fact. You've been very good to me, with the kidnapping and the trial, and…"

The words stuck fast. The images, the events after that verdict, impossible to articulate.

"Everything that's happened," Newman continued. "I just wanted to tell you I appreciate it."

He pulled his dressing gown tighter around his chest, despite the comfortable warmth of the ward. Outside, most of the sky was covered in a silver shroud, only a few forlorn patches of blue remaining, a dying memory of the sunny days that were.

"When my leg's better," Newman went on, "I'm going to step back from the day-to-day running of Roger's Rugs. I'm going to dedicate myself to my charity work. I plan to set up a foundation in Annette's memory."

He bent down, shifted the weight of his plaster-bound leg and wriggled the protruding toes.

"I should never have jumped. You were absolutely right. It's not what Annette would have wanted and it's not me. It was cowardly and I've never been a coward. I just wanted to apologise."

He reached out a hand. Dan was aware of Adam's eyes, sharp upon him, but he shook it anyway.

A nurse walked over and fussed around, straightened the blanket over Newman's knees and offered the visitors a cup of tea. Adam declined, with just a terse shake of the head.

"Anyway," the businessman said, "I don't expect you came here to listen to me going on about how sorry I am. How can I help you?" He smiled again. "Have you come to release me from arrest?"

Adam still wouldn't reply, so Claire said, "I think it's a moot point whether you were actually under arrest. As I remember, we didn't get through the caution before you... got a little upset."

"So, how can I help you then? Have you got some news about the investigation?"

And now Adam did speak. But all he said was, "Kind of." Just two words, but as ominous as a shark circling in the water.

"Which means?"

The detective folded his arms. "Here's the problem, Mr Newman. We've investigated everyone who might have a reason to want to harm the Edwards. We've looked at their motives and their movements. And this is the same old issue we keep coming back to."

He paused while a cleaner walked by, pushing a broom back and forth.

"No one has a motive and opportunity like yours. No one wanted the Edwards to suffer so much. I've heard what you say, about not killing them and it not being in your character. But frankly, I don't believe it. So, in answer to your question – no, we haven't come to release you from arrest. It's quite the opposite."

Claire caught Dan's look. Their differences were gone in a shared sympathy for this man. And there was concern too, at the direction in which Adam was forcing the investigation.

He was working through the words of the caution. Newman said nothing, just stared at him. A hand grabbed at the crutch, propped by his wheelchair. He gripped it hard, as if he wished it was the detective's throat.

"Now, do you have anything you'd like to say?" Adam concluded.

The businessman didn't reply. He looked stricken, immovably static. It was perhaps disbelief, maybe anger, or a collision of the both.

"In which case, we'll leave you – for now," Adam continued. "And in case you were thinking about another of your little disappearing acts, be it wheelchair bound or not, I wouldn't bother. There'll be a cop on the entrance to the ward."

Still, Newman said nothing. That hand was gripping and releasing, gripping and releasing the handle of the crutch.

Adam headed for the door. Claire and Dan exchanged a glance and dutifully followed. Neither could look at Newman. But a noise made them stop.

It began as a low growl, but grew fast to become a roar, like a jet preparing for flight. It was Newman, his face contorted in a frightening manner. What calm the man had found was turned to ash in the furnace of his fury.

"You idiot, Breen!" he yelled. "You're a fucking fool! You can't catch any criminals, and now you're persecuting an innocent man. You're a prick man, an absolute arsehole! I'll get you for this."

His hand scrabbled for the crutch, drew it back and sent it flying across the ward. It barely reached Adam, clattering forlornly at his feet, and he kicked it contemptuously aside.

★★★

On the drive back to Charles Cross, the car was filled with silence. On several occasions, Dan thought about trying to break it, but the look on Adam's face suggested that would be unwise. He was preoccupied to the point of reverie. Battles were being fought, time and again, in the detective's mind.

Dan tried to find some respite from the demons of the case in comforting memories. But all he could think of was the trick he'd pulled to spend the night with Katrina. What was a triumph of resourcefulness had now begun to feel like shameful deception.

And here was Claire, just inches away. A woman who loved him and hoped for a future with him, however unworthy he may be.

Just half a mile from the police station, as they reached the end of Mutley Plain, the car got stuck in a traffic jam. A delivery lorry had broken down, a small mishap leading to the predictable gridlock that is always the way with England's overcrowded roads.

Dan's mobile rang. It was a withheld number and that meant work. He ignored it and then listened to the answer phone message. It was Lizzie, and in full ranting force.

Newman's solicitors had been on the phone. They were ringing all the media in the kingdom.

Their client had called a press conference at the hospital to attack the police in the most forthright of terms. Incompetent, blundering and negligent were the words the solicitors were using. It would be highly newsworthy.

As she reached the end of the message, Lizzie's tone changed. Another point Newman would be making was that the police were so inept, they appeared to be relying upon the input of a journalist to help solve the case. She wondered if Dan might know anything about that?

Lizzie's voice was as subdued as Dan had ever heard it. Intensity and insanity he was used to, but this was disconcertingly different.

Yard by painstaking yard, they neared the end of the jam. Adam rolled down a window, looked to Claire and finally spoke. "You don't think Newman did it either, do you?"

She let the car trundle on, before admitting, "No sir. I have to say, I don't."

"Because of that reaction?"

She nodded. "It just wasn't like any I've seen before. It wasn't that strange kind of relief that the game is over, or the standard defiance. It seemed… heartfelt."

Adam tapped a hand on the dashboard. He sounded so deflated it was painful. "I fear you may be right."

"That's not to say he wasn't involved," Claire added. "I think he's got the brains and the motivation. But I think he'd need someone else, to either help or encourage him."

"Which brings us back to the conspiracy theory," Adam replied, thoughtfully. "But who could he be working with? The only one who doesn't have an alibi is Parkinson. And I can't see him being involved."

Claire guided the car around the lorry and onto the roundabout. She had something else to say, Dan could see, but was struggling with it. The gate at the back of Charles Cross ground out its guttural welcome.

Adam moved to get out of the car, but Claire said, "Stop a moment, please, sir."

Her voice had changed. It wasn't the usual measured calm, but instead had taken on a querulous tone. It was almost a fear of what she needed to release.

"Yes?" Adam replied.

"This is difficult for me to say, but I think I have to."

In the back of the car, Dan sat still and silent. Never before had he heard Claire speak like this.

She flicked at her hair, and then said, "I think I have an idea who might have killed the Edwards."

"What?" Adam yelped. "Who?"

"It's difficult…"

"Templar, you mean? Do you think it's Templar?"

"No."

"Ivy?"

"No. Not Ivy either."

"What, Parkinson then? Surely you don't think it's him?"

"No, I don't."

Adam looked baffled. "But they're all the suspects we've got. There is no one else. Claire, what are you talking about?"

She swallowed hard. "I think the killer may be one of us, sir."

"One of us? What? Who? Claire!"

Once more she hesitated, before saying, "I think it might have been Katrina."

CHAPTER THIRTY-SEVEN

Amongst the mass of the professions a detective is one of the hardest to shock, and an experienced investigator the toughest of all.

It might be the years of prying into the terrible details of the foulest of horrors the human race can inflict upon its kin. The countless sleepless sights of bodies, dismembered in the clinical coldness of an insane killer, or in the bloody, slashing rage of passion. It could be the accumulations of corpses that many detectives have to face at some point in their careers.

Or it can be the simple day-to-day corrosion of lies. The expectation of deception that picks away another little chip of humanity each time. Or the foul abuse that is whispered, shouted and screamed. Or the threats of a bloody revenge, no matter how long it takes, a criminal's vengeance one day sure to come.

All this Adam had known in his years as a police officer and so had become largely insulated from shock. But it was clear now, in the windows of his eyes.

"I did say it wasn't easy, sir," Claire repeated.

"You're not wrong there," the detective replied, with feeling. "Go on then, let's hear the worst."

The first part of Claire's argument was straightforward. Katrina had got to know Annette well – perhaps too well.

"I noticed a real closeness between them. In court, when Annette was upset, it was Katrina she wanted to run to."

"Carry on," Adam said, thoughtfully.

"Look at Katrina's reaction since the Edwards were murdered. She's not exactly been showing great commitment to catching the killer. Not like she did when we were trying to get Annette back."

It was growing hot in the car. Dan wound down a window, but a glance from Adam prompted him to close it again. This was no conversation to risk being overheard.

263

"She's a cop," Claire continued. "She knows how to commit a crime and not leave any traces. She could easily have seen a case like that gas explosion in Plymouth before and got the idea how to kill the Edwards from it. She knows a fire is the best way to destroy evidence."

"Ok," Adam said slowly. "Anything else?"

Now Claire hesitated. There was more difficult terrain to come. She looked straight ahead, out of the windscreen and up at the police station.

"There's her – well, character. There's a kind of detachment about her. It's a certainty, a conviction that what she thinks is right. It's the sort of dissociation we've seen before in many killers."

Adam watched a police van reverse carefully from a space and head out of the gates. A patrol car followed it.

"That's all highly speculative," he said. "Where's your actual evidence? There's nothing solid to it."

Claire waited for a few seconds, before saying, "Actually, there is."

And now she looked around, at Dan. Throughout the conversation he had been doing his very best to keep quiet – hoping the two people in the front of the car might forget he had ever existed.

But Claire was a detective – a good one. And that meant he knew exactly what was coming next.

One day he would have told her. He would have confessed it. He'd agreed that with Rutherford. One day, when he was able to stand before her, he'd finally tell her that his mind was clear. When he knew their future.

He would apologise and ask for forgiveness. Say he didn't know what he was doing. That he was confused, unbalanced, vulnerable – all the excuses so familiar to men throughout the ages. He had never imagined the confession would come in the back of an unmarked police car in the yard at Charles Cross.

"Dan?" Claire prompted, gently. "There is evidence, isn't there?"

"Well, I don't know – I mean…"

"What Dan's trying to say is that he's been seeing Katrina."

Their eyes were fixed upon him. One set, the eyes of a detective and a friend, the other those of a detective and a lover. Dan could have been a naughty child, fetched by his parents and taken home from school. The fun was over and a mighty reckoning had begun.

"I, err – well…" he gulped.

"Haven't you?" Claire persisted.

The thinness of air had become curiously thick.

"I don't know about seeing. I mean, I might have just—"

"I know," Adam cut in, ruthlessly. "Of course I know. I was just hoping you didn't, Claire."

"No, I knew too. I wasn't sure whether to be angry, or pity him. But I don't hold it against him – not too much, anyway. He's never been the best when it comes to emotions."

"I hope he's learned a lesson," Dan's newly appointed father replied.

"Yes," Claire agreed, before softening her voice and adding. "And I very much hope he sorts out that strange mind of his soon."

They both looked at him, as if parents united in their disappointment, ire and indulgent fondness. And amidst all this, the subject of their rue sat quietly because there was nothing else to do.

"On the day Annette committed suicide, later that evening, Dan sent a text message to Katrina," Claire said. "Ostensibly, it was a few words to share the shock of what happened and check she was coping. In fact, it was designed to get together with her that night."

Dan was still finding the way of a Trappist the only available option.

"But he didn't get a reply," Claire continued. "Instead, the next morning, Katrina apologised for not texting back, saying she was preoccupied. It was when we were at Homely Terrace, after the explosion."

"I recall," Adam said.

"That, in itself, was an interesting insight into her character," Claire went on, coolly. "I think it was partly to goad me. And looking back, I think she also couldn't resist giving us a clue. That it was her who'd killed the Edwards."

Adam swore and loosened his tie. "You're saying she didn't want to see Dan because she knew she was going to kill the Edwards that night?"

Claire didn't reply. There was no need.

A seagull swooped down and landed on the bonnet of the car. Adam waved an irritable hand. It gave him a contemptuous look, but deigned to fly off again. The detective stared at the air it had vacated, working away at Claire's words. And they were everywhere, confined in the small space of this car.

"This is bloody far-fetched," he said, eventually. "Katrina's got an impeccable reputation. She's run loads of these cases."

"But never one quite like this."

"I know her track record. She's handled some huge kidnappings."

"When the subject's been a 17-year-old girl? Who she's got so close to?"

"Yeah, but – I just can't see it."

"I don't like it either, sir. But you must admit it's feasible."

"Well…"

"Which means we've got to check it."

"Maybe."

"She broke the golden rule. She got involved. And you know what that can do."

Adam rolled his neck and rubbed a hand over the stubble of his chin.

"Ok, go check it out. Talk to the staff at her hotel. And get the CCTV, too. But Claire…"

"Yes?"

"Be damned discreet."

They got out of the car and headed towards the back door of the police station. They were only metres away when it opened and Katrina stepped out.

"Afternoon," Adam said brusquely, and pushed past. Claire followed, without a word.

Katrina watched them go, one eyebrow raised. Dan put on the vaguest of smiles, mumbled a greeting and also edged into the corridor.

Stepping out into the grey light of the afternoon, from the darkness of the police station, those eyes had looked particularly vivid. The brown was warm and burnished, the green as bright as a jewel.

Dan wondered if, in the months to come, they would be captured on the front page of every newspaper and labeled the most beautiful eyes a murderer had ever possessed.

★★★

The time was coming up to two o'clock, the scheduled start of Newman's press conference. Dan rang Nigel and asked to speak to Phil.

"I need a favour."

"Are you ok? I mean, Lizzie's—"

"I'm fine. I just need your help. You're at the hospital?"

"Yeah, they're doing the conference in the garden."

"I need to hear what's said. Can you leave the line open and put your phone down near Newman?"

"Why?"

"Don't ask."

Dan switched on the phone's speaker. There were a couple of bumps and thuds and some muffled, background conversation. Adam came to stand beside him, in the corner of the MIR.

"Deputy Chief's due in a couple of hours. I'd say we've got until five."

"Snap."

"Meaning?"

"That's as late as I can leave it before I miraculously resurface, hopefully to tell my editor I've been undercover but now I'm back with an exclusive on who killed the Edwards."

They were alone in the room, but Adam lowered his voice anyway.

"What do you think about whether Katrina might have…"

"I don't know what to think. But I know we've got to check it."

"Yep."

"And if Claire's right, apart from being a flash of genius, it might just save us. On the subject of which…" Dan nodded to a pile of papers in the other corner. "That's Katrina's stuff."

"No!" Adam protested. "It could be personal, it could be confidential. I can't possibly start going through a fellow officer's notes."

"You're right. It's only our futures at stake."

Another silence. Both men looked around the room. At the felt boards, the clock, the windows, but never the papers in the corner.

"I could do with a coffee," Dan said airily. He nodded to his phone. "It might ease the pain of what we're about to hear."

"Good thought."

"But – oh darn."

There followed a vigorous pocket patting display, which would have prompted derision even from a junior school drama class. "I don't have any money."

Adam folded his arms. He somehow managed to produce a look which was both knowing and disapproving. "I suppose I'll have to go, then."

From the phone's speaker came the sound of chairs being shifted and background conversation. The door to the MIR clicked closed.

Dan checked over his shoulder and walked nonchalantly across the room.

"How messy," he said to himself at the hillock of papers. "These could do with tidying. But I'd better make sure there's nothing important before I move them."

He checked through the pile. There were lists of the suspects' alibis and details of which officers had been assigned to the various inquiries. Nothing interesting. But at the bottom he found a pocket notebook.

It was full of the details of various cases, dating back a year. But towards the end, Dan found one page which was all doodles.

In a variety of styles and sizes, time and again, were written the letters *PP*.

The door opened and Adam returned, carrying two coffees. He made a point of shuffling in backwards.

"Good timing," Dan said, from his seat on the windowsill. "The press conference is about to start."

★★★

A resonant voice broke from the phone's speaker. It asked for quiet in a way that made it clear the words were an instruction, not a request.

"Thomas Mortice," Adam observed. "The head of one of the local solicitors. They're good – and expensive. Newman must be serious."

"Ladies and gentlemen," Mortice was saying. "You'll be more than a little taken aback to learn my client, eminent local entrepreneur and tireless worker for a range of charities, is under arrest. Let me assure you, we believe this to be the most ridiculous folly on the part of the police. It is, perhaps, a bizarre reflex action which comes about because they are unable to bring to justice those who really did kill Martha and Brian Edwards. We will naturally be challenging the allegation robustly. However, given that Mr Newman is technically a suspect, I have advised him only to read a statement."

The speaker rustled and clicked. In the background, they could hear the whirring of camera motors. Dan could see each lens turning to find Newman. He would be sitting in a wheelchair, probably against a backdrop of flower beds, a sheet of paper in his hands, the smartly-suited figure of Mortice protectively by his side.

Newman began in a voice which was quiet, but rang with indignation. It didn't sound as though he was playing to the crowd.

"I have always had the greatest respect for the law," he read. "I have always believed the British police have a very tough job, but that they do it marvelously well. When Annette was kidnapped I had every faith they would bring her home to me – and they did. I was indescribably grateful for their efforts."

Newman paused. Dan imagined him turning a page or working down to the next paragraph. Whoever wrote the script had done it well. First, build up your victim. Love them good.

And then, in a second of turning, bring them crashing down.

"But now," Newman continued. "Now…"

Dan could see Mortice stretching out a reassuring arm, telling him it was right to go on, that what he had to say must be aired. The cameras were tracking in their shots for the close up of Newman's anguished face.

These would be the words that counted. The sentences which were repeated, time and again, on the radio, the television and the internet, reprinted in papers and magazines.

"I've never committed a crime in my life," Newman went on. "But the police somehow convinced themselves that I have. Despite the lack of any evidence whatsoever, they have accused me of killing the Edwards. Me, a grieving father. Me, without a stain on my character. I have been accused of murder."

Again, his voice caught. The faint sound of trees whispering under a growing breeze slipped from the speaker. Adam was staring at it, unblinking, a hand pulling at his chin.

"I hardly need say that I am entirely innocent," Newman continued. "I do, however, need to tell you that I find this accusation gross, disgusting and offensive. I have attempted to help the police in every way I can and this is how they react. It has shaken my faith in our police service terribly, which is why I asked you all here today. I felt I needed to speak out."

His voice was growing louder, the words more impassioned. Adam was shaking his head, but still staring at the phone's tiny, grilled speaker.

"I believe the police have accused me of this crime because they are too inept to find those actually responsible. I regret having to say this, but I feel I must. I believe the officers I have encountered are incompetent and should be removed from the case. I would also like to see disciplinary action taken, such has been their lamentable inability to do their jobs properly."

Newman paused, for a breath, a drink of water. When he resumed the statement his voice was calmer, but the words no less powerful.

"As an example of their incompetence, I have personally witnessed this. The police appear to be relying not on experts in explosions, fires, experienced investigators, or any such thing but instead on the input of a local television reporter."

★★★

The rain began to fall, beating upon the line of windows in the MIR. Dan and Adam stared out at the city. People were sheltering under briefcases and magazines, or with jackets pulled up over their heads. The rain poured into the ruined church as it had since those wartime years of destruction. Traffic began to tail back from the roundabout. Cars, buses and lorries switched on lights and wipers.

On this September day, it felt as though summer was finally leaving the stage. Autumn was taking on the performance, with winter waiting, gloating cold in the wings.

"That's us fucked, then," Adam announced, bitterly.

He paced over to one of the computers and found a news website. Newman's diatribe was already the lead story.

Dan's mobile had rung three times, but there was no way he was going to answer it. The only caller could be Death.

The first messages were from Nigel and El. Both recounted what Newman had said, and both sounded worried in ways far out of character.

"I somehow doubt I'll be ok," Dan grunted, in response to the familiar modern-day question his friends had asked. "And as for where you'll find me – probably busking tunes at the nearest subway in an attempt to earn my next meal."

The third message was from Lizzie. In a voice as calm as an assassin, she instructed Dan to call immediately.

"What do we do?" He asked.

"Resign now and save them the bother of sacking us, I'd say."

"Adam!"

"Have you got any better ideas?"

Dan returned to his study of the scurrying city. Far out to sea, a sparkle of lighting flinted the sky. "There must be something we can do."

"Like what?"

"Like – what if Claire's hunch is right? If we can crack the case, Newman's attack will be neutralised straight away. It'll be put down as the rantings of an unbalanced man and forgotten. All the media will concentrate on is the killer being caught. You can take it to the Deputy Chief to show him the case is sorted, I can take it to Lizzie as an exclusive."

Adam found his phone and rang Claire. After a muted conversation, he clicked off the call and turned to Dan. "It's not looking good. None of the hotel staff remember Katrina going in or out the night the Edwards were killed. And they're pretty sure they would have."

Dan tried not to sound desperate. "She's a resourceful woman. She could have slipped by them."

"Which is exactly what Claire said. She's going through the hotel CCTV. It'll take a couple of hours."

Their eyes crept to the clock on the wall. The time was a quarter to three.

"And," Adam concluded, "I'd say a couple of hours are about all we've got."

★★★

They resumed the vigil at the window. The storm was moving closer, riding on the growing might of the westerly wind. With each white dagger, they were buffeted by an accompanying thunderclap, rocking the sky.

"Are we just going to stand here?" Dan asked. "Just hope that Claire can save us?"

"What else do you suggest? We don't have any other leads."

"How about going back through the case? A quick brainstorm, to see if there's anything we've missed."

Adam's voice was far from enthusiastic. "If you like."

They started with the suspects' alibis, then moved on to the men's characters and relationships with each other. Dan wrote brief notes on a sheet of paper on one of the boards. They went through Parkinson,

Templar, Ivy and finally Newman looking harder and harder for that hidden diamond of a giveaway hint.

"I might have changed my mind about Newman," Dan said. "That attack on us – it shows he does go in for revenge, despite what he might say. What if it was a desperate last bluff? He knows the game's up. It could be an attempt to force us to pull back from him."

"That's possible," Adam replied. "But we still come back to the same old problem. We've got no real evidence against him. In fact, it's worse than that. His neighbour gives Newman half an alibi – or three quarters – depending on how certain she's feeling."

Dan tapped the board with his marker pen. "Do you know what bothers me about his alibi, or whatever percentage of it?"

"What?"

"It's how bloody convenient it is. It feels odd. He says he's up all night, ranting and raving. But only at the very moment our killer's waiting to let off the car alarm does Newman start making a real noise which should wake the neighbours."

"That's interesting, granted – maybe even suggestive," Adam said slowly. "But if it was deliberate, it throws up two problems. Firstly, it didn't really work. The alibi the neighbour gave him wasn't great."

"That might just have been bad luck. It doesn't alter the fact it could have been his plan."

"The second problem is bigger. If it was him in the house, deliberately giving himself an alibi, then it couldn't have been Newman who did the killing."

Dan thought for a while, before pronouncing the rueful verdict, "Bugger. I thought I was onto something."

More lightning flickered across the sky. The rain was coming in hard, pounding on the windows of the MIR. Droplets shattered as they hurled into the glass.

"Unless," Dan said, "We go back to the conspiracy idea. What if Newman was deliberately giving himself an alibi because he was part of the plan to kill the Edwards, but someone else was involved, too?"

Now Adam did sound interested. "Then who? And how?"

Dan grabbed the sheets of paper documenting the suspects' alibis. He started sketching arrows between the four men, jotting down thoughts, potential connections, the movement of the pen becoming faster with his excitement. Adam peered down at the growing mass of writing.

"What is it?" he urged.

Dan inked in a couple of numbers and stood back from the sheet. White light and a thunderclap filled the room. The time was just after three o'clock.

Two names were ringed, encircled again and again, two columns of timings alongside.

"That's it," Dan gasped.

CHAPTER THIRTY-EIGHT

Once more, they were drawn back to the plaza.

The car park stood in its far corner, the stark concrete lines softened by the relentless rain. The white discs of headlights bumped and trundled around its floors as they made a slow escape. Inevitably both Dan and Adam looked to that high, southernmost edge from where first Annette and then Roger Newman had jumped.

Beside the car park towered the Civic Centre, columns of windows shining through the gloom. A gang of forlorn workers huddled under its ramshackle old portico to share their nicotine slavery. People emerged from the sliding doors, hesitated at the sight of the elements' welcome and then began miserable runs through the rain.

Atop the courts the Lady of Justice stood, solitary in the face of the storm. Lighting played around the scales and sword. Watery pellets hurled mercilessly into her body, running along her outstretched arms and cascading onto the courthouse.

Another thunderclap shook the sky. Like an unwelcome guest unwilling to take their leave, the storm had settled above the city.

Behind the courts, concealed in the gloom, lay Catherine Street, so narrow it felt filled by the rain as it rebounded from wall, tarmac and tile. And that one doorway where, a little more than six months ago, a white van had been parked, waiting. Where Annette Newman had bent down to offer her charity and where all this had begun.

And now was coming to an end.

★★★

Adam had tumbled down the stairs of Charles Cross and into the office behind the front desk. A harassed sergeant was trying to ensure a passable masquerade of cleanliness, modernity and efficiency, ready for the regal visit of the deputy chief constable. Protest as the man may about needing every available officer, Adam insisted on a driver to take them to the plaza.

A ten minute walk had become a ten minute drive, so snarled up was the city by the weather, but at least they were arriving dry.

Dan's phone kept ringing and resolutely he ignored it. Messages were being left from a range of fellow hacks all wanting a comment about Newman's claims. There was even one from Phil, the poor trainee sounding wretched as he rambled through the apologetic request.

"I'm sorry, but I know you'll understand I've got no choice. It's obvious it was you Newman was talking about. Everyone's saying so. I have to ask, even though you're a colleague, and, well... my mentor."

Dan found his chest feeling curiously tight. It must be the pressure of the storm. He deleted the message before he had to hear any more.

The time had moved on to twenty past three. They were on Royal Parade, at the back of a line of cars and buses. Adam briefly debated whether to run for the plaza, but quickly decided against it. They would save little time, if any, and be soaked in seconds.

"Come on, come on," he kept urging the poor young constable who was their driver, as if he might have a magical ability to slip through a solid block of traffic.

Dan tried to distract himself by staring at the two buildings, standing stoically together in the rain. Perhaps Parkinson was in a break between meetings. He would see the police car pull up and wonder what new torment it might bring for his undistinguished life.

Templar would be in court, presiding over another case, counting away the last few days of his long career. He would be prickling at the verbosity of a procrastinating barrister, a trademark hand tapping impatiently on the bench. Or perhaps the judge would be in his chambers, delighting in another swing of the Newton's Cradle.

As for Ivy, he would be standing at the back of another courtroom, another trial, perhaps alongside the hapless people who were fate's choice for this week's victims. Offering a sympathetic smile and a guiding arm, and ready with those tissues for the tears he had seen so many times.

The car edged on and gained a few more precious yards. They were almost at the plaza.

★★★

"Any word from Claire?" Dan asked.

"I imagine you might have noticed if my phone had rung and I'd been talking on it," was Adam's horsewhip of a retort.

Dan didn't bother replying and the detective continued, a little less piercingly. "How sure are you about this?"

"Not sure at all. It's just as I said. I've got a theory. It feels consistent. It fits. It's just the same old problem – proving it."

"Which has been the trouble at every twist and turn throughout the whole of this damned case," Adam grunted. "Which leaves us with just the one chance. And what do you reckon our chances are?"

Dan didn't answer. He turned to watch a party of young children kicking their way through the rain, jumping and stamping in the lines of puddles. A car horn sounded, another quickly joining it. A cyclist picked a careful way past the line of traffic, rain running from every angle of her coat.

"So, then – our chances?" Adam said again.

"All I can say is that he's the weak link. If there is a conspiracy, he's our best chance of cracking it."

★★★

The car was misting up. Adam rolled down a window and was attacked with a face full of swirling rain. He swore and wound it up again.

The rows of headlights picked out the diagonal lines of the downpour. Spray rose from the road as the raindrops pounded their attack. The storm had brought a premature darkness to the land, as if forcing the afternoon aside and ushering in an early night.

All around was the sound of the coming autumn. Tyres cut through the standing water. The rain beat, rattled and drummed on windscreens, pavements and umbrellas. Engines idled, exhaust fumes mixing with the encompassing mist.

And the smell, too. The relief of the land after days of baking dryness. As plants, hedges and trees opened their leaves to drink in the gift of the skies.

The drains struggled, overwhelmed by the unaccustomed load. Tonnes of oil-sheen water frothed and gurgled, chasing down to the greedy, waiting sewers. Leaves patterned the streets, beaten from the trees by the force of the storm.

The sky vented its anger, stretching colourless as a blackboard. To the west hung a little hope, a lighter shade of graphite amongst the dominance of the slated darkness. But it was far off and forlorn. For now the rain held sway, its moment finally here, delighting and rejoicing, unwilling to relent.

The line of cars moved once more and won another tiny gain of the road's territory. They had reached the plaza.

Dan and Adam opened the doors and began to run through the rain.

CHAPTER THIRTY-NINE

The storm swirled around them. Its wrath made real the impact of every individual raindrop upon the inconsequential shields of skin and clothing. Each blow felt propelled by a catapult of the heavens, with a heavy momentum and an exacting aim.

Dan took a hit to his eye. He recoiled and squinted as he ran through the attack of water. Adam was doing the same, a hopeless hand raised to try to deflect the assault. It was as if the storm had taken offence at these two foolish humans breaking cover and directed all its mighty firepower upon them. They were only yards across the plaza and already stained, streaked and disheveled.

Adam's mobile began to trill. He fumbled it from his pocket and glanced down at the dim light of the display. The detective veered sideways, slamming into the side of the Pepperpot café and finding the relief of shelter under its awnings. The noise of the rain beating down was so loud he had to shout.

The name on the display registered *Claire Reynolds*. But what news she had to tell was unclear. Adam uttered only a series of prompts, "Right? Go on... really?"

The café owner looked hopeful but Dan put on an apologetic expression and the man went back to his book. It was the kind of day when he might expect to get through a fair portion of its pages. No one was venturing out in Devon's version of the monsoon season.

Adam had almost finished his conversation. He was saying he had to go, but that Claire should come to the courts and they would talk more later.

"It wasn't Katrina," Adam said, slipping the phone back into his jacket. "Not that I ever really thought it was. The CCTV at the hotel is comprehensive. She has a meal in the restaurant. After that, she goes up to her room. And that's where she was when someone was breaking in to the Edwards' house and setting off the car alarm. She's on the fifth floor. There's no way out of the hotel which isn't covered by CCTV."

"And that's it?"

"Just about."

"Just about?"

"Claire said there was one oddity, but it's hardly relevant."

"Try me anyway."

"It means nothing."

"I'd like to hear it. You know how I like odd details."

"You'd like to hear more about Katrina, you mean."

"Just the detail, please."

Adam flicked some water from his face. "She asked for a very early morning alarm call. Just before dawn. The receptionist remembers, because Katrina said the forecast was for another beautiful day. She would be going back to London soon and she wanted to see a Devon sunrise first. The CCTV shows her going up to the roof terrace of the hotel just after five in the morning and then back to her room again fifteen minutes later."

Dan nodded and said thoughtfully, "Does it now?"

★★★

A young, but burly security guard led them up the stairs of the courthouse. Adam had rung ahead while they were in the police car, to outline his requirements.

"He definitely doesn't know we're coming?" Adam asked the man.

"No sir. He'll just be asked to report to the office."

"And he won't be told who's here, or why?"

"No sir," the guard replied, patiently. "It'll be exactly as you asked."

"You'd better hang around at the end of the corridor. But discreetly please, not as though you're guarding a nightclub."

For the first time, the man looked more interested. "Is there going to be some action? I wouldn't mind a bit of that. I get fed up with just checking bags and confiscating knives."

"I doubt it," Adam replied. "But I'd appreciate your help, just in case."

They were shown into Templar's chambers. The fine old clock on the mantelpiece said the time was twenty to four. They had an hour, perhaps a few minutes more, to solve the case.

Dan noticed he was leaving little black circles of drips on the thick pile of the carpet. With a thought of Rutherford he shook himself, discarding a shower of droplets. His jacket and shirt were heavy with the soaking. He stood by the radiator and tried to dry himself.

As for Adam, he appeared not to notice how wet he was. The detective paced back and forth across the room, hardly standing still for a second. He studied some leathery old books on the shelves, then crossed to the window and stared out.

The storm had lost none of its vigour. Rain continued to lash the deserted plaza. Another flash of lighting speared across the sky, the thunder no more than a half a second behind. It rattled the wooden panels of the room.

Adam stalked over to the door and rested an ear against it, before returning to the window.

"Are you ok?" Dan asked.

"Fine."

"Really?"

"Yes."

"Really, really?"

"No."

"What are you doing?"

"I'm thinking."

"What about?"

"Nothing."

"Come on."

"Ok then," the detective snapped. "I'm thinking about the next few minutes. I'm thinking about how to handle this interview. How, if I get it wrong, if I don't get a confession, I'm off the case, facing a disciplinary and maybe even the end of my career. If I'm lucky, I might be giving out parking tickets. So, I'm thinking about exactly what to say, and the best way to crack the case. At least that's what I'm trying to think, when I'm not being interrupted."

Dan fielded the cudgel of a hint and quietened. He paced over to the judge's desk and set the Newton's Cradle to work.

Click, clack, click, clack...

To pass the waiting time, Dan studied the paintings on the wall. All were gloomy oils of Dartmoor scenes. They reeked of being created on an intemperate day by an artist in a dour mood.

A trickle of water wound its way down Dan's neck, and he pulled tetchily at his shirt. Adam was gazing out at the multi-storey car park, one foot tapping on the carpet.

He turned as footsteps settled outside.

★★★

The wooden panels edged open and Jonathan Ivy stepped into the room. He saw Adam and Dan and stopped.

And in that moment, just that one single second, Dan knew. It was in Ivy's face. Something changed. It was a realisation, an understanding, a sudden knowing. The pale disc of his features lost another tone of colour. The thin line of his mouth twitched.

He had been exposed. He was part of a conspiracy to murder that resulted in the deaths of a brother and sister. Finally, his role had been revealed.

For Dan, it was an effort to keep his legs strong and not allow his body to sag back against the paneling of the wall. The long hours of the investigation, the lack of sleep, the pressure, the emotion, all now settled upon him. The invisible weight climbed onto his back and fastened a grip around his throat.

But yet he stood. For riding dominant above, the highest banner, the one which conquers all challengers, was hope. More powerful even than the storm outside, a tropical wave of sheer relief.

The tension was gone. The future was clear. His, Adam's, both were saved and safe.

They were going to be all right. They would survive. They had come through this ordeal and would fight on.

The case was solved. The police would have their charges. *Wessex Tonight* would have its exclusive. Roger Newman's attack would be cast aside, forgotten in the frenzy of the revelation.

Dan would still be a television reporter, Adam a senior detective. They would remain friends and continue to investigate cases together. The unseen powers above would persist with their tacit tolerance.

It's unorthodox, they would huff, in their backroom cabals, *but they get results. So we'll run with it – for now.*

Adam stood before Ivy and recited the words of the caution. And buckled by the density of understanding the man's strength gave way. Adam caught Ivy before he could fall and eased him down onto one of the chairs. The folds of his robe wilted around him.

"How – how did you know?" he gasped.

"We got there eventually," Adam said, without a hint of sympathy. "You led us quite a dance, it's true, but we got there. We usually do."

"But – how? He said it was brilliant. He said we could never be caught."

Adam snorted. "Do you know how many times I've heard that? It was clever Ivy, that I'll grant you. But it wasn't brilliant. As you're going to realise in the years you'll spend in jail."

The usher lowered his head into his hands. "But he said it was perfect."

A loud thud echoed in the room. It sounded as though it came from the far corner. Adam glanced to Dan, nodded a prompt, and he walked over. Dan checked the drapes but found nothing. He opened a cupboard and a cabinet, but met only files, stationery, and a decanter and glasses.

"There's no one here," Dan said, walking back to Adam. "It must have come from next door."

Ivy was still doubled over, breathing heavily. The odd sob emerged through his hands.

"That's enough melodrama," Adam said. "You were big enough to kill, you're big enough to face the consequences. It's time to get you to the police station."

The usher half rose but collapsed back onto the chair again.

"Come on!" Adam ordered. "Start walking or I'll get some cops here and we'll carry you out in front of everyone."

Ivy gripped at the sides of the chair and pulled himself to his feet. "But he said it was perfect," he bleated. "He had it all worked out. He said we couldn't possibly be caught."

"You won't be taking all the blame, if that's any comfort," Adam replied. "We know you were just a little follower, doing as your master told you. Newman's under arrest, too. It's all over."

CHAPTER FORTY

The day of the Edwards' acquittal and Annette's suicide kindled a fury, scorching and searing, incandescent and irresistible. It was the most powerful of fires and could only be quenched by one remedy.

Vengeance.

That was how Dan described it and rather well he thought, in that familiar self-satisfied manner. But Adam just scowled and told him to get on with it. The *it* in question was his theory. The realisation of how the Edwards were murdered.

The end of the trial had left four bitter men and some unfinished business.

"And unfinished business," Dan narrated, "Is so dangerous. Sometimes, it has to be tackled. It can't be buried, hidden from, or forgotten about. It just has to be faced. It can be that powerful."

Adam rolled his eyes and repeated the words which he had used so many times in moments like this.

"Will you please – just – get – on – with – it. We don't have time for your drama."

They were in the police car, being driven through the rain, preparing to confront Jonathan Ivy. Adam had demanded one further run through of the theory, one last playing out of the scenario just to be absolutely sure. So much rested on them getting it right.

The way the Edwards had been killed and by which man.

Or, as they now knew, which men.

"The bitterest of the bitter, the most prominent of our four suspects has to be Roger Newman, as we've agreed from the start," Dan continued. "With the Edwards acquittal and, on top of that, what he had to witness…"

Both Dan and Adam looked to the distance and the highest levels of the car park, rising in the grey mist of the downpour.

"This is what I think happened," he went on. "Newman is set on revenge. For all that they've done the Edwards have to die. But how to go about it? I'm guessing he remembers that court case, the one where the gas company was put on trial. And that gives him an idea. He looks it up, in an internet café somewhere, so there are no traces on his own computer. There's not much time after Annette dies, but enough probably, given his determination. Plus, what he's discovered is ideal. He can kill the Edwards on his own, without the risk of them fighting back. But, as always, there's a problem."

"He's going to be the prime suspect," Adam observed. "And he knows it. So he needs an alibi."

"And he realises the only way to get one is if he has an accomplice," Dan picked up. "So – who does he turn to? There's one very obvious candidate. Someone he's known for years. Someone he's sure he can trust. Someone who thinks they owe him. A man who's ripe for something like this, because he's already spent years in the courts seeing justice not being done."

Adam nodded. "Step forward, Jonathan Ivy."

"They get together and talk. There are no emails, no phone calls, as we know. I don't think Ivy needs much persuading. He thinks the Edwards deserve what's coming to them. He's seen Annette die in front of him too, remember? And he thinks Newman's plan is flawless."

"Ok, that makes sense. But how did they do it and still manage to have alibis?"

"Ah, that. Now that was the clever part."

★★★

Dan took out his notes and traced through the interlinking arrows and scrawled annotations. There were so many. The case had to be one of the most complex he had ever worked on.

How would he describe it in the little diary he kept hidden in the drawer beside his bed? Justice would have to feature somewhere, or a parody of justice. Something twilight, or in the shadows.

"We went through the times which the suspects would need for their alibis and came out with the spread of 3.15 to 4.10am," Dan continued. "That's the period one of the four would have to be away from home in order to get to the Edwards place, break in, start the gas running, crack the light bulb and get out again. Then he'd have to wait for enough gas to fill the house before setting off the car alarm."

"Agreed."

"But that's where we made our mistake. We assumed it was probably just the one man committing the crime, so his alibi had to take in the whole of that 55-minute period. But this is where Newman was clever. He realised if two people were involved, neither would need to be away from home for anything like as long. So, they could give themselves much better alibis. Perhaps not watertight, but enough to make sure they weren't prominent suspects. Combine that with the destruction of any real evidence, as Newman knew would happen in an explosion, and they should be safe."

"How does it work with the two people being involved?" Adam prompted, rather sharply.

"One other point first, because it's important. If you'll indulge me?"

"I indulge you too much."

"Then just a little more, please. We made the assumption that the murderer was one person acting alone – that prompted me to think about just how committed we really were to solving the case. I wonder if we might have been a little sloppy, because we had sympathy with whoever killed the Edwards."

"Take me through the part about the two people and their separate alibis," Adam insisted.

Dan closed his eyes as he imagined the events of the night.

"Assume Newman's alibi is genuine. He is at home at about 3.45am, throwing things around and shouting himself hoarse. I thought that was a little too convenient, and this is why – he is indeed doing it deliberately, to give himself an alibi. It was just bad luck his neighbour was in a daze and couldn't be a hundred per cent sure it was him. But it was. So – he's certainly at home then. But that's not to say he was home at 3.15, or much before 3.45."

"So he definitely couldn't have set off the car alarm," Adam said. "Because it starts wailing at 3.57. He couldn't get to Homely Terrace in time."

"Exactly. But now look at Ivy's alibis – and I'm using the plural deliberately here. He's emailing Templar in the run up to the time we're interested in and then looking at websites during the moments someone is breaking into the Edwards' place. So, he can't have done that bit. But! The remainder of his alibi is entering the PIN to watch the porn. That happens just after 3.45. It's not a bad attempt at an alibi for the last part of the period we're interested in. But just because he's entered the PIN, it doesn't mean he actually has to be at home after he's done it. With a happy coincidence, there's just time for him to get to Homely Terrace, find a car with an alarm, set it off and disappear again."

Adam thought his way through the scenario. "So, we've got two men involved in a conspiracy. One does the actual breaking in and starting the gas, then goes home to establish his alibi. The other comes along later and sets off the car alarm, having already established his particular alibi.

"And it all fits. The timings work. And look at the men's characters. Newman's the most motivated, so he does the dangerous part, the actual breaking in. Ivy just has to come along and set off the alarm. That's easy. He could even tell himself he's hardly done anything wrong. After all, he was pretty convincing when we interviewed him."

They sat in silence for a couple of minutes as the car waited for the traffic to move. Dan traced a pen across his notepad one more time, following his theory.

"It all sounds plausible," Adam said, at last.

"Any advance on plausible?"

"Potentially convincing, then."

"You could do even better than that."

"All right, all right. You don't have to vaunt your cleverness. But there's still no evidence. Or, at least, nowhere near enough for a conviction."

"So you'll have to do your hard cop bit and push him into a confession. Which might be the tricky part."

"Don't worry," Adam replied, determinedly. "I'll sort that out."

And the detective had been very much as good as his word Dan thought, as he stood in the judge's chambers staring at the man dabbing at his eyes with his robe. The breaking of Ivy and the concluding of the case had proved much easier than he'd expected.

The time was just before four. Only a few hours away from the sweet respite of going home. First, Dan would have to drive to the studios and face Lizzie. But given the exclusive he had to offer, there was little to fear.

Afterwards, it was the actual broadcast to negotiate, and then finally to the flat. A cuddle with his beloved dog and perhaps a jog around the park together. The ordering of a take-away to celebrate the successful end of another case and a couple of pints of whatever dusty tins of beer were left in the back of the cupboard.

The only other business of the evening was the phone call Dan would have to make. It wouldn't be easy but really, that wasn't so very important. He wasn't even sure he blamed her. And nothing could ever be proven, of that Dan was certain. Nonetheless, he wanted to tell her, just because he could.

And tomorrow, not so far away now, delicious normality would resume. At least for as long as ever it did in his ridiculous life.

★★★

Adam put a hand under Ivy's arm and began guiding him towards the door. But the usher was a dense weight as he struggled to put one foot in front of the other. He was whispering something, but too faintly to hear.

"Come on man, enough of your stalling!" Adam barked. "It's over. We've got you and in a few minutes we'll go and get Newman."

Still Ivy's lips were trembling as he tried to find the words.

"What're you bleating about?" Adam snapped. "This is your last chance before I have you carried out."

Ivy looked up. His face was a study of misery, crumpled and sodden with tears.

"Roger," he managed. "Why poor Roger?"

"What?" Adam said. "What're you talking about?"

"Roger… why have you arrested poor Roger?"

Adam stared at him, looked harder, penetrating the man's mind. There was no deceit: that was far beyond him now, no space for doubt. Ivy was genuinely baffled.

"Shit!" Adam yelped, and sprang for the door.

CHAPTER FORTY-ONE

Adam tumbled out of the room. At the end of the corridor, the security guard was feigning interest in a couple of maritime watercolours. It was as convincing an act of innocence as a bloated cat sitting by an empty fishbowl.

"Are you alright, sir?" the man asked.

"No, I'm bloody not. Who gave us that room?"

"I'm sorry?"

"Why were we using Templar's office?"

"Because His Honour offered. He's out working on some big legal thing. He heard you were coming to do an important interview and wanted to help."

Adam swore with sufficient velocity to make even the guard grimace. He led the man into Templar's chambers.

"What's your name?"

"Collet, sir. Tom Collet."

"Ivy's under arrest and you're going to stand here and guard him. He's going nowhere until we come back to get him, understood?"

The usher had taken the opportunity to slump back onto one of the visitor chairs. With the gown falling around him, he resembled the debris of a human loosely wrapped in black cotton. Tom Collet drew himself up to his full and imposing height.

"He's going nowhere," Collet proclaimed, in a voice of which a regimental sergeant major would have been proud.

Dan stared from Adam to Ivy and tried to make sense of what was happening. From sailing full speed aboard a luxury liner, he now felt shipwrecked and castaway.

The case had been over. Ivy and Newman were under arrest. In a stroke of inspiration – if he did say so himself – Dan Groves, amateur investigator of note, had uncovered their conspiracy.

He had even begun rehearsing for the *Wessex Tonight* broadcast.

Tonight, we can exclusively reveal who the police believe killed Martha and Brian Edwards, Craig would intone. *Our crime correspondent, Dan Groves – who was integral in the breakthrough, as I hope he won't mind me saying – joins us now to tell us more...*

And now what?

"Come on," Adam ordered and began running towards the stairs.

It was all Dan could do to force his legs to start moving and trail bewildered in the detective's wake.

★★★

Claire was waiting in the lobby by the court's main doors, trying to ignore the admiring looks of the two security guards. Her hair was tussled from the rain and she wore it well.

Outside, the storm unleashed its venom. A waterfall poured from the small shelter of the entranceway. The trees in the plaza were being battered incessantly.

"Are you alright, sir?" she asked Adam, who had grown so disheveled he was beginning to resemble an explorer emerging from a jungle expedition.

"I wish people would stop asking me that," he grunted.

A couple of people stopped to watch the strange scene, but Adam didn't even register them.

"Where's Templar?" he barked at one of the guards.

"His Honour?" the man corrected.

"Whatever. Where is he?"

"He's gone out."

"No shit. Did he tell you where?"

The man smiled, revealing teeth which had encountered far too many cigarettes in their unhappy lifetime.

"You know, he did. He made a little joke with us. His Honour likes his jokes – well, sometimes he does. I don't know—"

"Where," Adam cut in, forcefully, "did he say he was going?"

"To the car park." The man pointed across the plaza. "The multi-storey, over in the corner."

Adam swore again. He made to head for the doors, but stopped. "And what the hell was funny?"

"Oh, it wasn't that. It was what else he said."

"Which was?"

"You won't believe it."

"Try me."

"He said he had a gun. That was very funny, I thought. He had a gun, he was in a mean mood and to be sure to tell that to anyone who came after him. Can you imagine it? His Honour with a gun? Now, that'd be some scary form of justice, wouldn't it?"

★★★

Without a hint of hesitation Adam headed out of the doors and into the rain, beckoning Dan and Claire to follow.

It was like walking into a weatherborne assault. Hissing droplets beat into their faces. Their hair, coats, jackets, trousers were pulled wildly around. The whipping of the air made it difficult to catch a breath. They ran down the steps and onto the plaza, bent over against the onslaught.

The wind was tormenting the young trees, bowing them one way then another. The concrete was slippery with a patina of sodden leaves. Puddles were everywhere, deep and distorted with the waves of the pounding weather.

Within seconds, the rain had soaked them through to the skin.

"What's going on?" Claire gasped to Dan.

"No idea. I thought the case was sorted."

A car drove past, sending a cascade of water over them. It made no difference. They could have been swimming and stayed drier. They jogged around a line of benches, the rain sounding a tattoo on the wooden slats.

Adam reached the car park and stopped in the lee of its shelter. He leaned on the doors, tried to gather his breath.

"What the hell is going on?" Dan gasped.

"We got it wrong," the detective replied. "*You* got it wrong."

"What?"

"Wrong! Who offered us the loan of that room?"

"Templar, according to the guard."

"And what did we hear at the end in there, when we were arresting Ivy?"

To the east, a flash of lightning lit the sky. Dan waited for the thunder to abate. "A thud. But that was just someone next door dropping something, wasn't it?"

"Was it? What if that was someone who'd been listening in? And then deciding it was time to get away?"

"Well, I mean... I suppose it's possible," Dan flailed. "But – who? Why?"

A strange noise, a kind of low groan came from Claire. It was the sound of painful realisation.

"You'd better tell him," Adam said. "It might be easier, coming from you."

Claire abandoned her usual diplomacy and did, hard and direct. "It's not Newman."

"What's not Newman?" Dan gaped. "Not Newman what?"

"Not Newman who killed the Edwards."

"What? But I had it all worked out."

"It's not Newman," Adam interrupted. "Will you please get that into your head?"

A spray of rain swirled around them, flying leaves spinning in the vortex.

"If it's not Newman, who the hell is it?" Dan asked.

Adam gave him an exasperated look. "Think man!"

"Well, it can only be... Templar?"

"Brilliant! You got it. Well done you! He offered his chambers so he could listen in to the interview with Ivy."

"But we had it all worked out. How Newman and Ivy killed the Edwards."

"Almost," Claire said. "Except – substitute Templar for Newman."

"But Templar's got an alibi. Those emails he sent. To the Ministry and—"

"And he more or less told us how he did that," Adam snapped. "Remember he was going on about managing to book a round of golf at St Andrew's, despite being in court? He set up some program to send the emails at a specified time."

And all Dan could do was repeat his word of the moment.

"But—"

"But nothing," Adam yelled. "Just get it into your head. It was Templar and Ivy. Templar did the breaking in. He knew everything he needed because he presided over that bungalow explosion trial. He was the ringleader. He got Ivy to go along with it and set off the car alarm. While Ivy did that Templar was back at home phoning his bank, establishing the rest of his alibi. When Ivy was blubbing after we arrested him he kept saying, 'But he said it was perfect, he said we couldn't be caught'. The 'he' wasn't Newman. It was Templar."

Dan leaned back against the concrete of the car park wall. The world has shifted and he was struggling to cope.

"Shit," he whispered. "And I was so sure. So – what do we do now?"

Adam nodded grimly to the doors. "Let's see if we can prevent it becoming a hat trick of jumpers, shall we?"

★★★

Adam was about to reach for the door handles, but Claire stopped him.

"Sir, the guard said Templar may be armed."

"So?"

"So, we'd better think about how we handle this."

"He was bluffing to stop us following. A judge wouldn't have a gun."

"Just like we thought a judge wouldn't commit murder?"

Adam took his hand from the door. "What are you saying?"

"That we ought to at least consider the possibility he's armed. We should get the firearms teams here."

"There's no time. He'd jump."

A man of action as ever, Adam wasn't to be deterred. He reached once more for the doors, but Claire barred the way.

"All right, we'll face him. But one thing first…"

"What?"

She looked deliberately at Adam's left hand. "You're a married man with a teenage son. Whereas Dan and I…"

She let her eyes slide over to the crumpled, downcast and unusually quiet journalist who was propping up the car park wall.

"We don't have anyone else."

Adam shook his head. "No way. I'm the senior officer. I wouldn't let you take the risk. It has to be me."

"But sir—"

"No! That's my final word. Now, come on. We've wasted enough time."

Claire studied him and smiled. It was a look filled with respect and fondness, even through the wind and rain.

"I thought you'd say that. Ok, sir, you win. But before we go up there, I need a quick word – in private."

She opened the door and ushered Dan into the car park. Claire turned back to Adam and with remarkable speed and strength shoved him away. He stumbled under the surprise of the attack and she darted through the doors.

From her jacket, Claire produced a pair of handcuffs.

"In case I needed to arrest Katrina," she explained. "I was quite looking forward to it."

Quickly, Claire locked one cuff around each of the handles of the double doors. From outside came an angry hammering. The doors rocked back and forth, but the handcuffs held them firmly closed.

"Sorry sir, but you didn't leave me any choice," she shouted at the wood.

Claire beckoned to a dazed Dan and began jogging up the stairs.

CHAPTER FORTY-TWO

Something in Dan's expression must have given him away, and probably with some panache. He'd always prided himself on being able to adopt a decent poker face, as the expression had it, although Botox face might be more appropriate for the modern world.

A reporter often required such a talent for dealing with people whose views may be irritating or even abhorrent, and equally so for the agreeable. Neutrality was the course a good hack had to sail.

Dan took in the cramped and smelly stairwell and saw it roughly this way. Outside the doors, securely locked by handcuffs, was the platinum path to safety. There also was the man he had followed through many an ordeal and unspokenly come to think of as his protector.

Up the stairs was a land Dan had long tried to avoid, one known as mortal danger. It was quite possibly occupied by a man who was not only seriously unbalanced, but also armed.

And on the steps, waiting for him, was a woman about whom he didn't know what to think.

All this must have registered as plain as semaphore, because Claire gave him an understanding look and said, "I know you're not the bravest. But now's a chance to redeem yourself."

"Err – in what way?"

"In my way."

Dan made no move whatsoever for the stairs. He might as well have grown roots.

"You know I'm right," she added. "We don't have anyone else. Mr Breen has a family."

"I've got Rutherford."

"I'll look after him if you're killed."

"Who looks after him if we're both killed?"

"We'll worry about that later," she replied, with a logic which would have impressed even the most dogmatic of politicians. "Now come on! We don't have long before the boss works his way up the ramps."

She hopped down a couple of steps, found Dan's arm and began to pull. But still he resisted. Claire let her grip ease, took his hand in hers and gently pulled again.

★★★

One by one, Dan counted off the levels. Details of the floors lingered in his vision.

The allotment of chewing gum blossoms of Level One. It must provide a meeting place for youngsters with nowhere else to go. And if that was the location of choice, they really were short of options.

Level Two boasted a ticket machine, its cheerful lights flashing a slow rhythm. It was designed like a tank to repel the inevitable attacks of the criminals, vandals and angry motorists.

"Any progress on sorting out your feelings yet?" came Claire's voice from over her shoulder.

"Not really."

"Not really?"

"Ok, not at all then."

"You're going to have to sometime."

Dan thought he would concentrate on conquering the stairs and didn't reply. The human brain could commonly only cope with one powerful emotion at a time and fear was the current resident.

A sudden and discomforting worry nagged. What if Claire was deliberately leading him into danger, as a punishment for Katrina?

Dan ushered the thought away. It was scarcely helping.

Level Three was the most nondescript. A small black patch of an oil stain dirtied one corner. Its heavy smell lingered in the fetid air. The thick plastic coverings of the lights made the stairwell dim and tinged with green.

Outside the storm was still grumbling, but further away. Dan thought he could hear sirens. The fire brigade would be on the way again, but this time accompanied by police firearms teams. His clothes were soaked through and, despite the warmth of the day and the exertion of climbing the stairs, Dan shivered.

Level Four was a gallery of graffiti, an accident of colour.

"How's Rutherford?" came Claire's voice again.

"What?"

"Your dog, remember? How is he?"

"Is now the time?"

"Just asking."

"He's fine."

"Just fine?"

"Fine."

"How'd you feel about me popping round and us taking him out for a walk sometime?"

"If I'm still alive, gladly."

She continued climbing the stairs. A small pile of discarded newspaper filled the corner of the stairwell of Level Five. Some showed evidence of an attempt to start a fire.

Two more floors to the roof. Dan noticed his legs were starting to move more slowly.

"Come on," Claire encouraged from somewhere above. "We're almost there."

"Exactly," Dan muttered.

Level Six was the *Floor of Signs*. Visitors were advised about a range of prohibited behaviours in the dictatorship of the car park. They included, improbably, a particularly strident ban on camping.

Above, a door slowly opened. Daylight spilled into the stairwell. A breeze ran down the floors. They were almost at the roof.

★★★

Claire was waiting inside the door. She'd crouched down and pushed it open with an extended arm. Dan hesitated, half way down the steps.

"What are you doing?" he asked.

"Seeing whether he was going to take a shot as soon as we appeared," she replied.

Dan sat down heavily on one of the concrete steps.

"Come on," she said. "You can do this."

"Are you sure about that?"

"Do I have to take your hand again? Are we going out there hand in hand? How'd you think that would look?"

"I don't think I care."

"I do. Come on. It's important not to show fear in situations like this."

"I'm not sure I've got that option."

"Dan!"

He got back to his feet and joined her. Together, with Claire taking the lead, they edged out onto the roof.

★★★

Dan braced himself for the gunfire, but there was nothing. Just the sound of the rain, beating on the tarmac and the wind, magnified by the height and whistling around them. It was like a tempest in their faces.

There were only four cars on the level. A modern Mini, close to them, a couple of older cars further along and a large, black Jeep. It was in the corner where Annette and her father had jumped.

"That's where he'll be," Claire said. "But we'll have to check the other cars first. We don't want him jumping us from behind."

She began walking, step by careful step, towards the Mini. It was spotless, had the shine of a showroom, even in this weather. Claire knelt down to look under the car, checking for signs of anyone hiding on the other side. She inched her way around the bonnet, treading silently, before turning to Dan, putting a finger to her lips and shaking her head.

They moved on to the next car. It was an old, red Ford, streaked with rust. A wave of wind hit them, Claire paused and then began carefully pacing around the faded silver of the front bumper.

Something moved. Fast and darting, running through the rain. Claire sprang back, arms outstretched, ready to fend off the blow.

Dan felt himself tense. He wanted to run forwards to help her, protect her, but his legs weren't responding.

More rain, more wind, pummeling into them, spraying chaotic patterns in the pools and puddles on the tarmac.

The doors to the stairwell banged under the assault of the gust. Claire and Dan both span around. There was nothing, just the ghost of the wind.

From the side of the Ford a seagull appeared and danced across the tarmac. Claire shook her head and continued around the car. There was no one, nothing.

She ruffled her hair and held up a couple of fingers. Two more cars to go. But to Dan, it was obvious where Templar was hiding, as evident as if a great neon arrow was pointing down from the sky. He was behind the Jeep, watching them, quite possibly tracking every movement with the barrel of his gun.

Dan's mobile rang. He jumped, fumbled for it and switched it off. It was a withheld number, the newsroom again. Lizzie demanding to know where he was and what was going on. The answer to both those questions he preferred not to think.

The time had slipped on to ten past four. If they could find Templar, if they could persuade him not to shoot, if there was no siege, if he would submit, if he would confess, all would be well. Dan's career would be saved, Adam's too. But first, there was a daunting course of *ifs* to navigate.

Next was a battered, green Renault. Claire approached, crouched down, checked underneath, warily circled the bonnet. Dan hung back, peering through the opaque greyness of the cloud of weather. She disappeared around the car, then quickly stood and held up a thumb. Nothing.

They began making for the final vehicle on the roof. The Jeep had some of the bunches of flowers that had been left in Annette's memory climbing the low concrete wall around it, a few scattered by the onslaught of the elements.

"I'm going to need your help," Claire whispered.

"Err – how?"

"You'll have to go around one side, I'll do the other."

Dan wasn't surprised by the faintness of his voice. "Me?"

"You."

"Why?"

"Do you really want to know?"

"Maybe," Dan gulped.

"It might make Templar hesitate. It means he won't know which of us to shoot first. "

Claire smiled and, for what must have been the first time in his life, it wasn't a look Dan found anywhere close to being reassuring.

"Come here," she said, and kissed him gently on the lips. "That's for luck."

She looked him in the eyes and kissed him again. "And that's for you. Now, come on."

★★★

Below, a line of fire engines had parked along the street. The yellow bags were being inflated once more. Police cars had cordoned off the plaza. Dan thought he spotted men with guns running across the expanse of concrete but he looked away before he could be sure.

He followed the low concrete wall, step by step, silently, towards the Jeep. A few metres to his side Claire was peering at the corner.

There was no movement, no sign anyone was there. Just the odd swirl of the incessant wind and rain.

They were twenty metres away. Claire slowed her pace, gestured to Dan to do the same.

The Jeep was a big, silver box, parked slightly askew in the rectangle of white lines. It made for good cover, plenty of space to hide behind. It was spattered with mud, the green and white of a Devon flag proudly positioned within the back windscreen.

Flowers flapped in the wind. A chip of gravel crunched under Dan's foot.

He stopped. Claire did the same. But there was nothing. No movement, no reaction, no attack.

They stepped onwards. Fifteen metres now.

Claire edged a little further away, to get a better angle to see around the Jeep. More thunder rumbled in the distance, but the rain was a little lighter now.

Ten metres.

Still no movement from the Jeep.

Claire stopped. She crouched down, then kneeled, angled her head, her cheek close to the tarmac. She scanned under the chassis, stood again and shook her head.

But those wheels were plenty big enough to hide a pair of legs. And a man, one who was waiting patiently, nursing a gun. Biding his time until he knew he couldn't miss.

They paced on, their steps even slower now. They were only five metres from the Jeep.

Once more, Claire stopped. She mouthed, *ready?*

Dan took one very long, very deep breath, hoped it wouldn't be his last and nodded. Claire held up her hand, four fingers and a thumb outstretched, and counted down.

Five, four, three, two, one...

In unison they lurched forwards, ran for the Jeep. Dan headed for the boot, Claire the bonnet. They reached the target at the same time.

Dan expected the levelling of a gun barrel, turning to point between his eyes, a blinding, burning blast, an explosion of roaring, deafening sound. And then the black oblivion of instant death, the sudden plunge from light to darkness.

But there was nothing. No one. Only the fading flowers, flapping in the wind.

★★★

They found Adam on the plaza, standing outside a police van, impervious to the rain. His hair, usually springy and fastidiously styled, had become a mat of dark moss and his suit was black with saturation.

Dan caught a glimpse of himself in one of the van's windows and grimaced. Even Claire had the decency to look a little disheveled. No one was at their best in the appearance stakes today.

"Sir, about what happened outside the car park," she said to Adam. "I apologise, but I thought it was for the best. I fully expect to be disciplined, of course," she added.

Adam looked her over and did his best to assemble an expression of disapproving authority. But it largely failed.

"Then consider yourself disciplined," he said, fondly. "If you'd been killed, I'd have been furious. But as you're ok, forget it. So, where's Templar?"

Dan shrugged. "He's outthought us again. He's probably miles away. What he told the security guard about going to the car park was a lovely diversion. It gave him loads of time to escape."

"And now he could be anywhere," Claire added. "But we'll find him."

"Maybe," Adam replied. "But not in time to save me – or Dan."

As one, they checked their watches. Dan's said it was twenty past four, which meant probably around half past. Brian Flood would be arriving at Charles Cross at any moment.

Back in the *Wessex Tonight* studios Phil would be editing the story of the day. Roger Newman's outspoken attack on the police and the journalist suffused with such extraordinary arrogance to presume he could play an important role in the investigation. The funeral requiem was being readied.

"Haven't we got enough to save ourselves?" Dan asked, trying not to sound desperate. "Now we know who killed the Edwards?"

"Nowhere close," the downcast Adam replied. "In fact, it's worse. Newman's attack still stands and we've let the mastermind escape. I'm going to look even more stupid than before."

Claire laid a hand on his shoulder. "Come on, sir. You cracked it in the end."

"More by blundering around than good judgement." He sighed and wiped some rain from his face. "Ah, come on, I've had enough of standing here feeling sorry for myself. It's time to face the wrath."

Adam was about to start trudging back towards the courthouse when a shout stopped him. It was the security guard and he was running and waving.

"Just make my day even better," Adam grunted. "Let me guess – Ivy's escaped?"

"No sir," the man replied. "It's Judge Templar. He wants to see you."

"What?"

"Most insistent, His Honour was. He even made me run through this weather to tell you. He says he's in Courtroom Number Three and wants to see you right away."

CHAPTER FORTY-THREE

Through the glass panel of the door they could see Templar, sitting high at the head of the court. He was writing, a fat fountain pen moving quickly back and forth over a sheet of paper. The judge occasionally stopped to think before continuing with his task. He wore his grey wig, his red and purple robes and had positioned a gavel by his side.

Adam turned to Dan and Claire. "The good news is – no sign of any weapon. The bad news – no sign of any sanity either."

"There's plenty of space under the bench to hide a gun," Dan observed.

Claire ignored the latest outbreak of faintheartedness. "I can't believe he'd have called us here if he just wanted to start shooting. He could have done that earlier when you two were talking to Ivy. Or he could have gone to the car park and waited to shoot it out with us there."

Adam checked his watch. The time was just before half past four. "If we're going to crack this case and save ourselves, it has to be now."

Claire nodded her agreement. Dan hesitated and did the same, but without anything like such commitment.

Adam held a quick whispered conversation with the tactical firearms commander, who was standing by the stairs. It was clear from the look on the man's face he didn't approve. Dan could hear the odd phrase.

"It's going completely against standard procedure... Surely better to hold him there until he decides to come out."

But Adam wasn't in a mood to heed advice. The discussion was brief and the order given.

Armed police officers were deployed at both ends of the corridor around the door to courtroom number three. They were dressed all in black, wearing body armour, and moved fast and silently, despite the weight of their pistols and semi-automatic rifles. Some knelt, others half hid behind walls.

All were soaking wet, a legacy of the operation to surround the car park. When the security guard passed on his message, the marksmen had followed Adam into the courthouse, their faces full puzzlement. A firearms call to a court, with a judge as the subject, was hardly their usual fare.

The rest of the building was quietly evacuated, ushers and security guards herding people towards the front entrance. There they stood, a huddled group, sheltering as best they could from the rain. Across the plaza the firefighters were packing up their inflatable bags, ready for use another day.

Word of what was happening had reached the media. A cordon was in place around the courthouse and behind it stood photographers, reporters and cameramen. Nigel was amongst them. By no means for the first time in his life of joining Adam on cases, Dan found an unspoken wish welling in his chest – that he was standing in safety beside his cameraman, rather than here.

The firearms commander beckoned to Adam. "The Deputy Chief Constable will be here in ten minutes."

Adam paced back to Dan and Claire, waiting by the double doors of the courtroom.

"That settles it," he said. "I'm going in. The only question is whether you two should come."

"I'm coming," Claire replied. "I was ready to face him in the car park, I am again now. Plus, Templar's old school. He might just react better to me."

"Thank you," Adam nodded. "Dan?"

"Well, Templar doesn't like the media, and he didn't think much of me before. I don't want to antagonise him. Maybe I should just—"

"Dan's coming," Claire interrupted.

The three held a look. The curious triangle that linked them still held strong. They would fly or fall together. Inside the court, Templar was still scribbling at his piece of paper.

"Right," Adam said. "Let's do it."

★★★

Claire pushed the door gently open and Adam stepped carefully into the courtroom. Templar didn't look up from his notes.

The detective took a pace inside, then another. Claire and Dan followed. There was still no reaction from the judge.

Rain beat down on the skylights. The room was a little too warm, just as it had been when the jury returned their verdict in the trial of Martha and Brian Edwards.

Adam stopped in front of the rows of seats in the public gallery. Templar had shown no sign of acknowledging their arrival. He was too intent on what he was writing.

Claire shifted her position. One of the old wooden floorboards creaked a loud, complaining sound. They waited, sure now that the judge would speak. But the room was still, the only sound the unending, battering attack of the rain.

Adam took a breath and coughed loudly. And now, at last, Templar looked up. He stared at them, those piercing eyes following the line of their wary and watchful faces, scrutinising, just as he did with everything that happened in this court.

They must have looked a strange incarnation of the coming of justice. All three were soaked; their hair still dripping with rainwater, their jackets dark with the outpourings of the storm. Each of them standing with hands behind their backs in the well of a deserted courtroom, facing a judge who the years had journeyed to become a murderer.

Templar prodded at his wig. "Ah, there you are," he announced, brusquely. "It's about time. I was beginning to wonder when you were going to turn up."

He pointed to Adam. "You, Breen. I imagine even you managed to spot the clue about where I might be – given that I instructed that guard to come and tell you. I see from your appearance you followed my little feint to the car park. I thought that would appeal to your sense of melodrama."

Adam rode the blows without comment. He hesitated before replying, and even here, even now, the judge of so many years standing in this court still demanded the respect of the title he had long worn.

"Your Honour," Adam said, carefully. "I'm not sure whether you appreciate this, but we're here to arrest you—"

"Yes, yes, I know all that," Templar interjected. "God knows I've presided over enough miserable trials to have heard it sufficient times. We'll get to all that nonsense in a moment. But first, I have something to say."

He pointed to the benches below where the solicitors and barristers normally sat. "Step forwards, will you? Come on, hurry up. I have some remarks upon which to address you."

★★★

Dan couldn't help but glance around the room. At the jury box, where Parkinson delivered that extraordinary verdict. At the dock, where the Edwards stood, waiting for the decision on their fate. And then behind, at the public gallery. Where Annette and Roger Newman sat week after week, as the trial went about its judicial progress.

It was only a couple of days ago that the case had ended – but it felt a long time indeed.

"Right, then," Templar barked. "Before I begin, I think we need a little accompaniment, do we not?"

He reached under the bench. Dan saw Adam stiffen, his body tense, ready for the appearance of a gun. Claire was doing the same. But in Templar's careful hands was carried only the Newton's Cradle. He smiled fondly, set it upon the polished wooden surface and began the silver balls swinging.

Click, clack, click, clack...

"That's better," he exclaimed. "Now, one last matter requires attention before I begin summing up in this, my final case."

An accusatory finger singled out Dan. "You, Groves. You're supposed to be a reporter, are you not?"

"Yes, Your Honour," came the startled reply.

"Take some damned notes, then. This is an important part of the story, is it not? Something you will doubtless be wishing to report upon? It would at least be welcome if you could make some reasonable attempt to get it right – for once."

Dan reached into his satchel for a pen and pad. His phone was there, switched off to avoid the endless calls and messages. An idea formed. A couple more seconds pretence of fumbling and all was in place. He held up his notebook and did his best to smile disarmingly at Templar.

"About time," the judge chided. "Do I have to think of everything for you people? Right, pay attention. This won't take long. In fact, it's rather remarkable that after all these years I have so little to say by way of my concluding remarks."

Click, clack, click, clack…

Templar studied the piece of paper and drew himself up in the chair. His voice boomed as he projected it around the old wooden panels of the courtroom.

"It is often said that justice is a game. But if that be the case, then it is a game in which one side is heavily disadvantaged, like a football team of the full complement of eleven playing a five-a-side ensemble. And not content with this handicap, the state appears set upon ever further attempts to neuter its ability to find any form of justice. It bestows an increasing weight of rights upon the criminals, whilst eroding those of the victims."

Templar paused and looked up to check they were all listening. And they were, how they were. Strange, extraordinary and bizarre though it may be, this was the most compelling of confessions.

"In my years upon the bench, it seems to me that Lord Denning's fine old quotation – 'Justice should not only be done but manifestly and undoubtedly be seen to be done' – has taken on a new meaning. In these modern days, justice should neither be done, nor be seen to approach anywhere remotely close to being done."

A droplet of rain dripped from Adam's jacket, landing in time with one of the clicks from the silver spheres. Claire pushed her fringe back from her brow but kept her eyes set on the judge.

"I can no longer keep count of the number of cases which I have presided over where the needs of justice have fallen far short of being satisfied. When first I became the resident judge in this court, it was with great pride that I would arrive here, and look up to the Lady of Justice, standing tall above us. These days, I fear I have come to see her as a figure of shame."

Click, clack, click, clack...

Templar's voice fell to a confiding tone. They were in the confessional together, edging towards the heart of the man.

"At this point, I must raise one personal matter, and it is an issue of a dreadful irony. My comfort and companion throughout the difficult times of my changing views was my lady wife, Eileen. She was the most doughty of rocks. And then she was taken from me. The result was a man whose life had been spent serving justice suffering the gross injustice of the loss of his lifelong companion and best friend."

Dan was writing fast, taking down quote after quote. But now he paused, for even the most hackneyed of hardened reporters would have been moved by the pain in the judge's words.

"I turn now to the trial of the Edwards, the case in point," Templar intoned, his voice stronger. "It encapsulates all that I have outlined. A trial where it is so very obvious what the true outcome should have been but yet again where that ending proves elusive. It was then I decided to take matters into my own hands."

Overhead, thunder rumbled once more. Templar waited for it to die and then turned over his sheet of paper.

Click, clack, click, clack...

"In conclusion, I say this. Please show mercy to Usher Ivy, who played by far the minor role in our conspiracy and who acted entirely in my thrall. And I would ask you also to try to understand why I did what I did, and ask yourselves the question – whether it was truly wrong?"

The judge rested the piece of paper. He reached out and stopped the swinging of the silver spheres.

Stillness and silence settled on the courtroom. Templar studied the two men and one woman, lined up below him. And they looked back. Perhaps now with a different view, but still an inescapable duty.

Adam waited, then took a step forwards. The old wooden boards creaked with the movement. When at last he spoke, the words were quiet and measured.

"Your Honour, I hear what you say. And perhaps I can understand it, maybe even sympathise. But I must now tell you that I have to place you under arrest for the murders of Martha and Brian Edwards, and—"

"I have not finished," Templar barked suddenly, with all a judge's authority. "By no means."

And now came something entirely unexpected. Templar's face changed. It twitched into a grin, followed by a broad smile. He even began chuckling to himself, the sound eerie in the empty courtroom.

"This was all phased out before my time," he giggled. "We're far too politically correct for anything so sensible now, sadly. These days it's all community service and psychiatric assessments, as though a crime isn't a damned crime. But I've always wanted to do it."

Templar fumbled under the bench once more. This time, he brought out a black cap that he placed slowly and deliberately upon the top of his wig. And if that was not shock enough, following the small square of dark silk came a gun.

CHAPTER FORTY-FOUR

It was a quirk of history, but so portentous that it resonated through the years.

In his law classes at Journalism College, Dan had been taught about the legend of the black cap. The stories of the culmination of a murder trial and the judge donning the cap to pass a sentence of death were still told by older hacks at retirement gatherings and reunions. They were often marked as the sole moments of stillness in the hubbub of the evening.

The impenetrable quiet in the courtroom. The movement of the judge's hand towards that little square of black fabric. The inevitable gasps of the crowd and the look on the face of the defendant.

These days it had become a curiosity. Something for museums, books and bedtime stories, no longer needed in a modern courtroom.

Until today, this stormy afternoon, and Templar.

The judge was staring down at them, the laughter gone and any hint of humanity banished in another of those mercurial swings of mood. His face was intractable, as hard as the Dartmoor granite.

Before him, Dan, Claire and Adam stood in a line. It was as though they were waiting to find out who would be condemned. Dan let his eyes slip to the expressions of his companions. From the looks chilling their faces, creeping like the crystals of a frost, it was clear they knew far too well what that black cap signified.

The smile returned as Templar began checking the gun. It was a revolver, a bright and polished body and a dark handle, curved with the crescents of finger grips.

"Came from some relative in the war, never found out which one," he chuckled. "Dad always kept it. He said you never knew when you'd need it. And damned right he was, too."

The judge turned the wheel of the gun and stroked the brassy, honed bullets. Dan could see Claire calculating the distance to the bench, whether she could make it in time to grab the weapon. But it was too far, too difficult to clamber over that last parapet of the wood. Templar would have plenty of time to take aim and shoot. Instinctively, with no thought as to the meaning of the simple gesture, Dan found himself taking Claire's hand to hold her back.

Templar raised the gun and pointed it at the glass walls of the dock.

"Bang, bang! That sure beats handing out suspended sentences, eh? You know, sometimes I think I missed my moment. I'd have been much happier parking the old black cap on my head. I'd have them hanging for bloody shoplifting, let alone murder."

Templar beamed around the court. To the lawyers, jury, public gallery. All were there in his mind, all intent upon this, his final case.

The whiteness of a distant lightning bolt lit the gloom of the courtroom and more thunder rumbled overhead.

"Now then," he said. "To our final business."

He levelled the revolved and pointed it at Adam.

★★★

It had started as a game, this life as an unofficial detective. The first case had been serious, yes, but ultimately just a deception. A clever riddle to be solved and little more. For Dan, in those days, it had been entertainment. A distraction, a reinvigorating new world at a time when he was growing stale in a job he had known since college.

Only after a couple more cases, when he was confronted by the enormity of true suffering and violent death, did Dan understand the gravity of that which he had become a part. And now, on this rainy afternoon, he was facing the end himself, as surely as if summoned before the reaper.

"Your Honour," Adam spoke out, his voice remarkably calm, "it doesn't have to be this way."

"This is my court and my judgement. I shall be the one who decides which way it has to be."

"But—"

"There is no but. There is only now. I invited you here to witness my summing up. That issue has been concluded. There remains just one further order of business."

Templar stroked a hand over the barrel of the revolver. It looked so long, so lethal, so very effortless in its ability to guide that killing bullet.

"Judge Templar," Claire said, gently. "I think I understand what you've been going through. I've sometimes felt the same myself in this job. But how does it help, doing this? It won't bring back Annette. It can't change the past. How does more death make anything right?"

The flint of the man's expression softened. "Ah, Ms Reynolds, I appreciate your thoughts. At this final moment, please allow me to say that you were always one of my favourite officers. A diligent and talented investigator but, as I hope I've shown, justice can be a fickle and flighty visitor to our world. I thank you for what you say, but I cannot agree with it. This is the end I have chosen, and so it must be."

Dan saw Adam's eyes flick to him. Many times the detective had joked that the reporter who became his friend did so in part because he possessed the legendary gift of a silvered tongue.

And so Dan tried to think of some powerful logic or moving emotion to save them. He scoured the furthest edges of his mind for a beautiful intervention. And at this time of greatest need, the canvas remained steadfastly blank.

He was too afraid to think. And the second of opportunity was lost.

"So then," Templar intoned, "as we have no blindfolds available to us, you may wish to turn around."

"Your Honour—" Adam tried, but was overridden.

"Turn around, Inspector."

Dan began to turn, and a strange memory formed. It was a story he'd once covered, a suicide, a young woman who had been made redundant from the job she loved. She wore glasses but had taken them off before jumping from the top floor of her office building. The investigation uncovered the curious insight that most people who wore glasses would remove their spectacles before jumping.

And in this case, a bullet in the back of the head was surely preferable to the last living second of witnessing it tearing between your eyes.

"I'm not turning around," Claire said, firmly. "If you're going to do this, you do it face to face."

"Very well, Ms Reynolds. If that is how you wish it."

Outside, through the glass panels of the door, Dan thought he could see a marksman. But the movement was fleeting and he couldn't be sure.

To his side he heard Claire draw in a sharp breath. Adam let out a low murmur.

Dan could sense the revolver raising. He wondered who would be shot first. If it was him, at least he wouldn't have to suffer the sound of the bodies of his comrades falling and that horrendous wait for his own turn.

Another movement at the door. Dan was almost sure it was edging open.

But then again, if he was the first to be killed it would mean no chance of salvation. No time for the marksmen to storm the courtroom and disarm the judge. And something was happening outside. Feet were striding, running.

A loud click made Dan start. It sounded like the movement of a trigger, but it was the Newton's Cradle. Templar had set those silver spheres in motion once again.

Click, clack, click, clack...

"This is your final chance to turn around," the judge announced.

"No," Claire replied.

"No," Adam affirmed.

More thunder boomed overhead, more pounding rain. Dan tensed his body, wondering if he would live long enough to know how the burning passage of a bullet felt. He waited for the shot.

But it didn't come.

The door to the court was opening.

★★★

So much Dan may have expected then. A rifle barrel, the red dot of a laser sight finding a target on Templar's chest and killing him in an instant. Perhaps a negotiator, dressed in helmet and body armour, edging through the door.

Maybe stun grenades, smoke, tear gas flying through the air. Shouts, a tumble of armed police flooding the court, pinning down and protecting Adam, Dan and Claire and overpowering the judge.

Nothing so dramatic came to pass. The door opened to reveal Katrina.

She stood in the doorway, just stood. Arms by her sides, not threatening, not fearful, but calm.

"Hello, Judge Templar," Katrina said, in a gentle voice, but which carried easily across the courtroom.

"Ms Harper," he replied, with similar composure. "It is a pleasure, as ever. But you arrive at a crucial point in the proceedings. Hard though this is to say this to one as engaging as you, it may be better if you left."

She took a step into the room and let the door ease shut.

"I don't think so."

Templar allowed the revolver to lower from its bead upon Adam. He rested the gun on the bench, but his fingers were still firm on the handle and his expression intensely watchful.

Katrina paced further into the room until she was level with the edge of the public gallery. "I hope you don't think ill of me, but I was listening at the door," she said.

"Then you will have heard all I said. I have nothing more to add. My case rests."

He lifted the gun again and ran a finger over the grooves of the chamber. "I do, however, suspect those gathered here may have been suffering from a misapprehension which I must correct. They were never at threat. I am a man who believes in justice, not murder."

Templar guided the gun back and forth through the air, as if conducting an orchestra, and placed the tip of the barrel carefully against his temple. With his other hand he adjusted the black cap so it was set perfectly square upon his crown.

"It is time for the sentence to be carried out."

"No, it is not," Katrina replied, emphatically. "There's one more submission for the court to hear. It's my appeal. And if you believe in justice, then you have to allow for an appeal."

She walked further into the courtroom, every step a challenge. The footfall fell in time with the *click, clack* of the cradle. She was level with Adam.

Templar watched every movement, but said nothing.

"Your Honour, I heard your – closing speech, may I call it?"

"You may."

"I found it very powerful. Very moving."

The judge inclined his head. "Thank you, Ms Harper. Coming from one as eloquent as you that is a compliment which I cannot fail but to appreciate."

"And I agreed with much of what you said. As I believe would many people."

Adam was trying to catch her eye, warn her of the danger they were facing, of how quickly the man's mood could shift. But Katrina was focused only on Templar. Dan glanced down at his satchel. The little red dot on the side of his phone was still alight.

If they got out of this alive, all would be well. But, as he had thought so many times before, *if* was a very small word which often carried far larger implications.

Templar nodded slowly. "Thank you again Ms Harper, but I fear I fail to see the point you are trying to make."

She stepped past the dock, her elegant figure reflecting in the glass, and rested by the witness box.

"Why not make your point to the whole world?" Katrina asked.

"In what way?"

"The most effective way – in person. Every word argued well to a watching public. I believe they would find it compelling."

"I believe I already have." A disdainful finger pointed to Dan. "That is why I summoned the media here."

"Yes, Your Honour, but he's just one journalist. Why not a whole court full? And not just that, but solicitors and barristers, a judge, a public gallery? The case would attract international attention."

Click, clack, click, clack...

Templar considered her words, a hand tapping on the wood. "You are suggesting I give myself up and submit to a trial?"

Katrina stepped forwards again. She was almost at the bench. Dan could see Adam assessing the distance between her and Templar, calculating whether she could reach the gun before he had time to shoot.

"You could represent yourself," she said. "You were such a fine advocate."

Templar reached out and stopped the silver spheres. The room felt suddenly quiet without their rhythmic sound. Even the rain had eased, to just a gentle spray pattering on the skylights.

"And why should the court grant your request?"

"For several reasons."

Katrina began to climb the steps to the bench. She eased open the small wooden gate that led to the great chair where the judge sat. He made no move to stop her, but kept the revolver pressed to his head.

"Careful, Ms Harper," Templar warned. "This court requires sound arguments, not ill-advised heroics."

She stopped and held up her hands. But she was only feet from Templar.

"Your Honour, I believe you still want to live. The plan you put together to set off the explosion, the way you provided alibis for yourself and Jonathan Ivy, was brilliant. It's clear you didn't want to be caught."

The barrel of the revolver was drooping.

"And then there's the rest of your life," she continued. "What about your memoirs? And you were looking for another partner, weren't you? That's not the way of someone without hope. There are so many women who would love to know someone as principled and engaging as you."

319

"Visiting me as I spend the rest of my days in a tawdry prison cell, like some common criminal?"

"I don't believe so. Given your skills as an advocate, along with the emotional trauma you've suffered, a murder charge could never be proved. A jury would have sympathy with you, as would the rest of the world. You could be the catalyst for reform of the legal system – in exactly the way you've spoken so passionately about wanting."

In the distance, more thunder rumbled. Katrina moved forwards once again. She was standing above Templar now. He had lowered the gun to the bench, but it was still in his hand.

Dan, Claire and Adam all watched, all wondering what she would do. Katrina was much younger and fitter than Templar. She could easily end this. Grab the revolver and give them the few seconds they would need to restrain the man. He would be carried out in handcuffs, the case finally over.

But all she did was stand there, staring down at the old man wearing the black cap and grey wig, his face as soft as an opium dream.

Katrina reached out her arms. Templar looked up and found those mesmeric eyes.

Slowly, laboured with a great weight of emotion, he released the gun and cuddled into her.

CHAPTER FORTY-FIVE

The storm battered the city anew.

From the vista of the bay window Dan watched, Rutherford at his feet. Fork after bolt of lightning flickered and struck, the great percussion of the heavens following in their wake. The rain cascaded down, beating on the trees and plants of the garden and the protective shield of the double glazing, distorting the world in a flood of water.

Darkness had fallen early tonight, the power of the elements a foe too formidable for the day's light. It was an omen of the shorter, colder days to come.

"No run for us," Dan told Rutherford. "But we'll do one tomorrow, I promise old friend. I've been neglecting you, haven't I? Are you ok just to sit here and chat tonight? There's lots I want to talk about and you've got the short straw of listening, as ever."

The dog rested his chin on Dan's thigh and accepted a gentle stroking, his manner of a graceful acquiescence.

"I don't think I've ever had a day like it," Dan continued. "So, where to begin? Perhaps some refreshments?"

In the kitchen he tried once again to ignore the yearning of the surroundings for modernisation. Some days it felt as if the cooker, fridge and cupboards had formed a union to lobby for retirement. Dan found a tin of beer at the very back of a dark recess and tried to ignore the urgent requirement to do some shopping.

"You'd think a man of my age would have learned to look after himself by now, wouldn't you?" He asked Rutherford, as they returned to the lounge.

They settled back to watching the storm. It was moving out to sea, carried on the changing wind. The city was quiet tonight, few car headlights moving, the people cowed into shelter by the onslaught of the skies.

Dan gave Rutherford a biscuit and positioned his water bowl in a corner of the bay to give the dog minimal opportunity to make his traditional mess.

"Where do we start? Well, let's be a good hack for once and begin with the headlines. They go like this. Firstly, we're safe. Adam's still in his job and has been praised for cracking the case. And I'm still gainfully employed too. That little exclusive I brought back for Lizzie means all is well. It was bloody close, though."

***

It was just after five o'clock by the time Templar had been disarmed and arrested. Dan ran out to find a taxi and headed back for the studios, urging the driver to a frenzy of haste. On the way he called Lizzie to explain what had happened, put the engineers on standby to help and sent a quick text message to Phil.

As can be the ruthless way of news, a programme running order that had been nurtured for hours was discarded in an instant. The story Dan brought would dominate to the exclusion of all else.

"I want as much as you can do, I want it fast and I want it good," Lizzie demanded. "And after you've done all that, I want a word. No, I want several."

The first task was to listen to the recording of Templar's confession and the moment of his arrest. The quality of the sound the phone had picked up wasn't brilliant. But it gave the viewers a very clear and dramatic understanding of what happened in the final minutes of the case.

As Dan expected, Roger Newman's attack was dropped. The story of the day was a judge, a man appointed as a guardian of the law, committing murder in the name of his personal reckoning of justice.

It must, by Dan's recollection, be his longest studio appearance. Segment after segment of Templar's speech he introduced.

Phil had been disappointed, to overstretch a euphemism, that the story he was carefully cutting about Newman's press conference was dropped. It was the lad's break, a chance to show what he could do. But the text message of a little earlier had done its work.

In one hasty discussion, twenty minutes before *Wessex Tonight* took to the air, Dan said, "What we could really do with is some background on Templar, to get a flavour of the man. His biggest cases, that sort of thing."

"Good point," Lizzie replied. "But there's no time now."

"Hang on – Phil, weren't you looking at Templar's career because you had that great idea for doing a profile when he retired?"

"What?"

"You were, weren't you?" Dan insisted.

"Err, yeah. Sure."

"So you've got all you need – his history, the works? All researched and ready to go."

"Um – yes."

"You're on!" Lizzie snapped. "Don't just stand there, get writing."

But Phil, either in a brave or misguided mood, insisted he had one more element to add. He'd discovered that Amy Ailing, the young woman who was injured in the gas explosion, had recovered well. She was expected to leave hospital tomorrow.

Lizzie accepted the offering as another flourish in what would already be an impressive sequence of reportage. She bathed him in the warmth of a rare "well done". The young man's strides were long and light as he went about preparing his contribution.

After the broadcast Dan took the long walk to Lizzie's office where she raised the comments Roger Newman had made.

His face was never built for a look of cherubic innocence. It was a mismatch akin to sending a rowing boat to do the job of an icebreaker. But Dan looked as blameless as best he knew how. He suggested Newman must have witnessed his closeness to the investigation – purely as a reporter doing his job, naturally – and come to an errant conclusion.

A knowing stare was the fizzing return of serve, but no more was said. Dan took his leave and made for the flat.

***

Rutherford had never been bothered by a storm, unlike many of his kin. The dog itched busily at his ear, decided such exertion was more than sufficient for a quiet evening, and lay down.

"I got a call from Adam earlier," Dan told the contented Alsatian. "He's going to charge Templar tomorrow. He's got another commendation for solving a 'highly complex and immensely demanding case' – in the Deputy Chief Constable's words. So, we blunder onwards to fight another day – whatever that may bring."

The central heating rumbled into life. It was that dreaded turning point of the year when it had to be switched back on. Rutherford lifted his head and shifted position to favour the radiator.

"Here's something that will interest you, hound. It's about Claire."

At the sound of the sacred name, the dog was back on his feet.

"Between you and me, she was magnificent in the case," Dan continued. "I don't think I appreciated just how brave she is. It really is about time I sorted myself out with her."

Rutherford, unsurprisingly, didn't reply. But he did somehow manage to produce a look that was laced with more than a hint of reproach.

"Anyway, we had a quick chat earlier. We agreed we're going to have a walk at the weekend – that's all three of us naturally. It won't be a summit, or anything heavy like that, but we will try to talk about, well… you know…"

The dog's look appeared to change to one of expectation.

"Oh, do I really have to say it? All right then, we're going to try to talk about – the… future."

Together they sat in silence, watching as another fork of lightning played over the sea.

"There's something else I've got to tell you," Dan said, when the celestial display had calmed. "You won't be surprised to hear it's about Katrina."

★★★

In his limited experience of the phenomenon of the woman, Dan had come to think that dealing with Katrina was like trying to catch a cloud. So before he made the call, he planned out what to say.

"Congratulations," was the opening gambit.

"On what?" she asked, with an element of wariness.

"Is there more than one thing?"

"In my life there could be many."

"I'm talking about persuading Templar not to shoot himself, or anyone else for that matter – particularly me. It was clever the way you played him, making it sound like a court case."

They talked a little more, on the safe ground of the tension of those final moments in the courtroom, before Dan said, "Actually, you're right. There was something else I wanted to congratulate you on."

"Oh?"

"I'm not sure quite how to say this, but try – how to commit a crime by remote control."

"Meaning?"

"I think you put Templar up to it."

A silence filled the line, before Katrina said, "What in the world might make you think that?"

"Just the obvious. That you became close to Annette, so you had the motive. That you knew Templar, and better than you let on, I think. It was apparent when you were talking in the court. You had that meeting with him after Annette killed herself, which you yourself set up. I can't help wondering what you might have said there. There's also the fact you were well aware Templar was more than a little unbalanced. And you know exactly how to manipulate people."

"Which all sounds like your wonderful imagination working even more overtime than usual. It's all entirely circumstantial, if even that."

"Which is exactly how you'd make it look, of course. Which, in turn, is why I'm surprised you left a clue."

And now there was a coldness in her voice. "I have no idea what you mean."

"You couldn't resist going to have a look, could you? To see if the idea you planted about the gas explosion might just have come to fruition."

She chuckled, but without humour. "It's a lovely idea, but I didn't leave my hotel that night."

"Which is absolutely true, the CCTV shows it; as well you knew it would. You could hardly turn up at Homely Terrace without it looking suspicious, could you? So, you popped up to the hotel roof instead. You knew you'd see the aftermath from there."

Katrina sighed. "What a terribly suspicious mind you have. It must be the journalist in you." She paused, before adding, "I hope you haven't shared this strange fantasy with anyone else. You'd make yourself a laughing stock."

"I haven't, don't worry. What's the use? There's not a particle of proof. And Templar won't say anything. He's too old fashioned and gallant to cause trouble for you. Besides, he wants his trial to be all about what justice in this country really means. Bringing you into it would only muddle the message. I just wanted to let you know that someone is aware of what you did."

"Interesting," she mused. "Because I know what you did too."

And so a conversation which, according to Dan's plan ended here, diverted rapidly from the script.

"What I did?" he queried.

"That night in the bar. When I asked you what *heterochromia iridis* was, to see whether you were worthy of spending the night with me. When you went to the toilets to 'think about it', as you said. You looked it up on the internet on your mobile, didn't you?"

Dan let a couple of seconds pass. "When are you going back to London?"

"Why?"

"I'm only interested."

"Does it make your life harder, or easier?"

"Just – different."

They began saying goodbye but Dan noticed a final scrawl on his notepad.

"Katrina, one more thing?"

"It's three hours by train, another ten minutes on the tube and five minutes' walk after that."

"What is?"

"The distance from Plymouth to my flat."

"It wasn't that."

"Really?"

Dan closed his eyes. In the darkness of his thoughts all he could see were her eyes, and those unique, contrasting colours.

"Really," he managed.

"What was it then?"

"Why the Ankh? Your tattoo?"

A smile warmed the line. "Think about it. You're not that dense, however much you might sometimes play the fool. Bye bye – for now."

★★★

The night was slipping ever onwards, the time coming up for ten o'clock. Rutherford yawned, and Dan did the same.

"Maybe it's time for bed, eh dog? But I don't think there's much hope of sleep yet."

He walked over to one of the bookcases and found some writing paper and a pen.

"Anyway, there's one more task for tonight. I've got to write to Roger Newman. I want to apologise for thinking he killed the Edwards and try to do something to make amends. I was wondering if I could help with the foundation he was talking about setting up in Annette's memory. Maybe I could give some careers talks or mentor young people who might be interested in the media."

Dan tried drafting a few lines, but the words wouldn't come. He paced around the lounge, tidying the odd book and plumping the cushions on the sofa.

In the kitchen, he put away a line of plates and tried to scrub a stain from a work surface. The effort resulted in the mark becoming ever more prominent.

Dan headed to the bedroom, thought about changing the sheets, but took no more than a second to decide against it. Such a chore was always one for tomorrow. In the bathroom he wiped the sink and watered the spider plant on the windowsill. Rutherford dutifully followed the intinerant, domestic odyssey.

"I just can't settle," Dan muttered. "But I've got an idea. How do you feel about an unusual night out?"

As ever, Rutherford didn't argue, which is one of the great benefits of the ever-loyal creatures that are dogs. Dan filled a container with water, took the duvet, a blanket and the whisky bottle and ushered Rutherford through the rain and into the car.

The streets were quiet. It was a drive of only five minutes to the city centre and the multi-storey car park in the corner of the plaza. Slowly, one by one, the Peugeot rumbled up the levels until they reached the roof. There were cars on the lower floors but this high it was deserted.

Dan parked in the corner where Annette and Roger Newman had jumped. He switched off the engine, cuddled Rutherford to him and together they watched the storm.

Lightning Source UK Ltd.
Milton Keynes UK
UKOW051802300413

210000UK00001B/13/P